Doomsday!

It was a small thing at first; a barely detectable blip on a display in the heart of a heavy fang that had alarms wailing. Moments later, the alarm was silenced when the ship was blown to pieces by capital ship missiles.

The destruction of Vasuk was noticed, and the Shan fleet turned to investigate. It took the destruction of another heavy fang for the horrible truth to dawn.

The Murderers had returned.

Hard Duty

by

Mark E. Cooper

Published by Impulse Books UK

Published by Impulse Books UK August 2012
http://www.impulsebooks.co.uk

PUBLISHER'S NOTE
The characters and events in this book are fictitious. Any similarity to real persons living or dead, business establishments, events, or locales is entirely coincidental and not intended by the author.

Books are available at quantity discounts. For more information please write to Impulse Books UK, 18 Lampits Hill Avenue, Corringham, Essex SS177NY, United Kingdom.

Cover Art: Mark Brooks
Cover Design: Samantha Wall

A CIP catalogue record for this book
is available from the British Library.

ISBN: 978-0-9545122-3-1

impulse
books uk

Printed and bound in Great Britain
Impulse Books UK

Acknowledgments

Special thanks go to Sylverre, Terri, Anne, Scott, Arlene, Sharon, Star, Rob, Erick, Lindi, and all the others hanging out at my favourite writing group. Last but not least, I want to thank Dave Milne for reading an early draft of this book.

Thanks everyone.

1~Discovery

"Captain to the bridge!"

Captain Colgan turned over and slapped the intercom button. "What is it, Francis?" he said, still groggy from sleep and squinting at her in the glare of the comm's screen. "Lights one third!" he barked in annoyance, and his cabin brightened.

"Sorry to wake you, sir," Commander Groves said contritely, but the excitement Colgan heard in her voice did not diminish. "We've picked up a transmission."

He frowned at that. They were a long way from the core, and even the Border Worlds were a distant memory out here. Only exploration vessels such as *Canada* herself dared venture into the deep this far.

He sat up and began pulling on his uniform. "Source?"

"Mark has categorised it as unknown sentient, sir. I've logged a possible first contact," Groves said for the log, but then she broke procedure and grinned. "This is it, Jeff, I can feel it!"

He understood her excitement, but kept his own voice neutral. "I'm on my way. Continue first contact procedures and log everything to chip for immediate transmission. Better download what you have so far to a drone... just in case."

Groves straightened her shoulders, gave a crisp nod and cut the circuit.

That had wiped the grin from her face, and well it should. The last time anything like this had happened, the Alliance had been embroiled in a war with the Merkiaari that had nearly seen Humanity exterminated. That could not be the case here; Merki transmissions would have been recognised instantly. Not only that, the ship would be at battle stations and running for home at max. That they weren't doing that was reassuring. Groves knew what she was doing, but what was to stop these transmissions coming from another murderously vicious species?

Nothing.

Colgan made his way to the bridge; by the time he reached it, he knew what he had to do. He racked his helmet beside his command station and took his seat.

"Anything further, Francis?"

"Nothing yet, sir. Our course and speed are unchanged. We have a transmission from an unknown source bearing zero-niner-zero by one-three-two degrees approximately thirty light years out. Mark is coddling his computers while they chew on the data, but I doubt we'll know much for a few hours."

Thirty lights? Maybe a day to get there... not very far at all.

He pursed his lips as he considered his options.

Survey missions were considered hard duty stations since by definition ships and their crews were out of contact for prolonged periods. His orders left him a good deal of leeway because of that, but if he chose to go with his first impulse of abandoning their current survey in favour of investigating Mark's transmission, he had better be right about his reasons for doing so. He needed more data.

"What can you tell me, Mark?"

"Well, sir, they're definitely not Human," Lieutenant

Ricks said, ignoring the laughter coming from helm and tactical. "They're not Merkiaari either."

That sobered everyone. The fear of meeting a Merki warship was very real, but it went with the territory. No one ever found anything by staying home.

"You've told me what they aren't, now tell me what they are."

"Sorry, sir, my analysis is incomplete. I've isolated multiple sources and they all seem clustered in the same region of space. At this range it's difficult to tell, but I think they're mobile. Call me crazy, but I have a hunch what I'm receiving originates aboard a convoy of alien ships. Sorry, sir, that's the best I can do from here. I can't make head nor tails of the language. It's a miracle we received anything at all—I'm getting mostly leakage."

Colgan winced. Leakage was dangerous. Unsecured communications was one reason the Merki had found the colonies so quickly. Nowadays, where tight beam comms (TBC) couldn't be used, foldspace drones were to eliminate leakage. TBC was secure, but it was limited to ships in close proximity. It was essentially a modulated laser pulse... like blinking flashlights at one another.

Drones were different. Given enough time their foldspace drives had enough capacity to cross the Human sector of the galaxy. They were slower than using courier ships, but where speed was not an issue, drones were the best way to keep Alliance worlds in contact with each other.

He wished there was a faster way to inform HQ of Mark's discovery, but they were too far out for speedy communication. The closest Alliance world to *Canada's* current location was Northcliff. He doubted they had a courier ship on hand. If he sent the drone there, Northcliff Port Control would simply re-upload the data to another drone and pass it up the line. No, it would be better to launch straight to HQ and damn the delay. He instinctively felt that the fewer people who handled Mark's data the better.

It would take a drone maybe five months to reach HQ, and that was pushing its drive to the max—not really a good idea in this instance. Drive failure could leave the Admiralty ignorant of his intentions and whereabouts until he launched another drone with an update.

"I want a full diagnostic run on the drone," Colgan said. "Make absolutely certain that its self-destruct is armed and functioning."

Groves cocked her head in surprise.

It was extremely unlikely for anyone to track and run down a foldspace drone in flight. Theoretically they could be intercepted, but Fleet had ensured that anyone tampering with one would get a nasty surprise.

Yeah, like a nuke in the mega-tonne range going off in his ship!

It was locking the barn door after the horse had bolted as far as the Merkiaari were concerned, but who knew who else might be listening?

"Who else indeed?" he muttered under his breath.

"Diagnostic complete, Skipper," Lieutenant Ricks said. "All systems nominal. Self-destruct is in the green."

In the green meant that the nuke was primed but safe. It would become active and dangerous the moment it reached minimum safe distance from *Canada* after launch.

Colgan swivelled his station forward again. "Download everything to the drone—ship's log to date as well. Set drive parameters to eighty percent."

"Updating the drone now. Destination?"

"Destination Sol. Alliance HQ."

Lieutenant Ricks keyed the drone active with his command codes, and programmed its computer. «Destination set. Ready to launch, Skipper.»

«Launch.»

«Aye, sir, launching… drone away… drone has entered fold space.»

«Very good.» Colgan turned to the helm. «Plot a course

for me, Janice. We *are* going to have a look at these people, but I don't want a whisper of our presence to reach them. Clear?"

"As crystal, Skip!" the helmsman, Lieutenant Wesley said.

"Very good."

He waited for the course to be laid in, all the while wondering if he was about to go down in history or down in flames. Had Captain Tibet wondered the same thing when he hailed the first Merkiaari ship to enter the Human sector of the galaxy? Somehow, he thought he probably had.

And we all know how that went. Please God, don't let me be responsible for another war.

"Course laid in, Skipper. Foldspace drive is hot."

"Execute," Colgan said without the tremor in his voice he felt must surely be there.

"Executing."

* * *

2~Memories

Fire. The dream always began with the memory of fire. The buildings burned unattended, the bombardment never ending and ongoing. The shrieks of incoming shells and explosions a constant background noise to accompany Eric's panting exhausted breaths. He didn't have the time to worry about the falling glass and steel. None of them did. The Merki troops were also oblivious to the danger. Both sides had been killed by it, neither side could avoid it. The city was dead except for the combatants. Most of the population centres had suffered the same fate.

The battle of San Luis seemed never-ending. The war had brought it here months ago, and neither side seemed able to overcome the other or admit defeat. The Merki had lost hundreds of ships and millions of troops. The Alliance had lost hundreds of ships and millions of citizens and troops. The system itself had changed hands many times while the ground war continued unabated. The Alliance was currently in ascendance in space, and had managed to fend off the last Merki push. For the first time, the Alliance had prevented reinforcements reaching the planet's surface and it was having the desired effect. Slowly, the Merki had been pushed back and whittled down.

The regiment was here entire. That never happened. Never. The risk of losing every combat capable Viper by committing them all to one place and battle had always been deemed too high. Yet the madness of San Luis had needed something to smash the stalemate, and when General Burgton had seen the pathetic remnants of San Luis and its people, most half mad and starving, that madness had gripped even him and infected the entire regiment. There was no going back now, no strategic withdrawal, not after seeing the cities carpeted with the bodies of their people.

Eric and the others had gone a little crazy then, and the General had let them. Vipers never allowed themselves to lose control. Their stability relied upon discipline, and the loss of it could lead to malfunction and death. It need not be enemy action that killed a Viper. In the event of serious malfunctions a unit would be scrapped for the good of the regiment. An insane Viper would be a horror to behold.

Eric ran up the street screaming his wrath, not mimicking Merki battle cries as he often did, but simply letting out the berserk rage he felt at the fate of this world's people. He fired his rifle from the hip into the stampeding Merkiaari's backs as he ran. His comrades were doing the same thing, and roaring their hate. None cared that they were running into their own artillery barrage. The other Alliance forces with them faltered and halted their advance, not willing to follow them into that hell. None to blame, and no shame in it. It was sense for them to stop and consolidate the gains they had made, but Eric and the others were all in melee mode and boosted to the maximum their enhanced bodies could take. To them, the world had slowed to a crawl. It seemed easy to dodge the flying plascrete and falling steel from buildings being blown apart by high explosive rounds pouring in upon the enemy. All illusion of course. The world hadn't slowed at all; the Vipers had sped up, and they did take casualties despite their speed, but nothing like as many as unenhanced soldiers would. Melee mode meant every resource Eric had was reserved for offence with nothing saved for defence except speed. It was god mode for a Viper, and rarely used because it threw caution to the wind. Wounds were ignored, everything but battle was ignored until a unit reached that critical point when he would go into automatic shutdown and hibernation. Hibernation in the midst of battle was death all too often.

Blinking blue icons on Eric's display witnessed units down, in hibernation or dead he couldn't tell, awaiting pickup. Dozens and dozens of his comrades were falling to Merki fire and indirectly to the dangerous environment of artillery inspired shrapnel, but there were hundreds more leaping over the debris of civilisation, leaping high to climb buildings like crazy alien spiders in an effort to gain good firing position, or leaping craters and mounds of bodies to rend their enemies. It was chaos.

Eric reloaded his rifle and screamed his hate at the enemy again. He selected full auto and poured fire into them. Grenades. He used his entire supply as soon as the thought occurred; his borrowed launcher using his targeting data in a lash up that worked only because it pointed the same way along the rifle's barrel. No way to use range data. Just point and shoot and adjust on the fly.

Someone leapt past him and was blasted back, taking a shot that would surely have killed him if it had hit. Blood sprayed over him, and he wiped his face on his already dripping sleeve. He spat the coppery taste out of his mouth and stepped over the still twitching body of his comrade as another blinking icon added itself to his sensor grid. This time, he noted, the unit was definitely in hibernation. Not dead. The thought should have been a relief, but every emotion except hate was a weak and distant thing. The thought uppermost in his head was taking the injured man's ammo supply. He used his knife to cut away webbing, and then tied it roughly across his chest like a bandolier. It didn't seem out of place; there were others already hanging from his armour. Most empty now. He didn't bother cutting them away.

Grenades and power cells. Good.

It meant he didn't have to stop yet. He gave no other thought to the downed unit behind him. He was in hibernation and that was all that could be said. Nothing but evac would help him now, and that wouldn't happen until the Merki were cleared out.

The street ahead was blocked, one of the towers had fallen filling the street with debris. The retreating Merki bunched up and artillery control took full advantage by hammering them in the tight confines of the blocked street. The aliens, starting to panic now, turned to enter a side street. Eric turned aside without a second to consider the danger and ran through flames. The partially collapsed building was fully engulfed; the heat unbearable on exposed skin, but he was a Viper and any amount of pain could be endured if it meant he could kill more Merki.

Damage and warning alerts flashed upon his display as the temperature soared around him. He wanted to hold his breath against the smoke and pollutants in the air as well as the heat that seared his throat and lungs, but he couldn't. Not and run. His armour smoked in the heat, and he had a moment to worry about the power cells and grenades so recently acquired. What was the flashover temp of the regiment's power cells again? He didn't have the time to check. Nothing to do about it anyway. He smashed through an already burning door, shot away a partition wall that divided offices, and saw windows overlooking a street. He dove toward them as the ceiling gave way above him.

Other Viper units noticed his new direction and followed, but they were fighting their own war and Eric didn't have any advice they would listen too. It was every unit for himself this late in the battle.

Eric crashed onto the street gasping and choking on the pollutants released from burning synthetics, but TRS (Target

Recognition Software) didn't care about anything other than its programming. It acquired the Merki without his input and he opened fire on automatic even as he rolled into the road. The entire action took milliseconds, and he didn't intervene. He poured fire into the snarling aliens; other units bursting into the street did the same. The shrieking of dying aliens blotted out the roar of the nearby blazing buildings for an instant. Return fire hammered the street and buildings around him. The Merki troopers were in such a panic, their fire discipline was shot to hell.

Eric got to his feet, dodged left, right, left and jumped reaching for a handhold on a building ahead. He crashed into the wall, missed his grip, and fell toward the ground far below. He reached for another hold, anything to arrest his fall as the wall rushed by. Failed again, and kicked hard at a ledge as it flashed past him, launching himself away toward the next building over. He grunted as he hit the target building awkwardly. Damage alerts flashed, but it was nothing serious. Left shoulder only, but it hurt and made his arm tingle. The arm felt slower of a sudden, but usable. The building had taken damage, the wall blasted to ruins, and he had smashed down on jagged broken plascrete. It was well though. A better firing position and one with better handholds. He hung by one hand, kicked and shoved himself up until he could hook an elbow in the nearest cavity blasted into the wall by RPG (Rocket Propelled Grenade) attack, and rained fire onto the Merkiaari. He emptied his rifle into them and then pumped grenades as fast as he could. Slowly the enemy withered away to nothing. Eric snarled as Vipers ripped and bludgeoned the bodies in a berserk frenzy, reducing them to bits and red paste. He wanted to join them in that, but he was sane enough to realise he couldn't kill the Merki any deader than they already were. The last few red icons on his sensors winked out one by one.

It was done.

Eric let himself fall to land in the street. He reloaded his rifle and noted its power was low. He swapped cells taking a pair off the charred bandolier across his chest, and shoved grenades into the launcher he had taped under his rifle. He wished he had a properly integrated weapons system, but the new rifles were still in development. The standard Alliance rifle and launcher couldn't accept targeting data from a Viper, and output was lower, but even so he would have like to have one. His temporary lash up worked, but that was all that it had going for it.

"Burgton to all units," the cold, deadly voice of the General was clear on Eric's comm, and every Viper within Eric's range paused to listen. "Operation Clean House complete. Proceed with Operation Annihilate. Burgton clear."

Eric turned as did every surviving Viper, and pushed himself to a ground consuming lope, heading south. Behind him, the artillery paused for a moment, and then it thundered again at a new target. South. Operation Annihilate was the codename for the endgame of this entire campaign. Burgton wanted to teach the Merki a lesson they would never forget. As he had said in the meeting where it was conceived, they would turn San Luis into the Merkiaari's vision of hell... it was already Eric's.

Eric left the city and reached the rally point. The Wolfcub class landers were coming in hot; scores of them howling down upon Eric and his comrades as if stooping upon prey. One after another they came in, ramps already down and ready to accept the Vipers. Landing struts slammed down, and the Vipers raced up the ramps even as the dampers were recoiling. Moments later the landers went to max thrust and threw themselves skyward so hard that G-stress greyed even a Viper's vision. Eric groaned as the seat edge cut into his thighs.

Behind them, navy shuttles crewed by Viper medics and navy corpsmen flew over the burning city on SAR (Search and Rescue) missions to retrieve the fallen. Eric watched a real time view by satellite as they homed on the beacons indicating downed Vipers awaiting pickup. He hoped most would be carried into orbit and back to the ship for repairs, but he knew many would go into cryogenic storage when they arrived to await their final journey back to base and a last appointment with the regiment's archive.

He broke his link to the satellite and closed his eyes, trying not to see the faces of the fallen, but Vipers never forgot anything. Nothing at all.

Computer: combat mode.

The world sped back up as he dropped back to his default condition. Alerts began appearing upon his display, some flashing for his attention. Priorities. His processor wanted instructions. Did he want to enter maintenance mode? Hell no! He would be fighting again soon. He would rely upon combat mode for now. True, it would take longer to repair his damage that way, but it would be repaired and still let him fight. His decision caused a cascade of new data to be displayed. A shortlist of needed repairs and the wireframe graphic to go with it as if he didn't already know where it hurt. The worst damage was to his left shoulder, but it wasn't serious. The rest were burns and some loss of lung capacity. Damn smoke. All was repairable without need for outside intervention.

>_ DIAGNOSTICS: 87% COMBAT CAPABLE
>_ IMS: REPAIRS IN PROGRESS.

Eric glanced at the others, but none acknowledged him. They were all busy with internal business, same as he had just been. He was glad to see Ken Stone had made it, and Dick Hames. Both were good friends, and had been enhanced with him in the same group. Enhanced together, trained together, and often fought beside one another. Dick's armour was heavily pitted and scared from enemy fire, but he seemed essentially intact. He could see other faces he knew, all looked weary, and all were ready to fight again. He pretended not to notice the missing faces, preferring to imagine them safe and aboard the other landers.

"What happened to your hair, bro?" Stone said raising his voice over the noise of the engines.

Hair? Eric reached up and realised he was burned bald on his right side. His helmet hadn't protected him from it, probably made it worse. It had been damned hot in that building.

"You like it?" Eric said. "New style I call Merki Barbeque."

Stone grinned and some of the others laughed. "Hell of a thing. You think we get to go home after this one?"

Eric shrugged. "No clue." The Alliance was still on the back foot and barely holding on. He doubted they would go home, but even if they did, it would be a short respite. "Don't worry about it. You'll get to increase your score—"

"Incoming Merki Interceptors! Brace for high speed manoeuvres!" the pilot shouted over the comm.

Eric tugged on his harness straps hard to tighten them. He hugged his rifle to his chest, clamping it there with folded arms as the Wolfcub lurched going to max thrust. It spun upside down, veered left and suddenly a gaping hole appeared in the floor between Eric's feet. He looked through the hole, pursed his lips in thought, and turned to toward Ken who looked a bit sick. Well, it had been very close

"I don't think we—" Eric began as the lander was hit again and fell out of the sky, already disintegrating."

The pilot screamed, "Brace, brace, bra—"

>_ 0559:59 CLOSE ARCHIVE FILE #0000063577982-3996-SL
>_ 0600:01 DEACTIVATE MAINTENANCE MODE... DONE.
DIAGNOSTICS: UNIT FIT FOR DUTY
ACTIVATE COMBAT MODE... DONE
TRS... DONE

Sensors... Done
Targeting... Done
Communications... Done
Infonet... Done
TacNet... Done... Scanning... No units/
stations found
>_ 0600:05 Reactivation complete

Eric's eyes snapped open, and the dream faded away back to storage. He was in his rack aboard the tramp freighter, instantly alert as always. His programming wouldn't allow anything else of course. His 0600 wakeup call was better than gospel as far as his processor was concerned. Not that it knew or cared. It was just following its programming. Some days, more and more as the decades rolled by, he thought he was just doing the same.

"All behaviour is programming one way or the other. Mine is just more so," he murmured frowning at the thought.

He was a Viper. A cyborg soldier designed to kill Merkiaari in milliseconds, and he performed that task extremely well. They all did of course, the Vipers, the one hundred units that were all that remained of the once powerful SAG. The Special Assault Group had been created to augment the 501st Infantry Regiment's offensive capability during the Merki War; it's mission back then to seek and destroy the alien invaders wherever they were found. Eric and his comrades had done so with extreme prejudice, and their reward?

Continued existence.

Eric sneered at the familiar hurt. Existence. They were lucky the Alliance hadn't decided to deactivate them all. They were feared and respected still, but mostly feared. No one was comfortable in a room with something that could kill three metre tall alien monsters in the blink of an eye. None would seek them out to get to know them, not knowing what they thought they knew of the cyborgs who won the war for them. That war was long over, or in hiatus if you believed General

Burgton's predictions. Unfortunately, Eric and the others did believe him; it wouldn't be long before the Alliance needed them all again.

Eric swung his legs out of his rack and went through his routine.

At precisely 0620 he was groomed, dressed, and ready to debark the ship. His duffel was ready to go; he had packed it last night. There was nothing in it he really needed, but as a prop it added to his cover story. He wasn't Eric Penleigh right now. He was Eric Martell, ex-merc looking for a cause. The clothes he wore and the kit in his duffel all helped with his image. He had aged his brown uniform coverall well, and it had no insignia—he had unpicked them all himself exposing the darker cloth beneath. It was actually a civ design, but it was the right type and no one could tell now that the insignia had been that of a cleaning company. It made him look like what he was pretending to be. A dishonourably discharged merc.

The ship began its final approach to station. Nothing to do but wait until docked. He sat on his rack and waited staring at the bulkhead in silence. How many times had he been on missions like this now, on missions that could have been identical except for location?

WORKING...

Eric sighed and ignored the list of codenames as it scrolled past on his display. He didn't want an answer to his question. He knew the answer was in the hundreds. It had been rhetorical, but his processor didn't care and continued its task of filling his vision with holographic data. It wasn't really holographic of course. It only seemed to hover before his eyes like a holotank display. No one but he could see it and not even he cared to read it. His internal damn computer was too literal, and Vipers could not forget anything.

Anything at all.

He was programmed with perfect recall; the idea had been to make them all better killers by making target acquisition at a glance instant and perfect. The routines in his programming were complicated and numerous. Together they were called Snapshot, and there was no way to turn it off. Not even his death would shut it down, well, not immediately anyway. He had seen comrades take careful aim and one final shot after they were already dead just to take their killers with them. It was freaky as hell, and scary. That would be him one day.

>_ 563

Eric sighed when the total blinked on and off. He erased the list with a coded thought and his vision cleared. Five hundred and sixty three missions the same as this one, or close enough for his damned literalist processor to count them. That probably meant a similar amount just outside its acceptable parameters. Its true/false subroutines were distressingly precise and were something every Viper had to take into account when asking for data. The days of real A.I computer architecture were centuries in the past, Douglas Walden and his hacker rebellion had seen to that.

Over five hundred missions like this one, and hundreds different enough to be excluded from the list, and they all meant nothing. The days when his battles did mean something ended with the Merki War. He spent his time now killing other Humans, not murderously vicious aliens bent on genocide. It was enough to make a statue weep.

How far they had fallen.

The Alliance and the regiment was all he had. All any Viper had really. They were his two reasons to exist. The General ordered and he obeyed. The General said the coups and mini wars had to be managed. So they were managed... by Vipers behind the scenes when that was possible, and when not possible the General had the President's ear. Orders came down, and off they went to war once more... or battle at least.

They had to keep the peace when it could be kept, and divert or bring the wars to a swift conclusion when it could not. The Alliance must remain strong when the next Merkiaari incursion occurred. And it would occur soon. Five years the General estimated. Just five more years and his existence would have meaning again.

>_ 0700:23 DOCKING COMMENCING.

The sound of grapples and maintenance lines connecting were clearly audible. He could have used his sensors to detect people on the ship and station but there was no need. He could have slipped into the security net on the station and accessed a live feed of the ship's final approach. He used to do that, he remembered. Long ago that was. He did not think on it too hard now; if he did, his processor would resurrect one or more memories and replay them. The damn thing was programmed that way.

He checked the synthskin glove on his right hand, but as before it was intact and hiding his weapon's data bus. The data bus was the only obvious external difference between his enhanced body and a standard Human. The other one, his primary node was at the base of his spine and hidden by his clothes. As long as the glove remained undamaged, no one would know what he was.

>_0710:12

He watched the seconds tick by. The time on his display was set to Thurston local, as were the ship's chronometers. That was standard for all ships when jumping in system. Made things easier to manage—traffic patterns and the like. Ships received the correct time and other information like trade prices and news bulletins from the beacons.

The sounds died away and Eric stood. He threw his duffel up onto his shoulder and left his cabin to join the few other passengers debarking here. None of them spoke. All of them were civilians of one kind or another. No tourists here, but then the Betty wasn't a cruise ship. It was a freighter and only took a few passengers aboard to supplement meagre profits way out here in the Border Zone. Eric supposed these people were down on their luck spacers, they had the look. They would most likely be seeking a ship docked at station to take them on as crew, or to take them to another port where they could try again.

Eric followed the ramp out of the ship and stepped dockside. Multiple alerts competed for his cybernetically enhanced cerebrum's attention, but he ignored most of them. As always, his sensors and programming leaned toward tiresome completeness. What did he care that leaving the ship had exposed him to an atmospheric pressure drop of a few hectopascals? Did he give a fuck that the station's atmosphere was nitrogen rich and its temperature a few degrees low? No, but did his processor care, did it ever take instruction from him to suppress pointless alerts when there was no risk of harm to him? Of course not.

Nothing to do but keep on keeping on as they say.

"They are full of shit," he growled. He shifted his duffle on his shoulder, took a deep breath, and folded himself away letting his cover personae take over his features. "Just another day on the job," he whispered, the weariness in his voice not registering in his own ears after all these centuries.

Eric marched across the dock toward arrivals and departures board. He stopped, looking blankly at the departures section and was bumped from behind. He pasted on an annoyed expression and turned to see who had walked into him, already lowering his duffel to the floor.

"Oh excuse me, so sorry," the stocky black man said. "Wasn't paying attention there. Worried about my flight... can't find it on the boards."

"Don't worry about it," Eric growled turning to look up at the departures again.

"No really, you must forgive me. You will won't you, and shake on it?"

Eric gritted his teeth noticing the grins from those close enough to hear. He rolled his eyes at them and mouthed the word silently, "Bethanites!"

The onlookers grinned wider, nodding in sympathy.

Eric put on a smile and tuned toward the man again. "From Bethany's World I assume?"

"Why yes! How did you know?"

This time the laughter was loud enough for the tourist— he must surely be one as he was dressed in flamboyant colours and ridiculous looking printed patterns—to notice. He looked around uncertainly, his smile slipping and Eric was suddenly tired of the pretence.

He held out his hand for a shake. "I'm Eric, honoured to meet you. I recognise your scrupulous manner as being from Bethany. I visited there once."

"Ah, you are too kind, Eric. My name is Kenneth Hartley-Browne. Glad to make your acquaintance."

Eric clasped Ken's hand.

>_ CONNECTION REQUEST. ACCEPT [Y]ES/[N]O?
>_ Y
>_ CONNECTION ACHIEVED... STONE, KENNETH.
MASTER SERGEANT 501ST INFANTRY REGIMENT,
SERIAL NUMBER DGN-896-410-339.
>_ INCOMING DATA PACKET... DOWNLOADING.
>_ DOWNLOAD COMPLETE.

Eric shook Ken's hand and palmed the key card he held. "Sorry to leave in such haste, but my shuttle departs soon."

Ken smiled. "Quite all right. I must away to find my own transportation. Good bye to you."

"Good bye," Eric said and watched one of his oldest friends walk away.

Suddenly he couldn't leave it like that. What if this was

his last op? No one stayed lucky forever. Stone was already out of sight but that was no problem. He could have hacked into station comms easily enough, or used his built in comm. No one would have been the wiser. They didn't know to monitor Viper freqs, and if they had they would have received encrypted bursts of data that to them would have amounted to garbage or background noise. TacNet (Tactical Network) was a quicker built in system dedicated to Viper systems alone. Totally secure. He quickly accessed it and contacted the only other Viper in the entire Thurston system.

"Ken... just wanted to say thanks. For everything," he said silently, his words encoded by his processor and sent on their way.

"No big, just another recon op."

Stone's voice came to him as if his friend were standing a few feet away. He thought he was worried about the op, easy enough mistake he supposed. "It's not that, Ken. It's..." he couldn't voice it. "It's just..."

"Are you okay, brother?" Stone said, sounding concerned now.

Brother, yes, Stone was his brother in every way that mattered. His family—his birth family—were long dead and their descendants didn't know him, but he still had brothers and sisters in the regiment. Everyone wearing the snakehead patch was family. He felt better remembering that; he wasn't alone.

"I'm coming back there," Stone said.

Eric cursed himself. He had taken too long to answer. Stone's blue icon, clearly visible on his sensors among so many green ones denoting the civs on the station, reversed course.

"No, Ken. You have somewhere to be, yes?"

"Tigris, but it can wait. You need me now."

"I'm okay, feeling my age I guess. I just didn't want to let you go without saying it's been an honour serving with you... in case, you know?"

"Bro... I feel the same. Nothing is gonna happen to you;

not now, not ten years from now. Besides, the General says we have an appointment in five to kick alien butt. You wouldn't want to miss that, right?"

"Wouldn't miss it for anything," Eric said grimly. He couldn't kill enough Merkiaari in a thousand lifetimes to make up for what he and the rest of the Human race had lost. "Go, I'll be fine. That's an order if you need one."

"Nah. I knew you were fine. Stone out."

Eric watched Ken's icon on his sensors. "God bless," he whispered and turned his attention back to business as Stone headed for his ship's dock.

He had no idea what Ken's mission on Tigris was; probably something along similar lines as here on Thurston. It had no bearing on his own mission that he could see. Ken was often tasked with information gathering missions. He would be sent out to find trouble spots and assess whether the regiment needed to get involved. If it did, he would report that and facilitate any follow up missions by providing intel, or weapons, or any number of other useful things. The download would have any data Eric needed to succeed in his own mission, and the key card was probably to access a cache of weapons or something interesting like that. No doubt there was trouble on Thurston somewhere. The authorities might not even know about it yet, but it would be there simmering and ready to boil over. He wouldn't be here otherwise and Ken was like the proverbial trouble magnet. If there was something here, it would have come to Ken's attention one way or another.

Eric found a departing shuttle easily enough, but first there was customs and immigration to go through. Basic stuff out here in the Border Zone. Thurston wasn't an Alliance member world and its citizens enjoyed a more liberal way of life. That was good and bad. Good when people played nice. No one liked too much government red tape and observation. Bad when people didn't play nice and flouted laws designed to keep the peace and ensure everyone had a fair shake.

Thurston used to have a dictatorial government based upon corporate ownership of resources. Such company owned planets were numerous enough out here in the zone not to raise too many eyebrows, but Thurston had moved beyond that now and was making a serious bid for Alliance membership. There were prerequisites for that. Democratic rule being only the first hurdle.

"Identity please," the trim looking woman wearing the blue uniform of a customs official said.

"Eric Martell, here looking for work."

"Planet of origin?"

"Alizon," Eric lied. He had no fear that his fake identity would fail. His simcode implant, though the same as millions of others implanted at birth in the core worlds and an integral part of his spinal column, was special in one important detail. It was programmable. His processor had quite a few identities saved in its database. "Where's your scanner?"

The woman grimaced. "It's on the fritz again. We're still working the bugs out of the system; only had them six months."

And there went another of the liberal benefits of living outside the core worlds on its way out the airlock. Babies born on Thurston from now on would have the simcode implant fitted. It was one of the indicators that real core world type civilisation had reached here. Not everyone would be pleased by that. Fertile ground for the kinds of problems he was often sent to deal with.

"So," Eric nodded. "What next?"

"Sorry for the inconvenience, but I'll need a blood sample before an identity card can be issued."

Eric nodded. "That's fine," he said and let her walk him through the procedure.

The old card system would be in place for decades to come. It would take that long for simcoded citizens to become the majority here. Until then, Thurston would have a hybrid system of DNA checks backed up with old style fingerprints and holographs.

When she was finished he had a shiny new I.D card. He passed through immigration and boarded the first available shuttle down world. He found a seat easily; the small fast little boat was barely half full. He didn't bother stowing his duffel but secured it on the seat next to him with its safety belt. The cabin staff nodded at his precautions and didn't say a word. Things were always more relaxed in the Border Zone, but shipboard safety wasn't one of those things.

With time on his hands, he decided to open Ken's data and find out more about his mission. So far, all he knew was that he would be busting heads on Thurston. His missions always had that in common, and mostly involved him infiltrating somewhere to do it. Solo ops and escaping alive were his personal way of keeping score. After centuries of fighting, there wasn't much else to use. He wondered how Ken coped, because back in the day he had used Merkiaari kills for his personal scoreboard, but now? With the regiment mothballed, it wasn't as if rank had any meaning to him or any Viper.

Eric grimaced, his thoughts heading toward a place he knew well; one he didn't want to revisit. "Going through the motions. All of us... all is programming," he murmured.

"Sir?"

Eric cursed himself. Dammit he was slipping. He hadn't noticed the steward arrive. And he had said that last aloud! Dammit, he was acting like... he shuddered. He was acting like a classic whigout wannabe—a malfunctioning unit fit only for termination. No! He was fine. He was rock solid stable, he was!

"I'm fine," Eric said, making a guess the steward was offering refreshment. The steward nodded and made to move on. Eric stayed him a moment with a raised hand. "How long to undock?"

"As the pilot said, sir, a few minutes more for traffic to clear our space."

Shit, he had missed the announcement too. "Thanks."

"You're welcome, sir."

Eric let the steward go and turned his attention inward again. He pulled up his diagnostics and ran a full scan. While that was running, he opened the download and forced himself to wait calmly for the scan to complete. He wasn't a damn burnout, he was just distracted. It happened. Being enhanced didn't make him less Human in that aspect at least.

The mission was a snoop and scoot. The data provided plenty of background information for him. Interesting. The current president of Thurston was the son of the old one, who had been an unapologetic bastard of mega proportions, but strangely not in the people of Thurston's eyes. He had limited his particular brand of vicious single-mindedness to political and business enemies, and allowed the citizens of Thurston quite a bit of freedom. Very clever of him really. They loved him for it, and never realised he was only letting them have what they were entitled to anyway. Of course, he was one of the founders of the company that owned most of the planet, and employed most of them in his mining operations. The planet was named for him!

The current President, Martin James Thurston, was cut from different cloth. Educated on Earth he had brought true democracy to his home planet when his father died and he took over. Raised to the presidency by acclamation, he immediately set about undermining his own power by legislating a five year term for the presidency, and throwing away his own lifetime position. At the same time, he instituted wide spread reforms that made the existing parliament more than just a tourist attraction and into what it was meant to be.

His father must be spinning in his grave, Eric mused. Of course introducing a proper parliament with real powers and political parties meant Thurston was on course to join the Alliance—a stated goal of the current government. Such things as real democracy and political safeguards were required for membership, and it was that proposed membership that had sparked the need for Eric's mission.

As always, democracy had enemies. In Thurston's case it had the so-called Freedom Movement to deal with.

In his father's time, such a terrorist group would never have flowered into a real problem. Dictatorships did have uses, and one of those was making troublemakers disappear. Eric had a lot of sympathy with that sort of thing. He preferred making such people vanish as well, but dictators never knew when to stop. Too many innocents tended to die needlessly, and that was something Eric did not approve of. According to Ken's data, Thurston had requested aid from the Alliance to deal with the terrorists and it was granted. An Alliance Marine battalion commanded by a Major Stein had been landed to take care of business. They were not yet in position to take out the Freedom Movement in its entirety, but they had been in action a few times on a smaller scale.

His mission then was to infiltrate the Freedom Movement and report to Major Stein with everything needed for the Marines to clean house. Thurston would then complete his intention of dragging his planet into the big leagues—full membership of the Alliance.

>_ DIAGNOSTICS: ALL SYSTEMS WITHIN
ACCEPTABLE PARAMETERS.
>_ UNIT FIT FOR DUTY.

Eric had known he was fine but seeing it confirmed was good. He wiped the report from his display knowing the diagnostic would be logged and archived automatically.

Eric closed his eyes as undocking commenced and gravity abruptly dropped away. The shuttle was a civilian vessel and too small for internal gravity fields, but it still had mass. Manoeuvring under thrust had an effect similar to gravity. Eric ignored the tug on his harness as the shuttle backed away from the station, and continued reading his brief.

Travel time down to the port was less than an hour. The shuttle's departure from the station was good timing as the pilot was able to descend without needing to orbit the planet first. He didn't waste time or fuel, Eric noted, as the buffeting increased enough to be jarring. It was not on the same scale as a combat drop of course, but it was a speedier and more violent re-entry than the usual sedate ride one would expect. Eric had to wonder why. The other passengers were concerned and whispering questions that none had the answers to. He had no more information than they, but he could make better guesses based upon experience. Either there was some kind of emergency or the pilot had been given standing orders to land as fast as possible. With the threat posed by the Freedom Movement in mind, Eric would put money on the pilot having orders to push the envelope and land fast. Eric didn't care either way; a quick descent worked in his favour.

With wings glowing and fuselage darkening as its nanocoat battled to absorb the heat of re-entry, the shuttle bore into the atmosphere of Thurston toward a landing at the main spaceport just outside the capital.

Thurston was a well planned and developed example of a border world. Most had one or two cities sited conveniently in temperate zones of the available continental masses. Usually cobbled together to provide the basics, the cities would be sited close to something of interest usually a geological formation. Rare earth elements for example, needed in nanotech engineering, or heavy metals needed for use in power systems used in spacecraft. The housing in such cities had more in common with barracks built for mine and industrial workers, than the architectural marvels to be found in the core, but Thurston was different.

Thurston had more than a dozen decent sized cities already. In the core they would be classed as large towns, but make no mistake, out here in the Border Zone they *were* cities. And they were spread out on each of the eight continents with plenty of space to grow. Each one had its own representatives in Thurston's parliament, and all were modern with up to date services. Eric had never seen such a well thought out example of colonisation. Not even the most powerful giants of the Alliance such as Alizon or Garnet had been given such a good start.

Thurston had potential, Eric mused. Serious potential and the General had foreseen it. In a century or less, Thurston would be a power in the Alliance and its location within the current confines of the Border Zone made it a prime candidate as a future sector command node for the navy. Eric pursed his lips imagining it. Like the Kalmar Union, Thurston could become the centre of its own political entity within the Alliance. Whether it would or not, a Fleet base located here was a given, maybe one with full scale yard facilities and those were rare. Thurston did have excellent resources in the form of two large asteroid fields to feed a yard's smelters. It even had four gas giants for fuelling refineries. It was bloody perfect...

If.

If things could be managed and guided in the right direction.

It would take decades, a century even, but the General had centuries and the vision to guide the Alliance down the correct path... his path. Eric shuddered. Burgton scared him sometimes. If Eric hadn't known him so well, if he didn't know that Burgton's every waking and sleeping moment was dedicated to the good of the Alliance and the Human race, he would have shot him in the head when next they met. But he did know him, and he would continue to obey him as would the rest of the regiment no matter what was asked of them, because they did know, all of them, that Burgton was always right. Scary right. So when he said there would be another Merki incursion within five years, they knew it would happen and that the Alliance needed to be prepared for it, even if it didn't know it was being prepared. Missions like this one, and others Eric knew nothing about, were all part of it.

Eric skimmed the data Ken had put together picking out interesting facts and figures. The planet was firmly in the grip of global warming he noted, but it was a natural occurrence. The geological survey commissioned before colonisation placed Thurston in its cretaceous period. Every square meter of land was covered by steaming jungle. There were mountains visible from orbit and the cones of extinct volcanoes rose out of the vegetation like the bones of some great beast, but everything else was either water covered or teeming with native life. There were no ice caps and as a result sea levels were high. No deserts either. Thurston had eight continents. If he included the small island chains in his calculation, land equated to more than fifty percent of the surface area, and Thurston was not a small planet. It was twelve percent larger than Earth for example, and populated by Thurston's unique brand of wildlife.

"More dinosaurs," Eric grumbled. "Really? What the hell is it about the lizards that they evolved on every bloody planet we like?"

He was no scientist gleefully labelling the wildlife, but the few pictures Ken had included looked like dinosaurs to him. Big buggers some of them, and although a lot were vegetarian living off the vast jungle canopy, some were carnivorous. Eric studied one of the meat eaters and compared it to other critters he had seen over the past two hundred years. It looked like a mutant crocodile—huge jaw full of ripping teeth, no molars that he could see. Long narrow body with a ridge of horned spikes along the spine for protection, and stood twice a man's height on four feet each having four clawed toes. The front legs each had a long curved spur, probably a vestigial toe, but what did he know?

Computer: compare current image with known Earth dinosaurs. Query: what is closest match?

>_ WORKING

>_ DESMATOSUCHUS: DINOSAUR, LIVING ON EARTH THROUGH THE TRIASSIC PERIOD. APPROXIMATELY 245MILLION YEARS B.C. CARNIVOROUS LIZARD ANALOGUE. REF;

LINK CROCODILE. REF; TEXAS. REF; MASS
EXTINCTION.

Eric had no idea what Texas had to do with it, but he had to
agree it did look like a crocodile; a super-sized croc that spent
its time eating dinosaurs under the jungle canopy, and not
soaking itself in a swamp. Or maybe it did, and just came out
for a snack. A hundred ton snack.

Eric snorted at the whimsical turn his thoughts had taken.
The point was, old Desmond the super croc was only one
danger among thousands hidden all over the planet. The
jungles were dangerous places, which meant most of the
population went everywhere armed. That was common in the
Border Zone where protection was a personal responsibility.
Often border worlds had little or no police force, and when
they did their jurisdiction rarely reached beyond the city
limits. Thurston did have police and emergency services in the
cities, but had no way to extend that protection to its people
if they left civilisation and entered the wilds. The wilds could
be described as everywhere not under plascrete... everywhere
outside the cities or mining compounds in other words.

Ashfield, Thurston's capital and centre of government, was
as modern as any city to be found in the core worlds. It was
just smaller, maybe a tenth the size of an average city. Despite
that, the port had been built full scale and would rival the
best facilities to be had in the core. Impressive foresight on
somebody's part as it must have cost an immense amount.
Eric couldn't have made that decision he realised. He just
didn't have the vision, but someone did. Someone had faith
in Thurston's future enough to force the issue. The founders
must have bled credits for decades after colonisation. Even
now, the port was only using about five percent of its capacity,
but if President Thurston could make his reforms stick, if he
could defeat his political opponents, if he could rid himself of
the Freedom Movement, and if he could persuade and cajole
enough members of the Alliance council to ratify Thurston's

application to join the Alliance, then that huge investment would suddenly be realised. The spaceport and the station in orbit above it would become the most important assets the planet owned eclipsed only by the resources waiting to be mined below the planet's surface and within the asteroids.

If.

A lot of ifs had to be turned into certainties, and that was the real goal. Like dominoes falling, Eric's snoop and scoot mission should lead to Stein's marines taking out the Freedom Movement, which should clear the way for Thurston to drag his planet closer to full Alliance membership, and decades down the line Burgton's plan for Thurston would be realised.

Eric snorted. And maybe he was just over thinking it. Maybe the General just wanted another scumbag terrorist outfit like the Freedom Movement knocked on its arse. Eric could relate. He had spent too many years of his existence doing just that. Grandiose plan or simple plan, he was here and would see to it that the Freedom Movement did not prosper. He really didn't like people who set bombs and killed innocents.

Eric finished reading through Ken's data and waited for landing. He had a place to start looking for a contact man and enough background information to be confident of his ability to get inside the Movement. Where that would lead him he didn't know. Wherever he ended up, he would succeed. He always did and always would until one day he didn't.

Eric's lips quirked. A little uncertainty was good for him. No way to think of random chance as just programming.

The shuttle came in hot but the landing was smooth and Eric silently congratulated the pilot. He briefly wondered if the guy had been navy. The steward came around a few moments after the shuttle finished taxiing off the runway and opened the hatch. Eric was quick to take advantage of his seat position and was the first to leave.

The port was a modern one. He didn't have to use a ladder to leave. There was a proper debarkation tube leading to a lounge. It was empty. He glanced around the lounge, his sensors trawling for threat and anything of interest. He didn't expect any dangers, but caution was ingrained after all these years and his programming backing it up was immutable. Data flickered over his vision, some coloured to attract his attention. When it did, the data blinked on and off briefly and parked itself onto a growing list. His attention danced all over his display, pausing briefly as this datum or that caught his notice, though there was nothing for anyone else to see. If they were close enough maybe they would see his eyes moving a little as he changed focus, but he doubted it. He knew what to look for and even he rarely noticed another Viper doing it.

He focused upon the list and with a coded thought selected the Infonet node in the lounge.

>_ Infonet: Logon Eric Martell account number #08965bHu532AsW... Done.

A new window popped up on his display and Eric ran a quick search as he followed the signs in the lounge toward the exit. He wasn't surprised to find a lack of security. All of that was up at the station for outsystem arrivals and departures. Any departures from the planet though, even shuttle departures bound for the station from the other side of the port, would be another matter. Security and customs would be on that side and they never slept.

Most spacecraft were unable to land and would use the station to unload and load cargo, but most wasn't all, and out here in the border zone raiders were a concern. Pirates took ships, but raiders were another breed. They not only jacked ships, they jacked stations and even colonies if they could get away with it. Their ships had landing capability, and Fleet was stretched thin out here. Raiders weren't the only concern for colonies like Thurston. Smugglers could quickly undermine fragile economies, but Thurston had another worry right now. Gun runners. The marines really wouldn't appreciate a ship full of weapons making landfall, especially when the only customer was a terrorist group like the Freedom Movement. Security would be tight right now with a continual over watch by navy hotshot pilots patrolling in low orbit.

Eric found what he was looking for and dismissed the Infonet window.

>_ INFONET: LOGOFF [Y]ES/[N]O?
>_ Y

Eric left the lounge but instead of heading outside for a taxi, he turned right. His search on Infonet had been for the bank that matched the key card Ken had slipped him. Banks at spaceports and on stations were common. They catered to spacers who needed quick access to funds or a secure place to leave their gear. Crew on freighters with a regular run found it easier and cheaper to stash their stuff in a deposit box rather than continue paying for an empty housing unit. Eric knew he wouldn't look out of place, even in his less than pristine faked up merc uniform.

He walked into the bank and got in line. There were a few early risers making transactions before catching a shuttle up to the station. The android bank tellers didn't care of course. When it was his turn, he slid the key card into a slot in the countertop and chose option three.

"Thank you, ma'am," the android said. "A Human member of staff will be with you shortly. Please take a seat."

"I'm not a ma'am, I'm a sir," Eric said because he was bored and twitting the droid appealed to him. "Male you know?"

"Thank you for the correction. Correction logged. Please take a seat ma'am. A Human member of staff will be with you shortly."

Eric sighed, already losing interest in the game. "All is programming... you poor bastard." He wasn't sure who to feel the more sorry for; an android following its programming and completely unaware of it or himself who followed his while denying it.

"Next please," the android said.

Eric moved away and took a seat.

Five minutes later he was escorted down to the vaults beneath the building. It was a typical example of its kind and Eric considered it no better than medium security. Plenty good enough for its purpose of storing its customer's gear, but not something governments or military would consider using. Security systems were in place—Eric's sensors had picked up their emissions—and the facility itself was fine—fire and bomb proof—but without simcode recognition the entire system relied upon keycards and passwords. Still, he wasn't here to critique the security arrangements, though he had done that before. He had done pretty much everything before... many times. He was here to collect whatever Ken had stashed for him.

The armed guard stopped at the last door after passing a dozen similar doors and tugged his uniform tunic straight. He inserted his card, rapidly entered a code while shielding the key pad with his body, and then stepped back as the door slid aside.

"After you, sir."

Eric walked inside and waited for the guard to lock him in. The sound of the locks engaging were quiet but Eric's enhanced hearing picked up the sounds easily. Good. He didn't want to be disturbed. The guard would wait outside the door for hours if need be. They were paid for more than weapon's proficiency after all. They were hired for their discretion and lack of curiosity too. He had pretended to be one once, he remembered. Long ago. It had been a cover for an assassination op. Not his favourite type of gig, but the guy had really pissed Burgton off by proposing to demobilise the regiment a few decades after hostilities with the Merkiaari ended. The guy's suicide had been big news back then.

Eric turned toward the opposite end of the barren room and located the interface. It was a small pedestal about waist height with a simple keyboard and card reader. He inserted his card and typed the password Ken had given him in his download.

Velox et mortifer.

It was the regiment's motto in Latin. Swift and Deadly. Vipers were definitely that among other things, but at their most basic, swift and deadly described them well.

The password was accepted and the sounds of machinery starting came to him from beyond the far wall. The wall was grey and featureless except for a panel painted with black and yellow caution stripes about a metre square. A minute went by. The brightly painted section of wall slid out into the room attached to a steel bench or table with a metal box sitting on it. Eric opened it and surveyed the contents.

There was duffel like the one he already had and containing many of the same things. He pulled everything out and quickly inventoried what he had. Uniforms, toiletries, minicomputer, three wands topped up with funds each drawing on different banks, a Raytheon .50 semi auto pistol and a pile of loaded magazines, a small stash of hard currency in the form of platinum wafers—platinum was still universally accepted even if frowned upon by governments—and a shoulder rig for the pistol.

He eyed the weapon unhappily, not having time to strip it now, but he did a quick visual on it. It was battered and old seeming, but that would be camouflage. He worked the action listening to its smooth sounding mechanics and nodded when he pulled the trigger. Eric knew Ken would not have supplied an inferior weapon, and Raytheon made good ones, but a slug thrower no matter how good wasn't his preference. They had limited ammo capacity compared with pulsers, very limited when they were large calibre like this one, and had a low recycle rate. Vipers could pull a trigger repeatedly on the order of 0.18 to 0.25 seconds apart and do it all day if necessary. If he tried that, the Raytheon would jam. The regiment's custom made weaponry was designed to stand up to such punishment;

this thing would fire one round and break.

Pulsers were more forgiving. They were generally fully automatic and a single trigger press could fire a three round burst or empty hundred round magazines in seconds depending upon settings. His new toy's extended capacity magazines only held ten rounds. The standard for this weapon was six rounds he seemed to recall. He was pleased to have any weapon since he came here unarmed, but had to wonder at Ken's choice. Maybe there was a reason for it, but give him a good pulser any day.

Eric quickly unsealed his uniform, letting it hang from his hips, and put on the shoulder rig. It wasn't a convenient way to wear it, but he wouldn't go around blatantly displaying the rig either. He loaded the pistol and chambered a round, before holstering it and pulling his clothes back into order.

He stuffed the clothing and toiletries back into the box along with the unwanted duffel, and swept everything else into his own already bulging duffel—he didn't want to carry two. He wanted his right hand free. He slammed the lid closed and went to retrieve his card from the consol. The moment he did, the vault's hidden machinery activated and the box slid into the wall to be whisked away to storage.

Eric summoned the guard with a quick press of the call button next the door, and moments later he was led out of the vaults and back to the bank proper.

"Will there be anything else, sir?" the guard asked when they reached the main floor of the bank.

The guard's hand didn't stray toward the weapon on his hip even once on the trip back, though he was well aware Eric had armed himself. Eric appreciated professionalism like that. Alert but sensible was good for a position like a bank guard. No doubt he had warned his chain of command somehow, because although Eric hadn't picked up anything on sensors on the way back, there were more security personnel suddenly in evidence just loitering.

"I have everything, thanks," Eric said with a small smile

at the wary look he imagined he saw deep within the man's eyes.

The guard smiled professionally. "A good day to you then, sir."

"And to you," Eric said and turned toward the doors.

Eric orientated himself just outside the bank using his internal 3d map of the port and headed toward an exit and hopefully transportation to a hotel. He found a taxi outside easily; he was pounced upon by a driver before he could even raise a hand. Not many customers this time of day maybe, but Eric wasn't in the habit of taking chances.

Computer: initiate full spectrum security scan. Range out to 500 meters.

>_ SENSORS: FULL SPECTRUM SWEEP IN PROGRESS.

Eric let the driver take his duffel and lead him to his taxi. He stowed the duffel in the trunk and even opened the rear door for him. Eric hesitated for just a second but shrugged internally and climbed in. He could rip the door off if the driver tried to lock him in.

>_ SENSORS: NO THREATS DETECTED.

A bit late now he was in the car, but good news all the same. He didn't need to attract attention before he was even settled in.

The driver got in behind the controls and turned to lean over his seat. "Where to, my man? If you want me to take you to the mines, I can do that. Have to go airborne though. Will cost extra."

"No mining for me. Now if they were fighting a take over and needed some extra muscle?" Eric said easing into his role as an out of work merc. Corporations of all kinds had their own armies to protect their investments or they hired merc companies to ease the way in "negotiations" with rivals.

The driver's eyes narrowed. "Our companies are honourable, they don't use or need mercenaries," he said with distaste for Eric thick in his voice. "I guess you could try out for a security guard or something." He didn't sound enthusiastic.

Eric didn't laugh, but the driver's instant dislike of him made that hard. It was cheering that decent people like him still existed; people who believed in a world where mercs weren't wanted or needed. He was wrong of course, but that didn't make the guy's sentiments less warming. Maybe Thurston could stay clean of the corruption that lead to underground wars between mega corps, wars between hired armies fighting and dying not for a cause but for pay. Maybe it could keep the shadowy world of organised crime that infested the underbelly of the core worlds at bay, stopped at Thurston's interface with the rest of the Human sector of the galaxy—the station. Eric doubted it. The Alliance grew, Human's colonised new worlds in ever greater numbers, and things changed, but Human nature? That never would. Until it did, there would always be a need for people like him willing to fight violence with violence.

"We'll see," Eric said. "Take me to a hotel; somewhere not too pricey but close to the action."

The driver nodded and turned back to his driving, and Eric entertained himself by watching the world go by.

The road out of the port arrowed straight for Ashfield, the land between still untouched and pristine, meaning jungle covered it. Having such a large section of real estate left virgin was a conscious decision Eric suspected. The original settlers had planned things very well in other areas, why not this? It was a good idea regardless of reasons, but was probably done for safety. Shuttles were quite safe, but accidents still happened. Besides, Ashfield wouldn't stay small forever.

"Where did the name come from?" Eric said. "Ashfield."

The driver grunted and gestured out the window toward

the direction they were travelling. "The mountain, it's an extinct volcano. The survey people named it Mount Ebra after one of their guys slipped and broke a leg or something. Whatever. The point is the geologists say this whole place, the city, the port, the land all around here is the ash field left over after Ebra blew its top. So when they decided to build here the name was sorta natural, you know?"

Eric nodded. "I like it."

The driver grunted.

"You sure Ebra isn't just dormant?"

The driver shrugged. "The geologists say extinct, and they should know. Be a bit of a bastard if they were wrong though, eh?"

Eric laughed. "Yeah. Ever heard of Pompeii?" Eric craned his neck to see the huge cone-shaped mountain. It was a big bugger, looming hugely over the city even at this distance. "Why do we Humans keep daring things like volcanoes to kill us by building in their back yards?"

"Dunno, but it's really pretty country here," the driver said with a grin.

Eric watched the jungle wondering what was looking back at him from under the trees. Something was. His sensors were active as always in combat mode, pretty much his default setting, and was picking up all kinds of unknowns. His data on Thurston was pretty good he would judge. Most new colonies in the border zone couldn't or wouldn't pay for the best studies, but Thurston had paid good money for what it did have. The surveys of its resources, and that included fauna and flora on top of the usual geological maps, were quite detailed he would judge. No doubt there were gaps, there always were, but the data was good and well presented. Eric remembered Desmatosuchos the super croc. Was ol' Desmond under those trees watching dinner drive by? Some of the amber icons on his sensors could be dinosaurs of one kind or another. They were big enough anyway.

"Any trouble with the wildlife?" Eric asked as he watched

a herd of something on his sensors amble along parallel to the road hidden by the jungle. "Maybe you have safaris?"

"We sure do!" the driver said enthusiastically. "Both I mean. Hunting is big here. Most of us do a little hunting when we get the time. Safaris, yeah we get them in the season. Brings in the tourists you know? Not around here though. Government pays for a cull every once in a while to keep the city safe, but some of the dumber dinos still come calling looking for a free lunch."

Eric smiled, imagining it. "Sounds like fun."

"Can be," the driver agreed. "Mostly it's a pain though. Road closures and waiting for a crane to carry the carcass away. They weigh ten even twenty tons some of them. Can bust stuff up before you know it."

The contacts on his sensors must be deemed safe enough, Eric mused. Maybe they were vegetarian or something.

They entered the city and ten minutes later found them stopping outside the St James Hotel. Eric used one of his wands to pay the driver. He chose the one he brought with him, not those Ken had left. He didn't know the usernames and passwords set on them yet. That information would be on the minicomp, or should be. He authorised payment and slid his wand out of the receptacle before climbing out of the car to get his duffel. The driver popped the trunk for him without getting out. Eric grabbed his duffel and closed the trunk. The driver raised a hand out his window and drove away.

Eric watched him go, studied his sensors for a brief moment watching for threats and movement patterns that might indicate he was of interest to someone, but found nothing to concern him. Good enough. He entered the hotel to get a room and some quiet time to study his brief in greater detail.

The St James Hotel was a three star establishment, it said so right on the door he passed through, but three star on whose scale? The award sticker and plaque didn't say. Going by the decor and general feel of the lobby, Eric expected good food but nothing fancy, high prices but not extortionate, and generous sized rooms. Other facilities would probably come under the heading of extras. Eric had seen the best and worst that money could buy in his time; the St James Hotel would rate on his own scale as first class but not top class. There was a difference, mostly in how much useless and fancy pampering a guest wanted or was willing to put up with. Eric had learned to put up with quite a bit but he had never learned to like it. He was a soldier first and his tastes were a soldier's tastes. Good food, comfortable bed, and within walking distance of some action at a price he could justify come debriefing was all he needed. Not that the General ever asked him how much a mission cost. He had underlings to handle budgets. He just wanted to know successful completion yes or no. If yes what were the results, was a follow-up mission advised? If no, what the fuck was Eric doing back then?

Eric grinned. He never went home to report failure. Not after the first time or two just after the war. That was something they had all learned. The General expected results and within reason didn't sweat how success was achieved. Obviously the regiment's exposure was out of the question and was mission critical. No mission could be called a success if it resulted in knowledge of Viper involvement getting out, but apart from that Eric had a free hand. He was expected to get the job done with minimal collateral damage and loss to the Alliance. Note that didn't mean loss to him, or Thurston, or even Thurston's citizenry—Burgton could be ruthless when needed—it meant what it said; loss to the Alliance was to be minimised. Eric left those calculations to the General. He decided what an acceptable loss was in the greater scheme, and losing Thurston was not an option.

Thurston would become part of the Alliance. Eric would remove anything or anyone standing in the way of that.

"How may I help you?" The concierge asked and smiled a pleasant but false smile. His eyes flickered disdainfully at Eric's well-used duffel and worn clothes. "I'm afraid our prices might be... ah, a little beyond your means."

"I doubt that," Eric said feeling annoyance rise at this petty little man. "Here, take a look."

Eric inserted his credit wand into the desk and activated the balance display function. The concierge's eyes widened at the figure it showed. It was stupid, but Eric felt vindicated when the man whitened as he realised he had insulted a very valuable customer.

"My apologies, sir. Your clothes made me think... never mind. Would you prefer a suite, sir?"

Eric nodded. "I'll be staying a while; a month or so."

"Very good, sir," the concierge said. He was back in his comfort zone and working his computer. "If you would fill in the register," he continued and indicated a screen set in the desk.

Eric picked up the light pen and quickly filled in the blanks with his false identity. "Send up a meal in an hour. Steak medium rare, eggs, potatoes, and a house salad. Is there a bar in the room?"

"Of course! Fully stocked, sir."

"Good."

Eric took his wand, the room key, and headed for the elevators. He glanced at the key. Room 402, fourth floor. He called the elevator and was alone with his thoughts on the ride up.

His first order of business upon entering the room was a sensor sweep. It was very unlikely he would find any surveillance devices, but he had been burned before in the most surprising ways. It cost him nothing to do a walk through while his sensors took the place apart.

>_ **Sensors: No threats detected.**

As it should be and as expected. He wanted a shower before the food arrived so attended to that next. After he was done and wearing a fresh uniform, he stowed his duffel in the closet but took a couple of spare magazines out and put them in his pockets. The minicomp and all his wands in hand, he relaxed in the sitting room and started work. Twenty minutes later and a lot wiser, he heard a knock on his door. He reached out to the hotel's rudimentary security system, slipped in, and accessed the camera in the hall. As expected it was room service at his door. He pushed his computer under a pillow and went to open the door.

"Your meal, sir," the woman said with a warm smile. "I think you will enjoy it. We have an excellent chef here."

Eric stepped aside to allow her to push the trolley inside. "In the sitting room, please."

The woman nodded and wheeled the trolley to where he indicated. She held out her scanner and Eric pressed his thumb to it authorising the cost, but he took a moment to key in a five percent tip. It would all be added to his bill.

"Thank you, sir," the woman said and sounded genuine. "You didn't need to do that. Service is all included."

Eric knew that, but he also knew the people who provided the actual service saw none of it and they were the ones who really needed it. Besides, he wasn't being completely altruistic. He had found simple kindness cost him nothing and sometimes benefitted him in unusual ways; like the time a barman had covered his back when he got jumped one night. He hadn't needed the assist, but the introduction of an old pulser rifle fired into the club's ceiling at the right time had certainly ended the fight before body bags had been needed. Kept his cover intact. Well worth the tip.

Eric shrugged. "I can afford it."

She smiled at him brightly and left.

Always a good idea to make friends rather than enemies, Eric mused, and besides, it wasn't all about the job. Sometimes he just liked to make someone smile at him. It made him feel like a real person again.

Eric ate his food and called for the trolley to be taken away. The same woman fetched it, and he again insisted upon tipping her. This time he had to talk her into presenting her scanner at all. It was charming, seeing her stammer and blush.

"If there is anything else, sir, ask for me by name. Moira."

"I will, Moira. Can you set my door to do not disturb on your way out?"

She nodded.

"Thanks."

Eric watched her leave on the security camera, and she did set the DND as asked. Good. He went back to work.

* * *

3~Undercover

St. James Hotel, Thurston, Border Zone

>_0559:59 CLOSE ARCHIVE FILE #0000063577982-
3996-SL
>_ 0600:01 DEACTIVATE MAINTENANCE MODE...
DONE.
DIAGNOSTICS: UNIT FIT FOR DUTY
ACTIVATE COMBAT MODE... DONE
TRS... DONE
SENSORS... DONE
TARGETING... DONE
COMMUNICATIONS... DONE
INFONET... DONE
TACNET... DONE... SCANNING... NO UNITS/
STATIONS FOUND
>_ 0600:05 REACTIVATION COMPLETE

Eric's eyes snapped open. He was back in the hotel and instantly alert as always. He stared at the ceiling in silence feeling the ghosts of his past slipping away from him and back into his memory, fading, and the ache of their loss dulled from knife sharp agony to the normal ache he always felt.

He swung his legs out of bed and headed for the shower. He had a great deal to get done and he wanted breakfast before he got down to it.

He didn't call room service but ate in the dining area. Bacon, eggs, toast, fried potatoes, lots of butter on his toast, and plenty of very strong black coffee. He gleefully ignored every warning his processor flagged up for his attention. Caffeine and saturated fats for god's sake, what were the programmers thinking? It was bad enough he had to imbibe the crap the design team had stipulated to maintain his systems—nanotech could do amazing things, but repairs and maintenance needed raw materials. His bio-systems used food just as god and nature intended, but his cybernetic enhancements needed much more. Viper ration packs tasted disgusting not because all Alliance rations did, but because they were laced with metal salts and other things designed to be broken down and used by his bots. Foul didn't begin to describe the crap he had to eat every few months or so. No one liked a Viper smoothie that was for damn sure.

When he finished eating, he left the hotel and walked the city streets, taking in the sights. Just another visitor, no particular place to be, looking around, blah, blah, blah. In reality he was watching his sensors intently, and building a three dimensional security map on top of the existing map he had downloaded from Infonet. Ken hadn't bothered with the city, not because he didn't have the time, but because he knew Eric's mission was not in Ashfield. That was understandable. Ken had his area of expertise, and Eric had his. Eric didn't care that the Freedom Movement was not based in the capital, Ken's data seemed to indicate that fairly well, but he did care that every target they had hit to date was here. So, that was why he spent that entire day and the following days building up a solid security map of the city; well that, and the fact he would need something to prove his worth to a Freedom Movement recruiter.

He spent the daylight hours of that week walking the

streets, riding in taxis, hopping from one train to another crisscrossing the city and using his sensors to trawl for electronic emissions. His night time hours were spent infiltrating computer networks so that he had as full a picture as possible. His data would impress, he had no doubt. Any Viper could take Thurston's security apart, but he had no plan to do the terrorists any favours by just handing it over to them. He would much rather slaughter them all, but that really wasn't his mission.

The day came when he was ready to make contact with the Freedom Movement. He wiped everything on the computer Ken had left, and then physically broke it into pieces before throwing it away far from the hotel. Nothing it had once contained would be recoverable. He didn't know how competent they were, but if anyone checked his room they would find nothing to suggest he was other than the merc he pretended to be.

He left the hotel and took a taxi to a cafe he had found his first day. He liked it because it fronted onto the plaza outside the Parliament building and he could watch the bustle. He often did that when time permitted, people watching he called it. He always wondered who they were and what they thought of the world around them. It was hard to remember what it had been like, being like them.

Being Human they would see people like themselves and buildings, sky and ground, vehicles going by. They would smell the scent of jungle vegetation on the breeze, and think nothing more about any of it. They would move through the world, oblivious. How wonderful it must be.

He envied them.

When he looked at the world he saw it through layers of data. He glanced outside the taxi at a pedestrian walking by. He didn't see people, he saw...

>_ WHITE MALE, DARK HAIR AND EYES, 1.9M TALL, 97KG, 33 YEARS OLD APPROX. UNARMED.

Threat potential negligible.
>_ Searching... no matches found.
>_ Search local databases [Y]es/[N]o?
>_ N

When he looked at a building, he didn't see architecture. He didn't see artistry or admirable design concepts. He saw stress points and weaknesses. He saw schematics with data appended in colourful boxes and lines leading to points of access, or places where the right amount of explosive would bring the building down, or damage it to varying degrees depending upon the mission's needs.

When he closed his eyes, he didn't see blackness. He saw sensor data scrolling by. If he shut that down, he couldn't while in combat mode, but if he could, he would see internal system data. The sky? Not really. He would see weather forecasts, thermal and atmospheric data, analysis of local conditions such as contaminants in the air, both chemical and bacteriological. There was just no way to separate himself from the machine side of him.

He was the machine.

The taxi let him out at the cafe after he paid with his wand, and he sat down at an empty table outside. He didn't wait for service preferring to use the table menu to order. He scrolled through the lists on the table top display and chose a pastry that looked good and a strong coffee he recognised from his hotel. A waiter quickly appeared with his order, its android features that of a young woman. A polite smile had been programmed into its features. The android set the food and drink before him and turned so Eric could pay. The receptacle for his wand was in its back centred between the shoulder blades.

The waiter left and Eric enjoyed his pastry.

When he was finished he used his wand in communicator mode and called his contact man. Ken had found the little weasel and promised money for an introduction. A lot of money. That was the reason for the platinum he carried.

"Hello?"

Eric glanced around watching visually and with sensors. None were paying him any mind but he set up a short range scramble regardless.

"The Cafe Reichard, Parliament Plaza. Thirty minutes," Eric said.

"Who is this?"

"No names. A mutual friend left something for you with me. You know of what I speak?"

The man swallowed audibly. "You have it?" He sounded scared but eager.

"Thirty minutes," Eric repeated and disconnected.

The time passed quickly, and it wasn't long before his tap into certain security cameras placed at junctions for traffic management revealed a face he had been watching for. The man wasn't alone.

Eric used the camera to zoom in and captured an image of both men. He passed that quickly to his processor and ordered a search. The first hit came up quickly and as expected from his own data. It was definitely his contact and the search had found his bio in Ken's download. The search continued and spread out into local networks after Eric gave it the go ahead. The second hit was the contact man again, and the data filled in some blanks but nothing interesting. His real name was Bryce Kanarion, not Syl Finnegan, the name Ken used for him. Eric had begun to wonder about that when more hits came up in quick succession. Eric grunted unsurprised by a short list of aliases, and now doubted Kanarion was the real name. It didn't matter. What did, was that Kanarion was a small time crook with contacts above his pay grade by an order of magnitude. Eric wondered how that had happened.

The first hit for the other man appeared and Eric turned his attention to his bio. Eric pursed his lips in thought as more data started coming in. Yi Zhang was no freedom fighter that was certain and it annoyed him. Zhang was just a little man, and Eric didn't mean his physical stature. Chinese ancestry didn't always lead to a small build, but it did quite often and had done so in Zhang's case. No, he was just a businessman, and not a rich one. He owned a small factory making machine tools. No doubt he sold most to the mines. How he connected with a terrorist group Eric couldn't fathom. Every new bit of data that came up reinforced his none violent nature and that made Eric pause in his assessment.

Everything pointed him in only one direction, but that wasn't natural. No one was this one-dimensional. Everyone had something to hide even if it was only stealing office supplies. Not so with Zhang. If the data could be believed, he was a saint! That meant the data had been sanitized, but whoever did the work hadn't understood how to build a truly believable bio. This one screamed false. It said, 'look at me, I am innocent' or 'nothing to find here, go away now' or 'I love little animals, none violent is my middle name.'

Eric snorted; yeah right. Zhang was a player, probably small time as yet—his engineering business did seem real—maybe his shady side was a hobby or something. Eric chuckled at the thought. He would keep digging.

Kanarion was supposed to facilitate a meeting, but Yi Zhang could be nothing more than a middle man if that. If Kanarion expected him to pay full price for this introduction, he could think again. Damn him!

Eric followed the two men using Ashfield's cameras until they entered the plaza. He picked them out on his sensors and tagged them for targeting. Even slowed by the Raytheon inside his clothes, both would be dead before they could think of betrayal. Still, he didn't seriously feel threatened. He watched for any surveillance on himself or on his visitors and found none. He stood to greet them as they reached his table.

"Gentlemen, please sit," Eric said shaking their hands as if this were a normal meeting. Both men looked taken aback but did sit. "Kanarion... yes I know it's not your real name. You were supposed to introduce me to a certain someone. Mister

Zhang here doesn't fit the bill."

Kanarion's face darkened.

"If you think I'm paying you fifty thousand for this meeting," Eric went on. "You're stupider than you look."

"You!" Kanarion began in a rage, but his companion stopped him from leaping up with a hand on his shoulder. Kanarion sat back fully and hissed the words, "If you try to screw me, you won't live to regret it."

Eric grinned nastily at the blustering man. His targeting reticule pulsed redly, spinning and centred on his forehead right between the eyes. Kanarion was only a thought away from death; his companion too. Zhang was more sensible. He had moved a little apart from his friend after his initial instinct to restrain Kanarion. A quick assessing look was all Eric needed to assure himself they were both unarmed.

Eric leaned forward. "You had a job to do. You didn't do it. Why should I not just walk away? Oh, and by the way, threaten me again and I will shut your mouth for you. Permanently." Eric let Kanarion see a glimpse of the Raytheon under his arm, and smiled when he looked away. "No answer?"

"If I may?" Zhang said. "He can't help you, but he knew I could. He hasn't failed."

Eric sat back and regarded Zhang thoughtfully. He kept both men targeted, but had his sensors do a sweep looking for anything interesting. A wire frame representation of both men flashed up onto his display as the sweep commenced. A few seconds later a couple of places flashed amber on the models, but none red. A query showed Kanarion was carrying a wand, but although its carrier wave showed it was active for incoming comms, it wasn't in use. Zhang had a number of devices in his pockets. An inactive wand was one, the other two might be minicomps of some kind, but neither device was recording or active in any other way. Both men's wristcomps were active of course, but unlike Eric's military issue, they had no ability to broadcast.

Eric dismissed the sweep's results to concentrate on

Zhang.

"... knows to keep silent. If you agree?"

Eric quickly reviewed his log of the last few seconds, and nodded slowly as if thinking it over. Zhang had proposed paying Kanarion off so that they could get down to business.

"And you guarantee his silence?"

Zhang nodded. "He is my sister's husband."

Eric grinned, Zhang didn't sound happy about that. Eric wouldn't have been either. "Tell you what I'll do. I'll pay him twenty five thousand—"

Kanarion cursed.

Zhang whirled toward his brother-in-law. "Keep silent fool!" He turned back to Eric. "Go on."

"Twenty five thousand for him as payment for this intro, and he goes away. He doesn't talk about this and you guarantee it. Then, if you complete his job as you say you can, I'll pay you another twenty five thousand and you can give it to him or keep it yourself. I don't care which." Zhang began to agree but Eric held up a finger and pointed at Kanarion who was looking incensed. "Make me believe you can control him."

Zhang turned to his brother-in-law. "You were always a disappointment to my family," he began and Kanarion's face darkened. "But this time you accidently did something right by calling me. Don't ruin it. I swear I will give you the twenty five thousand. On my honour. You know my word is good."

Kanarion nodded reluctantly.

"I know you think me a fool for keeping to the old ways, but remember this: keeping my word is not the only tradition I uphold. Vendetta is another. I swear if you speak a word of this, my sister will be a widow the next day. Do you understand?"

Eric blinked. Zhang didn't sound angry or upset. His heartbeat and other stats were unchanged, but Eric believed every word he'd said. Going by expression, Kanarion did as well. The suddenly scared man nodded jerkily.

"Good," Zhang said and turned back to Eric. "Satisfied?"

Eric counted out twenty-five platinum wafers as his answer and slid them toward Kanarion. The greedy man's hand darted out and made them disappear, his eyes glowing with excitement.

"Good bye, Kanarion. We won't meet again... we better not," Eric said evenly.

Kanarion stood and walked quickly away. Eric kept him tagged on sensors but left it to his processor to alert him should the man change his mind and return or do something else interesting. Meanwhile, Zhang had to be dealt with. He slid the remaining wafers of platinum to Zhang and the man pocketed them without counting them.

"I don't envy you," Eric said mildly.

Zhang grimaced. "My sister loves him and I love my sister. It would hurt her should I have to make good on my threat, but sometimes I think a little accident and a quick funeral for him would be better for her in the long run."

"Kids?"

Zhang shuddered. "No thank god, but she wants them. I must decide soon."

Eric pursed his lips, but then he nodded. This so-called businessman would be called something else on other worlds he had visited. Something a little more sinister. Crime boss sounded a little old fashioned and the image it conjured was a cliché, but that's what Eric was getting from Zhang's demeanour and conversation with his brother-in-law. Eric remembered thinking about Thurston's future when he first arrived, and how the station stood guard against crime, but it was obviously already here dirtside. And that was a problem of another sort. Why hadn't his searches found Zhang's shadier dealings? His digging still hadn't found anything of the sort.

> *Computer: Narrow search to Yi Zhang's immediate family. Include financials. Query: Is there any evidence of Freedom Movement affiliation and/or sympathies?*

>_ Working

Eric decided to probe a little while his processor deepened its search into Zhang's family.

"You said he did the right thing by getting you involved. Why?"

"Because I can do what he cannot. You are not the first mercenary I have hired on behalf of my... of friends," Zhang said.

Eric's eyes narrowed, he had been going to say something else. Family maybe?

"In my line of work, I have needed such before," Zhang continued. "My... friends heard that about me and when they found a similar need they came to me for advice."

"I see," Eric said and did see quite well. His processor had finally found the missing data he had needed to get a handle on Zhang.

Yi Zhang's company was family owned and run as Eric had expected, and although it must be a front for some criminal activities as well, it really did produce machine tools for the mines. It was a legitimate company, but one family member had not stuck around despite that. His brother, Hu Zhang and severed all ties and changed his name in an apparent effort to disavow its less than legal activities. A noble goal, but that was why a preliminary search had failed to find any links to Zhang. Hu Zhang, was now Daniel King, a politician opposed to President Thurston's policies. Eric realised immediately why Hu chose the name King. It was just a Romanised version of his real name, but his processor hadn't made the connection on its first pass. Yet another reason to regret the loss of real A.I computer architecture. An A.I would not have needed him to make the connection, it would have seen the obvious. Still, Eric had the data now; that was important, and besides, he had enough problems with a dull but obedient computer living in his head. He did not want to think about having a real A.I constantly with him. He didn't think his sanity would survive it.

"I understand you wish to join the Freedom Movement," Zhang went on after a moment. "Why? You are not from Thurston. Why do you care what happens here?"

Eric took a sip of coffee and frowned when the usual caffeine alert appeared on his display. He ignored it as he always did. "You know the answer. I don't care what happens here unless it inconveniences me. I'm a merc. Money interests me, nothing much else does."

"But you have money."

"Not enough."

"What is enough?" Zhang shrugged. "I'm a businessman and I've yet to find that elusive figure."

Eric laughed. "Same here. I don't want to join the Freedom Movement, I don't do causes. If the movement didn't exist here, I would go to a planet where it did. I'm not the type to follow a cause. I follow the money, period. Now that's not to say I won't stick around for a while you understand."

Zhang grinned but sobered quickly. "So it's just another contract for you. I can understand that. My friends will want to check you out, but assuming all goes well, I think you can consider yourself hired."

Eric raised a hand. "I don't come cheap, not even on the Guild's pay scale, but I can be had. Two mil for the duration of ah... of hostilities."

Zhang paled and then laughed. "Two million credits for one man is ridiculous. I could hire ten for that!"

"Ah, but they wouldn't be me. And besides, you wouldn't get ten on an open ended contract. I did say I would stick around for the duration. For all you know that could be years."

Zhang frowned. "True. Why would you agree to that?"

Eric grinned and retrieved the data crystal he had compiled over the previous week from a pocket. "I'm glad you asked. This is a free sample of my work. Give it to your friends. If they like it, I want the two million up front deposited to my account. You'll find details on here." He passed the crystal to Zhang. "In the very unlikely event they don't like what it contains, no hard feelings and I'll be on a ship away from here by the end of the month. Deal?"

Zhang nodded slowly. He was looking at the crystal pensively. "I will enquire."

Eric stood and offered his hand. "Nice doing business. I'm off to catch a show. Might even try to bag one of your dinos. Heard you have safaris."

Zhang nodded, still seeming distracted.

Eric walked away watching Zhang on one of the cameras feeding him live imagery. He smiled to himself as Zhang took out his wand and made a call. Eric froze the image and captured the name and number displayed on the wand. You never knew what could turn out to be important.

Saint James Hotel, Thurston, Border Zone

Eric returned to his rooms after the latest in a long list of leisure pursuits he had indulged in. He would rather have been on his way back to Snakeholme, but with no contact from Zhang or his friends, he had to stay here and pretend to be having fun.

> *Take in the sites like a tourist,* CHECK.
> *Go on a three day safari,* CHECK.
> *Take in a couple of shows,* YAWN AND CHECK.
> *Practice on the range, making errors like a Human just in case he was being watched,* CHECK.

It had whiled away the time, but he could have gone into hibernation mode if that was all he wanted. No, it was more to keep up appearances than to fill time. Surely he was being monitored, if not electronically then by Human means. He did still watch for surveillance, but he hadn't detected any.

It annoyed him, because without any kind of reaction to his presence he couldn't gauge his progress.

Eric checked at the desk for messages. None again, but that was expected. Zhang could leave one on the comm in his room if he wanted, or preferably on Eric's own wand. Checking at the desk was a sign of his impatience, nothing more. He wanted to be done with this, and go home, that was all.

He took the elevator up to his floor and quickly entered his room. As soon as he entered he froze, hyper alert, and the nano-sized remote he had left to guard the door reported in. Two intrusions within the last five hours. Why two? His sensors swept ahead, but found no one in the suite now, but someone had been here. Perhaps the hotel staff had stopped in to clean... no, he couldn't detect any aromas of cleaning products. Excellent. If not hotel staff, then it was likely a team sent to search his room. It was the kind of response he had been waiting for.

Well it took them long enough, Eric mused as he checked out each of his rooms. Someone had finally gotten around to searching his suite and installing listening devices. He wondered if it had been Major Stein's paranoia or whether the Freedom Movement had finally gotten with the program. Eric sighed. If there was one thing he hated more than terrorists, it was incompetent terrorists. Professionals could be expected to do certain things and were therefore predictable within certain parameters. With two hundred years experience, he had those parameters pretty well mapped now, but amateurs... he shuddered. They were a bloody menace.

The search of his suite wasn't a surprise; bound to happen eventually. What did surprise, and annoy, was how long it had taken for a reaction. His meeting with Zhang was nine days ago, and no money or other contact had been forthcoming. That was why Eric wondered if the search had been a marine operation. Stein had to be jittery now that the Freedom Movement had completed the op his data crystal had outlined.

Stein had not been happy when Eric informed him of the operation, and the expected results. It went against the grain to allow a terrorist group to successfully jack a government armoury that way, but in the end Stein had gone along hoping that casualties would be low and that getting a man inside the movement would compensate.

The Freedom Movement had gone in hard, neutralised the security net as instructed in Eric's plan, killed everyone in the building—five guards that late at night—and withdrew in a pair of armoury trucks carrying pallets of ammunition and dino hunting rifles. They were completely unopposed and unseen thanks to the network shunts he had included the specs for in his plan. Eric had ensured there were no pulsers, AARs, or RPGs stored at that particular facility when he chose it, and as soon as the op went down Stein had beefed up security at the places where such things actually were stored. That was fine. The Freedom Movement would have expected no less.

Bringing Major Stein into the loop had been a calculated risk. Eric knew he would need backup eventually, but he could have waited until later to make contact, but Stein was one of those forward thinking officers the marine corp. liked so much—an effective one. Eric preferred that sort too, but in Stein's case it could have short-circuited the evolving plan. Eric had needed to hustle when he realised Stein was going to make a move that would have made the data on the crystal he'd given Zhang obsolete. That would have ruined everything.

Getting Stein alone had been hard, but Eric had managed it, and the marine had taken it in stride when he realised what Eric was. Getting him to agree to delay his plans though, especially when doing so would almost certainly risk lives, had been a struggle. Eric never liked pulling rank. It didn't seem right to give orders to a major when his own official rank was lesser, but the truth of the matter was that Stein could have been the Commandant of Marines—unlikely in the extreme as it was an administrative position not a battlefield command—and he would still have complied... probably. Eric grimaced at the thought.

It was history and tradition that made Vipers command the other branches of the military on the battlefield, not rank or regulations, and Eric was careful never to abuse that. All of them were. They were feared and respected, but that respect never quite dulled the fear. No one in the regiment wanted to make that worse. Eric had to wonder how well that would work if they began recruiting again. He shrugged. It wasn't his problem.

Eric wandered his rooms as if bored, allowing his sensors to map the surveillance grid newly installed by unknown persons. It wasn't Stein, he decided as he traced more and more emissions. The gear was good tech, a little too good for the regular military. That was no insult to the marines. The marines wanted rugged gear, able to do the job and take abuse without failing on the battlefield, and military budgets also preferred it that way. A score of good solid units could be had for the price of a single highly sensitive and temperamental unit meant for true espionage. The tech in use here was not regular military issue, neither was it the absolute cutting edge, but it was spy stuff. The kind of thing a government agency would employ.

Eric frowned as another grid appeared on sensors. What the hell? Two surveillance grids in one place made no sense unless... he nodded and smiled in amusement. The high end gear probably was government. Thurston was up and coming, its agencies would need to keep pace. Unemployed mercs would surely be on the watch list especially considering recent events. Eric tagged that net as Thurston InSec for now and left it alone. It was active but passive in that the sensors had no offensive capabilities. The same couldn't be said for the other grid.

This one he tagged as Freedom Movement and hostile because it did in fact have offensive capability in the form of sonics and neurotoxin dispensers. Eric immediately hacked the net and disabled the weapon circuits but left the passives alone. No one would realise what he had done unless trying to trigger an attack. It was good but not high end tech; exactly what he had come to expect from terrorist organisations with off world backing, something he was seeing more and more as the decades rolled by. Maybe Burgton was right about that too. Burgton's theory of growth over stagnation within the Alliance was something the regiment often debated. They had the time and vision to see long-term trends—very long term. Their unique perspective and ability to collate data and statistics from all over the place gave Burgton an unparalleled ability to predict events.

After a moment's thought, Eric inserted a little subroutine into the hostile net that would warn him if someone sent a signal to attack. His hack would prevent the attack, but it would be good to know if one were attempted. Looking over his work, he carefully withdrew from the net, satisfied he was once again secure.

Nine days. That delay gave him some idea of the terrorist's capabilities he realised. Zhang must have handed the crystal to his friends that day; probably to his brother, but there was no proof of that. Didn't matter who; it was the timing that interested him. A day to get the data to someone with the authority to evaluate it, and maybe another day to decide to use it. Add to that a week to gather personnel and supplies to launch the op. Not bad, but not great. Probably supply issues rather than personnel. It was usually that way around.

They had proven his data sample was good with the attack last night. He could expect contact any time now. Fine then. He would step out for one final day of exploring. With the thought fresh in mind, he left the room and locked his door before making his way down.

He didn't have a destination in mind, so when the taxi driver asked him, he said to tour the city a while. The driver nodded and off they went. Eric had Ashfield mapped and in his database, so he simply let the man have his head and let the world go by without taking too much of an interest in any one thing, besides, the people interested him the most. He watched them as if they were some alien species just discovered. The children walking with their parents always perked him up. It was good to know that the cycle of life was unending. All the death he had seen was offset by new life. Not erased of course, his memories would never fade, but it did make him feel better seeing the children. They didn't know he existed and were better off not knowing the things he did. Their lives went on separate from him and unconnected.

Eric frowned as the taxi ventured away from the areas tourists were normally interested in. The buildings were less flashy, more utilitarian. A quick check of his map told Eric they were heading away from the city centre toward the industrial zone.

"Hey, I said I wanted a tour. I'm not interested in factories," Eric said in annoyance.

The driver ignored him.

What the hell? Eric used his sensors and sighed in annoyance. They were being escorted in front and behind by armed men driving identical cars. Government maybe. He could rip the door off and bail, but really, what was the point? It would only draw more attention to him. He could force the driver to pull over and let him out... no he decided, he would wait and see where this leads. Maybe it would be interesting.

Interesting was one word for it, he mused as the taxi pulled into a compound. Another word for it was surprising. The compound was part of Zhang's factory complex, and was full of loading and unloading trucks. Eric watched as one lifted off and flew low over the city as it clawed for altitude. Heavy bugger that one. He wondered about the cargo. He decided after a moment that his escort wasn't government. Bringing him here didn't make sense for that to be true. These were Zhang's men probably... or maybe his brother's. Eric readied himself for action when the taxi stopped and his door popped open.

He wondered briefly if they would try to disarm him. If they did, it would at least give him a point of reference. He needed to move the mission along. If they were hostile, he could at least take out this part of the Freedom Movement's operation. He would keep one or two alive for interrogation, and use the answers to target another cell. With luck, he would learn about their base of operations. There must be one if they really planned to overthrow the government. There was no way urban terrorism alone could do it; not now the marines were here with air support. No, they needed to field a proper force, and that would take logistical support—equipment and personnel. If they didn't have that, the Freedom Movement would be nothing more than an annoyance to any government, but Eric didn't get that sense from them.

"No tip for you," Eric muttered to the driver as he climbed out of the taxi. Or fare either, he thought.

The driver shrugged and grinned. He drove away leaving Eric facing the escort cars waiting for them to make a move. The car windscreens were dialled to black. The occupants might have weapons trained on him and he wouldn't know. His sensors detected four men in each car, and they were armed with pulsers by the emissions he was receiving, but that didn't tell him if they were out and pointed. Eric turned to watch as the security gate slid shut and locked him in. It couldn't hold him of course. He could climb it or the wall if need be. He turned on the spot letting his sensors do the work for now. He had three exit strategies mapped by the time a welcoming committee came out to join him.

"Mister Martell, forgive the manner in which you were brought here," Yi Zhang said. Beside him walked another man. His brother. Eric had his picture in his database. Both men were wearing high-collared business suits that befitted their corporate status. "Unavoidable I'm afraid. There have been developments."

Eric glanced at Zhang's outstretched hand but didn't take it. He would need his hands if this went sour. "Zhang," he said with a slight nod, "and this is?"

Zhang lowered his hand. "I think you already know, but in case I overestimated you, may I introduce Daniel King? Daniel, this is the man I told you about, Eric Martell."

King didn't offer to shake. "You have a novel way of gaining my attention, Martell. Your free sample certainly did."

Eric relaxed a little; this didn't feel like a prelude to an attack. "I've found it quicker and it usually works. I like to do my groundwork before meeting clients and getting down to the practical applications of what I can offer."

King didn't smile. "President Thurston's secret police are watching your suite. They have it wired."

Eric shrugged. "I know."

Secret Police indeed. King was trying to portray himself as a patriot fighting the good fight against a despot. Eric managed not to laugh. It was amazing really, how many of these people used the same rhetoric when justifying themselves. He had heard it all hundreds of times before. He was beginning to wonder if they had read the same terrorism manual, because they all seemed to be using it for their bullshit.

King blinked. "You know?"

"Of course. No need for concern, there's nothing for them to find there. Everything I need is in my head." He tapped his temple with a finger. He didn't tell them that he had found their surveillance as well as the government's gear. "All they have is my underwear and spare uniforms."

A splutter of laughter burst out of Zhang. He turned to his brother. "See what I mean?"

King nodded. "The two million will hit your account in..." he checked his wristcomp. "About twenty minutes. Come inside to wait. You have the means to check our deposit here?"

Eric nodded, patting the pocket containing his wands.

So, no attempt to disarm him and they would definitely assume he was armed. He would have in their place. The mention of the money clinched it. He was in the door... more or less.

King lead off and Eric followed. Behind him, car doors opened and eight men brought up the rear. Eric targeted each one, but did nothing outwardly offensive. It was precautionary only. He would do nothing to halt progress. He had gained some ground, but he wasn't in yet.

Zhang led them into an empty office, not his own Eric noticed and wondered why not. Maybe all his employees weren't in the loop. Eric glanced around as King took one of two swivel chairs near the desk. Zhang headed for the autochef. Eric turned as two of the escort entered the room and closed the door. Before it closed fully and they blocked any approach to it, Eric saw the other six men arraying themselves along the corridor outside. Not very trusting, he thought with an internal grin.

Eric didn't seat himself, but did take a coffee from Zhang when it was offered. He grimaced at the taste. He detested decaf. "Assuming the transfer goes ahead without problems, what do you envision my role will be?"

King turned his chair and looked up at Eric. "I'll assume you know the situation here so won't waste time reiterating. Normally I wouldn't be meeting with a recruit like this, but your unorthodox approach appealed to me. You're no ordinary recruit and I don't expect you'll need that gun under your arm. I have plenty of trigger pullers. I want you on my team devising strategy."

Eric nodded; smart man to be thinking along those lines. It was exactly what he wanted King to think, but he hadn't needed to guide the man. It being his own idea should bolster King's trust in him and give better access to what he needed. If they had just recruited him as plain soldier, he could have been posted as a guard at the arse end of nowhere and unable to learn what he needed.

"You are fortunate," King went on. "Your plan worked so well that it occurred to people I trust that you might be an operative working for our enemy. President Thurston isn't above using InSec for his own ends despite his so precious constitution."

Eric took note of King's sneering condemnation of his President. There was something personal there; it wasn't all politics, and Eric wondered what it was about, but King was still talking.

"... our base of operations. I won't tell you where you'll be working, and you will have no access to that information even while there. If you have objections?"

Eric shook his head. It was perfect. King wanted him to work on planning more raids from a secret location as a security measure, but he was a Viper. He could be deaf and blind and dropped anywhere on the planet and he would know where he was seconds later. He was only a thought away from a secure satellite link anywhere in the system. His designers would never have missed such a basic necessity. Many of his systems used the link. TacNet didn't actually need to use it—unit to unit links could be and often were used—but TacNet could use satellites to increase range when they were available. Sensors used them for keeping track of friendly and enemy units on the battlefield, and for navigation. Calling in air support without them could be a pain. The point was, King could call it a secret base all he wanted, but as soon as Eric arrived, he would know where it was and so would the marines. He would see to that. The Freedom Movement had just taken a huge step toward their extinction, and Eric a step toward heading home again.

He was pleased.

The time came and he went through the motions of verifying payment. He couldn't care less about the money and wanted to get going, but he had to play his part. A mercenary wouldn't overlook it, so he dutifully used a wand to check his balance. Two million had been deposited a few minutes earlier and he nodded to King.

"It's there. When do you need me to be ready?"

King raised an eyebrow. "I thought you understood. You

will leave from here directly, and no you can't go back to your hotel."

"Don't you trust me?" Eric said.

"Of course not. You will be escorted by my men at all times until you reach our base. Once there, you can move about, but not before then, and we won't let you leave without escort for any reason."

Eric shrugged. "I agreed to a contract for the duration of hostilities. Hope you don't mind if I make that duration short."

King smiled this time. "I like your confidence. You get to leave when we have won, not before."

"Understood. I estimate three to six months," Eric said. "But that depends on resources and your willingness to cooperate with me and use them as I direct. I don't need to take command or expect to, but I do need your fighters to at least consider what I say."

"They will do what I tell them," King said coldly, his eyes suddenly hard. "You will have access to our logistics data, and I expect you to evaluate what we can and can't do with what we have. I want ideas. If you have a way to increase our capability, I want to know about it immediately. You will be my advisor as far as my people are concerned. Advisor only. They won't take orders from you."

Eric shrugged. King was a paranoid bastard. "Okay by me. I'll need a way to talk to you, unless you're coming with?"

"No. I can't be away from the capital right now. I'll give you a number where you can reach me or someone I trust."

"Fine."

King stood and prepared to leave. He spoke with Zhang a moment before leaving the room. The eight man security team did not follow.

"Well," Zhang said and clapped his hands together cheerily. "I have transportation all arranged for you. Your... watchdogs? They will take over from here. Good luck to you."

Eric nodded to him and followed his keepers out of the

office. They led him outside and into the compound toward one of the transports he had seen earlier. He climbed into the cargo bay of the nearest when told to, and sat on one of the crates. His watchdogs climbed in to join him, and moments later the transport lifted off. He didn't know his destination, but using a satellite link he followed along and plotted a few points of interest. A minute into the journey he decided they were heading for the spaceport. He guessed they would be taking a shuttle somewhere. No matter.

He closed his eyes and leaned back pretending to sleep.

* * *

4~Sanctuary

"Do you see him?" Tahar whispered, his black-tufted ears stood erect and alert atop his grey furred head.

Shima tried to penetrate the gloom beneath the trees and find what her father had seen, but the shadows were too deep, and her eyes blurred with the distance. She silently cursed them for not being as keen as his. Sometimes she felt like clawing them out of her head. At least then she wouldn't see the disappointment on her father's face every time he looked at her. She knew where the Shkai'ra stood. It was a warm and peaceful presence within her mind, very different to the fierce glow that was her father. The breeze suddenly shifted in her favour, teasing her with the Shkai'ra's scent. Her claws slid from their sheaths and dug into the moist soil beneath her paws. A frustrated growl rumbled deep in her chest.

"Do you not see him even this close?"

She wanted to howl in despair at the pity she heard in his voice. "I feel him my father… I almost see him," she lied. She knew which sub-species it had to be. There were a great many of the Lesser Shkai'ra at Sanctuary East. She doubted it could be one of the much rarer black tailed variants of the species. "A

Lesser Shkai'ra. A big one, yes?"

Tahar's ears flattened in distress at her lies. "No. He's black tailed—barely adult and very small."

He was disappointed in her. She could feel it. The pain that caused her was worse than anything else she could think of. Her father was the best hunter and tracker in her family. Chailen, her younger sib, might grow to be as good, but she was barely adult. It was too soon to be certain.

"I…" she began, but she couldn't finish her apology. She lowered her head almost to the ground in shame.

Her father pretended not to see a reason for shame. "Come. I will take you closer so that you might see."

He crept forward still on four paws like a shadow, then froze with his right forefoot raised. His ears pricked and swivelled, listening for danger hidden in the dense undergrowth. The sun was lowering in the sky, deepening the shadows and heralding the arrival of Sanctuary East's night hunters. His whiskers drew down and his nose twitched as he scented his quarry. Shima waited motionless, less than two paces behind him. The breeze shifted and she caught the scent of the Shkai'ra again. It was calm and unaware of them.

Tahar eased his paw to the ground, and with his head low between powerful shoulders, crept toward his quarry. Left forefoot, right hind foot and pause. Right forefoot, left hind foot and pause again. Shima mirrored her father's movements and was concentrating on him to such an extent that she failed to notice when her sight finally resolved the Shkai'ra.

Tahar stopped and looked back at her in question.

She was so close to the beast that one pounce would have been enough to take it down. The Shkai'ra was a young male, barely old enough to forage for himself. Although his fangs rivalled hers, his other weapons were still undeveloped. Two knife-sharp horns presaged an impressive rack that would eventually grace his proud head.

"He's beautiful," she whispered almost inaudibly, and Tahar flicked his ears in agreement.

The Shkai'ra froze in mid-chew and Shima held her breath. It raised its head warily, looking for the source of its unease, but Tahar's pelt was a mottled shadow, and Shima took after him in her looks if not in her abilities. It failed to see them. The Shkai'ra used his wickedly sharp hooves to dig for more roots and went happily back to his chewing.

Shima took one more step and slowly raised herself onto her hind legs. She could almost reach out and touch him now. One more step and she reached forward. The Shkai'ra turned to look back and froze. The moment stretched out into an eternity. She stared into those innocent eyes in wonder, feeling connected to her ancestors as never before. It was so easy to think of herself as one of those primitive hunters. She would have known nothing of the wider world back then. She would have known nothing of engineering, or genetic farming methods—known nothing of history or philosophy. Her only concern would be the wellbeing of the clan and her people, her only task to hunt for food and protect her clan.

The moment passed.

She felt the barest of touches on her outstretched paw and then the Shkai'ra was gone in a blur of speed. She would never forget that moment or the feel of its hide as long as she lived. She watched it race into the trees until she lost it to poor vision. She could still sense it running blindly away from her—still scent its fear on the breeze. There was nothing wrong with her other senses. It was only her eyes that made her a cripple among her people.

The Shkai'ra was long gone when Tahar stood tall once more and led Shima back to their camp. She looked back once but the wonderful beast was lost to her. She could no longer even sense it. She and her father were its natural enemy. It didn't know it was safe from them. Sanctuary East was a preserve. The Shkai'ra weren't the only species to need such a place, but they were the most endangered.

"We must leave before the sun sets," Tahar said when they reached camp.

"I know," she said. "I'm sorry I lied. I wanted you to look at me like you do at Chailen... I'm sorry."

She ducked her head, looking at the ground and not at him. She was tired of seeing the disappointment on his face, but his anger would be worse. She busied herself tidying their supplies. They would be ready when it was time to begin the long walk out of Sanctuary East and back to the world. She retrieved her harness and slipped it on. It's weight felt odd after so long wearing nothing but her pelt.

"You are my first cub," Tahar said softly from close behind her. "I love you no less than Chailen."

She forced herself not to turn. "Chailen is special. You *should* love her more."

Tahar sighed. "Look at me. Please look at me. I can't keep talking to your tail."

Her jaw dropped open in amusement and her ears quivered of their own accord. He used to say that when she was very small.

"Stop trying to make me laugh."

"Laughter is good."

Tahar led her to the fallen tree they had been using as a table. Visitors to Sanctuary East were encouraged to take only the minimum of supplies into the preserve. Harming the animals was against the purpose of the preserve, and bringing technology other than an emergency beacon was discouraged. It was a matter of pride among those who came here to bring only what their ancestors had used.

Tahar sat upon the fallen tree beside her. "I am proud of you, Shima, so very proud. So what if you cannot hunt like the great Jasha? I cannot either, nor could anyone if you believe the stories. We are no longer hunters, Shima. We are beyond such things now. Hunting is not important any longer." He mimed grasping something and throwing it away. "It's a hobby, nothing more. You and Chailen are the future; I am the past as much as hunting is."

"Don't say that! You are great, everyone knows it."

He snorted. "A great fool for not teaching you better. You have surpassed me in all that matters, Shima. You make me proud to be your father, but you don't see it, do you?"

"I see disappointment when you look at me."

Tahar's eyes widened and his ears flattened. "I have *never* felt that. I have been angry on occasion, amused quite often, but never disappointed. *Never* disappointed, Shima." In a hushed voice he said, "What you see is my guilt, not disappointment."

"I don't understand. You're not disappointed that I lied—that I cannot hunt?"

"That you felt you needed to lie is my failure not yours. You can hunt well enough. You don't need eyes for that, but as I said before, it doesn't matter."

She *could* hunt after a fashion. The Harmonies were strong in her, and her nose and ears were very keen. Not much of a compensation for her poor sight, but it was better than nothing.

"Your mother wanted cubs very much."

"I know—"

"Hush. You don't know this. She could never tell you, and I... well, I'm telling you now. When your mother and I were first mated, we worked together."

"I know this," Shima protested again. "You and she were system controllers up at the new station."

"Hool Station, yes. I know that's what you were told. We did not work there, Shima."

"But everyone knows."

Tahar flicked his ears in agreement. "Everyone knows because that's what we told them."

"You lied to everyone?"

"Not everyone. My father knew, and so did Elder Harman. It was Harman who asked my father to bring Nidra and me to him."

"I don't understand. What has this to do with Chailen and me?"

"It was a time when our people believed that we would re-build the Great Harmony among the stars. We had succeeded at so much in such a short time. So why not? Our scientists were discovering new things almost at every turn. It was a wonderful time. After the war, Child of Harmony became more than ever a special place to us. It proved we could leave our homeworld and survive."

Tahar looked around at the trees. "Harmony is old, Shima. All planets are of course, but it feels old. Do you understand?"

Shima flicked her ears affirmatively. "Everything is known, every place has been found—"

"And explored, yes. Child of Harmony feels different. The gravity is wrong, the air a little too thick. The sun looks too big... do you understand what I'm saying?"

"Everything feels new?"

"That's it exactly. Everything is new. It makes you feel that anything is possible. You will see that for yourself when we land at Zuleika."

Shima flicked her ears in agreement. She was looking forward to it. She would miss Harmony, but her studies were complete and it was time to use them on Child of Harmony. This was their last cycle before the ship took them to their new home.

"Your mother and I worked on a project that we hoped might give our people the stars. Oh, we didn't design it, but we helped build and test it."

"Test what?"

"A new kind of drive," Tahar said staring into the distance at only he knew what. "We were all very excited. Your mother and I were tasked with designing a process and implementing it for the construction of the prototype. It was a massive coil assembly."

She leaned forward eagerly. "How did it work?"

"It didn't work. Oh, we built it to specifications all right, and within deadline too, but the drive fused solid the first time it was tested. The second was the same and the third. Your mother thought it might be the phase lock."

"Phase lock?" Shima recognised the term, anyone would. "You mean you worked on the FTL project?"

"Yes."

She stared at her father hardly able to believe what she was hearing. The faster than light project had been the culmination of Shan space development, and a complete failure. FTL had been proven an impossibility and the project was shut down.

"Your mother published her theory and was asked to join the design team. She accepted of course, it was a very great honour. The fifth prototype was built. I was so proud of her, Shima. Nidra's ideas seemed to work. Computer projections were almost exactly as predicted, but she was concerned by the slight difference in her calculations. She stayed aboard the ship to supervise the initiation of the drive. I found out later she had feared a core failure. The drive was activated and the core failed as Nidra predicted."

"And mother?"

"She was injured, but she healed." Tahar sighed unhappily. "We didn't know, Shima. We couldn't have known."

"The project was abandoned wasn't it?"

"Yes. Prototype Seven blew up on activation and destroyed the ship. The entire crew was killed—all two hundred. Your mother cried for days. They were our friends, Shima. It was her design that failed and she felt responsible. The project was terminated and we returned to Harmony. We wanted to start again. We thought that having cubs would help us forget the past, but we didn't know."

"Know what?"

Tahar's voice was very low. "Nidra gave birth to six cubs the first time, Shima. You had five sibs, but all except you were born… wrong. They died. The kin mothers said it happened sometimes and that we should try again. So we did."

Shima stared at her father in pained disbelief.

She had asked her mother a long time ago why she had

given birth to only one cub. It had happened not once but twice. Two litters with only one cub each was very rare. Five cubs was average. She had feared another genetic fault might have been passed to her like her weak eyes. When her time came to have cubs, would she also be cursed with small litters? She had nagged her mother and her mother's kin to send her for tests. They had tried to reassure her, but at her insistence and with the blessing of Elder Kerani, they had sent her for genetic testing. The results were both good and bad. Bad for her sight, but good for her future cubs—it was very unlikely that she would pass on her deformity to them. As far as anyone could tell, her litters would be normal in every way.

She shouldn't grieve for her five lost sibs—she had Chailen, and Chailen had her, but she did. Why hadn't they told her?

"Nidra wanted to try again straight away, Shima, but I said wait. That's why you are three orbits older than Chailen. Nidra had four cubs the second time—it was horrible." Tahar swallowed and went on in a voice choked with grief, "Nidra nearly died and Chailen as well. The other three were... *malformed*. They couldn't have survived."

She clutched her father's paw. "Was it the accident?"

Tahar's ears struggled erect. "Yes. The FTL drive is unlike others. It... I cannot explain it so that you can understand, but when it is activated it uses space itself to create a gateway to another place. When the core failed, Nidra was exposed to that other place for a tiny moment, but that is all it took.

"When everyone realised what that meant, it was already too late for your mother. Orbits later she died still believing a way could be found to survive in that place, but the elders disagreed. The project was terminated. The other place is just too dangerous, Shima. No shielding known would be adequate to protect us from it, and without it FTL is impossible."

"You should have told us, father. Why didn't you tell us?"

Tahar looked down. "Guilt. Chailen is lucky to be alive. All the tests say she is perfectly healthy—a miracle the healers said."

"And me?" Shima said softly.

She knew what he was going to say. She had known for a long time that she would be blind long before her middle years. It was a genetic disorder. Little was known about such things, though research was ongoing. What she did know was terrible enough. She had a degenerative disease of the inner eye—the part healers called the retina.

Tahar squeezed her paw. "Your mother died from the effects of the accident, and your sight is poor because of it. I hope you can forgive us... *forgive me* for not telling you the truth," he finished in a whisper.

Shima hugged him while inside she shrieked in anger. It was not him she blamed. It was fate. Even now she would not say that the FTL project should have been abandoned. She was its victim, yet she believed the elders were wrong to cancel the project. What did the future hold for her people if not the stars? Where would everyone live? Would there be feuding among clans like before the Great Pact? Her hackles raised and a shudder ran through her.

"You're cold, Shima. Let us go now."

She did not want to stay here any longer. Child of Harmony awaited her. "Let us go."

* * *

5~Survey

Captain Colgan stepped out of the lift onto *Canada's* bridge and paused just inside watching his crew with pride. Months spent hiding in an asteroid field belonging to an alien species, and they were still as excited and as dedicated to the task as they had been on day one. He could feel their excitement and shared it. It was a heady feeling, knowing he was doing something important, and yes, momentous. The anticipation they had all felt upon emergence from foldspace had not gone away or even lessened. They were learning new things at every turn.

Colgan was eager to be on with his day, but the dimmed lighting warned him that he had a few minutes yet before the watch changed and *Canada's* day cycle began. He was early, something he normally avoided so as not to appear like a mother hen. If there was anything spacers liked less than a captain who didn't trust them to do their jobs without supervision, he didn't know what it was.

A minute or so passed and slowly the lights came up full. Behind him the lift doors opened and day watch personnel filtered onto the bridge. Colgan smiled and nodded greetings as they murmured their good mornings. He had never been one to insist on formalities like saluting, certainly not on his own bridge, but some did have their place and good reasons behind them...

"Captain on the bridge!" Lieutenant Ivanova announced precisely on time, informing everyone she had passed command authority to him.

Like that one, Colgan thought wryly. "Carry on," he said heading for the just vacated command station. Anya removed her helmet from the rack and Colgan replaced it with his. "Anything to report, Anya?" he asked as he took his seat.

Ivanova grinned and rolled her eyes at the chuckles from the others as they handed over their stations to their opposite numbers of the day watch. "Well yes, Skipper, now that you mention it, there are a few small things." She leaned over Colgan's shoulder and with a few deft keystrokes displayed a summary on his number one monitor. "It's all there, sir; nothing to report—no malfunctions or incidents shipside, but plenty about the Shan as usual."

Colgan smiled. There was always a raft of knew intelligence about the Shan every morning. In fact, so much data was flooding in that his crew couldn't keep up. Over ninety five percent had to be archived for later study, but what else could they do? They needed an entire university of researchers to keep up with things. Instead, they had a couple of hundred eager sailors to help *Canada's* small but perfectly formed science department. Most of the crew had little to do with the actual day to day survey work that was *Canada's* mission, most were concerned with running and maintaining the ship's systems.

"Thanks, Anya, have a good rest."

"Thanks Skipper, but we thought we would head over to the rec-room for a few hours and watch the feed."

Colgan nodded. Shan watching had become something of a communal pastime amongst the crew. The big screens rarely showed anything else these days. The crew could access data about the aliens and their planets from any terminal on the ship of course, and the ones in the rec room were always busy with people doing that, but for generating a buzz there was nothing better than watching a live feed from the remotes. Colgan did it himself on occasion, but for entertainment, he preferred to study the Shan alone in his cabin. He would have to announce another lecture soon. He had more than enough new stuff already, and his last lecture was two weeks ago.

"Have fun then," Colgan said.

"Thanks, Skipper," Ivanova and her merry band said, as they left the bridge together.

Colgan watched them go with a smile, then touched a control to turn his command station to face front again.

The main viewer had a tactical overlay of the entire system displayed; the many coloured icons monitored and updated by *Canada's* computer represented Shan ships and stations. The system was a rich one, something that pleased Colgan on behalf of the Shan. It meant they could trade and compete with member worlds of the Alliance when they joined, but more importantly, they could maintain their independence if that's what they chose to do. It wasn't Colgan's job to protect the Shan from his own people, he was here to learn about them and encourage them to join the Alliance, but he felt a responsibility to do it anyway. He honestly believed they would benefit greatly from membership, but he also knew there were downsides. There were sharks in the Alliance— member worlds with economies based upon exploiting others—who could do huge harm here. He was determined to arm the Shan with knowledge of these dangers, and others... like the Merkiaari.

Compared to many Alliance systems, this one had very little space traffic in the outer system. That was because Shan ships preferred to work closer in. With two habitable planets, something that still amazed and excited Colgan, much of the space traffic clustered in that region would be freighter traffic.

There was plenty of it. More than an Alliance system would use in similar circumstances, but that was understandable—Shan ships were slower. They made up for the lack with numbers.

Further out and the system became the almost exclusive preserve of the Shan navy, and it was to these ships that Colgan's attention was drawn. They were beautiful and deadly. White hulled and sleek, they looked built for speed, but again that was deceiving. Colgan knew they were much slower than *Canada* and his ship wasn't by any means fast. The *Exeter* class cruiser was an old design and most had been decommissioned or converted into survey ships just like *Canada* years ago. Slow or not, the Shan ships were still a threat to the mission and had to be watched. Normally that would be his XO's job at Tactical, but Colgan had decided after a couple of months in system without being detected to allow *Canada's* computer to handle it while the officer of the watch, himself on this occasion, monitored the situation ready to intervene if necessary. That was why the tactical overlay was prominently displayed on the main viewer. Francis meanwhile, was having fun learning about the Shan by overseeing the current survey operations of the Shan colony world. Colgan had a deal with her to trade places in a few hours so that they could both keep current with the ship's operations and the Shan.

Thinking about keeping current brought Anya's list to mind, and he turned his attention to his station's number one monitor. While his crew worked quietly and efficiently around him, Colgan used his control wand to highlight items of interest on the display, and open the associated data packets on his number two monitor. Splitting his attention between the two displays and the main viewer, he worked undisturbed for almost two hours, when Baz Riley interrupted him with coffee.

Colgan took a sip and sighed. "God that's good. Thanks, Baz."

"You're welcome, sir," Baz said and moved to supply the others with their mid morning coffee.

Colgan finished his drink and then turned his attention back to the main viewer. Another Shan exercise was underway, and he was struck once again by how familiar it was all becoming. Their ships were always training or running fleet exercises in the outer system. They sometimes used asteroids in the outer belt for target practice, just as Alliance Captains would. It was all very normal, and Colgan shook his head at the thought. It made him wonder about things. Fundamental things, like what it all meant that a Human ship could travel all this distance to find alien beings doing the same things as people back home. He was no philosopher, but he thought it boded well that he could see similarities between the two races on the ground and in space.

There were many differences of course.

Shan, like Humans, were mammalian but unlike them, they had evolved from felinoid quadrupeds into a race comfortable walking on two or four legs. On four legs, they were faster than a cheetah, but unlike a cheetah's max range of about two hundred metres, Shan could chase prey for kilometres before tiring. They had reasons for evolving such a turn of speed. Their prey was even quicker in some cases, and some had serious defences in the form of horns and fangs. Seeing a Shan chasing something so fast was amazing.

Outwardly, Shan were as different as could be from Humans, but they were alike in other ways. They built cities and spaceships, formed relationships and had children, laughed and cried just as Humans had always done. They had different expressions and language, different philosophies and dreams, but despite it all Colgan had very high hopes they would kindle something great for his own people, something that could dispel the fear of non-Humans that the Merkiaari had fostered in mankind—a pan-species Alliance.

It could happen. It really could happen in my lifetime... if I don't fuck it up. Please, don't let me fuck it up!

The Alliance had to grow; it had to throw off the lethargy and gloom inspired by the fear of the Merki. Over the last two hundred years the Alliance had been inward looking, its exploration of space half-hearted at best. Consolidation had been the watchword for two centuries, and yes, it was important to safeguard what they had, but expansion was the only cure for what ailed the Alliance now. The infighting and mini wars between member worlds had to stop before they got out of hand. They had to look outward again.

The Merkiaari were a terrifying foe, but Humanity had beaten them once and would again, alone if it had to, but what if it didn't have to? If they could only do this right...

Colgan took a deep breath and forced himself to relax. They wouldn't screw up; he wouldn't allow it and neither would Francis Groves. His XO was of similar mind where the Shan were concerned. When President Dyachenko learned what they had discovered here, Colgan was sure he would see the possibilities and get the Council to offer the Shan people membership in the Alliance.

He must.

The first drones should be arriving at Sol any day now. Depending on the response and how quickly a follow up mission could be put together, Colgan estimated he had four to six months before another ship could possibly reach him with new orders. He had no idea what those orders would be. There were many possibilities. He might be ordered to return to his previous survey mission, or to hold here and assist the contact team he hoped would be sent. No way to know for sure, but he hoped *Canada* would be ordered to stay.

Commander Groves entered the bridge a couple of hours later to relieve Colgan so that he could go play. He smiled wryly at the thought, and removed his helmet from the rack.

"You have the con, XO," Colgan said heading for the lift and tucking his helmet under his arm. "Call me if you need anything."

"Aye sir, I have the con. Have fun!"

Colgan looked back trying to look stern. "I am embarking on serious study, Commander, not *having fun*."

"Oh, of course you are, Skipper. Silly of me," Groves said and the others laughed.

Colgan grinned and waved as the lift doors closed. "Deck two," he said and the lift jolted into motion.

* * *

AGRICULTURAL RESEARCH CENTRE, CHILD OF HARMONY.

Shima bent to examine the damaged plant and her ears flicked in puzzlement. She glanced up toward Adonia and asked again. "And you're sure this field hasn't already been tested?"

"I already told you, it was assigned to us. No one has been out here since sowing Area Six."

Shima's tail rose and waved briefly over her shoulder in annoyance before she forced it to be still. It wasn't Adonia's fault that she sounded like a grumpy elder talking down to a particularly difficult cub. Adonia was senior in years and experience, but Shima had been placed in charge of evaluating Area Six, a position Adonia felt was rightfully hers. Shima sympathised, truly she did. Adonia was part of the team that had pioneered the variants of grain currently being grown here, and as such knew more than Shima how much work and time it had taken to get this far. Adonia felt there was no one more qualified than herself to evaluate the crop, but there were rules. Child of Harmony might not be Harmony, but it still followed the Homeworld's rules and regulations and they stated that no one involved in a project was allowed to evaluate their own work. Those regulations held true in all forms of research, not just in genetics. Shima believed they were proper and good, but they were almost designed to cause ill feeling between researchers. Shima's own projects would have oversight when the time came, and knowing her luck, Adonia would be assigned to write the report.

"I know you did, Adonia, but see here?" Shima indicated

the damage with a claw. "Someone has been taking cuttings here."

Adonia's ears flattened and she stalked forward to glare at the offending stalks of grain. She paused when she saw what Shima had found and straightened to look around as if expecting to see someone running away clutching his booty.

"Perhaps some animal?" Adonia said a little more deferential now that she knew Shima wasn't using her position frivolously. "It happens."

Of course it did happen, and part of the reasoning for open field tests like this was to see how the crop stood up to local conditions, but no animal she had ever seen or heard of had caused this damage. It was too neat, the cuts too precise. Her own sampling kit would leave wounds similar if not exactly the same.

Shima flicked her ears and stood erect. "Well, it doesn't matter. I will choose another few plants to sample and we can move on."

Shima chose plants from different rows and sections of the field at random labelling each cutting with the time, date, row and field numbers, before putting each in its own sealed sample container. She tagged each plant she cut with her name embossed on a red plastic label so that anyone coming out here could see it and would know who to refer to with queries. That was procedure, and she followed it to the letter, especially now she knew that someone had failed to tag an earlier sampling. She wondered why anyone would want to hide taking a simple cutting like that. She shoved the thought away as irrelevant to her work and moved to the adjacent field. Adonia's again worse luck.

Twice more in different fields, she noticed signs of surreptitious sampling of the plants and no tags left behind to explain matters. It was very puzzling. She didn't draw attention to what she found this time. There was nothing to be done about it now and such cuttings did not risk the parent plant in any case. Still, it made her wonder if perhaps the

elders had sent someone to make an independent inspection...
a verification of their reports? Such a thought angered her. Did
the elders think they would falsify reports? How dare they... no
wait, there was no evidence of that. No evidence of anything
really. It could just as easily be another researcher wanting to
run his own tests, but why do it this way. Anyone at the centre
who wanted to could come out and take cuttings any time
they liked. All they need do is ask and leave their own tags.

Shima was just finishing up and was about to return to
Adonia who had sat out the last field's inspections in the car,
when she found the culprit. She didn't know at first that it was
responsible for the cuttings, and didn't think about it when
she saw movement down low among the plants. One moment
she was sitting on her haunches writing out a label, the next
she had sprung full stretch in a dive to capture the... it. What
under the Harmonies was it?

Shima stared at the thing gripped firmly in her paws. It was
some kind of machine, not an animal at all. It struggled in her
grasp, but she held it easily. It was shaped like a flattened ball
and had shapes and designs moulded into its dull grey surface.
Her father was an engineer, and she recognised a remote when
she saw one, but what was it doing here? Tahar and others
used such things but only in space where it was too dangerous
to go, or was simply easier to programme a remote to do the
work. Shima had never thought to find one in her fields.

Holding it with one paw, she held it up to her face and
sniffed. It smelled alien, like nothing she had ever encountered.
Little doors opened in its sides and mechanical arms reached
out probing its surroundings. Shima watched in fascination as
it reached all around itself, obviously trying to find what had
caught it. It touched her paw and tried to lever her fingers up.
It didn't hurt, but she moved her paw and took hold again in a
place it couldn't reach. The arm retracted and the door closed.
Another opened and another arm came out, a different one
because the end terminated in something she recognised as
a sampling tool. It was used for making cuttings. She wasn't

letting that touch her.

Shima turned the device over looking for its off switch. It still struggled in her grip, but had no obvious means of propulsion. Maybe it was using anti grav like the hover cars? Shima wondered if Tahar knew that engineers had managed to miniaturise things to this degree. She decided to give it to him. He would enjoy taking it apart and learning how it was done. She turned it over looking for an off switch and found more hatches. She forced a claw into one and popped it open. She recognised the controls for what they were, but she frowned at the markings on each one. None of the characters made any sense to her, but above the keypad there were two more buttons coloured red and green. She pushed green, thinking that green obviously meant safe and this cursed thing would only be safe when off, but nothing happened. She pressed red and the remote became a dead weight in her hand. Good enough.

Shima put the deactivated machine in her bag with her sample containers and went to join Adonia in the car. She decided not to mention her discovery. She didn't want to make a fuss, and besides, if she told anyone someone might claim it before Tahar could look at it. Behind her, two more grey shapes slipped out of cover and began taking samples unworried that their brother had been captured. They were very stupid machines and didn't recognise what Captain Colgan would call a shit storm, even when confronted with one.

Shima didn't notice.

* * *

Aboard ASN Canada, asteroid belt, Shan system

Specialist Yager glanced worriedly around and back to her station. She had to tell someone, but the captain was still here and he would yell at her and... she sighed morosely. It wasn't her fault, really it wasn't. She was a good avatar driver.

Nothing like this had ever happened to her before. Sure, she'd had her share of glitches come up, who hadn't? But she had always been able to get herself out of trouble. Why, once she had gotten a commendation when one of her remotes went dark on the job. She had saved it, and many thousands of dollars, using a pair of recon drones to find it and another sampler remote to bring it on home. She had deployed them on her own little SAR (search and rescue) mission complete with a properly planned search grid and everything. It got a few laughs from the guys and free drinks. It was a good story, but this time she was fucking screwed, and she knew it.

"Captain?" Yager said quietly still feeling sick. This reaming was gonna hurt. "I sorta have something to tell you."

* * *

"Say that again?" Colgan said calmly. He was quite proud of how calm he sounded.

Yager's face heated. "I lost a remote, Skipper. I mean I know where it is but... but... well, it's gone." She swallowed sickly and the rest came out in a rush. "Oh crap, I screwed the pooch! Shit sir, I know I did but I don't see what I could have done different! The Shan woman... female? Whatever, she was busy doing her own thing and I made my boys all hunker down out of sight, but she saw one of them somehow. I don't know how, sir. I can't believe she saw it, but damn she was fast! She was on me... I mean the remote. She grabbed it faster than lightning and I couldn't get free."

"Where is it now?" Colgan said noting the misery on Yager's face and swallowing the temptation to comfort her. This little disaster had potential. Oh yes indeed, it had potential to spiral right out the airlock, the system, and the entire stellar neighbourhood. "I assume you are tracking?"

Yager mumbled something.

"What?"

"I can't track it. She shut the fucker down! Excuse my

language, sir... sorry."

Colgan nodded, not caring about Yager's slip, he had more on his mind. "Play back the incident for me."

Yager seemed glad to be able to do something. She quickly faced her station and began working it with speed a precision.

Colgan watched as Yager's team of remotes took their samples and analysed them. He remembered reading some of the results of prior samplings. The crop had grown now, another month and it would be harvest time. The Shan were not as advanced in genetics as the Alliance, but from his reading of past data taken from these same fields earlier in the growing cycle he knew the Shan were within sight of some pretty spectacular breakthroughs. They had been huge advances when the Alliance made them. Given a hint here, a hint there, the Shan would leap decades ahead of where they could be if left alone. They had the understanding right now to implement current Alliance genetic enhancement methods. They just needed a little push and the technology to make use of what they learned.

"Here she comes, sir. See, I sent them all into cover?"

Colgan nodded. Two of the samplers were in the irrigation channel and there was plenty of foliage to cover them. One was in the next row over from the Shan female. Yager had told it to go to ground and it had done so before the Shan scientist arrived. Yager was right. It shouldn't have been detected, but it was.

"Holy..." Colgan hissed as the alien dove toward the remote from a crouch. She had just leapt at full extension like a cat after a mouse. She caught her mouse, and started examining it. "Well..."

"Yeah," Yager said sourly.

Colgan watched as the remote tried to free itself, and winced when the Shan female popped the main access hatch in its underside. Talk about luck, she had opened the right hatch first time. Opening any of the others would have dumped the contents of its sample bays.

"And lights out," Colgan said as the female hit the off switch on her second try. "Okay, we need damage control here. No saying what she is going to do with it. She might not tell anyone, or she might go screaming about aliens to their version of the newsies. She might do something else entirely. Nothing we can do now, no matter what she decides. Tell me about samplers, Yager."

"Like?"

"Like how screwed are we if they take it apart. Like can they find the others using anything they can learn from it? Can they find the satellite relays, and backtrack the data feed to us?"

Yager whistled silently and frowned in thought. It was obvious she had thought about some things in advance but not that the satellites might be endangered, and certainly not the ship.

"Okay, they will learn that someone not Shan is in the system, no way will they miss that, sir. The remotes are not very advanced compared to their own tech, but there are some differences. There's the anti grav for one thing, and then the controls are all labelled in English. They can't find any of the others we have deployed, but I'm sure they will guess we have them down there. They all use different channels and they're all encrypted. They will *theorise* the presence of the relays," Yager winced at Colgan's sharp look. "The transmitters aboard our equipment, any remotes the Alliance uses for that matter, are low powered. They have to be for security. The Merkiaari taught us that, sir."

Colgan nodded. "So they will figure out the satellite relays exist. Can they find them using your sampler?"

"No sir, but they can start a search. The relays are relatively tiny things and stealthed real good, and I mean *really good*, sir. The Shan would literally have to stumble into them. I'm pretty sure they won't find them, sir. The area they need to search is vast."

Tension eased in Colgan's shoulders. "Good, and what about us?"

"If they don't find the relays, they can't use them to find the ship," Yager said quickly and obviously vastly relieved to be able to say something positive.

"If they don't find the relays," Colgan repeated.

"If," Yager nodded.

"If they do?"

Yager swallowed. "If they do, they can't find us if we move, but they could take the relay apart and figure out its range. They will learn we are in the inner belt somewhere. I mean, we could be running silent anywhere in range of our relays. We don't have to be in here, but they will think of the asteroid belt first, won't they, sir?"

Colgan nodded. "I would."

As far as Colgan could see, there really wasn't much point in relocating. Not yet. They couldn't retrieve the remote, and without that there was nothing he could do to stop whatever happened from happening. All he could do was watch and be prepared to move if and when the time came, which he was already doing anyway. So, the only thing he need be concerned about was preventing any more losses, and especially in the same location. The Shan female might, unlikely though it is, keep silent about the incident. She might not think the remote was alien tech. She might be dim as a stump and think it was home grown. Hey, it could happen right? Whatever she did now, finding more of them in her back yard would be a bad thing.

"Right, recall all your remotes and move to another sector well away from this one. This place is now off limits to everyone. Let's hope she doesn't tell anyone, but if she does, I am not letting them get their paws on any more of our stuff. Clear?"

"Clear, sir."

Colgan nodded and walked away frowning in thought. Yager slumped in her chair, relieved to have avoided a reaming, but then stiffened when Colgan turned back to regard her. "Oh and Yager?"

"Sir?"

"If I catch you running missions so close to a populated area again, I'll have your arse up on charges for negligence. We're not playing games here. I know you're good at your job. I don't need you trying to prove it with stunts. You could have sampled that field during local night and avoided all this. Are we clear?"

"Very clear, sir!"

Colgan turned away and pretended not to hear Yager say, "Holy shit," under her breath.

* * *

6~New Life

Shima didn't get the chance to give Tahar the device she had found, he was working on Hool Station and couldn't visit so soon after taking up his duties there, so she simply took it home and put it away as a surprise. She and Chailen still spoke with him every few cycles on the comm, telling him about work and friends. Chailen spoke often about Sharn. Shima had the feeling that unlike other times a male had caught Chailen's eye, this time it was serious. Tahar agreed privately that Chailen was smitten for good, but he wasn't concerned. He had talked to Sharn's family in confidence and had checked certain things were in order. They were in good standing with their clan; Sharn's father was warrior caste, while his mother belonged to the healer caste. She could trace her lineage back through the generations with many notable healers among her ancestors and was more than worthy herself to rank alongside them.

Unlike Tahar's own family of scientists and engineers, Sharn's had never been honoured with producing cubs strong enough in the Harmonies to join the Tei, but that was no black mark against them. Many fine families never reached so high, and Tahar's own had only three as far as his line could be traced. Shima's mother, Nidra, had been strong in the Harmonies just as Shima herself was, but Nidra's oldest sib, Thrand, had been the one invited to join the-clan-that-is-not and change his name. Tei'Thrand was greatly honoured in Shima's family, and Nidra was said to have been very proud of her sib and his achievements. Shima didn't know him well, but he seemed nice enough for an uncle rarely seen. Shima sometimes wondered if she might have been Tei if not for her deformity. Where would she have been now if not for her eyes?

She really couldn't say for sure. Shima loved her work, and couldn't imagine herself a warrior as many Tei seemed to choose. She could hunt as well as any, better than many in fact even deformed as she was, but to be a warrior trained to kill and destroy rather than follow her heart into research? She just couldn't imagine it. The-clan-that-is-not held a special place among the Shan, and Tei were honoured. No matter their chosen paths they were always leaders and advisors. Set above others, to lead, to advise, and to inspire with one's own performance... Shima thought it must be very tiring, but that is what it meant to be Tei.

Shima finished the report on Adonia's work and submitted it a few cycles after catching the remote. Her findings were all positive, and she was able to make good progress on her own work. Adonia moved from colleague to friend and introduced Shima to her family. They visited with each other and spent some of their free time together. Shima took Adonia hunting, and she seemed to enjoy it. Adonia took her to the coast where they walked on the beaches and climbed rocks or explored the caves. Shima's circle of friends grew and Zuleika soon became home. Child of Harmony and the city no longer felt so strange, though the planet still had the power to surprise. She might be working outside for cycles then suddenly notice all over again how odd the sun looked in the sky—so much bigger than back on Harmony. Or she might notice how thick the air was or how much stronger she felt, but then she would forget about it only to be surprised all over again when something reminded her.

Shima spent most of her evenings caring for Chailen when she chose her own home to return to instead of Sharn's after school, which was about half the time. Caring for her sib was not duty or chore but love. Perhaps it was because she was her only sib, perhaps not, but Chailen was special to her and Tahar. Next orbit, Chailen would be adult and would choose her own path. Shima didn't think she would follow Tahar into engineering, and certainly she would not be a scientist. Perhaps she would mate Sharn first. If so, she would probably become a healer. Sharn had the Harmonies given talent for it like his mother.

Adonia adored Chailen, as was only right, and of course wherever Chailen happened to be Sharn invariably was also. The four of them explored the city together sometimes, Adonia and Sharn conspiring under their breaths with heads together in an effort to find new things for Shima and Chailen to see or do.

Everything at home and at work was wonderful.

When Shima was finally able to give her father the present she had found for him, she didn't expect the reaction she received. He had been smiling and joking with her and Chailen, but then he took the gift box and his manner changed. He looked inside and paused in surprise.

"Where..." he reached inside and lifted out the remote. "This is..."

"I found it at work," Shima said oblivious at first to Tahar's strange reaction. "I was in Area Six. I had to sample some of Adonia's work for her quarterly inspection and there it was. Isn't it amazing? Where do you think it came from? I thought it was probably a remote sampler checking up on us, but why would the elders authorise something so silly? They can just read our reports any time they want—"

"The elders did not send this," Tahar said in a strange

voice. "Tell me again what it was doing."

Shima glanced at Chailen who gestured with her tail that she didn't know what was wrong either. "Well, I didn't see it do anything really, but I found some of the plants had been damaged. Sampled but not tagged properly. I was tagging one of the plants myself when I caught sight of that thing and pounced on it. It did try to get away, but there are controls underneath. See?"

Tahar had turned it over and opened the hatch. His ears flicked acknowledgment. "Yes I see. These symbols... which one did you use to turn it off?"

"The red one."

"Red, you're sure?" Tahar said sounding puzzled. "Green surely?"

"No it was red. I tried green first and nothing happened. Why, what's wrong?"

"Probably nothing," Tahar said with false cheer. "Thank you for the gift, Shima. This is *very* unexpected." He raised the device to his face and breathed in to sample it. "Most unexpected, but greatly appreciated. Thank you."

Shima smiled. "I thought of you right away. I knew you would like it."

Tahar replaced the remote in the box. "I do, I can hardly wait to play with it."

Chailen laughed and Shima did too.

Tahar didn't.

* * *

Tahar could hardly keep thoughts of the alien device out of his head all that cycle, but finally night fell and he was able to take his treasure to his workroom and delve its secrets. Alien. There was no doubt in his mind it was alien, but how could such a momentous thing come into his cub's hand and then to his just like that? It was incredible! It was like the opening chapter to a saga where the hero stumbled upon some great thing that would change the world. He snorted. This was no heroic saga, but the device certainly had the power to change his world... or its masters did any way.

Thoughts of the aliens themselves sobered him. He really should report this find and hand it over to the decon team that would surely be despatched to spirit it away, but he just couldn't do it. He had speculated on alien origins for years. Engineers like him could hardly fail to do so when so much of the tech they worked with was based upon alien principles and designs gleaned from the war years. Most modern Shan tech had a basis in Merkiaari artefacts left behind by them. Antigravity drives for example, used in planetary transport everywhere today, were little different than those found within the Merkiaari grav sleds used to attack his people hundreds of years ago. The principles derived from those hated war machines were the foundation of the tech used to produce artificial gravity within Fleet ships. The stations in orbit could not have been built without alien technology to base them upon and many other things taken for granted now would not have been thought of without it. His people had much to be proud of, but without the war they would be far behind where they were today. Perhaps still in ships without gravity and powered by solid fuel rockets of all things!

No, he wanted to play with his present first. He would report the discovery. He would. But he wanted to satisfy his curiosity first. Nidra would have loved this, he thought wistfully as he entered his workroom and set the box down on the table. His mate had always felt that the Merkiaari were just one of many aliens 'out there' waiting to be discovered. Tahar had to admit it made sense. Why would the Merkiaari have warships and weapons unless they expected to need them? Obvious really. They must have encountered other races before. That observation was one reason Nidra had been so determined to make her designs work, which in turn led inexorably to the accident and her death.

Tahar stared down at his gift. "Well my love, it's time to

open the box and learn what has come calling this time."

He wasn't completely irresponsible. Trouble would find him for doing this regardless, but to lessen the consequences he recorded everything he did with full voice and video capture on his comp. He raised the device out of its confinement and discarded the box. Holding it before him, he turned it over and around so that he had a record of every side and surface. He used a claw to point out the various hatches and spoke calmly and clearly.

"Definitely a remote akin to those I use up at Hool Station. Shima said this one was taking samples of plants, so it's not likely to have welding equipment aboard it or electrical testing sensors like one of mine. It's very light. I don't recognise the material. I don't think it's made of metal, or if it is, it's unlike any I have seen or heard of used by us. Shima said she used the red button to deactivate it. I'm going to try the green now to see what happens."

Tahar gripped the thing firmly and pushed the green button. Nothing happened at first but then Tahar realised its weight had diminished further. Carefully he released the device and allowed it to float unrestrained. He was delighted by this evidence that it used antigrav for propulsion. Of course he had suspected it from the moment he saw it—there were no thruster ports or wheels, so what was left? His people had so far failed to make antigrav drives in such a compact form. That was how he knew it was alien and not home built. Besides, it literally smelled alien. This remote, insignificant in itself, would revolutionise how antigrav drives were made. His clan would do anything to own this thing. With it they could design an entirely new generation of tech.

Tahar shivered, his delight tainted by dark thoughts as he foresaw some problems. If the knowledge was released in the wrong way, it could cause chaos. The makers of current designs could be ruined. He chewed his whiskers in concern but could see no way to avoid it. It wasn't his place anyway. Perhaps the elders would release the knowledge to everyone all at once so that no one was given unfair advantage. Whatever, that decision was far above him.

He watched the device hovering and realised it wasn't going to do anything else. That told him something as well. Its pilot was no longer in control of it. It wasn't one of the self guiding pre-programmed models he sometimes used for repetitive tasks. If it had been, switching it on should have been enough to trigger its programming. That it waited for input seemed to suggest it needed a driver. He didn't have the equipment here necessary to replicate a control station. A shame, he would have enjoyed putting it through its paces. He would have to be satisfied learning its secrets through dismantling. He took hold of it and turned it off.

The next cycle dawned with Tahar still hyper alert. He had segs of recordings and a box of alien tech parts. He knew he could put it all back together but didn't see a need. Besides, when the authorities saw it they might ask him to reassemble it and join the team to investigate its secrets. He would give up his place on Hool instantly if offered that. He had no doubt big things would come of Shima's discovery. He wanted to be part of something great again. With that in mind, he knew who he needed to inform first; Nidra's favourite sib, Tei'Thrand.

Tahar knew perhaps more than was good for him about the clan-that-is-not. For instance, he knew through Tei'Thrand that all was not as harmonious within that clan as perhaps it appeared to be to outsiders. The war had broken more than the Great Harmony. It had caused factionalism within Tei ranks. Tei'Thrand belonged to the most progressive group, those who believed in change and pursuing the dream of creating the Great Harmony anew amongst the stars, but they had taken a huge blow when the FTL project failed so disastrously. Since then, their opponents had held sway.

Tei who opposed change couldn't seriously be called regressive, no matter Tei'Thrand's scornful use of the word to describe them. They didn't want to roll back history and return to a time when clan fighting clan with crude stone and bronze weapons was the norm, but they did want to limit progress to small incremental steps. Very few of them chose outward looking castes such as the scientists, and none were spacers—ever. Tei'Thrand's group embraced space and the Fleet. All of Fleet's ship commanders belonged to that progressive outward looking group.

There were of course Tei who belonged to neither faction. Those who saw merit in both stances or were for harmony no matter how it be achieved, but by their very natures they did not have a strong voice in Tei councils. They were always seeking conciliation and tried to mediate between those they thought of as the extremists of their clan. Negotiation and compromise was their position in any dispute. Not a strong position to start from. They were never warrior caste.

Tahar checked the time and decided to call Tei'Thrand right away. The male wouldn't mind being awoken for this, not once he watched the video in the data packet Tahar had prepared for him. He wasn't sure what would happen, but something would and wanted to be a part of it. That might be tricky to achieve if Tei'Thrand decided to keep the information quiet. He could easily suppress it, telling only those he trusted within his own clan. Or the elders might order Tahar to surrender the device and keep his silence. All kinds of scenarios played out in his head as he waited for his call to be accepted.

Tei'Thrand appeared on the screen. "Tahar! How good to see you, it has been too long."

Tahar bowed his head. "Tei, an honour as always. I apologise if I woke you."

"Not at all. I was already up... meetings later. I wanted to get a few things done before that. How are you and the cubs doing, settled in now?"

"We're fine. Chailen is making friends fast as always. Too fast," he growled thinking of all the males who came sniffing around her those first few cycles. Tei'Thrand laughed, and

Tahar gestured his embarrassment with a dip of shoulder and tail. "I think we should block out some time for her mating ceremony soon. She hasn't said so, but I think Sharn is the winner. I doubt she will choose her caste before mating."

"Hmmm. Normally I would not approve of that order of things, but I know Sharn's family and their clan is solid. They won't let the pair stray too far from the proper path."

That was Tahar's feeling as well. He had investigated Sharn's credentials as was only proper, and had found nothing to fear. He would make for a good mate, and his clan had many fine healers within its ranks. Perhaps Chailen would be inspired to join them.

"Listen Tei, Shima has found something that you need to see. It's a little... well, shocking. Can I send you a packet? I would like to wait while you watch if that's all right?"

Tei'Thrand blinked. "Well, if it's not too long."

"Eight segs, but I don't think you will need to watch the entire thing now. You will understand after watching the first tenth of a seg, maybe right away if I know you."

"You intrigue me, Tahar. And yes I know you did that on purpose! Very well, send it."

Tahar did so with a few deft keystrokes and waited.

"I have it... hmmm, you were not joking. A big video file eh? Let's see..."

Tahar watched Tei'Thrand's puzzled expression dissolve as he played the video. It didn't take even a tenth of a seg. Tei'Thrand's ears were quivering with excitement after watching the opening sequence.

Tei'Thrand focused upon Tahar again. "Where is it now? Does Shima know what she found; does she know to keep her silence?"

"I have it here with me, still disassembled, and no, Shima doesn't know what we have. She thought the elders sent it to check her work." Tahar smiled at the thought. Tei'Thrand didn't. "No point in alerting her by telling her to keep it a secret."

"Agreed. I'm coming over to collect it."

Tahar hesitated. "About that—"

"No games!" Tei'Thrand snapped. "This is momentous news. Astounding... dangerous."

"I am aware," Tahar said stiffly. "There are many people I could have notified. I chose you for a reason."

"We are family, Tahar, but this goes beyond that."

Tahar waved that away impatiently. "I am not trying to blackmail you, you idiot!" he snapped. "The thing is yours regardless of what you decide to do, but I would appreciate a little consideration. I *did* come to you after all."

Tei'Thrand relaxed. "Apologies. Yes, you did come to me. What consideration?"

"When the time comes, I would like to be included somehow. My work up at Hool is..."

"Boring?" Tei'Thrand said with a laugh.

"Unsatisfying," Tahar qualified. "I miss the time Nidra and I enjoyed on the FTL project. That was a once in a lifetime thing I know, but now? Surely something will come up, even if it's limited to in system propulsion."

Tei'Thrand inclined his head. "Your background is consistent with any team set up to research that sort of thing. I would not have to try very hard to have you included I am sure. Nidra... I wish..."

"Yes. I wish too, every morning and every night," Tahar said sadly, but then straightened. "Thank you. I will expect you here shortly."

"I'm leaving now," Tei'Thrand said and closed the connection.

Tahar sat back and stared at the blank screen thinking about what he had set in motion. He had no doubt that Tei'Thrand would turn this discovery into something that would benefit the progressive thinkers of his clan. Tahar had no problem with that; he had a lot of sympathy for their beliefs and his caste would as well. Things were going to change again, hopefully for the better, but change they would.

That would not make the traditional land bound, and some would say backward looking, Tei happy. They could make things difficult.

"I wonder what the elders will say about it," Tahar mused.

Not that he would ever learn that. He doubted there would be any announcement of this discovery. No, the alien device would quietly disappear but suddenly new discoveries would just happen and researchers would announce a breakthrough. That is how Tahar expected things to proceed. No mention of aliens he was sure. They didn't need a panic amongst the populace, but quietly the Fleet commanders would be told to keep extra vigilant. Tei'Thrand would use back channels or something like that. Tahar had no real idea what Tei'Thrand planned to do, but he would surely do that at the very least.

Tahar would have been very surprised indeed if he had known Tei'Thrand had no plans to inform anyone but a handpicked group among his own clan about the device, and would have been even more surprised if he had known that group had allies within the council of elders itself.

* * *

7~Abducted

Professor Brenda Lane stormed into her office to find it being ransacked. She had been informed just moments ago that a dozen people in uniform had descended onto the building looking for her.

"What the hell are you people *doing?*" she yelled upon entering her office. "You," she said, pointing to a man with a lot of colourful ribbons on his chest. "Tell them to put those back."

The soldier glanced at her then away without speaking. He was reading a page of notes from a compad and took no further notice of her, even when she stood glaring up at him from just a pace away.

The items Brenda was referring to were her reference texts. Two women in uniform were stripping her shelves, and placing everything into padded aluminium cases. She hurried forward and tried to take the current book the soldier was holding, but the woman was built like a gorilla and wouldn't let go. Brenda turned away only to find a man stripping her computer files.

"What the *hell* is going on?"

"Don't worry Ma'am, I'm being real careful."

"I don't care. You leave that alone," Brenda said trying to shoulder him aside.

"Now don't do that, Ma'am, I have my orders." He gently but firmly moved her aside. Another man stepped forward and barred her from approaching the terminal.

"What orders?"

"If you will calm down, Miss Lane, I will explain."

Brenda whirled toward the door and found the owner of the new voice. He was a general or something. His chest was covered in flashy ribbons. She stalked over to tell him off, but before she could get a word out, he spoke again.

"First things first. You are Professor Brenda Lane?"

"You know damn well I am. Who the hell are you?"

"Commander Freylin. You are *the* Brenda Lane—professor of exobiology, and xenology?"

"I said yes, dammit!"

"If you will come with me please?"

"I'm not going—*hey!*" Two very large men laid hands on her. "Let me go or you'll be sorry."

The navy ratings smirked. They hustled her out the door, and were followed by two more as escort. Freylin walked quickly through the corridors ignoring her squawks of outrage.

"Help! I'm being kidnapped, somebody call security!"

People poked their heads out of the classrooms and labs as Brenda screamed bloody murder. James went further. He stepped out of his classroom and confronted her kidnappers.

"What do you think you're doing? I demand an explanation."

Brenda silently cheered.

Freylin frowned in annoyance. "And you are?"

"Professor James Wilder."

"Professor of what might I ask?"

"Palaeontology."

"Has that any links with exobiology or xenology?"

James frowned. "With exobiology certainly... in a way. Palaeontology is the study of life in the geologic past. It's the analysis of plant and animal fossils. Exobiology deals with present day life on other planets, so you see there is a tenuous link."

"Enough of the lectures, James," Brenda said in exasperation. "Can't you see I'm being kidnapped?"

James flushed. "Quite right. Sorry, Brenda." He glared at Freylin. "I must insist that you let her go."

Freylin ignored him. "Fossils? They can be found on any life bearing planet?"

"Of course."

Freylin nodded thoughtfully, and then shrugged. "Jones, Hopley," he said to the two unencumbered ratings. "Professor Wilder will be accompanying us."

"Aye, sir," Jones said and moved to take Wilder in hand.

Brenda shook her head in exasperation. James protested and tried to free himself, but Hopley moved to take his other arm. Seconds later, they hustled out of the building.

"See here, you can't do this," James said.

Brenda grinned even while thinking nasty thoughts at Freylin. "I think they can James."

"But I haven't done anything."

"Neither have I, but here I am... *and* they're ransacking my office. They're stealing everything not nailed down."

"Not stealing, borrowing," Freylin said absently as they reached the car. "That reminds me..."

Freylin turned to his driver and ordered James' office ransacked similarly. The man saluted and ran off to see to it. Brenda and James were bundled inside the car followed by their keepers.

"All right!" Brenda shouted. "Stop pushing me will you?"

"Do you promise to be good?"

She fumed, but what was the point of struggling when she had no chance against the two muscle-bound gorillas. "I'll be good," she grated between clenched teeth.

It went much easier after that. James was quick to agree when asked the same question, and Freylin sat opposite them to await his driver.

"Where are you taking us?" Brenda said.

"Yes, and what's it all about I would like to know." James turned to Brenda. "You aren't a subversive are you?"

"James," she gasped in outrage. "I have no idea what's going on."

"All will be explained to you," Freylin said as his driver climbed into the car and started the turbine.

As the car pulled away, Brenda noticed a military loader pull up and receive the cases containing her files and reference texts. What the hell was going on? "Am I being arrested for something? Deported?"

"*Deported!*" James blurted in shock.

"You're not under arrest. We need your help with something." Freylin raised a hand to prevent further questions. "That's all I will say until you join the others."

"What others?" she demanded but Freylin stubbornly refuse to answer.

Brenda fumed in silence for the rest of the journey.

Their destination was a surprise. The spaceport seemed an unlikely place for a meeting, but then this entire thing was pretty damn unlikely. Freylin climbed out of the car followed by James. Brenda hesitated, but one look at her jailers was enough to make her climb out hastily. They didn't lay hands on her this time, but they hovered close as if expecting her to run. She wouldn't do that. Electrified fencing surrounded the spaceport.

"This way." Freylin said and led the way inside the terminal building, but instead of heading toward one of the gates, he turned right and entered the V.I.P lounge.

Once inside, their keepers left them to roam freely through the lounge, while they joined others like themselves standing guard at the exits. Relief swept through her. James and she were not the only ones here against their will. Being kidnapped didn't seem so bad when there were a dozen of you. It was silly, but she felt safer in a group. More than that, she felt comfortable with the people in this one. She recognised them. They were all highly respected scientists in the fields of exobiology, xenology, linguistics, physics, astrophysics... she knew them all, though James seemed not to. He was the odd one out. He was only here because he had intervened in her kidnapping.

"I'm sorry I got you into this, James."

"Not to worry. This is the most excitement I've had in years."

Brenda smiled at that, but she could see he was tense. "Let me introduce you around. We might learn something of what is going on."

"Good idea."

They mingled with the others listening for titbits of information. Nothing anyone said made the least bit of sense, until another woman was hustled into the room by two burly navy types.

"—listening to me? I'm going to *sue you!*" Janice Bristow shouted through the door.

Brenda grinned. "Hello, Janice."

Janice whirled still glaring, but then she brightened. "Brenda! It's been too long. And who is this handsome fellow, a new man in your life?"

She felt herself blushing. "This is a colleague of mine. James Wilder, this is Janice Bristow. Janice was my mentor way back when I first decided exobiology was my thing."

"Pleased to meet you," Janice said and shook James' hand. "Xeno, or exo?"

"Err, neither I'm afraid. Palaeontology."

"Palaeontology?" Janice frowned in thought. "That doesn't make sense."

"He tried to stop them kidnapping me and got swepped up as well," Brenda explained.

Janice's face brightened. "Thank heavens for that. For a

minute there, I thought I had it all wrong."

"You know what's going on?" she asked eagerly. "What?"

"It's plain to see, Brenda. She never could see what was right under her nose," Janice confided to James.

James grinned.

Brenda spluttered. "I so can see what's under my nose!"

"Well then, you should have worked it out by now. The bloody navy waltzes in and kidnaps a dozen pre-eminent scientists from the fields of xeno and exobiology among others. All their work is stolen; all their possessions are packed up. It's simple."

"Janice," she growled. "Just tell me will you?"

Janice beamed. "The Merkiaari are coming back."

James inhaled sharply in surprise, but before he could demand an explanation, or a source for Janice's shocking reasoning, Freylin returned to the lounge with another man in tow. Brenda recognised him instantly, as did most of the people in the room. It was Admiral Rawlins. Rawlins was First Space Lord, which meant he was responsible for everything that was wrong with the military. She scowled. His presence could only mean things had gone from bad to worse.

"Ladies and gentlemen," Freylin announced as he led Rawlins toward the podium and the microphones set up at the front of the room. "Ladies and gentlemen, if you would all kindly take your seats, the explanation I promised will now be forthcoming."

"Admiral?" Janice yelled over the hubbub. "When are the Merkiaari coming?"

There was a stunned silence as everyone turned to Rawlins to hear his answer.

"My dear lady," Rawlins began, but Freylin leaned in to whisper her name. "Professor Bristow, you're not here to study the Merkiaari. They're old news and let us hope they remain so. You're here at my invitation to see something I hope will be a boon, not a bane to the Alliance. Now, if you will take your seat, I will get started."

Janice grumbled and Brenda grinned.

Rawlins waited until everyone was seated. He glanced briefly at a compad, and began an obviously prepared speech. "Ladies and gentlemen, the Alliance needs your help. I apologise for the manner in which you were brought here, but secrecy is important. A while ago, one of our deep space survey vessels received a transmission coming from ships of unknown origin. An investigation was undertaken, and it was discovered the transmission originated from an unexplored system." He turned to Freylin. "The first slide please."

The room darkened and a picture was projected upon the wall. The room erupted into excited whispers as first one slide then another was shown.

"Two of them!"

"Absolutely unheard of!"

"Both inhabited do you think?"

"Probably. Look at that atmospheric ratio... pollutants indicate industries."

"My God, she's right."

Rawlins raised his voice to calm their excitement. "I'm sorry for the primitive method of displaying this information, but time is short and the lounge is not equipped with a holotank. You can view everything we have aboard ship should any of you be interested." He grinned and received laughter in return.

"Interested he says. My God, this is the greatest opportunity this century!"

"For the last two centuries."

Rawlins nodded. "It's a great opportunity, and a great responsibility. I'm sure you all realise why I can't let you tell anyone outside of this room about the Shan."

"Shan," the name was whispered throughout the room.

Brenda squeezed James' hand and grinned at him. He looked stunned, as did many in the room. The news was fantastic. "Can you believe this?"

James looked down at her hand in his and shook his head.

"No."

"The fools would panic..." someone was saying behind them.

"People can handle it surely? We've known for centuries that we aren't alone."

Rawlins broke in before the whispers became a full-blown debate. "I can't take the risk. The President has decided to keep this information secret until the Shan have been contacted. I want you to journey to their system to learn all you can about them. We have much to tell them, not least, we must warn them of the Merkiaari. If we could find them, then so can the Merki."

Brenda cursed under her breath. Rawlins and the bloody navy were going to screw it up again. "You would infect the Shan with Humanity's prejudice regarding the Merkiaari?"

Rawlins frowned. "I hardly think one could call it prejudice, Professor?"

"Brenda Lane."

"The Merkiaari are dangerous, Professor Lane. They attempted genocide in their war against us. Is it fair to leave the Shan ignorant and perhaps in danger? Do they not have the right to decide for themselves whether the Merkiaari pose a threat to them?"

"I suppose so," she said unhappily. "As long as it *is* their decision and not one forced on them by us."

"I have no intention of forcing the Shan to do anything. I want them to be our friends, Professor. For that to happen they need to learn to protect themselves. Every day that passes, their ships are broadcasting the whereabouts of their homeworld. That has to stop before the Merki find them. We all know what will happen if they continue as they are."

"That is a militaristic point of view. There are those among the scientific community that support the idea of communicating with the Merkiaari. I'm of the opinion that they can be reasoned with, and should be."

Rawlins' smile was condescending. "That's your opinion

Professor, but I could find billions who would disagree with you. I do not have the luxury of taking such chances with the lives of our people. If the Merki want to talk to us, they know where we are, but I will not go to them when doing so risks lives."

Brenda would have argued, but the majority of her colleagues were more interested in speculating on the best method to communicate with the Shan.

"Now then," Rawlins said and silence descended once more. "We come to the point where you have a choice to make. You can volunteer to join the contact team we are sending to the Shan, or you can go with Commander Freylin where you will have all knowledge of the aliens wiped using hypno."

"Outrageous," Janice spluttered.

Brenda agreed. How could he justify such a thing as mind wipe, when it was only ever used in the most heinous of criminal cases? It was more than outrageous, it was an unthinkable misuse of the legal system.

"Not at all," Rawlins continued smoothly as if unaware of the shock he had caused. "I cannot allow news of the Shan to leak out. You will not be harmed, I assure you. Hypno is a well proven technique. Those of you choosing to go, please rise and walk through the door behind me. You'll be met and shown to the shuttle. Those choosing mind wipe, please remain seated and you will be attended to."

There was a moment of silence before everyone stood and trooped out to the shuttle on mass. Rawlins looked insufferably pleased with himself. Brenda stood and began to follow Janice to the shuttle, but then she realised James was not with her. She turned back to see what was keeping him. Janice stopped by the door and waited for her to catch up.

"Come on, I want an aisle seat."

James remained sitting and looked wistful. "I'm not going."

"Of course you are. Come on, Janice is waiting."

"You go on. I'll wait for the hypno people."

Brenda frowned uncertainly. "You mean it. Why not come... is it me?"

James snorted. "Of course not. Look, I'm here by accident, Brenda. You're the reason I'm here, not my expertise. I'm not needed for the mission. If Rawlins knew, he would have barred me from his presentation. There see, here he comes now."

Brenda turned to find Rawlins heading her way. She took James' hand and pulled him to his feet. "You're coming even if I have to drag you there," she hissed under her breath.

"Is there a problem?" Rawlins said.

"There's no problem, Admiral, I'm not—" James began.

"Feeling well," Brenda burst out. "Nothing to worry about. I'm sure it's just the excitement."

James began to protest, but she elbowed him in the ribs to shush him. Rawlins was frowning. He turned to Freylin and raised an eyebrow at him. Brenda begged Freylin with her eyes not to say anything.

Freylin cleared his throat. "Hmmm, I'm sure *Invincible's* doctor will screen everyone aboard ship, sir. Captain Monroe was briefed thoroughly on our current thinking regarding first contact procedures."

Rawlins wavered. "May I?" He took James' arm and queried his wristcomp. It reported no health warnings. "We can't possibly risk contaminating the Shan. If he's ill, and his bots haven't taken care of it..."

She nudged James and whispered. "Please?"

James looked doubtful, but he nodded finally. "It's just butterflies, Admiral. I'm feeling better already."

"Very well." Rawlins turned to Freylin. "Signal *Invincible*. I want a full medical workup performed on him the moment she's secure from jump."

Freylin nodded. "I'll see to it, sir."

"Good." Rawlins turned back to Brenda. "The shuttle won't wait forever. I suggest you hurry."

She took James by the arm and dragged him toward Janice

where she waited near the door.

"What was all that about?" Janice said as they hurried to the gate.

"Nothing," Brenda said. "Everything's fine now."

* * *

8~Decisions

Professor James Wilder ambled along the decks of *Invincible* feeling sorry for himself. Why had he agreed to come along? Hypno wasn't so bad. He knew the rumours about the government turning people into loyal robots was just paranoia. It was used for more things than punishing serious crime. It was commonly used in medicine for one thing. Hell, anyone watching the latest release of Zelda and the Spaceways was agreeing to be submerged into the action via hypno.

Hypno didn't worry him, but Brenda did. She would be more than a little annoyed if she knew how he worried for her, but that didn't change how he felt. As a student of history, he knew the past wasn't all that rosy, but he couldn't help thinking that the days when armoured knights fought for a lady's favour were better than today. He might have been a lady's champion. He certainly fantasised about it enough, but instead of charging the foe, he was on a mission where his area of expertise wasn't even needed.

Women can be so intimidating at times.

He stepped around a maintenance detail working on a section seal. He eyed the circuitry hanging from the access port as he passed by, and stepped over the power feeds lying on the deck, but none of it meant anything to him. A crewman—crewwoman? Whatever, she scowled at his nosiness and he raised a hand in apology.

"Sorry," he said backing away.

They were strong, women were—independent and career orientated. Where once they would have waved from the battlement as he rode to war, now they went to war, and he waved instead. He grinned at the image of Brenda standing over the gates of some castle waving, and shook his head. She would be galloping at the head of the army not awaiting his return.

James turned a corner oblivious to his surroundings and those who populated it. He had let Brenda think she had talked him into coming along with her enthusiasm for meeting the aliens, but his fear for her was the real reason. The thing was, the data now seemed to show there was not the slightest chance of any danger from the Shan. Unlike the Merkiaari, they were civilised beings. He was sure they would be open to reason. So then, he was redundant twice over. Brenda didn't need a protector and wouldn't accept one even if she did, and his expertise was useless here. He was feeling out of sorts—bored and restless. Hence this little stroll, which was becoming a habit of his.

He was so distracted by his melancholy thoughts that he found himself confronted by a sealed hatch without realising where he was. He laid his palm over the scanner hoping it would open. Fleet was extremely security conscious for obvious reasons. Wherever this hatch went—Fleet called doors hatches for some reason—it was not sensitive. It slid aside, and he stepped through.

"Oh!" James said in embarrassment. "I didn't know..." he said backing up and preparing to flee.

"That's all right, sir," a crewwoman said sitting on her bunk and watching a game of chess in progress.

"Yeah, come on in. You don't play chess do you?" another

said.

He nodded. "As it happens I do. The name's James—James Wilder?"

"Yeah I know," the chess player said. "I'm O'Malley—Trish to you. The big ugly one is Sam Lundquist, but we just call him Swede."

James nodded at the man on the upper bunk. He was a truly huge example of a Swedish hero out of legend. Bulging muscled arms stressed the material of his uniform to bursting point even while relaxed. Good thing Fleet uniforms stretched to fit all types.

"Good to know you, Swede," he said with a polite nod.

"Likewise," the giant rumbled.

"You're from Earth then?"

Swede shook his head. "Kalmar."

"Kalmar… then why do they call you Swede?" The worlds of the Kalmar Union were on the periphery of explored space.

"My folks settled on Kalmar from Earth," Swede explained. "The locals called us Swedes because of the way we looked, and the name stuck. I kind of like the image you know?"

James nodded. Swede certainly looked the part anyway. James acknowledged the others with a nod and received names and specialities in such profusion he had no chance to remember them all. He did associate certain faces to names, but not many. The man they called Whiz looked like one of his students back on Earth—a gawky kid name Andrew. Whiz was named for his ability to fix anything just by glaring at it. Then there was Pug—real name Edward Stockely. His nickname came from the state of his face, which was bruised and battered most of the time, and ugly all of the time. He liked to fight anything in a uniform different to his own. His nose had been broken so many times, the doctors had given up repairing it—hence the nickname.

O'Malley waved James forward and indicated a bunk near her and the board she was studying. He sat and glanced around. Dozens of eyes were on him. Some of the crewmen smiled or nodded, others looked speculative, many had been reading letters or books on their compads, but now they were watching him.

"Crew quarters," O'Malley said absently and not looking up from the board.

James blinked. "What?"

"You were wondering what this place is."

"I was. How did you know?"

"She's psychic," one of the others said and laughed.

The comradely feel here was strange to him. He was used to his colleagues fighting him for position and tenure, not laughing and trading friendly insults. Maybe he had missed something when he chose teaching instead of adventure in the navy—nah, too many rules to follow.

"Are you?" James said when they quieted.

"No, but I can see you're pissed about something," O'Malley said and moved her bishop to block a possible mate in three.

James could see a way around the trap Trish had laid. He smiled at O'Malley's opponent, but he did not speak. Whiz frowned at the board obviously wondering what he was missing.

"Going to talk about it?" O'Malley asked.

James shrugged, why not? "My area isn't really suited to the mission. To be honest, I'm feeling a bit left out."

O'Malley snorted and all the crew shook their heads at him in disbelief. "Tell him Swede."

"Yeah Swede, tell him," they chorused.

"Tell me what?"

"Civs," Swede said in disgust. "You know what we do when that sort of thing happens to one of us?"

James shook his head thinking that he should find out.

"I'll tell you. The Chief gives him a job, or the Captain does if he's an officer, and tells him to learn fast."

Laughter and insults rained down on him, but James gave

as good as he got. There were advantages to being a historian after all. He knew a lot of cuss words.

"It's not that easy," he said when his new friends quieted. "It takes years of study to become a xenobiologist or exobiologist or any of the other disciplines needed for the mission."

"You're a prof right?" O'Malley said and James nodded. "That makes you clever right?" James nodded again. "In Fleet, we work as a team. We don't go out looking to be heroes and saving the day on our own. We leave that crap to the Marines."

"You're saying I should just join in and help out?"

"Course! Everyone needs a hand now and then, and besides, you might learn something in the process."

Could she be right? He knew next to nothing about most of the things needed for the mission, and it would take longer than he had to learn, but what else did he have to do? Nothing.

James stood to leave. "Thanks guys. It's been fun, but I've got work to do." Before heading for the hatch, he leaned down to whisper into Whiz's ear.

Whiz grinned and made his move. "Check and mate," he said in glee and everyone howled in laughter.

"Hey!" O'Malley cried in outrage. "You cheated!"

Catcalls and more insults rained down from all sides as the others pounded Whiz on the back in congratulations.

"No way, he cheated! Jimmy told him the move I tell you. It's not fair..."

The hatch slid shut on O'Malley's cries of woe and James chuckled. With his hands in his pockets, he whistled a popular tune as he made his way to the briefing room. Captain Monroe had turned it over to the contact team for their studies.

He supposed this was a momentous time for the Alliance, but he knew the old saying with regard to living in exciting times and took its meaning to heart. So much could go wrong, but his colleagues—so busily collating the data they had been given access to—were the cream of the scientific community.

Rawlins couldn't have chosen a better team to ensure a smooth first contact. James knew he wasn't in their league, or Brenda's worse luck.

James strolled into the briefing room a short time later and watched his colleagues at their work. Linguistics would be critical to their efforts. He decided to have a word with Professor Singh who was the leading man in the area. Janice Bristow also took a keen interest in linguistics, but her main area of study was exobiology. She was too busy to help much, though James was sure she wished to. He crossed the room and stopped behind the busy man.

"Professor Singh?" he said softly, and Bindar looked away from his work to frown up at him. "May I have a moment of your time?"

Bindar hit the pause icon on his terminal and removed the earpiece he was using. "It's good to see you, James. We've missed you around here. Where have you been?"

Bindar sounded genuinely pleased to see him, which made James feel like an idiot for not thinking of this sooner.

"Making friends with the crew. I was wondering if you needed any help?"

"Well..." Bindar said uncertainly. "This is an exhausting task, James, and ordinarily I would jump at the chance, but linguistics isn't something you're really familiar with."

James smiled and sat next to the Professor so that he might explain. "Both of my areas aren't needed Professor—"

"Call me Bindar. We're friends, James."

"Thank you, Bindar. As I was saying, my area of expertise isn't required. I was rather at a loss for a while, but then someone advised me to help out with whatever the rest of you needed."

Bindar's face brightened. "That *is* a different matter. A lot of this is simply menial work at this early stage, any college student could do it..." Bindar's face darkened in embarrassment. "I didn't mean to suggest that you... ah anyway, what I'm doing is isolating and cataloguing the verbal exchanges *Canada* obtained for us. It's painstaking work, and I must warn you, James, it's rather boring."

James grinned. "That's okay. I'll do that and you can begin the translation. Would that be agreeable to you?"

"*Agreeable?*" Bindar cried almost bouncing in his seat. "My dear *friend*, I would be eternally in your debt! We have so little time to learn what we need to contact our newest neighbours. Your sacrifice will help immeasurably!"

"I wouldn't call it a sacrifice."

"*I would,*" Bindar said forcefully. "You haven't been listening to those awful recordings for weeks."

James laughed and swapped places with Bindar so he could take over the terminal. Bindar sat and switched on another screen and brought to life his software. He had designed it to make the translation easier, but the database of known words was empty at present. He would begin filling it soon enough. When he was done, they would all start to learn how to speak the alien's language.

James inserted an earpiece, but he didn't start just yet. He went through the professor's work studying and learning as he went. It was fascinating, and he soon saw the pattern Bindar was imposing on the chaos. Bindar had been listening to the recordings and picking out the individual words before cross matching them for context. For instance, he had a list of words always, or nearly always, spoken at the end of a sentence. He had tentatively labelled the set as phrases of leave taking; in English, a comparison might be good-bye, or see you soon. Other sets were labelled as nouns and adjectives, while still others were broken into groups such as words with a technical bent. Those came from ship to ship communications. The only column completely empty was labelled *Common Phrases* and James wondered why that was so, but Bindar was busy. He decided he knew enough to begin.

He keyed the terminal to resume, and winced at the yapping growl of Shan speech. He lowered the volume and began to make out what he was supposed to be listening for.

The yaps and growls appeared to be some kind of emphasis placed on the words. He heard it at the termination of each sentence mostly, but certain words always had emphasis put on them. He reversed the recording and listened while reading *Canada's* observations. He tried to associate the words with observed movements of the ships.

Ha! He had one already. He typed the word *Chakra* into the noun column. The Shan crew seemed to use the word a great deal. Perhaps it was the name of their Captain?

Interesting...

* * *

9~Checkmate

Brenda watched James chatting with Bernhard and smiled secretly. A couple of weeks ago, James had wandered around doing nothing and feeling sorry for himself, but now everyone was clamouring for his help on their projects. Bindar was the first to see him as something other than a fifth and unneeded wheel, but he certainly hadn't been the last. When he ran out of recordings to transcribe, James was swamped with requests for help on other projects to the point where he was the busiest among them. He was on his third project now. Brenda was determined to have him next.

"You should marry him," Janice said in an offhand way as she paged through her printouts.

"Don't start that again."

Brenda was tired of Janice badgering her. Didn't the woman ever let go? It had started with a mention of how good James was with Bindar, and then how nice his eyes were, and then how good he looked in uniform, and then back to his work. On, and on, and on, for two whole weeks. She just never gave up.

"If you won't marry him, at least take him to bed."

"*Janice,*" she hissed through gritted teeth.

"You're attracted to him, and he to you, so what's the problem? You don't have to marry for life. Just keep him for a few years then trade him in."

"Ha, ha. I'm not you, Janice."

"Obviously. If you were, you wouldn't be turning into an old maid."

Brenda winced. Janice was only teasing, but it was too close to the mark for comfort. She was fifty years old—a third of her time gone already and she was still alone.

"I'm sorry," Janice said with concern. "I didn't mean it, you know that don't you? I just want to see you happy, kiddo. Don't live your life regretting what might have been."

Brenda shrugged uncomfortably. "I have my work... we're part of something huge here. I don't need—"

"Crap," Janice whispered crossly. "Hey, this is me, Janice remember? I taught you about boys and where to get them— remember? I *know* you, Brenda. I've seen you with other people's kids. I've seen you standing alone watching them."

"So I like kids. So what?"

"So you want some. I had mine early, so I could watch my great-great grandkids grow. If you don't get off your duff and start breeding girl, you're going to miss it all."

"I could adopt, I could even have one implanted. I don't need a man to make babies."

"No, no, no. Don't even go there. *I* don't need a man to make babies, but you definitely do." Janice looked her directly in the eyes. "*Definitely.* Besides, kids aren't everything. A husband makes for a great bed warmer, and they're fun at parties."

Brenda grinned, but then looking at James she sobered. "He's not interested."

Janice sighed. "Again you fail to see. He's the strong silent type—he's shy."

"Shy? The man is fifty-two years old!"

"So? Age doesn't cure all ills, Brenda. Some people go

through life without actually *living* it."

Brenda flushed. That described her as much as it did James. When she didn't answer, Janice shook her head again and went back to work. Brenda could almost hear her friend's thoughts; they were so obvious. You just can't help some people, Janice was thinking, and she was right. She was right about a lot of things. Brenda *was* lonely. Her career had been one long series of successes, and at the time it had seemed like all she wanted, but as the years rolled by, she was seeing things differently. What real difference did it make who discovered this thing or that, as long as someone discovered them? She had only one life to savour; she should be living it to the max.

She watched James preparing to leave. "I'll see you later," she said to Janice. Taking a firm hold upon herself, she met James at the hatch. "James?"

"Hey Brenda. What can I do for you?"

Take me to bed like Janice suggested?

"Take me to... dinner," Brenda said lamely and cursed herself for not following through.

"Sure. How about tomorrow?"

"Why not now? It's about that time."

"Sorry, Brenda, can't do it," James said reluctantly. "I have something on tonight."

"Oh," she said in disappointment. What if it was one of the crew? It had better not be, or she would... what? She had no call on him. "Can I come?"

James raised an eyebrow in surprise. "Sure, glad to have you." He palmed the hatch sensor again.

Had Brenda more courage, she would have said something different, something Janice would have approved of, but the words stuck in her throat. She was like a schoolgirl on her first date.

"So, where are we going?"

"Crew quarters," James said glancing at her and then at the time displayed on his wristcomp. "C-Shift doesn't go on duty until twenty two hundred."

Twenty two hundred? That uniform was going to his head.
"And that's good?"

James smiled at her. He had a really good smile. "Very. I have a tournament to win."

Brenda refrained from asking, but she was wondering when he had made the time to find friends among the crew. Maybe during his sulking period? Janice was obviously wrong about him. If he made friends so easily, he couldn't be shy. That was a depressing thought. If he wasn't shy then he just wasn't interested in her. She felt like begging off now, but it was too late. James palmed open a hatch and stepped into C-Shift's quarters.

"Hey, Jimmy, how you doing?" a crewman said with a grin.

"Great, Swede, where's Trish?" James said looking around and taking no notice of the giant man as he pulled his uniform on over naked skin.

"In the shower. She won't be long. Can you take her?"

"No problem," James drawled with a grin.

Brenda was staring at the giant. He was huge. He had blonde curly hair and blue eyes, and muscles... *muscles everywhere!* Her face heated when she realised she was staring at his abs, and imagined what she would have seen if they had arrived a few moments earlier. *God!*

"Hey, Jimmy, where are your manners boy?" A battered looking man said, as he walked by and hooked a thumb toward Brenda.

"Oh, sorry guys." James' face flushed. "This is Professor Lane. Brenda, I want you to meet my friends from C-Shift, *which*," he said loudly in a parody of conspiracy. "Is rumoured to be the only one that knows what it's doing."

"Damn straight. C-Shift rules the night," someone yelled loudly.

James grinned. "Yeah, but not the day!"

Brenda looked on in confusion.

"A and B shifts run the ship during the day cycle," James

explained.

"Ah," she said finally catching on. These people had just awoken and would be going on duty at ten. They had hours yet, but they were moving as if there wasn't time.

"The little one is Whiz, and you know Swede," James said pointing out his friends. "The hairy one is Pug for obvious reasons and…"

Brenda smiled at James' friends, and received nods or an occasional handshake in return. James was completely at ease, but Brenda felt a little uncomfortable with so many sailors close by. The military was an unfortunate fact of life in the Alliance. She had so far managed to keep her distance from those who killed people for a living, but these were James' friends. She would try to make an extra effort not to upset anyone.

"Ready to have me wipe the deck with you, Jimmy?" a woman with wet hair and a towel over her shoulder said as she came in.

She was wearing her uniform, thank goodness, though no one seemed prudish here. Living so close together would eliminate such childish concerns in a flash.

"Hi, Trish. You have no chance, as you well know." James ushered Brenda forward and in front of him. With his hands on her shoulders he made introductions again. "I want to introduce you to a good friend of mine. Trish O'Malley, meet Brenda Lane. Trish has delusions regarding her chances of beating me in chess matches."

Brenda was finding it hard to stay smiling. This O'Malley woman was staring at her in challenge, but when she looked at James, it was like a cat looking at a fish within reach of her claws. Remembering her promise to try hard at being nice, Brenda kept a smile plastered on her face and shook O'Malley's hand.

"Let me finish dressing, and I'll be with you," O'Malley said to James and hurried away.

James sat on a bunk near the chess set, and Brenda hastily

claimed a space next to him before one of the others stole it. Whiz looked disappointed, and sat on the other side of the aisle instead. A good many were interested in the contest it seemed. The upper bunks were full of spectators.

"Are you all right?" James said. "You look a little pale."

"Fine," Brenda said shortly still thinking about O'Malley, and how she would like to snatch her bald for looking at James that way.

"You sure?"

She relented a little. "I'm fine, James. Can you beat her?"

James shrugged. "Oh sure. I usually do win. Well, three out of five anyway."

"Great," she said not caring one way or the other. "How many are we doing today?"

"Just the one for the title if you like."

"Title?"

"Champion of C-Shift," James said with an embarrassed chuckle.

Brenda laughed and bumped him playfully with her shoulder against his. "You're not part of C-Shift."

"Sure he is," O'Malley said as she sat down opposite James. Her hair was miraculously dry now and styled to accentuate her high cheekbones. It annoyed Brenda immensely. "He's an honorary member."

Everyone agreed.

Brenda watched the game but was bored very quickly. She didn't play, and so didn't understand the differences between the pieces. An hour went by as a move by James was countered by a similar move from O'Malley, and nothing seemed resolved. Both players were taking the game seriously, but the spectators came and went only to come back again to check on who was winning. This was a routine they seemed to have acquired over more than a little while. Brenda imagined James and O'Malley sitting together for hours during the week's long journey playing chess and chatting.

She didn't like it one bit.

James took more pieces off the board than O'Malley, but he didn't seem pleased when his opponent took a tall one of his—one of a pair that looked alike.

"Bishop," Swede said. "He's a goner for sure."

"Is a Bishop important?" Brenda whispered.

"Can be. If he can protect his king, he might last a while longer."

"Which one is the king?"

"You serious?" Swede said incredulously. "That one," he said and pointed.

"Do you mind?" James said in annoyance at Swede's finger hovering over the board.

"Sorry." Swede grinned at Brenda and rolled his eyes.

"Jimmy is worried," O'Malley said with a smirk. "He should be, there's no way he can take me now."

"Oh, I can't?" James moved a horse that Swede said was called a knight.

O'Malley smiled. She moved a piece like a castle. "Check—"

James pounced the instant O'Malley released her castle. "And checkmate."

"Wahoo!" Swede yelled. "No one saw that one coming; he suckered her."

"Wait," O'Malley yelled over the congratulations coming from all sides. "I can still take him."

"No," James said confidently and turned away from the board.

"I can." O'Malley glared at the offending chess set. "It's… checkmate," she sighed.

Laughter and insults rained on O'Malley, but she yelled a lot worse back at her tormentors. Everyone howled with laughter.

"Another?" O'Malley asked hoping to get her own back.

"Not tonight, Trish," James said with eyes only for Brenda. "I have a dinner date."

"Your place or mine?" Brenda asked with a smile.

"Mine." James took her arm like a lord with his lady as they left.

Brenda liked that. A lot!

* * *

"I didn't know you cooked," Brenda said pushing her now empty plate aside and reaching for her coffee.

James smiled. Plastic plates and plastic cups were hardly romantic. Where was the candlelight he had imagined, or the red roses in their silver vase? If he lit a candle in here, he would have alarms screaming all over the ship, and a very irate captain bearing down on him. Fire in space was not a laughing matter.

"Oh... you know," he said with laughter bubbling below the surface. "Living alone you learn how to press a button like a pro."

Brenda laughed.

She could laugh, but it was true. Aboard ship, autochefs were the only source of food and drink, but with a little careful button pressing, it was surprising how good a meal one could concoct. He had practiced and learned some good combinations on this journey. Brenda seemed to agree.

"I've known you for years, James, yet I don't know you at all."

James pursed his lips and shrugged. "Not much to know. Boring and dusty professor of history—"

"And palaeontology," Brenda cut in with a grin.

He smiled and inclined his head. "And palaeontology. He has tenure in Oxford, the pre-eminent university of the Alliance." He leaned forward and in an exaggerated whisper said, "On *Earth* yet."

"Stop clowning," Brenda said laughing.

"I'm not clowning."

Brenda's laughter died. "You don't have to hide from me, James."

"I'm not hiding, what makes you think I'm hiding?"

"Will you stop? You always hide behind jokes and witty remarks. You don't have to, not with me, and not with the others. It's *you* that everyone likes, not the front you put up."

He didn't know what to say. He did seem to have made friends here, but he always joked around. Sarcasm was his middle name. But was it really? Didn't it start to be this way when he turned thirty-five and still unmarried? He couldn't remember; it was too far back.

James took a sip of his coffee and shrugged. "All right. I'm unmarried, no family to speak of, no prospects—"

"You're doing it *again*, James. You should stop putting yourself down. Tenure at Oxford is no small thing. If you think it is, ask those who try without hope for what we have."

Brenda was right, but it seemed a small thing way out here. They had passed through the Border Zone and were into the void of unexplored space now. What mattered out here was the team, and its goals. The Shan had to be warned about the Merki, and hopefully they would then join the Alliance for the betterment of both races.

Brenda finished her coffee but waved away James' offer of a refill. "What of your parents? They must be exceptionally patient to put up with you."

"They're dead," he said flatly.

Brenda gasped. "I'm so sorry! How did it happen?"

"They were killed in a meteoroid collision on the way to Mars. A pebble the size of my fist hit the station. It was a freak accident, never happened before or since as far as I know."

James had been devastated. He was only twenty-nine when he received the news that he was alone. He had expected his parents to be with him until his hundredth year at least, but they had died instantly in the decompression of a transit tube. Three more steps, and they would have been safe behind an emergency hatch, but they hadn't known to hurry. No one had. The hatch had slammed shut in their faces within microseconds of the pressure drop being detected thereby

142 Mark E. Cooper

saving the station, and sentencing them to death. The hatch saved thousands of lives on the station, but at the same time it killed a dozen people in the tube including his parents. The government hailed the designers of the station as heroes. A dozen dead was a small thing, he thought bitterly.

Brenda reached across the table and held his hand. "James I..." she squeezed his hand again. "Can I have a tour?"

"A tour?" James said looking up in confusion.

"What's through there?"

"The..." he flushed. "The bedroom."

"Show me," she said quietly and pulled him to his feet.

Brenda led him into the room and turned to face him. She slowly removed her shirt and trousers to stand before him clad only in her panties. A moment later, she stood in her bare skin. She was so beautiful.

"Brenda I..." his voice broke.

"Shush," she said and came into his arms.

The feel of her in his arms was... and her back was *so smooth*. They kissed, and the world went away for a minute. His uniform fell away as if by magic and they were suddenly on the bed kissing and stroking each other.

"Lights—" James began but Brenda said no.

"I want to see you, all of you."

He smiled. "Lights full." He didn't notice the slight increase in illumination as he lost himself within her.

* * *

Aboard ASN Invincible at jump stations

"Time?" Captain Cynthia Monroe asked her helmsmen.

"Two minutes to translation, Skipper. Jump drive in the green, jump stations report ready to jump," Lieutenant Keith Hadden said without looking away from the chrono on his board. His finger was hovering over the manual override, ready to intervene should the computer fail in its task.

"Good," Monroe said. She turned to Commander Hamilton at scan, but Hamilton was already concentrating upon the data her station was displaying. Monroe left her XO (executive officer) to her work and nodded to Lieutenant Davin instead. "Sound battle stations, Martin."

Martin Davin, a veteran of navy service nodded and the strident wailing of the alarm sent men and women scrambling for their stations. Some buttoned themselves within weapons blisters, and brought laser cannons to life while repeatedly running diagnostics on targeting software; others were careening down corridors and into central damage control, yet more were climbing into hard suits so that, should the unthinkable occur, they could work in vacuum to save the ship when damage made working in sealed uniforms unsafe. All over the ship, men and women pulled on their gloves and sealed their uniforms. Helmets went on, and life support hoses were pulled from consols to be connected to ports waiting to receive them in their uniforms. Connected to the ship, those armoured cables and airlines represented life for three hundred and twelve passengers and crew.

"Battle stations report manned and ready, Skip," Davin reported.

"Good. Time?" Monroe said.

"Thirty seconds," the helmsman responded.

"Tactical on main viewer," Monroe said looking away from her small repeater displays.

"Aye, sir," Commander Hamilton said.

The endless otherness of fold space was replaced with a blank screen. That would change as soon as the ship translated into normal space. The sensors would then have something they were designed to handle to work with. Sensors in fold space were basically useless for anything beyond visual range.

"Ten seconds," Keith Hadden at the helm said into the silence.

"Point defence online, Skipper. Targeting computers active, autoloaders functioning normally," Irene *Weps* Bishop said.

Monroe nodded, but she didn't answer; she was bracing herself for the jump disorientation to come.

"Five seconds, four..."

"Shields to maximum," Hamilton ordered.

"Aye, sir, shields show maximum attained. Power levels equalising, negative draw on auxiliary generators."

"...one. Translating!"

ASN *Invincible* jumped...

Monroe's head rolled back against the restraint. The bridge was twisting like a screw. Her crew were frozen, unaware of her regard. She felt sick to her stomach as the jump turned her ship inside out and her with it.

Falling...

    ...Twisting and falling and...

Monroe's eyes rolled up and she sagged in her restraints. She was unaware that she was drooling into her helmet. Her mind shrieked in disorientation as her body became disconnected from her control. She felt nothing now, floating and spinning and falling. It was all in her head, but real for all of that.

Falling...

    ...Twisting and falling...

        ...and here!

"Oh God..." someone said and gulped air in an effort not to vomit.

"Trans—" Hadden panted. "Translation complete, sir. Point two five seconds elapsed."

"The referent," Monroe gasped. "Have we acquired the referent?"

"Scanning... scanning... scanning... referent attained!"

"Precautionary: charge the jump drive," Monroe

snapped.

"Aye, sir. Charging the drive from auxiliary."

"Contact!" Commander Hamilton sang out. "Multiple contacts... my *God!* We jumped into the middle of their entire fleet!"

"Weps, stealth mode active maximum!" Monroe snapped as the shock brought her back to the here and now. It was such a sudden turn of events that her stomach forgot to be sick any longer.

"Aye, sir. Fields spinning up—fifty percent, seventy five, one hundred percent, sir."

"Talk to me, XO," Monroe said intent upon the viewer showing them well inside weapons range of the alien ships. "Were we seen?"

"I don't think so. They're on some kind of manoeuvres. It would be a miracle if they saw us for the few seconds we were visible."

"Keep an eye on them. Helm, new course..." Monroe said and glanced down at her displays. "New course, zero-four-five by one-two-eight degrees."

"Course plotted and laid in, sir."

"Best speed!"

ASN Invincible swung and leapt onto a new heading roaring across the system toward the outer asteroid belt that her tactical display insisted lay not far away.

"Time to the belt?"

"Three niner minutes, Skipper," Hadden said.

Monroe nodded. "Show me those ships, XO."

"Aye, sir. Targets designate: Alpha One through Alpha Thirty," Commander Hamilton said and brought the ships onto the viewer one after another. They were beautiful and deadly looking. "Heavy cruisers, tentative assessment: *Excalibur* class heavies."

"*Excaliburs* eh?" Monroe said. "That's a lot of muscle."

"Yes, Ma'am. Targets designate: Beta One through Ten. Light cruisers."

"Class?"

"Hard to say, Skipper. They look fast but have limited weapons. We have nothing like them. The Merki would kill them too easily. If I had to, I would class them as weak *Sabres*."

A weak *Sabre* class light cruiser they could handle with ease, but not the heavies. Still, *Invincible* was here to avoid conflict, not start it. Monroe began rattling off orders one after another without pause.

"Continue on course. Point defence to standby, shields to standby, secure from battle stations! Stealth mode remains at maximum while within this system. All clear?"

"On course, zero-four-five by one-two-eight degrees," the helmsman said quietly confirming *Invincible's* heading.

"Aye, aye," Bishop said and began punching her keys to comply.

"Aye, Skipper," Lieutenant Davin said and his voice boomed throughout the ship. "Now hear this: Secure from battle stations, secure from battle stations. That is all."

"Very good," Monroe said rolling her shoulders trying to free herself of the tension that had set up shop in her. "We seem to have come through unscathed. Let's try to keep our record clean shall we?"

Everyone sighed and chuckled, all except Commander Hamilton who kept her eyes glued to her screens tracking her targets. That was as it should be. Fleet didn't like taking chances and neither did Monroe.

* * *

10~Visitors

Anya Ivanova leaned way back in *Canada's* command station and stretched. She groaned as her vertebrae shifted and popped. She sighed and sat up straight again. At 0200, it was hard to keep alert. Sitting in one place was not helping.

"I'm going for a quick walk around the deck, Steph." Anya said, but Second Lieutenant Stephanie Mills did not answer. "Steph?"

Stephanie looked up from the plot with a frown. "Something has the Shan stirred up, ma'am. I have four heavies converging on one of the light cruisers. I don't know what to make of it."

"Hmmm," Anya joined Steph at the consol. "Might be part of the exercise they're running..." she broke off as she stared at the data being displayed. "Huh. That's no training exercise."

"That's what I thought ma'am. See here?"

Anya frowned at the icons Steph pointed out. "Yes... Where was the cruiser when you first noticed this? Did you record it?"

"Yes ma'am, of course. The Skipper was very insistent."

Anya smiled. The Captain had been very thorough about recording everything they observed about the Shan. He would have made a good teacher, she often thought. He held weekly lectures for the crew about what he had learned from his studies.

"Replay your scan on the main viewer would you?"

"Yes, ma'am."

Anya took her place at the command station again and watched the recording. "Advance it to the point where the light cruiser breaks off."

The picture blurred as it raced forward then cleared as it resumed playback at normal speed. The light cruiser was on the edge of a formation of six light cruisers, itself the vanguard of the Shan fleet. An opposing force of eight heavies fled the pursuers, but suddenly the cruiser veered away without warning.

"That's it ma'am."

"Hmmm," Anya pursed her lips and leaned forward as she plotted the ship's courses in her head. "There was nothing to warrant this?"

"Nothing on my visual scan, no ma'am."

"Peculiar... peculiar to say the least." Anya frowned, going over all the possibilities and ticking them off in her mind. Ship malfunction... a possibility but unlikely. The ships were not slowing or trying to rendezvous to give aid to a stricken vessel. Collision avoidance? A very good possibility out there near the asteroid belt, but why not come back on course and rejoin the main body once immediate danger had passed, and why would the other ships leave formation to join the first ship? That left one thing she could think of, a dangerous thing but perhaps not unexpected considering where they were and the mission. "Back it up again would you?"

Stephanie worked her consol and the light cruiser appeared to reverse course.

"Overlay the scan with your system grid," Anya said and Steph did that. "Display location of the outer belt." There was something about the course change that suggested the outer belt was of interest to the Shan light cruiser. The schematic appeared and Anya knew at once that her conjecture was correct. The Shan were definitely interested in the outer belt and she knew why, or thought she did. "Scan for a jump signature, please"

"Ma'am?" Steph said puzzled.

"There might be traces of the translation."

"What trans... yes ma'am."

Anya knew what it had to be, but the Skipper would want hard data. While Lieutenant Mills scanned for the jump signature, Anya woke the captain.

* * *

Bee-beep, bee-beep.

Colgan groaned. It never failed. Whenever he retired late, something always came up that was guaranteed to wake him early. He slapped a hand down on the damn cut-off and blinked blearily into the viewer.

"Colgan."

"Sorry to wake you, sir," Anya said. "I have something you need to see. The Shan are all riled up, I think we might have company out here real soon."

"You think?" Colgan said rolling out of his bunk and reaching for his uniform. "What do you mean, you think?"

"Steph is running another scan now, but I thought you would like to be up here when the data came in."

"You thought right, Lieutenant. I'll be there shortly. Have Baz rustle me up a cup of something hot."

Anya grinned. "Black coffee coming up, sir."

Colgan broke the connection and yawned widely. He should have gone to bed early, but the Shan were so fascinating! How could anyone sleep when there was so much to learn?

An hour later, he was sitting at his command station nursing his second cup of coffee and frowning at the scan data. He could see why Anya was suspicious—he was too, but definitive evidence was proving in short supply.

"How is that sweep coming?" he said, turning to Stephanie. "Anything?"

"Something definitely came in, Skipper, but the traces are too vague to pinpoint the mass. It could have been one of ours, but I can't tell from the scan."

"Hmmm." That was about what he expected. "Helm, take us up slow. I want to take a peek over the top of my rock."

Janice grinned. "Aye, aye, sir. Z plus two thousand metres."

Colgan watched the asteroid they were hiding behind slowly drift down below them on his number two repeater display. "Keep a sharp eye on your scan, Lieutenant."

"Aye, aye, Skip."

Janice slowed the ship and *Canada* was finally able to bring all her instruments to bear. The emergence was confirmed almost straight away, but the culprit was still illusive. The last traces of drive activation were still dispersing and would be gone very soon. No scan tech ever born would have been able to tell what came in system from so little data.

"Concentrate your scan upon Alpha-One, Lieutenant. Let the cruiser lead you to them."

"Aye, sir."

Colgan waited and sipped his coffee. He glanced aside at the ship's chrono. A-shift would be on soon. "Steph, I want you to stay on this. Commander Groves will be up shortly. Bring her up to speed ASAP."

"Aye, Skip," Steph said happily. She wanted to stay and see this thing to its conclusion.

Shift change came and went with no sign that anything remotely like an intruder had ever entered the system. The Shan fleet turned back to its normal operations leaving the original light cruiser, designated Alpha-One, to its search. Sometime later, Stephanie and Francis were still whispering together as they puzzled over the master plot of the system they had displayed at their station. Neither woman had found what the Shan were looking for. Francis was exceptional at scan, and Steph was no slouch either. Whatever the intruder was, it was damn tricky.

"What do we know about that ship, Francis?" Colgan said and highlighted Alpha-One on the main viewer with his control wand.

"Not much, sir. Alpha-one: Shan ship in the light cruiser range. It was patrolling the zone when we came in. Since then, it has led two of their training ops with distinction. I would like to go aboard and meet her captain. I like his moves."

"Let's hope we get the opportunity."

"Sir?"

"What is it, Steph?" Colgan went to join her at Scan. He leaned upon the master plot's consol, reading the data absently "What have you found?"

"Could be nothing, Skipper, but see this?" Mills punched up another view. The current view cleared to be replaced by another sector of the Shan system. "Watch gamma-eight-niner, sir."

Colgan frowned. "I don't see anything—"

"There, sir. That's it."

For just an instant, something flickered into being. Vectors and velocity painted the target, but then it disappeared as it had come with no explanation. *Canada's* computer must have been as puzzled as Colgan felt because after a second's hesitation it deleted the data. Normally, if a target was lost from the scan, the computer would update the plot and paint the data yellow to designate a lost or stealthed target's presumed heading. It did neither of those things.

"A glitch?"

"I don't think so, Skipper," Mills said uncertainly. "It's as if the computer had picked up a ship with a faulty I.F.F"

Colgan frowned. "I don't follow."

"See, if I was a captain of say... a cruiser entering a possibly hostile system, I wouldn't want the Shan to find me."

"Obviously."

"Yes, sir," Mills agreed. "I.F.F might give the game away and it might not. Probably it would, but I wouldn't want to risk it either way, but what if I had to meet someone in that system?"

"Us?" Colgan noted the computer deleting another instance of the phantom target. "You think he's dicking about with his signature?"

"Yes sir, I do. It would be real easy to make our computer think it had a glitch. I know I could do it."

"From the inside," Colgan agreed. He could think of two ways right off. "But from *outside?*"

"Yes sir. I could do it."

"Hmmm." He wasn't sure he liked that, but now wasn't the time to think about it. Colgan turned back to his station. "Run a plot and extrapolate the phantom's probable entry point into the inner belt."

"Aye, sir."

"Janice?"

"Sir?"

"As soon as Steph gives you a course, I want you to take us there. Keep us down to five percent of max. That should keep the Shan ignorant of our movements."

"Aye sir."

* * *

Aboard ASN Invincible, approaching Shan inner belt

"Slow to one tenth," Captain Monroe said and swivelled her station. "Anything yet?"

"Nothing, Skipper," Commander Hamilton said. "They might have been detected and had to jump out."

"I doubt it. The Shan couldn't find us. If Colgan was careful, he should have remained undetected. What's that Shan cruiser doing now?"

"Still patrolling the belt skip."

"That's good." She turned to Martin at communications. "Keep transmitting."

"Aye, aye ma'am," Lieutenant Davin said.

It had taken them days to sneak away from the outer belt. The Shan had taken it upon themselves to run a training op of some kind almost in their laps. It had taken some skilful ship handling by Keith Hadden to extricate them. Now all they had to do was find *Canada* and her mission would be successfully completed.

"The report said that Colgan was using the inner belt to survey the system. Where the hell is he?"

"Could be anywhere by now, Skip. He's been here almost a year—" Kersten began without looking up from her plot, but then her eyes sharpened. "Contact! Target designate Charlie-one—Alliance survey vessel." She looked up and grinned. "It's *Canada*, Captain."

Cynthia smiled in satisfaction. "Helm, intercept course."

"Aye, aye. Coming to new heading three-four-six by zero-zero-two degrees," Lieutenant Hadden said, making the course correction and *Invincible* swung to port.

"Get me *Canada* as soon as we're in range, Martin. I want to say hello."

Davin nodded. "Yes ma'am!"

* * *

ABOARD ASN CANADA, SHAN INNER BELT

James stepped off the shuttle and into *Canada's* number two boat-bay. Brenda stopped beside him and took his hand. He smiled down at her, but she didn't see. She was looking around the bay with interest. The others whispered among themselves while half a dozen of *Canada's* crew trotted past and up the ramp to retrieve their belongings from the shuttle. Standing in a line ahead of the contact team was their reception committee.

Captain Monroe went to greet *Canada's* captain. James nudged Brenda gently and they tagged along.

"—my first officer Commander Groves. This is Lieutenant Ricks, my comm officer. Mark is the reason we're all here."

Ricks demurred. "It could have been anyone, sir. It was blind luck that I was on duty at the right time."

"Lucky for all of us," Captain Colgan said.

Monroe shook hands with Colgan's officers and introduced her Exec before turning to Janice. "This is Professor Bristow, George. She heads up the contact team. I will let her introduce you to the others."

"I am glad to know you Professor—" Colgan began.

"Call me Janice, please."

"As you wish, Janice. I am pleased to welcome you and your team aboard. I will have your things sent to your quarters. If you need anything, please let me know."

"Thank you, Captain, but the only thing we need is a place to work, and access to your computer and database. Let me first introduce you to the others." Janice said turning to James. "Professor James Wilder, history."

James smiled and shook the captain's hand. "Nice to meet you, sir. I'm looking forward to seeing what you have learned."

Colgan inclined his head. "Welcome aboard, Professor."

"Professor Brenda Lane, xenology and exobiology."

"Welcome Professor. I look forward to hearing your views on the Shan."

"Thank you, Captain," Brenda said and shook hands.

"Professor Bernhard Franks, cultural studies."

"Cultural studies?" Colgan said in puzzlement. "What do you study?"

"Rather it is whom do I study, Captain. I specialise in the Merkiaari. The President thought I would be useful."

Colgan raised an eyebrow at that. "I see. Welcome aboard, Professor."

"Professor David Harrison, biology," Janice said.

"Nice to meet you, Professor."

"Likewise, sir," David said. "You have a very fine ship here. I know quite a bit about the Fleet and—"

Janice interrupted with a gentle squeeze of David's shoulder. "Please, David. Leave that for later if you would."

"Sorry, Captain."

"Not at all, Professor. I am very proud of her. We'll find time to talk later."

"I look forward to it, sir."

"Sheryl Linden, physics and engineering design," Janice went on, and motioned Sheryl forward.

"I have heard of you, Professor," Colgan said pumping Sheryl's hand with enthusiasm. "If I'm not mistaken, you pioneered the development of the skip capable drive."

Sheryl shook her head. "You *are* mistaken captain. The ability is inherent within all fold space drives."

"Yes, but you made it possible to actually use it. Before your research, two out of three ships smeared themselves all over the quadrant whenever they tried it."

"It was simply a matter of proper calibration—" Sheryl began but stopped herself. "Forgive me, Bindar. That was rude of me."

"There is nothing to forgive, Professor Linden," Bindar Singh murmured quietly. "I am sure your achievements are more than worthy."

"Captain Colgan, this is Professor Singh. He is our linguistics expert," Sheryl said, introducing her colleague herself by way of an apology.

"Honoured, sir," Bindar said with a small bow.

"The honour is mine, Professor Singh. I have a lot to show you. We have been recording everything since the day we arrived. Much of it is verbal communication. Mark has been working on it, but he's not really trained in your field I'm afraid."

"I will start at once!" Bindar said eagerly.

"No hurry, Bindar," Janice said, and laughed gently at his downcast expression. "Let us get settled in at least. I'll call a meeting first thing tomorrow... have you a place for us to work, Captain?"

"You can have the briefing room whenever you need it, and all the labs are open to you of course."

"Thank you."

Colgan turned to Ricks. "Show our guests to their cabins please, Mark. Make sure they know how to use our equipment and can find their way around."

"Aye sir. If you will follow me please?"

Janice nodded and led the team after the lieutenant.

* * *

11 ~ Discovered

Tei'Varyk, commander of the light fang *Chakra*, was perplexed. It was unlike Tarjei to be wrong about something like this, but if she was not, where was the target? It had been long orbits since the Murderers of Harmony had destroyed the Harmony of Shan, but that made his people more vigilant not less. The Fleet had never been so strong, and it would get stronger still as new construction was added.

The Twin Worlds of the race had lived in peace for many hundreds of orbits, but then had come the *war*. War, he mused, a strange word that had no place in the mouth of any Shan. It even sounded alien, which of course it was. The race had no word for this thing that the Murderers called war, and so they used the alien word rather than foul the language of the race by adding one more harmonious. The elders were wise in this. How could something without harmony be given a harmonious word? It was much better to use the harsh sounding alien one to remind everyone what it meant.

Tei'Varyk glanced at the repeater display on his right side.

It was displaying a schematic of the outer asteroid belt with mining operations and other information blinking in the blue of known targets.

"Jakinda, come about to a new heading of... zero-zero-zero by zero-two-seven."

"I hear, Tei," Jakinda acknowledged the order. "He comes to a new heading: zero-zero-zero by zero-two-seven."

"Good Jakinda," Tei'Varyk said and turned his station toward his mate. "Tarjei, his eyes to maximum. Sweep a cone forty-five degrees either side of us."

"I hear," Tarjei said. "His eyes see nothing, but I am vigilant."

He flicked his ears in acknowledgment. "You are his eyes."

"I hear," Tarjei said dropping her jaw and baring her teeth in a smile.

With the press of a button, Tei'Varyk centred his station again and reviewed what he knew of this phantom target. It had appeared at the extreme edge of *Chakra's* envelope only briefly before submerging itself in the debris of the outer asteroid belt. A traveller (comet) he had thought, but it had not re-emerged from the belt, and there had been no impact detected. Tarjei, by coincidence testing *Chakra's* eyes at maximum, had locked up the object briefly, and the glaring red of unknown target splashed itself across half the displays on the command deck. The warning, sirens shocked everyone immobile for moments only before his finely trained crew responded as their training demanded. *Chakra* had turned toward the target, and his eyes had swept the belt at maximum range and power, but Tei'Varyk had failed to find any clue to the phantom's whereabouts. The elders had heard his report with worry evident in the way their muzzles and whiskers twitched. They ordered him to patrol the asteroid belt until a satisfactory answer was obtained. That was almost half an orbit ago—two seasons of searching and nothing to show the elders.

"Indications negative, Tei," Tarjei said unhappily. "I have failed you and him."

"Never say that," Tei'Varyk said harshly. "We will search until the end of the orbit if we have to. Do not concern yourself with failure. Look ahead in harmony."

"I hear," Tarjei said with her hackles raised and her tail restless. She was not in harmony.

The distress in Tarjei's voice was obvious. Her ears were plastered flat against her head—a sign of just how upset she was with her failure. Tei'Varyk saw the misery in her eyes before she looked away from him and back to her controls. He should comfort her tonight. They had spent so little time together while on this patrol. It was hard to remember the last time they were alone. Tarjei and he had been mated for only a short time. For all intents and purposes, they were still the strangers from far off clans they had been last orbit.

"Jakinda," Tei'Varyk said turning his attention reluctantly back to duty. "We have scanned every particle of the outer belt have we not?"

"Yes, Tei," Jakinda confirmed.

"Is there any area of the belt we cannot investigate properly?"

Jakinda was quiet for a moment. "No, Tei."

"Then it is not here," Tei'Varyk said with finality.

Jakinda turned away from his station to face Tei'Varyk. "If not here then where?"

"The inner belt is the only place to hide. It must be there."

"But that means it *is* a ship."

"Must be," Tei'Varyk said grimly. "Jakinda, new heading: best speed to the inner belt."

"I hear," Jakinda said and spun back to his consol. A moment later, *Chakra* swung toward the inner system. "Time to the inner belt... approximately four cycles."

"Good."

Jozka spoke up. "Should I inform the elders?"

Tei'Varyk hesitated. "No. If I'm wrong, it would be foolish to distract the elders. The rest of the Fleet will remain on patrol while we check the inner belt."

"I hear, but if you're right we may need help."

Tei'Varyk chewed his whiskers thoughtfully. *Chakra* was a light fang, but what he lacked in firepower, he more than made up with agility and speed. He felt confident they could escape any trap to warn the elders.

"*Chakra* is fast. If we find the phantom, we run it down and disable it. If we can't do that, we run for help."

"I hear, Tei." Jozka turned back to his station.

* * *

Aboard ASN Canada, inner belt, Shan system

"Dammit!" Captain Jeff Colgan said as he watched the Shan ship approaching.

The stupid fools were seen! They must have been!

Canada's bridge crew kept their eyes lowered to their stations as Colgan vented his spleen over the ineptness of a certain ship's captain, namely Cynthia Monroe. Monroe was skipper of the light cruiser *ASN Invincible*. Unfortunately, she seemed to believe the name extended to her own abilities.

"Get me *Invincible*," Colgan said through gritted teeth.

"Aye, sir," Lieutenant Ricks said, and moments later the Shan ship on the viewscreen was replaced by Cynthia Monroe.

"What can I do for you, Jeff?"

"I assume you're monitoring the Shan light cruiser."

"Of course."

"That ship has been patrolling the outer system without deviation since I've been here, Cynthia. Then you show up and it starts a search pattern. Why do you think it's heading here now?"

Monroe frowned. "It's *patrolling* not searching—"

"Don't give me that," Colgan began hotly, but then realising he was berating a fellow captain in front of witnesses, he forced himself to calm down. "You and I both know you were detected, but that doesn't matter now. That ship has just finished an exhaustive search of the outer belt and found nothing. Now it's coming here to do the same thing. That ship isn't going to give up until it finds us... or rather you."

Monroe's eyebrows shot up. "Me? What have you got in mind?"

"My mission is too important to abandon, and you're faster than me anyway. I suggest you run for it and allow the Shan to catch a glimpse of you before jumping out. With luck, they'll give up the search when they see you go."

"Dangerous, Jeff," Monroe said worriedly. "Without me you have no backup at all."

Colgan shook his head. "Not so dangerous as all that. Under no circumstances will I fire on the Shan, so adding your guns to mine is pointless. Besides, if you're careful you could sneak back in after the system settles down again."

Monroe nodded reluctantly. "Do you or the boffins need anything before I go?"

Colgan sighed in relief. "I can't think of a thing. I've no doubt the profs would like the entire Alliance database, but they'll make do. They had better!"

Monroe chuckled but it was a strained sound. "Well, if I'm going I might as well do it now. Good luck, Jeff."

"And to you."

The screen cleared to show the Shan ship decelerating hard as it approached the belt.

Colgan watched it come, and felt only admiration for a people that could build such beautiful ships. They were sleek and agile, but they lacked jump technology. They had fewer weapons than a Human ship of the same class, but for all of that they were beautiful. Human ships were never so fine looking—they were designed to kill Merkiaari, not look pretty.

"Split screen," he ordered. "*Invincible* on the left."

"Aye, sir," Ricks said and the screen changed to show both ships.

Invincible was manoeuvring. She had lain doggo against an asteroid for weeks, but now she was breaking for open space.

"Any indications that the Shan have seen her?"

"None, Skipper."

Colgan frowned. "Damn peculiar. They barely caught a glimpse of her when she came in, but that was enough to start a manhunt. Now when she strolls out into the open, they don't react at all."

"*Invincible* is still in stealth mode, Skipper," Commander Groves said. "Maybe the Shan can't see her."

Colgan pursed his lips, not sure he agreed. "She was stealthed when she came in. They saw her then."

"Maybe not," Groves mused. "Maybe they saw the jump signature."

"They don't have jump technology."

"True, but does that mean their sensors are inferior?"

"You're right." He had become so used to his technological superiority that he had assumed it covered all areas of ship design, but that was not proven. Just because *Invincible* was jump capable with superior weapons didn't mean she had superior sensors. "Inform *Invincible* of your thoughts, XO."

"Aye, sir," Groves said and keyed a channel open herself.

While his exec was doing that, Colgan concentrated on watching the Shan ship. *Invincible* was almost clear of the debris now. She would be firing up her mains any minute. Surely, the Shan would see that. They must.

"*Invincible* concurs with our assessment, Skip," Groves said.

Colgan nodded. "Sound battle stations, Mark."

* * *

Throughout *Canada*, the, siren screamed and her crew ran

to emergency and battle stations. In the bowels of the ship, damage control parties scrambled into hard suits, while elsewhere, the crew pulled on their gloves to seal their uniforms and put on their helmets. The system was a good one, proven time and again against the Merkiaari, but of course civilians had never needed to seal themselves into unfamiliar uniforms. There were difficulties.

"Ma'am, you have to twist it *clockwise*," an exasperated Chief Williams said to Janice Bristow, as he tried to make her stand still long enough to show her the proper way to suit up.

"Why didn't you say so?"

"I assumed anyone with half a brain would know that when you tighten something, it is *clockwise!*"

Brenda smirked, but then her face flushed when she noticed the plumbing connections in her uniform. "No way, that will never fit!"

Williams, looking harried, turned to see what the problem was. "Ma'am, these uniforms are proven technology. It will fit. They *always* fit."

"Put it on, Brenda," James said hustling her toward the hatch. He was already in his plain white uniform and was sealed except for his helmet. He had worn one since the first day of their journey, and was told he looked good in it. "I know it will feel odd, but without your uniform you could die."

"Easy for you to say," Brenda grumbled as she stripped in the privacy of an adjoining cabin. "You don't have a pipe the size of…"

"I get the picture," James said hurriedly. "You'll be pleased to have it if you're caught short."

"What?" Brenda's voice came muffled through the hatch.

"I said, you'll be pleased to have it if you're caught short."

Mumble, mumble, mutter!

"God, this thing is huge. Arghhh! Goddamn sonofa—"

"Are you all right in there?" He reached toward the scanner

to open the hatch. "Do you need any help?"

"You stay out there, I'm nearly done."

James smirked but he was pleased to see her come out fully dressed and sealed into her new uniform. It hugged her figure and suited her. Janice was putting her helmet on, and James did likewise. He looked around and found his colleagues all sitting and strapping in. He took Brenda's arm and led her to an empty seat where he helped her connect her life-support and strap in. He sat beside her and held her hand.

"The boffins are sealed and secure, sir," Williams said and strapped in nearby.

"Understood Chief. Keep an eye on them, they're important," Lieutenant Ricks said over the comm.

"Aye, sir."

* * *

"All stations report manned and ready, Skipper," Lieutenant Ricks said.

Colgan nodded. "Good."

"The civs are all secure, sir," Ricks reported again a moment later. "I have Chief Williams babysitting."

"Good work," Colgan said. "I'll have to schedule some training for them. They took way too long to get themselves sealed."

"They weren't wearing uniform, Skipper."

"Why the hell not?" he said and glared at Ricks, but he knew why. "From now on they wear the uniforms we supplied. No exceptions—it's damn dangerous."

"Aye, sir. I'll inform them."

Colgan nodded and dismissed the civs from his thoughts. "Weps, under no circumstances are you to open fire on the Shan."

"Aye, sir," Lieutenant Ivanova said. "Point defence?"

"Point defence free."

"Aye, sir," Ivanova said happily. "Point defence now active.

Auto loaders functioning normally, targeting computers online."

Colgan nodded. "Helm, be prepared to move on a moment's notice. I don't expect we will have to, but be prepared all the same."

"Aye, sir."

* * *

ABOARD CHAKRA, APPROACHING INNER BELT, SHAN SYSTEM

"Commencing deceleration," Jakinda announced.

"I hear," Tei'Varyk said. "Eyes to maximum, claws to standby."

"I hear, his claws are sharp," Kajika said.

"I hear, his eyes at maximum. Indications negative at this time," Tarjei said, but her voice was harmonious.

Tei'Varyk smiled at her. They had spent the journey to the inner belt alone together. It had been a wonderful time, full of quiet conversations and lovemaking. He felt much closer to her now, and knew she felt the same. They had needed the intimacy to cement the bond. They were truly mated now, and Tarjei was calmer and more harmonious for it.

He was too.

Tei'Varyk studied his displays and chewed his whiskers thoughtfully at what was reported. Nothing. He had been so sure, but it looked as if they would be searching for a long time just as before. He looked away for a moment, but his eyes snapped back to his display just as a red light blinked into being followed by numerals detailing velocity and vectors.

"Detection!" Tarjei shouted.

"Identify," Tei'Varyk snapped, as the computers realised the target was unknown and, sirens wailed. "Silence that."

"I hear," Jozka replied and cut the sirens.

"Unable to identify. Target: alien warship. Type unknown, class unknown. Weaponry exceeds our own by... *two* orders of magnitude—" Tarjei reported and continued detailing the target.

Order of two! That meant this alien ship was as close to a heavy fang as made no difference. *Chakra* was a light fang, fast and manoeuvrable, but the heavies were all weapons and power. Was this alien built along the same lines?

"Pursuit course," he snapped. "Sound alert!"

"I hear," Jozka said, and another siren growled throughout the ship making hackles rise.

Crew males and females dashed on all fours in some cases, in an effort to be first at their stations. Such primitivism was frowned upon usually, but not when the ship was on battle alert. Whatever worked, was the watchword in these cases.

Chakra swung nimbly onto a new heading.

Tei'Varyk's tail lashed with his excitement. He had to force it to be still. "Why did *Chakra's* eyes find him so easily?"

"Unknown, Tei." Tarjei tried to refine the data on the alien. "We found him, but the intruder was already leaving the belt at that time."

That was very wrong. Why leave the safety of the belt when *Chakra's* eyes failed to find him time and again? It made no sense. Things that made no sense lacked harmony and were therefore suspect.

"Fire to disable as soon as he's in range," Tei'Varyk ordered.

"I hear," Kajika said calmly. "Target locked, but still out of range."

"Inform the elders of what is occurring," he said without taking his eyes from the display. They were gaining, but much too slowly. How could a heavy fang, even an alien one, accelerate so fast?

"I hear," Jozka said.

Tei'Varyk pressed a control on his station and another screen lit. "Tei'Unwin, *Chakra* pursues."

"I hear, Tei. I have been monitoring."

Tei'Unwin was *Chakra's* alternate commander. It was

comforting to know that *Chakra* would be well cared for when Tei'Varyk was gone.

"I knew you would be. In the event *Chakra's* command deck is destroyed, you will command. I order the alien *disabled* at all costs, even that of *Chakra* himself."

"I hear," Tei'Unwin said grimly. "It will be done."

Tei'Varyk keyed the screen clear and noted the alien was pulling ahead. It was incredible. No heavy fang could accelerate like this.

"The elders say good hunting," Jozka said.

"I hear," he said. "Anything else?"

"They say *Hekja*, *Hoth*, and *Neifon* come."

His ears twitched and relief flooded through him. "I hear."

Three heavy fangs should be more than enough. The alien was still opening the range, but it was deep in system and would not escape. Even if he knew where the ship was trying to escape to, which he didn't, he was certain it could not... but where *was* it going? Tei'Varyk shifted uncomfortably at his station. Unanswerable questions always made him twitchy. This one had been asked time and time again without an answer. Who knew where the Murderers came from?

"Display current location of *Hoth*, *Hekja*, and *Neifon*," he said.

The viewer cleared and a tactical map of the system appeared. The three heavy fangs were moving to envelop the alien while *Chakra* chased him into the trap. It was too easy. He knew it was, but what else could he do?

Nothing.

"Go to maximum emergency power," Tei'Varyk said quietly and ignored the hisses of shock.

"I hear," Jakinda said prayerfully. "Accelerating to maximum emergency power."

Now they were gaining, Tei'Varyk noted with approval.

* * *

Aboard ASN Invincible, Shan System

"The cruiser is gaining, Captain. CIC reports that the three heavies will be in range in two minutes," Commander Hamilton reported.

Monroe nodded and studied the data on her number two monitor that CIC (Combat Information Centre) had gathered for her. She turned her attention to another of her repeater displays. Her number one monitor was currently mirroring in miniature the data displayed at Commander Hamilton's station.

"Very good, XO," Monroe said and turned to the helm. "Charge the jump drive."

"Aye, Skipper," Lieutenant Hadden said. "Drive will be hot in three minutes."

"This might be a little tight," she murmured uneasily. "Weps, point defence free, but no aggressive action. *Defensive* only. *Clear?*"

"Aye, aye, sir," Irene Bishop replied. "Point defence online, no aggressive action."

"Helm, go to evasive when necessary. Don't wait for the order."

"Aye, aye, Skipper," Lieutenant Hadden replied tensely and firmed his grip upon *Invincible's* stick.

* * *

Aboard Chakra, in pursuit of alien ship, Shan System

"Alien in range. Target lock confirmed... firing!" Kajika said.

Tei'Varyk watched *Chakra's* claws reach out to rend the alien ship, but Kajika missed. Tei'Varyk leaned forward to study the data more closely. No, he hadn't missed. *Chakra's* eyes reported a definite hit, but the alien was unaffected. Tei'Varyk's hackles rose and he shivered in fright. If *Chakra's* main energy mounts could not hurt it, what would?

"No effect," Kajika reported.

"Engage with secondary weapons, engage with everything!" Tei'Varyk gasped in shock when all his hits produced no effect.

"I hear," Kajika said. "Launching torpedoes, firing secondary mounts, firing primaries."

Tei'Varyk watched the torpedoes impact and detonate, but this time they definitely missed. Just as they reached terminal range, something detached from the alien and the torpedoes impacted it. Again, *Chakra's* torpedoes flew straight to the target, and again they were decoyed off track.

"Save his torpedoes. Go to maximum rate of fire on all energy mounts."

"I hear, Tei," Kajika said making the adjustment on his panel. "Firing energy weapons at maximum."

"*Chakra* slows!" Jakinda reported.

Tei'Varyk flicked his ears in agreement and watched grimly. *Chakra's* weapons were energy hogs. Maximum rate of fire was causing him to sacrifice energy normally reserved for propulsion.

"Continue action," he ordered grimly.

"I hear," Kajika said.

"I hear," Jakinda said. "Main propulsion heating beyond critical. Failure imminent."

"Reduce by twenty percent and continue pursuit," he said without fuss. He had been monitoring the situation closely on his own panel.

"I hear," Jakinda said in relief as *Chakra's* great engines cooled into the safe zone once again.

Chakra was losing the alien now, but it would remain in range for a while longer. The heavy fangs were just coming into range, and would have to take over from *Chakra* unless Tei'Varyk could somehow slow the alien. He could think of no way to do that. Everything he could do was being done.

"Alien wreckage detected," Tarjei yelped in glee.

"Well done, Kajika!" Tei'Varyk howled his own excitement.

"Continue action."
"I hear!"

* * *

Aboard ASN Invincible, Shan System

Damage control parties scrambled in the darkness trying to patch the hole in *Invincible's* defences. She had lost her aft launchers and boat bay, but worse than that; she was breached past frame two hundred all the way to two-fifty. Over a dozen crewmen were killed when shrapnel shredded their uniforms opening them to vacuum. Finally, power was restored and the full horror was revealed. Dead crewmen littered the deck with blood and fluids splashed over the walls where the absolute zero of space it had frozen it solid.

"All right people," O'Malley said coldly. "There's nothing we can do for them. Get that blast door shut. We seal this section or we can't jump."

Swede lifted the wreckage clear by main strength and forced the hatch shut. Men rushed forward to help and welded it in position. The damage control party moved on, repairing what it could, sealing what it could not.

On the bridge, smoke hung thickly, but no one took notice. Monroe raged at the loss of her people, but she would not be the cause of another interstellar war. She could not, *would not*, fire back. She grimly held to her composure and watched the heavies bear down on her.

"Damage control to bridge. She's sealed, Skipper, but I don't know for how long," O'Malley reported.

Monroe's eyes snapped up to Keith Hadden at the helm. "Execute!"

"Executing."

ASN Invincible gathered herself and jumped into fold space as a dozen torpedoes raced through the wake caused by activation of a jump drive. The tiny computer brains were no longer able to find a target, and as a safety precaution, they detonated.

* * *

ABOARD CHAKRA, SHAN SYSTEM

"Target lost," Tarjei said fiercely.

Everyone was grinning and celebrating their victory, but Tei'Varyk stared at the empty display in puzzled silence. There was something just before the final explosion, he was sure of it.

"Tarjei, look for debris," he said quietly and caused a profound silence to descend on the command deck.

"I hear. Scanning for debris, indications…" she said in stunned realisation. "Indications negative!"

Hisses of shock and outrage sounded from all sides as they realised the alien had escaped. How was it possible? One moment it was fleeing, the next it was gone. The explosion had blinded *Chakra's* eyes for a moment, but that was not enough time for the alien to escape.

Tei'Varyk studied his now empty tactical display. "Jakinda, search pattern at last known coordinates."

"I hear," Jakinda said and brought *Chakra* onto a new heading.

Tei'Varyk turned his station to Jozka. "Contact *Hoth*, *Hekja*, and *Neifon*. Tell them what we have discovered and ask that they search with us."

"I hear," Jozka said.

He flexed his claws in frustration. There was nothing on *Chakra's* display to say the alien had ever existed. Tei'Varyk flicked his ears in annoyance with himself and turned to Tarjei.

"Replay last action."

"Time index?" Tarjei asked.

"Just as the heavies fire their torpedoes."

"I hear."

Tarjei displayed the data frozen on the main viewer. Everyone, except Jozka who was busy talking to the commanders of the heavy fangs, turned to watch the screen.

"Advance at twice speed… stop," Tei'Varyk ordered when the scene reached the point he wanted. "Play at one half."

"I hear." Tarjei turned a control on her panel.

Tei'Varyk watched again as *Chakra's* claws reached out to tear and rend the alien. He noted the tiny amount of damage he had inflicted, and his lips rippled back in worry and fear.

"Slow to one tenth," he said.

"I hear."

The torpedoes approached at a crawl, and then it happened. Space itself shimmered and twisted. The alien ship seemed to glow blue for an instant before it twisted violently and disappeared. Tei'Varyk's shock was complete, and so was that of his crew. The alien had not been hit by the torpedoes and destroyed, it had escaped somehow. The torpedoes lost lock as they watched and detonated as they were programmed to do in these cases. The screen flashed white as the violence of the explosion overloaded *Chakra's* eyes, and then the star speckled black of space returned.

"The alien escaped us," Tei'Varyk said quietly. "Contact the elders, I must tell them what has happened."

"I hear," Jozka said.

"Reverse course back to where we first encountered the alien."

"I hear, Tei. *Chakra* turns to new heading, one-two-eight by zero-zero-two."

Why had the alien shown itself and then run? Was it possible there was more than one? It could be. They had been unable to find one, why not two or three or even more?

"The elders await," Jozka said.

"I hear. Call Tei'Unwin to take my place here. I will speak to the elders in my chambers."

"I hear, Tei." Jozka hunched over his consol.

Tei'Varyk stood and left the command deck. He was tired after all the excitement of the pursuit. He had been sitting for far too long, but strangely his legs felt wobbly. Fright. No doubt he would start shedding later. His people always shed when stressed—it was part of being born Shan. Would they ever find a cure for it? His people had made so many advances in the time since the war, that one would scarcely recognise the way they lived these days. The war wasn't all bad he supposed, though it was a shocking thought. If not for the war he would not be living in space, which he loved, commanding a ship that he also loved.

"Where do aliens come from?" he mused as he made his way along the empty corridor. "Other planets orbiting other suns obviously."

That being true, how did they travel the vast distances from one sun to another? Faster than light travel had been theorised by the elders since time began. It was generally accepted as being impossible, but what if it wasn't? The Murderers came from somewhere, and now these new aliens had also come. He had accepted that these aliens were not the Murderers of old. It became obvious as soon as he had a clear view of their ship. Maybe the blue light and the twisting was an FTL drive. But it was impossible... was it not?

Tei'Varyk growled irritably. He entered his chambers and keyed the terminal alive. The screen lightened to show three very old and grey-streaked Shan.

He bowed. "Honoured elders, I fear I have failed you."

"Nonsense, Tei'Varyk," Kajetan said from her position in the centre. She was the speaker for the elders. "*Chakra* was the only ship to detect the alien intrusion. The only ship to find them again, and now you are the only one to have noticed this new data. We are pleased with you."

"I hear, Kajetan. *Chakra* is on route to the inner belt to discover what the alien ship found so interesting. I have theorised that there might be more than one ship."

"Evidence?" Kajetan demanded.

"None eldest, except intuition. *Chakra* was unable to find the alien, yet he came out of hiding right before us knowing he would be discovered. This strange light and twisting may be a way to overcome the FTL restrictions we have long debated. If this is so, why did he wait to use it?"

"Why?"

"I believe he was luring us away from something he wanted to protect," Tei'Varyk said guiltily.

"Another ship?"

"Perhaps, or an asteroid base."

Hisses of shock and anger told him what the elders thought of such an idea.

"*Chakra* will hunt to find the answer," Kajetan ordered. "Is there anything you require?"

"Not at present, but I would advise you to hold *Hoth*, *Hekja*, and *Neifon* in readiness nearby. These alien ships are very fast."

"We hear. It will be as you ask. Good hunting."

Tei'Varyk bowed and the screen darkened.

* * *

12~The Next Step

James pushed aside his empty plate and stirred his coffee. How quickly things change, he mused watching Brenda eating her breakfast. A few months ago such a simple thing as sharing a meal with her would have seemed impossible, but now nothing did. Brenda's choice to move in with him was responsible for his new outlook on life, and he was so very thankful. He never wanted to be alone again.

"What are you thinking?" Brenda said.

"Hmmm?"

"You were light years away, James. I asked what you were thinking about."

James smiled. "I was thinking how much I love you."

Brenda's eye lit with pleasure. "Really?"

"Yes."

"I love you too, James. I know I don't say it very often, but I do. You know I do..." she frowned worriedly. "You do, don't you?"

He chuckled. "I know you do, but it's nice to hear it now and then."

Brenda shrugged ruefully. "I never was very good at telling

people how I feel."

"Me neither," James agreed. "Maybe we can learn together."

Brenda nodded. "I can't wait to show you off to my parents. They gave up on me and men a long time ago."

"I doubt that."

"It's true. They used to be worse than Janice with all their hints about marriage and wanting grandchildren." She shook her head gently. "When they find out about you…"

"They'll disown you?"

Brenda grinned. "No, they'll be the first Humans to reach orbit without mechanical aid!"

James chuckled. "Can't wait to see that."

Brenda finished buttering what the autochef insisted was a British crumpet. She knew better, as did he, but although it looked wrong, it actually tasted quite good. "What do you have planned for today?" she said and took a bite.

He sipped his coffee and then leaned back in his seat. "I have an idea on how to help Bindar. The translation is taking longer than he hoped—we haven't learned near enough phrases to attempt first contact."

"Hmmm, I know." Brenda frowned. "Janice is worried about him. He hardly sleeps. She says we're way behind schedule on the language side, and there's no sign of *Invincible*."

That *was* a worry. Captain Colgan said *Invincible* had planned to sneak back in system once the dust settled, but she hadn't yet. *Invincible's* damage had been light, and chances were good that her crew was fine. James was worried for Trish, Swede, and the others, but Colgan was very sure. He said the probable reason for her non-appearance was that she had been ordered to stay out. James thought it more likely that Captain Monroe had seen the mess they were in, and had decided to stay out on her own. Whatever the reason for her extended absence, *Canada* and all aboard her were running out of time.

Chakra had not given up when *Invincible* jumped out-system. If anything, the Shan captain was more determined to find them, not less. Hardly a day went by without *Canada's* battle stations alarm sounding. The first time had been so unexpected, it almost stopped his heart. What followed was a mad scramble to seal his uniform all the while trying to watch Brenda as she fumbled with the unfamiliar connections. The first thing he did after Colgan announced their successful evasion was teach Brenda how to use her uniform and its connections properly. He accepted no arguments. Only when she had shown him that she could seal her uniform, and connect herself to life support, did he relax enough not to watch her all the time. He only watched her half the time now... well, three quarters... maybe.

"How can you help him?" Brenda stood and dumped their plates into the autochef. The plates quickly disappeared to wherever dirty plates go aboard ship.

"Hmmm?" James said still thinking about *Invincible*. He hoped Trish and the others were all right.

"Bindar."

"I think I have a way around the speech problem. My historical studies have helped me there."

"That's great," Brenda said excitedly.

"I hope so. I plan to talk with the Chief about it. If anyone can make it, or know someone who can, it's him. What about you love?"

Brenda grimaced. "I'm still stuck on this harmony thing. I know it's important to them. They have so many sayings that link to harmony, but I can't get a handle on it."

James nodded remembering his own speculations regarding the harmony question. They all had their pet theories, but none of them were convincing to his mind.

"I hate to say this, Brenda, but I think you should move on. I agree it's important, but you can't afford to get bogged down with unanswerable questions."

"You're right." Brenda sighed. "I know you're right, but it

doesn't make sense. The Shan talk of the Great Harmony, and the Twin Worlds of Harmony, or the Twin Worlds of the Race living in harmony, when in reality they fly around in multi-megatonne warships and train everyone to fight. How is that harmony? Who do they fight—anyone?"

James shrugged. "I said I agree, but maybe the answer is more in my field. Maybe they did live in harmony in the past, and then something happened to change it. That might be the reason for the sayings you mentioned—they're all that remain of an older civilisation."

Brenda sighed again. "I'll move on, it's the only thing to do."

He stood and kissed her. "I'm sorry, but I think you're right."

They stepped out of their cabin and separated, Brenda to the briefing room, and James to find the Chief.

Finding the Chief wasn't hard as it turned out. James knew many of the crew by sight if not by name and prevailed on them for directions. He stepped into generator room four, and found a pair of legs sticking out of a consol with the Chief attached.

"Chief?"

"Yeah?" a muffled and distracted voice said from within the consol. "Whatdoyouwant?"

"I need help."

"Don't we all," came Williams' voice clearer now as he wriggled out of the tight space.

James grasped the man by the ankles and pulled him the rest of the way out of the consol.

"Thanks."

"The contact team needs a little help, Chief. We're falling behind schedule because of all these alerts. Every time *Chakra* turns up, we have to stop work."

"Yeah? Sorry to hear that, but what do I know about aliens?" Williams said scratching his head. "I can build you an autochef that makes the best pizza this side of Earth if you want, or beef up your pulser so it can knock out a tank with one shot—course you only get one, it uses a lot of power you know? But aliens…" He shook his head. "Nah, don't know any."

James coughed and smothered the laugh that threatened. "What I need is a device to convert our voices into the alien language, and the alien's voices into ours."

Williams' face brightened with interest. "A translator eh? Sounds interesting. I just might be able to help you there."

"Oh?" he said feeling his hopes rising. So easy?

"Yeah, come with me."

James followed Chief Williams deep into the ship until they entered a cluttered workroom that Williams called his own.

"See that?" Williams pointed to a piece of equipment with circuitry hanging out of it. It must have weighed as much if not more than James did and stood taller.

"What is it?" he said circling the thing and looking it over.

"That's the voice recognition unit for the ship's whole damn computer that is," Williams said with a glare for the offending item.

"Doesn't the ship… you know… need it or anything?"

"Nah." Williams smirked. "It's busted. The new one takes up a third the space this one does and costs ten times as much. I could probably fix her up for you."

James looked at the thing doubtfully. "Well thank you, Chief, but how will we carry it when we go aboard the Shan ship?"

"Carry it? *Carry it!* You never said nothing about carrying it."

James smiled contritely. "Sorry, Chief. What I need is something portable that will do the job, like… I don't know. Like a compad." He pointed to the mini-computer in Williams' top pocket.

"A compad," Williams said slowly. "Are you out of your

mind? A *compad!* How the hell am I going to get all that junk in one of these?" he said kicking the recognition unit and waving the compad under James' nose.

James stepped back a little. "I don't know, but the Captain said you were the best damn miracle worker in Fleet. He said if you couldn't do it, no one could."

Actually, Colgan knew nothing of this, but he would as soon as James could run over and coach him... ah, *tell* him what he was supposed to have said about Williams.

"He did?" Williams swelled, but then his shoulders slumped. "How the hell am I going to get all that crap in a compad?" He scratched his head in distraction. "Tight beam it? Nah, no bloody good around corners. What I need is a way to transmit without worrying about the damn leakage. The Alliance would make me a bloody saint if I figured that one out."

James nodded. Unsecured communications was one reason the Merkiaari had found the colonies so quickly. TBC (Tight Beam Communications) was secure, but the system was limited to ships in close proximity—it was essentially a modulated laser pulse... like flashing lights at one another. Where tight beam was impractical, fold space drones were used to eliminate leakage. Given enough time their fold space drives had enough capacity to cross the Human sector of the galaxy. They were slower than using courier ships, but where speed was not an issue, drones were the best way to keep Alliance worlds in contact with each other. All that was beside the point here though. As Williams said, TBC was no good around corners and fold space had no place within the confines of a ship.

Williams rummaged around in the junk pile. He grunted in satisfaction when he found a metre rule and turned back to measure the compad and recognition unit. He shook his head at what was revealed and double-checked his measurements.

"Can't be done... can it?" Williams muttered. "How about double thickness? Can't see why not. Bloody civs can sow bigger pockets for them."

That sounded promising. James was sure he could sow if he had to. He watched Williams working and realised he had been forgotten.

"I'll leave you to it then, shall I? I could come back to check on you or—"

"Where are you going?" Williams said and glared. "You can help me with this piece of crap for a start."

"Ermmm... I have no idea how to—"

"Course not, you're just a civ. Look, we have to fix this piece of junk and reinstall it. Only God knows what the skipper will say when I tell him about shutting the computer down."

James smiled sickly. Shutting the computer down while they were hiding from *Chakra*, was *not* a good idea. He had to see Colgan *fast*.

"I don't see how I can help you, Chief."

"How strong are you?" Williams said looking him up and down.

"Well, I don't know... why?"

"Coz you can help me hump this piece of junk over here that's why."

James helped him lift the recognition unit, and together they shuffled across the room.

"Damn civs..." Williams mumbled. "Trying to get me into hack with the skipper..."

James grinned, but then he winced as something shifted painfully in his back. He was grateful when Williams finally gave the word to lower his side onto the test bed. He massaged his back while the Chief hooked the unit up to the diagnostic computers ranged along the wall. James leaned from side to side and winced. It felt as if he had popped something in his back.

"Not enough exercise, that's your trouble," Williams said as he tested one circuit after another. "I do hope you ain't expecting me to program this translator of yours. If you are, you can forget it. What you're talking about needs something a lot more sophisticated than I can do."

James shook his head. "That's not a problem. Bindar, that's Professor Singh, has a program that runs on *Canada's* computer just fine. What we need is something that can hear voices and speak back in the right language."

"That's okay then. If his program runs all right now, it will run okay on what I have in mind."

James watched Williams run a diagnostic and wondered what he had started. "What *have* you in mind, if you don't mind me asking that is?"

"Don't learn if you don't ask questions." Williams straightened and waved a hand at the unit. "This crap is too damn bulky... heavy too." He eyed James as he stretched his back. "The new one... remember I told you about the new one that costs ten times as much?"

"Yeah, I mean yes of course."

"Well that one is tiny compared to this one. It's still too big for what you want, but it's small enough to make mobile. I have an idea how we can link into that compad idea of yours."

James realised he was staring. "You want to take out the new one and put that piece of... *you want to put that junk back in?*" he cried incredulously.

"Yup!"

Oh God, Colgan wasn't going to like this! He had to explain the situation before Williams said something and brought the wrath of God... well the wrath of the Captain down on him.

* * *

13~Predator and prey

"Easy, *eeeeasy*," Captain Colgan said as his ship navigated the clutter of the asteroid belt. He realised he was on the edge of his seat ready to pounce on the helm controls, and forced himself to sit back. Janice, *Canada's* helmsman, took no notice of his hovering presence at her back. "Steady as she goes, helm."

"Steady as she goes, aye," Janice verified automatically. She remained hunched over her controls and didn't look up.

Colgan glanced around his horseshoe shaped bridge. In front of him, on Janice's left, Anya Ivanova sat at tactical and monitored the feed piped to her station from Scan. Her job was to keep a wary eye on the Shan heavies, and update her targeting solutions. Colgan was determined they would never be used. The Shan heavies were waiting for *Chakra* to flush him out, but that wouldn't happen. He would never let himself be forced into the open.

Along his left side were two empty observer stations, while to his right, Commander Groves sat at Scan studying the data *Canada's* sensors provided her. She was tracking *Chakra*, and looking for a suitable hiding place. The plot table's colourful display hid her face behind shadowy patterns, and painted her uniform with scrolling alphanumeric lists of data. Colgan could almost read the current situation just by glancing at her uniform.

Behind Colgan's right shoulder, next to the unused holotank, was the comm shack. Lieutenant Ricks was monitoring Shan comm chatter. Opposite him on the other side of the bridge was engineering. Ensign Steve Carstens, their youngest crew member at nineteen, was manning the station. He had a direct link to central damage control. He monitored *Canada's* systems and despatched maintenance teams if required. A thankless task, but necessary. Computers were by no means infallible.

Colgan surveyed the faces of his crew one last time. Everyone was busy at their stations trying not to look at the tactical overlay currently displayed on the main viewer. It showed *Canada* trying to put distance between herself and the Shan ship they believed was named *Chakra*. They were sneaking away using the clutter of the belt to hide their movements. Although most of its stations were manned, the bridge was unnaturally quiet.

Lieutenant Ricks finished receiving a report and turned to relay it. "Stealth mode is still inactive, Skipper."

"*Chakra* is closing," Groves said a moment later.

Colgan nodded. The asteroid belt was like a maze, a perfect place to lose *Chakra*, but the Shan captain would not give up. *Chakra* would lose them one day and reacquire them the next. *Chakra's* skipper was learning his moves, but there wasn't a hell of a lot he could do about it. Not with three heavies lurking just beyond the belt.

Their game of cat and mouse had become serious. *Invincible* had jumped outsystem over three months ago, three months of silence spent hiding from the Shan hunters, but now *Canada* was in serious trouble. A minor collision yesterday with a piece of rock disturbed by the game they were playing, had since blossomed into a full scale disaster. The hit had been amidships, and had seemed of little consequence at first, but when the damage report came in, it revealed a more serious problem than scratched nanocoat.

The rock had damaged *Canada's* emitters, without which she was visible to *Chakra's* sensors. When active, stealth mode made *Canada* electronically invisible. She could still be seen with the naked eye of course, but one tiny ship in the vastness of space was almost impossible to spot. A ship hemmed inside an asteroid field without stealth, had few options but to hide behind a lump of rock and hope no one was watching from that side.

"Get me an update on repairs, Mark," Colgan said.

"Aye, sir." Ricks turned back to his station and contacted damage control.

"There's one," Commander Groves said looking up from the navigational plot her station was displaying. "Transferring to main viewer, sir."

The image on the forward viewscreen changed to display a section of the inner asteroid belt. *Canada's* friendly blue icon blinked on and off with her heading and velocity appended to it. *Chakra's* baleful red icon was closing on their previous position, like a hound on the scent of a fox. Groves circled an asteroid on the plot table, and the main viewer updated itself.

Colgan pointed his control wand at the circled asteroid, and copied it onto his number two monitor. Data denoting the asteroid's size and composition began scrolling down the right side of the screen. The computer analysed the data and highlighted the important points in red. The asteroid was big enough to conceal two ships the size of *Canada* with room to spare, but more to the point, it was of the right composition.

He highlighted the asteroid on the viewer with his control wand, and it began flashing. "Put us in the shadow of that one, Janice."

"Aye, sir. Manoeuvring... two percent only."

Two percent was nothing, but more thrust would disturb the smaller particles of the belt. With *Chakra* stalking them,

Colgan had ordered that two percent was to be used until further orders. So far it had worked.

"I have that update, Skipper," Lieutenant Ricks said.

"Let's have it."

"Five hours... minimum."

Hisses of shock went around the bridge. Groves looked at Colgan sharply. She would have made some comment, but his quick headshake silenced her. Everyone had assumed the damage to be minor and easily fixed, but now they knew that wasn't so. They were beginning to feel like the prey *Chakra* so obviously thought they were. They didn't need to hear their XO agreeing with them.

"Tell them that's unacceptable." Colgan's stomach began to seethe. "I want every swinging dick in damage control up to their elbows in circuitry right now."

"They already are, sir."

At the press of a button, his station turned to face the comm shack and Lieutenant Ricks. "Explain."

"The Chief says the rock we hit punched a hole right through the secondary control runs, Skipper. The entire thing fused solid when the overload hit the chips. They're having to make new emitters from scratch, not repair the old ones."

Colgan frowned. "I see." He should have known that already, but with *Chakra* bearing down on him, he hadn't taken the trouble to ask. He glanced at Francis and beckoned her over. She would have to sort this mess out. "Get down there and see what can be done to expedite repairs, XO. If we don't get those emitters back soon, I'm going to run out of hiding places."

"On my way." Groves entered the lift at the rear of the bridge.

Colgan turned his station to face the main viewer. "Display tactical overlay," he ordered. His eyes narrowed as the schematic appeared. "Remove all ships more than twenty minutes flight time from us."

He watched all ship codes disappear except *Canada*,

Chakra, and the three heavies that they had no name for. They were skulking about just waiting to pounce on anyone foolish enough to stick his nose outside of the belt.

"Centre overlay on *Canada's* current position and display previous hiding places."

The display was cluttered with the known positions of thousands of asteroids, but a dozen icons were blinking—his hideouts, each discovered and abandoned when *Chakra* bore in. They were widely scattered, but now that he looked at them all at once, he could see a pattern forming. That wasn't good. If he could see it, he knew damn well the Shan could.

It took a certain composition of metal asteroids to hide *Canada* effectively. Iron core, with enough nickel and molybdenum to camouflage her sensors and beam weapons. For the millionth time Colgan wished *Canada* was a light or heavy cruiser, almost any proper warship would do. *Canada's* beam weapons were mounted externally to save space for her labs. Her missile tubes obviously had to be internal for access to the magazines, but a warship had *all* of its weapons mounted internally. Only the muzzle of beam weapons truly needed to be exposed, and of course warships had sealable gun ports.

Not so *Canada*.

She had been converted from an *Exeter* class light cruiser into the survey vessel she was now. Most of her weaponry had been gutted to make room for her labs, her remote sampler storage bays, and her drone storage bays, which were oversized. Carrying extra drones gave *Canada* a greater range. Survey missions tended to be long ones. Sending back regular reports was part of that. Beam weapon and sensor grid construction both relied on alloys with heavy concentrations of certain metals, which would give the Shan a good way to find *Canada* if they knew what to look for.

Chakra knew what to look for, Colgan was sure of it.

All of his asteroid hideouts were of similar size and composition. It didn't take a genius to realise that all the Shan had to do was survey the belt for the correct type. When they did, they would have every possible hiding place he could use. Knowing his time was running out gave him a sharp twinge in his stomach. His damn ulcer was acting up again.

"Someone send for a glass of milk," he said grimacing at the pain in his gut.

"It's on the way, sir," Ricks said sounding concerned.

"Asteroid approaching, sir. Two thousand metres... passing fifteen hundred, sir. Twelve hundred... one thousand metres, sir."

"Knock it off, Janice. Just park us will you?" Colgan said holding his guts. Where was the damn milk?

"Aye, sir. Sorry."

He relented a little, no sense displaying his worry to his crew. It was important they believe he knew what to do even when he didn't.

"Sorry, Janice, but my guts are acting up."

"That's all right, Skip." Janice eased her charge closer and closer to the mountainous looking asteroid. "All stop. Grapples deploying... good catch, sir."

"Well done."

They had done this a good many times now, but grappling an asteroid wasn't easy. More than once they had grabbed one only to have the damn grapples wriggle loose. Asteroids might look solid, but they weren't always reliable. They sometimes shattered or separated when stressed. This time all went well. *Canada* pulled herself in close to the asteroid until it looked like a gigantic cliff on the bridge displays.

"One metre separation, Skip."

"Can't you get us in tighter than that?" Colgan said with a small smile.

Janice spun to look at him in outrage, and everyone laughed. She realised he was joking and smiled sheepishly. She turned back to her consol and went through her usual routine of shutting down all nonessential systems.

"Your milk, sir," crewman first class Riley said.

Colgan started. He hadn't heard Baz approach. He took the offered glass and drank the milk straight down. He felt the effect almost instantly. Excess acid, that's all it was. He had never had trouble with stress before this mission, but the constant threat of being destroyed, or worse, initiating hostilities with the Shan, was taking its toll on everyone. Doctor Ambrai wanted to adjust his IMS (Integrated Medical System), but the procedure would mean being laid up in bed for days. He didn't have time for that. Ambrai would have to wait until after the mission to reprogramme his bots. The milk would have to do.

"Thanks, Baz."

"You're welcome, sir." Riley took the empty glass and left the bridge as silently as he had entered.

Colgan turned his attention to the tactical overlay on the main viewer. He punched in a command on his control wand, and transferred the data to his station's number one monitor. The small repeater display gave him the ability to manipulate the raw tactical data without inconveniencing other stations on the bridge. In the heat of battle, his access to such data saved time and could save lives.

"Display *Chakra's* current position and heading," he ordered.

The main viewer cleared to show *Chakra* approaching, but it was obvious by her heading that the Shan had lost them once again. How many more times could he get away with this?

"Give me an all hands channel, Mark."

"Aye, Skipper. Channel open."

"Ah hmmm, this is the Captain," Colgan said. He always felt a little silly announcing the obvious. He cleared his throat and continued. "*Chakra* is still hunting us, but we're safe for the moment. I will keep you informed of developments. Keep to routine and stay out of the way of the damage control teams. That is all." He turned back to Ricks. "Call the boffins together in the briefing room and have Commander Groves back up here to take my chair."

"Aye, sir."

Colgan stood and stretched the kinks out of his back. He winced as vertebrae popped loud enough for him to hear. He had been sitting too long. He stepped around his station and went for the lift.

"If anything else breaks, call me," Colgan said before stepping inside. Everyone laughed, but as soon as the lift doors closed, his shoulders slumped and the false cheer dissolved from his features. "Deck two," he said and the lift jolted into motion.

What the hell was he going to do?

He was out of contact with the Alliance... who knew what the Admiralty would do when they learned the Shan had shot up *Invincible*? He could safely assume the Alliance wouldn't start a war over a single shooting incident, and that was good, but the only way out for his ship and those aboard her, was to make contact with the Shan and hope friendly relations resulted. He had to rely solely on the civs for that. Assuming the boffins had learned enough to do it, he would be going ahead with phase two of the President's plan without orders or even his sanction.

So be it.

The lift stopped and Colgan stepped out. The deck was deserted. His crew would be at their battle stations for a short while yet. They had learned through hard experience not to stand down immediately after an apparently successful evasion. *Chakra's* captain was a hellishly lucky bastard, and he could be unpredictable. The Shan skipper had nearly trapped *Canada* twice in recent days by using his shuttles as observers. By positioning them high above the asteroid belt's ecliptic, *Chakra* had used them like remote sensors. It was by the narrowest of margins and good luck, Groves had noticed and countered them in time. He wouldn't underestimate *Chakra's* skipper again. His crew would stay at battle stations until they were absolutely sure their evasion was successful.

Colgan entered the brightly lit briefing room to find twelve white uniformed men and women sitting around the cluttered table looking anxiously at him. The clutter represented months of painstaking work on their part. Printouts and compads lay on the table in such profusion, the high gloss finish of the simwood was completely hidden. All the wall screens were on—a dozen screens each displaying different aspects of the contact teams' studies. There were pictures of Shan going about their lives, pictures of their peculiar (to his eyes) cities. There were lists, and graphs, and god knows what else displayed wherever he looked.

In the centre of the table, the holotank was displaying one of the natives turning slowly within the holomatrix. The adult Shan stood on his or her hind legs—Shan sexes were hard to differentiate. To Human eyes, both looked almost identical. The females had underdeveloped mammary organs, hard to spot covered as they were by fur, while male genitalia was protected and hidden by what he could only describe as a pouch similar to that of a marsupial.

Colgan turned his attention back to those he had come to see. They had long since become familiar to him. In a way, they were part of his crew now. An unofficial, but vital part.

"I'm sure you know why I'm here," he began after he found a spare seat and made himself comfortable. "Since *Invincible* jumped outsystem, we've been on borrowed time, and it has just about run out. I have no option but to contact the Shan."

The twelve intent faces broke from concerned stillness into eager anticipation. Their excited murmurs filled the room. This was what they had worked for all these months—worked hard for.

"...contact the elders do you think?"

"...see how we can."

"Their language is full of..."

"...and what does harmony mean to them?"

James was the only one to pick up on what Colgan hadn't

said. "I have a question for the Captain."

Colgan nodded. "Ask."

"When did the drone arrive? We've been hiding or running since *Invincible* jumped outsystem. I don't remember you securing from battle stations long enough to pick one up, Captain."

"I'm sure you already know the answer, Professor. There was no drone. Our mission is unchanged."

Janice frowned. "Your career—"

"My *career* is my concern, Professor Bristow. I am one man. *Canada* holds the lives of two hundred and twelve within her. She, and all of you, are my responsibility. Don't think I haven't considered taking a chance and trying to jump out, because I have. There are three heavies skulking about out there. Three of them. We are no match for even one."

"Something else is bothering you... what?" Brenda asked him.

How she had guessed Colgan didn't know. "What do you think the Council will do when they hear about *Invincible's* battle damage?"

Concerned whispers erupted.

"Quiet down people," Janice called loudly. "What do *you* think they'll do, Captain?"

"Panic I shouldn't wonder."

"They wouldn't order an attack would they?" Brenda asked.

The silence was absolute.

"No," he said firmly. "We defend the Alliance, we do not make war on those not threatening us."

Brenda didn't look convinced. "But?"

"But, the Shan did fire on *Invincible* even though she was running and not threatening them. Some of our people are dead, Professor Lane. Our forces will be on high alert, but not, I think, charging here to the rescue. We are on our own. If I'm right, the Council will quarantine this system. The aliens have no jump technology, so that's all they need to do. None of that helps us or our situation. For all I know, our mission here has already been scrubbed."

Brenda clenched a fist and hammered the table in frustration. "The Shan only did what we would have done in their place. For God's sake, haven't we learned *anything* from past mistakes?"

Colgan frowned. "We learned plenty. We learned the galaxy is a dangerous place. We learned to be cautious while exploring, and vigilant in the defence of our sector. Finally, we learned to blow away the Merki wherever we find them."

Brenda reddened. "You all know my thoughts on the Merkiaari," she said breaking eye contact with Colgan and looking around at her colleagues for support. "The war needn't have happened if a team like this one had been sent to talk to the Merkiaari."

"You're wrong, Brenda," James said. "The Alliance was attacked without provocation on the border of our sector. We lost a dozen worlds before the alarm was even taken seriously. When it was finally understood what was happening, delegations *were* sent to talk to the Merki. None lived longer than five minutes."

Brenda glared. "That's because they sent military ships."

David Harrison, a professor of both sociology and biology raised his hand to attract Colgan's attention. "She's right, you know. The Merkiaari did fire first, but wouldn't we do the same in that situation? I know I would."

Colgan shook his head. "No. We would have hailed them first." At the sceptical looks he received, he explained. "It's standard procedure. When an unidentified ship jumps insystem, it's queried for its identity and intentions. Even an Alliance carrier with IFF screaming its identity, would be challenged before routing it to docking or wherever else it's heading. The Merki would have been challenged the moment they entered the system by port control if no one else."

"We'll never know now," Brenda said still looking sour.

"On the contrary." Colgan knew what was going through

her mind. She thought he was spouting the same militaristic garbage that she so vehemently denied was the truth. He was in a way, but it wasn't garbage. "A review of the ship's data recorders and logs recorded during that period is part of our officer training at the academy. I assure you the Merki were challenged repeatedly."

Brenda looked rebellious but a gentle squeeze of her hand by James calmed her.

"We're drifting a little far afeild here, Captain," James said. "You want us to contact the Shan in hope of opening full diplomatic relations at some future time?"

"In essence yes. I admit I'd be satisfied for now if you could just tell them not to shoot."

Colgan sat back to listen as the professors debated what they knew about the Shan. He idly picked up a nearby compad and glanced at it, but it was not very interesting. It was just a check list. He gathered up a few more and began building a tower while listening to the conversation between David and Brenda.

"He should be male," Dave said when asked about the speaker for the elders.

"Should be, or is?" Brenda asked.

"Well… Lieutenant Ricks tried to enhance the imagery for me, but I was still unable to see clearly. From what I've managed to glean from snippets snatched here and there, *Chakra* is commanded by a male."

"Where does that take us, David?" Janice asked.

"I'm assuming the Shan are male dominated like most Human societies were in the past. I know it's different today, but from what I've been able to determine the Shan still look at things that way."

"I don't agree," James said.

Colgan raised an eyebrow. James was not usually one to put himself forward at these things. Being the odd one out, he had little to contribute to the group that others weren't better qualified to offer. Most of the time he assisted the others on their projects. Everyone liked him, and all were glad he was there to assist, but they also realised his field was a little redundant in this situation.

"Why not?" Janice asked with encouragement in her voice.

James leaned his forearms on the table and interlocked his fingers. "It's this harmony thing."

Someone groaned and muttered that the harmony issue was a dead end.

"It's not," James said stoically.

"Prove it," Sheryl said with a smile.

James sighed. "You know I can't, but think it through. How can there be harmony if there's discrimination between the sexes?"

"There can't of course," Sheryl said. "But that's what I'm saying. Where is there harmony on the twin worlds of the Shan? Nowhere, that's where."

"You're missing the point, Sheryl. Their language is replete with sayings such as, and I quote: *Look ahead in harmony*, and what about this: *May you live forever in harmony*. Those are direct translations."

"If we have the translations right," Sheryl reminded him.

Before Professor Singh could protest that his work on the translation could do the job, Janice did it for him. "Those tapes are accurate. I would stake my reputation on it."

Colgan knocked on the table to draw everyone's attention. "You're staking a lot more than that, Professor. All of our lives depend on them."

That silenced everyone.

"I stand by them," Janice said.

"Those sayings are *old*," James said, taking back control of the conversation. "I hesitate to say they have a religious significance, but they certainly have a cultural one."

Bindar stood and crossed the room to the autochef. He selected coffee and took it back to his seat. "Religion can be a powerful factor in the development of a society. Look at the multitude of religions on Earth. Wars were fought over it; bombs were planted because of it. A powerful force it is, but I see no sign of a religion among the Shan. Their world is completely devoid of the things we associate with worship of a deity. What does that say about their culture?"

"That's my area I think," Bernard said. His area was cultural studies specialising in the Merkiaari, but as the Shan were only the second alien species to be discovered, he was the closest thing the Alliance had to an expert. "I do happen to agree with James on this. The Shan are remarkably open with each other, and lucky for us their communications security doesn't exist."

"They don't think in that way," Colgan interjected. "As far as they know, FTL is impossible and the only people in the system are Shan." He shrugged. "Up to a point, we were the same before the Merki War. We didn't concern ourselves too much with signal leakage, and where security was necessary, we just encoded the data stream. The Shan know nothing of the Merkiaari so…" He shrugged again.

"But they *do* know about *us*," James stressed. "They're going to start adding two and two, Captain. The FTL thing is already in the open. They saw *Invincible* jump outsystem. If I was an elder, I would be worried about talking in the open. If we don't contact them soon, the Shan will be the ones contacting us in a few years."

"We were in space for centuries before we cracked the problem. If they start now they will still take that long."

"You're wrong there, Captain." Sheryl said. "We didn't even know FTL was possible when we stumbled onto the answer. The Shan have *seen* it in operation. It won't take them anywhere near as long to figure it out."

Colgan frowned. Sheryl Linden was greatly respected in her fields of physics and engineering design. She was worth listening to. If she thought there was a risk of the Shan developing a workable fold space drive, then he believed her.

"Can we get back to the present issue?" Bernard asked

impatiently. "I thought you were desperate to have us perform a miracle for you."

Colgan smiled. "Quite right, Professor Franks. I do need a miracle. I need *Chakra* off my back. More, I need the Shan friendly and willing to allow me to fire off a drone to Alliance HQ."

"Well then," Professor Singh said. His area of expertise was linguistics, but unlike Janice Bristow whose interest in the area was secondary to her studies in exobiology, linguistics was his passion. "We have an extensive library of Shan verbal communication. Ship to ship traffic has helped us no end with the translation. The various broadcasts from the high orbitals, mining outposts, and planets have helped fill in a great many holes in our understanding. The—"

"Excuse the interruption, Professor," Colgan said. "Are you saying the tapes are not ready, or that they are?"

"I'm coming to that, Captain. I've been unable to eradicate all errors, but that's to be expected without a native speaker to converse with. Most Shan words are pronounceable after a fashion by Humans. Janice and I believe that in time we could learn to speak without artificial aid."

Janice nodded and gestured at the holotank. "Their physiology dictates the shaping of their language. As you can see, their mouths are completely different, more like a feline's muzzle than anything else I can think of. Certain sounds will probably sound odd to them, but we think they will understand the attempt."

"Yes," Bindar went on. "But for now, we will supplement the spoken word with the tapes you're so interested in, Captain. They *are* ready for testing. Though gaps remain, we believe they will suffice."

"Gaps," Colgan said without expression. "How big are these gaps?"

"We have perhaps seventy percent of the Shan vocabulary, or rather we believe so." Bindar was obviously uncomfortable with the uncertainty, but under such hardships as constantly racing to emergency stations whenever *Chakra* closed on them, it was remarkably good luck they had managed to reach seventy percent and not a figure much lower. "On the plus side, we have an extensive library of common phrases that will be very helpful."

"Take me to your leader, things like that?" Colgan said with a grin, and the others laughed.

Bindar sighed. "Not that one, Captain, but how about this: *we come in peace, don't shoot.*"

His laughter died. "I like that one very much. Can you teach it to me?"

"I'll dupe the chip for you, Captain. We should all start carrying the translators chief Williams tinkered together for us."

"Well done, Bindar," James said.

"Outstanding dedication. Can't wait to try it out my friend," Bernard said enthusiastically to the embarrassed professor, and the others chimed in with similar things.

Bindar blushed at all the attention. "Thank you, thank you all. Janice was extremely helpful."

Janice snorted. "I hardly knew where to start."

Colgan broke into the congratulations. "So, we have the means to converse with them. Now we need the opportunity."

James glanced at Brenda and then back to Colgan. "I've been thinking about that, Captain. It seems to me that *Chakra* is the only source of Shan we have available."

"That's obvious."

James nodded and glanced at Brenda again. She frowned obviously wondering what he was going to say. "I suggest we send one man in a lander well away from the ship and allow it to be captured—I volunteer."

"No," Brenda gasped looking at her lover in horror.

* * *

James took his time with his inspection of the lander. A week had passed since he volunteered for this mission; a week of intensive training and strained silences between him and Brenda. Both had taken their toll on him, but despite it all, the excitement of meeting a Shan face to face had not left him.

Despite their disagreement, Brenda had done her part. All week she had worked beside him, tirelessly helping him learn what he needed to know to make the mission a success. But at the end of each day, when they retired to their cabin, Brenda would eat in silence and then go to bed—without him. She had made it plain he wasn't welcome in her bed, not even to sleep.

James stopped and peered around the empty bay. He didn't want to leave without trying to straighten things out between them. He had hoped Brenda would come to see him off, but she hadn't yet, and he couldn't delay much longer.

After their last meeting with Colgan, Brenda was angry. It wasn't that she didn't understand why he had volunteered for the mission. She did... or so she said. What made her mad, she said, was that he hadn't discussed it with her before hand. He tried to explain that until that moment, he hadn't known he was going to volunteer, but she wouldn't hear excuses, and she was right. Although he hadn't known Colgan would pre-empt the President by going ahead with phase two without orders, James had long ago considered ways in which it could be done. His work with Williams on the translators was a big part of that. He tried to tell himself that he hadn't lied to Brenda, but deep in his heart he knew the truth. He had been working toward this mission almost since the day he offered his help to Bindar.

James climbed up the ramp to the shuttle, but stopped in the open hatch to look out at the empty bay. Brenda wasn't coming; he knew that now. With a sigh and a heavy heart, he sealed the hatch and made his way toward the cockpit. He was a damn fool. Brenda was everything he had ever wanted in a woman. She was funny, and passionate, and clever, and oh so beautiful. He loved her more than anything, so why had he let this wall develop between them? Their last argument had been the worst.

Brenda had tried to make Colgan let her accompany him, but the captain said letting a civ carry the mission was bad enough, he wasn't about to make the situation worse by adding another. The ensuing argument had nearly caused Colgan to send Commander Groves on the mission instead, but even he knew there was a greater chance of success if someone familiar with Bindar's work was there to operate the translators. Brenda knew that as well as anyone. The sneaky woman had studied up while helping James prepare for the mission. She knew as much if not more than he did now, and she had tried to use that to persuade Colgan to let her go with him. It hadn't worked.

James took his place in the pilot's chair and activated the lander's systems. "Alpha One ready for takeoff," he announced over the comm.

The viewscreen lit and Lieutenant Ricks appeared. "Alpha One, stand by for final instructions."

"Okay… I mean, copy that, Canada. Standing by."

Ricks grinned.

A moment later, Captain Colgan came on. "I'm depressurising the bay now." He turned to nod at someone out of view and then turned back. "Be careful out there, James. I don't want to lose you."

"I don't want to lose me either," James said with a grin. He sobered a moment later. "You'll look after Brenda if something should happen. It won't of course, but if it should?"

"She'll be fine, I'll see to it."

"Thank you, sir."

Colgan nodded and the screen darkened.

James took a deep breath and released the docking clamps. The lander was a dream to fly in simulation. Nice acceleration and good handling. The real thing was different enough to make him bite his lip as he eased it over the deck toward the hanger doors. As he approached, they cranked open to reveal the blackness of space populated by chunks of rock moving slowly by. As expected, *Canada* was already underway. He firmed his grip on the yoke.

"Here goes nothing." He throttled up the lander's main engine and shot out of the bay like a missile.

As soon as he was well clear of *Canada*, he eased back on the throttle and turned his ship toward the asteroid she had been using to hide from *Chakra*. He couldn't see the alien ship yet, but he didn't waste time. As soon as he was close enough, he used his manoeuvring thrusters to align the lander with the asteroid, before programming the computer to maintain the shuttle's position. The Shan should detect him easily.

With nothing to do until the Shan arrived, he decided to make himself a snack. He had missed dinner earlier. Brenda hadn't felt like eating after their meeting with Colgan, and neither had he. They had both been too upset. Brenda had locked the bedroom door against him, and hadn't even said good bye when he left for the boat bay.

He unbuckled his harness and floated across the cockpit toward the hatch. Landers like this one were too small to have gravity generators, but they did come equipped with a galley. As he approached the hatch to the main cabin, he glanced at the cases strapped to the deck behind the co-pilot's seat. They contained the gifts he and the others had put together for the Shan. One of them was filled with compad translators, while others were full of picture books and other things designed to teach Shan about the Alliance. The largest contained Williams' master unit, or what he called The Box of Crap. James grinned. Only he knew why Williams called it that.

He opened the cockpit hatch.

Brenda floated a short distance ahead of him. "It's only me," she said brightly.

James gaped. "I don't believe it. How the hell did you get here?"

Brenda grinned. "Magic."

"But I looked…"

"I was in the locker," she said hooking a thumb over her shoulder at her hiding place.

"You're going *back!*"

He turned and pulled himself into the cockpit.

"No I'm not." Brenda kicked against one of the seats and launched herself in pursuit. "*Canada* must be out of range by now."

"Brenda *please*. I need you to be safe."

Brenda pulled herself into the co-pilot's seat. "And I need to be here. If you want to be a hero, that's fine, but I'm staying."

James gritted his teeth. "We've been through this. We agreed it makes sense for me to go."

"Oh no you don't. You agreed, I never did and you know it."

"But you *said*—"

Brenda finished strapping in. "I said I understood the point you and the captain were making, not that I agreed with it. You *are* the odd one out, you *can* be spared, and you *do* want to do it. All that's true, but I love you and I'm not letting you out of my sight."

"I'll get the, Captain." He strapped himself in and searched the controls for the one he needed. He was so flustered he couldn't find it. "He'll make you see sense."

"It's that one," Brenda said pointing to a single control among dozens of similar buttons and switches.

"I remember my training, thank you."

"Well *do* it then."

"All *right*, I'm *doing* it!" James glared, and Brenda smirked. "Alpha One to *Canada*; respond please."

"*Canada* copies."

"I have a problem here—a stowaway."

Lieutenant Ricks' jaw dropped. "A what?"

"What is it, Mark?" Colgan said out of view of the

pickup.

Ricks turned away from the monitor. "Professor Wilder says he has a stowaway, Skipper."

"For the love of God, who would be stupid enough to... where's Professor Lane?"

"I don't know, Skipper."

"She's here," James said.

Brenda grinned and waved at the monitor.

Colgan was snarling something. "...have his damn hide. I told him to watch her dammit. All stop! Prepare to reverse course..."

"Contact," a voice sang out. "Bearing one-eight-zero. It's *Chakra*, Captain. She's coming fast."

"Sound battle stations," Colgan barked and the wailing alarm sounded. "Put Wilder on screen."

A moment later, the captain glared out of the monitor at Brenda. His face was red with rage, and she swallowed nervously. She opened her mouth to explain, but he began first.

"*Chakra* will have you in..." Colgan looked aside then back. "Three minutes if she doesn't blow you out of space first. I can't stay, and we'll lose TBC lock any second. For Chrissakes don't mess it up or I'll—"

The screen turned to fuzz.

SIGNAL LOST.

James flicked a switch and the screen darkened. He turned slowly toward Brenda with his jaw clenched and stared at her in silence.

Brenda shifted in her seat. "I'm glad we're together. *Glad* do you hear?"

"I hear you. I love you more than life, Brenda. I wish you had stayed aboard *Canada*. It's not safe here."

"We live together, or we die together..." she giggled. "I sound like a character in Zelda and the Spaceways."

"Let's hope we're still around for the next episode," James said peering out of the cockpit window looking for their guests.

* * *

14~The Chase

"He's running," Tarjei shouted in her excitement.

Tei'Varyk flicked his ears in agreement, but why run every time, why not fight? Every time *Chakra* found him, the alien tucked his tail and ran. And what about the other one? Firing into his ship should have made him mad enough to fire back, but he hadn't. Why? He chewed his whiskers in agitation. Why, why, why? He hissed and spat as if tasting something he didn't like. Unanswerable questions always left a bad taste. He *hated* that!

"Search for the asteroids as we discussed," Tei'Varyk said. "When you find the closest one of the right size, we will get there ahead of him and be waiting. He will not escape us this time."

"I hear," Tarjei said. "Lairs to your screen."

He studied his displays. "Remove any he has used before, Tarjei. I don't think he will chance using them again."

"I hear and comply."

Tei'Varyk noted the first ten or so had disappeared, but already there were numerous asteroids on his display and more appearing as he watched.

"Remove target asteroids that would require him to backtrack in order to reach them."

"I hear," Tarjei said and did as he asked.

"Good, very good." There was an asteroid almost exactly on the alien's current heading. "I believe I have him. Jakinda, new course—"

"New contact!" Tarjei said as the bridge alarms signalled an unknown target ahead.

"Silence that!"

"I hear," Jozka said and the alarm fell silent.

"Is it another light fang or a heavy?" Tei'Varyk asked intently. The aliens might be lying in wait for him.

"Neither, Tei. The target is at station keeping, and in the open a short distance from the alien's previous hiding place. The asteroid was occluding *Chakra's* eyes, but he sees him clearly now. It's small, no weapons of any kind." Tarjei looked up from her controls in confusion. "It seems to be a cub lander."

"That doesn't make sense…" A cub was useless in space. It was only carried aboard to ferry crew to and from a planet or mining base. "What's it doing now?"

"Nothing, Tei. It's waiting for us to kill it."

"Let us do that then," Kajika said eager to kill something after so long on the hunt with little to show for it.

"I hear, Tarjei," Tei'Varyk said ignoring Kajika's lapse in discipline.

He understood Kajika's feelings, but he didn't want to be hasty. He might learn the secret of the alien FTL they had witnessed. Although it seemed unlikely a cub would have the ability, there might be something interesting. He had to choose soon or he would over fly it. He hesitated a moment longer then turned to Jakinda.

"Bring us alongside the cub."

Hisses of displeasure surrounded him and Tarjei looked at him in worry. He flicked his ears at her keeping his face bland and she grinned.

"I will take this gift they have left me, and I will learn what they're about. I know where the alien fang will hide, do not worry. Look ahead in harmony and obey."

"I hear. Commencing deceleration," Jakinda said.

* * *

Aboard ASN Canada, Shan System

Colgan sighed as *Chakra* decelerated. "It worked."

"So far," Groves qualified. "You should have let me go, sir."

"I didn't know you spoke Shan, Francis," he said in mock surprise. "You should have said. It would have saved a lot of *work!*"

"We have the translators and—"

"XO, I'm no happier than you are, believe me, but Wilder *can* speak Shan enough to get by, and the translators are untested in the field. Besides, Professor Singh estimates gaps of at least thirty percent in the tapes."

They weren't really tapes of course. The so called tape was actually a complex bit of programming that no one but Bindar Singh understood. The program itself resided on a chip in the translator's master unit, and used an algorithm of Singh's own devising to access a huge database of Shan and Human words. The result was a master unit connected by a modulated carrier wave to compads that could, theoretically, allow a Human to converse with a Shan. There were so many things that could go wrong with the system, that Colgan felt almost physically ill thinking about it.

"I understand the reasoning," Groves said. "But civs are like sheep. They need a sheep dog to protect them."

Sheep dog? He grinned. "I'm the sheep dog?"

Groves laughed. "Well, I've heard rumours you're as hairy as one." Everyone chuckled at the by-play, and tension eased throughout the bridge. Groves and Colgan exchanged knowing smiles and then settled back to business. "Orders, sir?"

"Steady as she goes, XO. We hide and wait for Wilder to get in touch. He knows how."

"Aye, sir," Groves said and went back to her station at Scan.

Professor Lane had guts, he had to give her that, but she might well have ruined the operation. Wilder had been keen to go, but how keen could he be now that his lover was with him and in danger? He only hoped Wilder could overcome the handicap and still pull it off.

"*Chakra* is ninety metres from the lander, Skip," Groves said and then nodded. "*Chakra* is at full stop."

Colgan leaned back and crossed his legs. "Very good, very good indeed. Helm, continue on course."

"Aye, sir," Lieutenant Wesley replied.

* * *

Aboard Chakra, Shan System

"*Chakra*, at station keeping. Alien cub to his starboard," Jakinda said.

"Range to target one hundred heikke," Kajika added, but his earlier outburst did not re-materialise. He was only reporting on the condition of the target, as he should.

"I hear," Tei'Varyk said. "I will suit up and investigate this gift. Kajika, you will attend me. Have Tei'Unwin and Kon'stanji informed."

"I hear," Kajika said in excitement.

"I hear," Jozka said and spoke quietly into his pickup.

Tei'Varyk turned to Tarjei and then glanced meaningfully at Kajika. Kajika was so frustrated; it had to be relieved in some way. A little space walk seemed just the thing. Tarjei flicked her ears to show she understood, but she was far from happy about it.

"Tei'Unwin and Kon'stanji come," Jozka said.

Tei'Varyk stood and headed for the hatch. "Let us go now, the alien is far away and the cub awaits us."

* * *

Aboard Lander Alpha One

Brenda's knuckles whitened as she clutched the arm of the acceleration couch. "Oh, God, they're coming over."

James nodded but he was preoccupied. Brenda had seemed unafraid, but he heard the fear in her words. Some people used God as part of everyday speech without really looking at what that meant, but never Brenda unless severely stressed. Reducing *Him* to a mere word, an expletive quite often, seemed wrong to him, but even he did it on occasion. Where was reverence, where was simple respect in that? God wasn't something Brenda spoke of to him, though he knew she was a believer from her trips to *Canada's* chapel. When she unconsciously said it straight out like that, he knew she was scared.

"The outer door is open."

Brenda nodded but didn't take her attention from the monitors displaying the huge alien ship. "Have you checked the Box?"

"It's fine. I've triple checked it, but you could try your compad again if you want."

"Good idea." Brenda fumbled at the pocket on her right thigh. She snarled in frustration when the flap refused to cooperate with her. She was getting madder than hell with it when James intervened.

He reached out and captured her hand. "Shush, it's all right. We're together."

Brenda stopped fighting the flap to look into his eyes. "Forever?"

"Always."

Brenda leaned forward and they kissed for a long moment.

The insistent beeping from the instrument panel brought James up for air.

"They're here."

* * *

"At least they have courtesy, these aliens," Tei'Varyk said.

"I don't like it, Tei." Kajika ignited his thrusters for a short burst. "I will enter and hunt for danger." He drifted forward toward the open hatch.

"Be not so hasty. I am Tei, not you," Tei'Varyk said with his muzzle rumpling in annoyance. "When you are Tei, you may advise me, not before. We go in together."

In the end, Tei'Varyk managed to enter a token heikke before Kajika, but that was merely courtesy taking over at the last moment. Kajika could not, even after all he had said, ignore his ingrained habit of deferring to a superior. Once inside they looked around for a way to proceed. Kajika suggested cutting through the inner door with their weapons, but a blinking light next to the outer door solved the problem. Tei'Varyk pressed the red button and the outer door slid shut. With a pleased nod, he noted a breathable atmosphere slowly replacing the vacuum of space within the airlock.

"We can breathe the alien atmosphere at least. That is good to know."

"Why?" Kajika asked as the inner door began to slide open.

"It says we have something in common…" Tei'Varyk broke off when he was confronted by his first sight of a face so obviously not Shan.

This was the first time a Shan had met an alien since the Murderers of Harmony had annihilated almost ninety percent of them so long ago. Utter shock held Tei'Varyk immobile, but Kajika was a hunter first, last, and always. His reflexes were the best—he was the claw of *Chakra*. His paw came up smoothly with his beamer held ready, and his first claw twitched.

The weapon bucked, and the alien flew back.

"Noooo!" Tei'Varyk howled as the alien bounced limply from the seats and into the overhead.

"I killed it for you, Tei…" Kajika began.

Tei'Varyk shouldered Kajika aside and snatched his weapon away. "You have dishonoured me," he howled with hackles bristling with rage. "*Chakra is dishonoured!*"

"But it is alien."

"Can't you see? It is not of the Murderer's race, you brainless cub. It's too small, and where are its fangs and weapons?" Tei'Varyk growled and aimed the beamer between Kajika's eyes. "I should *kill* you for this."

"But I did it for you," Kajika whispered staring into the beam emitter without seeing it. "For you."

Tei'Varyk lowered the weapon sick at heart. He turned to find a second alien attending to the first. His hopes leapt. There was one left, perhaps something could be salvaged.

* * *

Tears scalded Brenda's eyes as she grappled with James' limp body. She pulled him down from the overhead, and finally strapped him into a seat. She was muttering all the while that he wasn't dead. In her heart, she knew he was gone, but still she went through the motions of her pretence.

"You're not dead, James," she said to his closed eyes. "I love you, and you can't be dead. Not so soon."

Brenda smashed open the medikit ignoring most of its contents as they floated through the air and clustered around the ventilation duct. She worked the nano injector repeatedly, pumping ten times the amount into him that would normally be required. It couldn't hurt him to have too many working on the job—she hoped. When she had done all she could, she finally did what she had been dreading. She laid her head upon his chest. Nothing... no wait, there was a slow beat.

"Oh God, thank you," she whispered and wiped her tears away.

The burn in James' uniform looked hideous, but Fleet knew the danger of fire in space better than anyone. The uniform had extinguished itself very quickly. She grabbed a pair of scissors that were floating by, and cut away the burnt material as carefully as she could. She winced as she pulled it free. Blood welled and floated on its way toward the ventilation duct. Blood flowing was good, she told herself; it meant James still lived. The weapon had cauterised the wound in his side, but her messing with it had broken it open. Still, as she watched, James' bots got on the case and the blood slowed. She cleaned the wound and snatched a medipad from those drifting around her head. They were self-sealing sterile bandages used on battlefield injuries to prevent infection. Brenda thought that a fine idea and applied it to his side. She frantically looked for something else to do, but there was nothing. His bots would save him, or... his bots *would* save him.

Brenda had been ignoring the aliens in the airlock, but now she looked at them, and felt nothing but loathing. She noted the smaller one had been relieved of his weapon and looked dejected. His ears were laid back, and his nostrils were wide as if facing into a strong wind. The taller of the two had also removed his helmet and was watching her.

Brenda ripped open her thigh pocket, and activated her compad. She would flay the hide off both of them for this.

* * *

The alien worked feverishly on its companion. Unbelievably, the thing... whatever it was, had survived a point blank shot from Kajika's beamer. Incredibly tough these aliens were. Just like their ships.

Tei'Varyk watched the second alien apply various things

to its companion, and noted the blood as it drifted by; it was red like a Shan. The creatures breathed the same air, though he caught a great many strange scents in it, and now another thing they had in common made itself known. Red blood. He breathed deeply and tried to distinguish the scents. Fear was prevalent, and with it came anger and pain. Both were from the second alien, and now that he was becoming used to it, he noted differences between the two. The wounded one was bigger and stronger looking. The other was slimmer and shaped differently in the front. The covering it was wearing hid many details, but he assumed it was female. The aliens didn't have fur on their faces, nor on their paws. Neither had decent fangs or claws, and their faces were horribly flat. They did have a kind of fur on their heads, but it was not what he would call a worthwhile amount. He tried not to think of them as sick, but the lack of fur made that hard. Shan shed for a number of reasons, fright was one, but the more common reason was illness. These... *things* were alien. Lack of fur was normal for them.

"Tei," Kajika warned as the female alien fumbled at a device of some kind.

Tei'Varyk began to raise the beamer, but remembering the last time, he lowered it ready to accept what would come. What he received was not what he had expected.

"You fatherless curs. You ### ### killed him," the device she held said in terrible Shan, but it was still undeniably Shan.

Kajika growled at the insult, but quieted at a rumple-muzzled glare from Tei'Varyk. Kajika had done more than enough this day. Tei'Varyk turned back in time to receive another flood from the alien, and noted she was speaking into something descending toward her mouth. The thing, an alien voice pickup he assumed, was anchored to what might be alien ears. Her ears, if that's what they were, were positioned oddly on the sides of her head, and not on top as was proper. They were immobile. How did the aliens express themselves?

"...came in ### and harmony, but ### do you ### do? You ### him! We ### to ### you to the ###!"

Tei'Varyk chewed his whiskers in frustration. There were too many missing words. It was obvious the aliens had been studying them, and now *Chakra* had forced them to act before they were ready. He heard the last word, not from the device she held, but from her own lips.

Merkiaari!

Tei'Varyk's ears plastered themselves to his skull. Shock heaped upon shock. How did this alien know of the Murderers? Was it possible that she had come from them?

"### ### ### to say ### yourselves?" The alien female looked from Kajika to Tei'Varyk and back impatiently. She scowled. "Well? ### the ### got your tongues?"

"Merkiaari?" Tei'Varyk said careful to enunciate the word clearly. "What do you know of the Murderers?"

The alien's face screwed up in an expression Tei'Varyk could not interpret. She said something that did not translate. She shook her head at the device she held, and tried again.

"### Merkiaari killed ### ### during ### war. ### of my people were killed, ### ### ### won in the end."

Killed *Humans*? Again there had been no translation, but Tei'Varyk assumed it was the name of their race she spoke. Humans had fought the Murderers and won but at terrible cost, the female said.

"Say again," Tei'Varyk said desperately trying to understand the gabble coming from the device the alien held.

"I ###, Humans ### ### in a ### war. We ### ### it the ### Merki War. ### worlds..." the creature screwed her face up, and raised a paw.

"What's it doing, Tei?" Kajika whispered.

"Teaching me to count," Tei'Varyk replied watching the creature pointing to her blunt claws and saying a word each time.

"But... yes, Tei," Kajika said miserably.

"...nine, ten. Understand?" the creature said. "Eight tens

worlds ### destroyed ### the Merki ### the ### Merki War. ### ### of my people died."

Eighty worlds, did he have that right? Eighty worlds had been invaded and seriously damaged with millions upon millions upon millions killed. *Eighty* worlds! The enormity of the Humans came crashing down upon Tei'Varyk like a herd of Shkai'lon. His people dared not make enemies of these aliens.

"It lies," Kajika said. "Eighty worlds is foolish. Why would they need so many?"

"I ### not lie," the alien spat angrily. "### you talked ### him ### ### shooting, he ### ### shown you."

"Ja…" Tei'Varyk coughed and tried to sound the alien name again, it made him feel as if he were about to chew his tongue. "*James*," he said slowly and noted the female's quick glance toward her companion. "He will live?"

"I ### so," she said and screwed her face up at the device she held. "Yes," she said and bobbed her head up and down.

Her action was what Tei'Varyk might have called a strange type of bowing before now, but he believed it was more likely to represent a Shan's flicking of ears to indicate agreement. The face screwing seemed to mean frustration, or perhaps irritation.

"My name is Tei'Varyk, and this is Kajika. We are sorry for your companion's hurt."

He ignored Kajika's protest at the naming. To name oneself in such a fashion was suggestive of a courtesy offered and received, but they had received none.

The alien listened to the device in her ear and nodded. "My name ### ### ###, and my mate's name ### ### ###. You ### ### of *Chakra*?"

The device couldn't handle the naming, but Tei'Varyk heard the alien's own voice naming herself and her mate. He was no longer surprised at what the aliens knew of him and the race. They had probably been watching him for a long time. The Human word for Tei was Captain… or so it seemed.

Tei'Varyk tried to bob his head instead of flicking his ears, and ended up doing both. "Yessss," he said using the Human word and mangling it only slightly. "I Captain."

The alien bobbed her head, and looked pleased if his judgment of her expression was correct. She checked her mate once more before beckoning him to follow her. She kicked against a seat to launch herself toward, he assumed, the cockpit of the lander. He watched as she floated out of sight through the hatch.

"Don't go, Tei," Kajika said. "It's all a trick. Eighty worlds, the Murderers attacking them. It's too convenient. They've come to confuse us, and make us weak before the Murderers come again."

"I am Tei. You will obey me. I will hear more and then decide what is to be done."

"I hear." Kajika bowed so quickly he nearly somersaulted in the lack of gravity.

Tei'Varyk rumpled his muzzle, and flattened his ears at such foolishness. Kajika was embarrassing him. He kept Kajika's weapon, but left his helmet next to James strapped into a spare seat, before pushing off to see what he could learn.

This cub, he absently wondered what the Humans called it, was designed to carry many Humans. So many seats were obviously meant for use. How many were aboard their ship? *Chakra* carried a hundred crew, but a heavy fang like *Neifon* carried almost *three* hundred. A mere cub with so much capacity probably meant the Humans used bigger crews than his people would think necessary.

Tei'Varyk followed the alien, no she was called *Brenda*. He followed her toward he knew not what.

* * *

15~Gifts

Brenda floated through the hatch and into the cockpit, when she would rather be looking after James. She knew his bots were working. The military used good ones, and unlike the less able civilian kind, they were designed for wounds like this, but she still worried. She tried to tell herself that sitting next to him and holding his hand would make no difference to his recovery, and that his bots were all that could save him now, but still she wished to be with him. Unfortunately, her duty to *Canada* called her to deal with James' abusers. She didn't much like that.

She turned and held herself in place by grasping the engineer's chair. The Tei, or was it just Tei? Whatever, he came in quickly followed by Kajika. She couldn't help her dislike of Kajika. He was the trigger-happy bastard who had shot James. Tei was looking at the controls and instruments with interest, but when she claimed his attention by the simple expedient of waving at him, he drifted closer and grabbed a panel to steady himself.

James and the others had planned this day well, but now that he was wounded, Brenda would have to follow through.

First, she had to sort out the compads. She opened a box of them and withdrew one, hesitated for a second, and pulled out a second for Kajika.

"For you," Brenda said into her mike, and the compads spoke in Shan. She grimaced as only the second word was translated and tried again. "A gift, yours to keep."

That was better, and Tei was pleased to accept them. He bowed to her. "I ### nothing ### offer ### in exchange, but ### come ### *Chakra* you ### ### my hospitality."

Brenda bowed understanding enough of what he said. She showed Tei how to use the compad as best she could by a few words and miming. She tried to show him that the words went into the microphones and then through the compads into the Box, before the Box sent them back out of the compads in the correct language. Tei flicked his ears, and then nodded in the Human fashion giving her hope that he understood some if not all of her explanation. Kajika was obviously not as interested as Tei was. He was holding his compad loosely, and hadn't put on his headset as Tei had done. The fit was not perfect, those mobile ears were a hell of a challenge, but it did seem to work reasonably well.

The next thing was to give them some basic information about the Alliance and Humanity in general. Where possible the literature had been compiled using hard copy diagrams and pictures, where that was not possible, Brenda would have to try to explain. Nowhere was jump technology mentioned, or any kind of astrographical data that might compromise the locations of Alliance worlds. Data of a military nature was absent also of course, but there was still a great deal regarding the threat the Merkiaari posed as well as day-to-day life in the Alliance.

Brenda had been against the inclusion of the Merkiaari material, but now it looked as if James had been right about the Shan. From Tei'Varyk's reactions, she knew that his people had met the Merkiaari before. It seemed obvious to her now that there *had* been a previous civilisation, perhaps the very

Harmony of Shan they had all puzzled over, and it had been shattered by war. Merkiaari were those the Shan named the Murderers of Harmony, and that made a great difference to her thinking. Before today, she had always subscribed to the view that the war was Humanity's fault for sending military ships to greet the Merki, but now she knew the Shan had also suffered through contact with the Merki. Once was an accident, but twice?

No.

Tei'Varyk was studying the pictures with great interest. He wasn't so much studying them, as flicking through to get a feel of what the folders contained. Brenda watched his ears flatten and prick erect, flick and twitch, all the time wondering what it all meant. He didn't appear upset as he floated with the folders hovering near to his paws, but some of what he saw must be confusing for him.

"Ask questions, I answer," Brenda said speaking pidgin Shan, which the translator obediently converted into English to the confusion of both Shan. She was about to repeat herself in English to cover her showing off, when Tei spoke. She had been understood after all.

"Why come?" Tei said copying her example.

"We hear talking. We come warn you to stop. Merkiaari find you when... when talk so *loud*. We know this. It happen to us. We talk quiet now."

Brenda was pleased with that. Most of the words had translated flawlessly, but she was not as pleased with the result it caused. Tei was agitated, and Kajika didn't look happy; his muzzle was rumpled and his ears were flat.

"Talk... talk is why they came? They no like talk?" Tei'Varyk said intently.

"No, no, no," Brenda said and shook her head. "They want to kill anyone not Merki, but not know where we are. They follow our talk... find us. They kill us and listen more. They follow talk, kill us again. We come here... try save you. We not know we too late."

* * *

Tei'Varyk believed her. So much made sense now. The alien fang running and not firing back, the other one always running and hiding, again without firing. Leaving behind two of their people in a cub lander was a desperate attempt to communicate, but would the elders believe it? He glanced at Kajika and saw the disbelief on his face, in the angle of his half laid-back ears, but Kajika wasn't a deep thinker. He was a hunter first, last, and always, which was good in a claw of *Chakra*. A Tei had to be more. He had to look at a situation and see not only what was, but what *could* be also. The Humans were a horrible danger to his people, but they could also be an incredible boon. Handled right, this meeting might see the Harmony of Shan resurrected stronger than ever.

"You... want be friends?" Tei'Varyk said in cub talk.

"Yes," Brenda said.

"You want help us kill Merkiaari?"

"If ### come, we stop them."

"No," he said feeling this was an important point. "Not *protect* us. *Help* us *learn* how to protect ourselves."

"We help you," Brenda said with her head bobbing. "Want you not hunt *Canada*—our ship. We need to send ### ### ### ###," she screwed her face up at the bad translation. "We need send message home."

Kajika hissed. "We can't let them do that. More might come."

"Quiet you fool," Tei'Varyk said but it was too late. The device had already told Brenda Kajika's words.

"You not help us send ### ### ###, we not help you," Brenda said quickly in reaction. "My Captain... my Tei say he not let you ### his ship. He say destroy ### himself first. You not ### ### you help ###."

Tei'Varyk's chewed his whiskers in annoyance. The alien was so angry, he could barely understand her.

"We have these two," Kajika said. "This lander might—"

"I won't tell you again. Be silent or suffer for it back on *Chakra!*" Tei'Varyk blazed in anger. Brenda had been friendly, but now the conversation had slipped over into hostile territory.

"I nothing, my mate nothing, ### cub ### nothing," Brenda said coldly. "Cub not ### our planets, little distance only… understand? Not go like *Canada* go. You learn nothing ### it. We ### be friends, but we not *give* you ###. A gift for a gift, ### we be friends forever. We not like Merkiaari; you not like Merkiaari. We kill them, help you kill them, but *Canada* small ship—not made ### fight. Help ### send message home… help come. *Canada* little ship. Made for explore— understand? Find new things, new places; not fight."

Brenda had let something slip, and Tei'Varyk's reaction to it told her that she had. She bit her lip and reddened. Did that mean she was embarrassed? It probably did, because she should be. Her ship was not for war, she said, but was instead for exploring new places. Imagine being in command of such a one, able to go anywhere and see anything.

He would revel in such a life. There would be new systems and planets for the taking, Shan venturing out and making those planets their home. A new and perhaps better harmony could be created. Not a warship she said. That was extremely useful to know. It said the alien ship would be easy to destroy, but he didn't want to. He wanted it all. He wanted the stars for his people. He had no doubt the Human Tei would see his ship destroyed before allowing it to be captured. He would do the same in the Human's position.

"I not say yes, I not say no. Elders say," Tei'Varyk said finally making a decision.

"You go back *Chakra*. Talk elders ### come back and say. We ### here," Brenda said.

Tei'Varyk flicked his ears in agreement, but then bobbed his head for good measure. He offered her the pictures back, but she said they were a gift. He bowed as best he could and she did the same before giving him a container to safeguard the talking devices and gifts.

* * *

Brenda knew she had gone wrong, but for the life of her she couldn't see how she could have done differently. She had slipped by telling Tei'Varyk that *Canada* was not truly a warship, but if *Chakra* fired on her, Tei'Varyk would still get a surprise. *Canada* wasn't a warship any longer, but she had been one once. She could still defend herself long enough to escape into fold space.

Brenda watched Tei'Varyk fit the compads and other things neatly into the container and seal it. They would be quite safe from the cold and vacuum of space. When they were ready, she escorted them to the airlock, all the time looking worriedly at James. Shouldn't he have awoken by now? Surely the bots had made an impression on the wound after all this time, but if they had, she saw no sign.

The Shan sealed their helmets and stepped into the airlock. Tei turned to face her. He raised a paw and Brenda did the same before closing the inner door and starting the exit cycle. She watched in silence as the outer door opened and her guests left.

"Brenda?" James croaked. "Did I miss anything?"

Brenda gasped and spun to see James looking at her with a grey and sweating face. She was by his side and kissing him before she had even thought to move.

"Are you in pain? Of course you are. I'll get you something my love; you'll be all right. I injected the bots, and Fleet has good ones and—"

"Shush, I'm not in pain," James said then grimaced. "Not much. I missed the whole thing didn't I? Some hero I turned out to be..." he said as his eyes slipped slowly shut.

"You sleep now. Tomorrow you will be well again," Brenda said and sat next to him holding his hand with tears of joy in her eyes.

ABOARD CHAKRA, INNER BELT, SHAN SYSTEM

Tei'Varyk stormed onto the command deck in a state of high excitement and agitation. The Humans could be the saviours of his people, but like all good things, there was another side to the story. What if the Humans came here, but did not allow Shan to learn their technology? What then? His people would be like cubs to them. His people needed friends and partners, *equal* partners, not some kind of master or parent.

"Kon'stanji, you are claw of *Chakra*," he said as he took his station from Tei'Unwin.

"I hear but…" Kon'stanji hesitated to ask.

"Kajika has shamed me. His punishment is reduction to alternate claw."

There was some little shock at that, but relief as well. For all they knew, the aliens may have killed Kajika. Only Tei'Varyk knew that if anyone had killed Kajika it would have been him, and it would remain that way.

Tei'Unwin had not yet left the command deck. Tei'Varyk wondered how much he should divulge. He had yet to speak to the elders about his meeting with the aliens. Would they expect him to keep the meeting secret? Keeping it secret might make it easier for them to ignore the aliens. That was something he would not allow if he had his way, but it was not his place to make such decisions. He chewed his whiskers and decided to risk their displeasure.

"We have a great opportunity before us," he began. "There are two aliens aboard the cub, and they are friendly."

Gasps and yips of shock surrounded him. Tei'Varyk dropped his jaw and waved his ears in amusement. What did Humans do when they were amused? He glanced at Tarjei and saw worry mixed with relief at his return. The worry was the same as on all the other's faces, but the rest was for him alone.

"You are certain, Tei?" Tei'Unwin asked. "Really certain they mean us no harm?"

"I'm certain of nothing. Never am I certain beyond some small doubt. You are the same or you would still be Kon'Unwin, but I feel they are not an *immediate* threat to us. I have been given gifts, and I have spoken with the female whose name is," Tei'Varyk paused and tried to sound the alien name. "*Brenda*. Her mate is *James*. I have been gifted with a device that turns my words into Human speech. They have the same devices to turn their speech into ours. It's not a perfect translation, but the errors are small enough for understanding."

"*Humanssss?*" Tei'Unwin sounded the strange name, but he garbled the last syllable. "They are not like the Murderers?"

"No, they are very different. They're much smaller and carry no weapons on their persons. They have no fangs or claws." He hesitated. "They say they came to save us from the Murderers... I believe them."

The command deck was silent, which was not good. Tei'Varyk looked around and saw complete disbelief on every face except Tarjei. She looked afraid for him, and worse, of him also.

"Tei..." Tei'Unwin began uncertainly. "May I have leave to speak with Kajika?"

Tei'Varyk flicked his ears. "You have my leave."

Tei'Unwin bowed and left in a scrabble of claws. He was in a hurry to verify Tei'Varyk's words, or refute them.

Tei'Varyk looked around at his crew's worried faces. They deserved more from him. "I know you doubt me. I have given the Humans nothing but my word that I will speak to the elders about our meeting. The Tei of the ship we have been chasing will not allow us to capture him; he will destroy him first. I would do the same if I was he. That ship has FTL capability beyond any doubt. The Human Tei will never allow us to take him."

"Then we should destroy him," Kon'stanji said. "Surely?" he added with his ears at half-mast.

"So, to, does Kajika advise me. I see..." Tei'Varyk said quietly and his crew leaned forward with baited breath.

"I see perhaps too much in these Humans, but the elders will decide. The Humans were attacked, as we were, by the Merkiaari. Eighty Human worlds were devastated. *Eighty.* Do you see what that means? I see a chance for our people to go out into the void and begin rebuilding the Harmony of Shan bigger and stronger than ever. I see Humans tracking down the Murderers with us and destroying them utterly. That's what I see."

"And what do the Humans see, Tei?" Tarjei asked.

"They see strength in numbers, I would judge. They came to warn and protect us, but I would have them help us learn, so that we might protect ourselves. We are not cubs. I would see us out there among the stars as equals."

* * *

16~Contact

Tei'Varyk chose his personal chambers to discuss the situation with the Humans. Besides James and Brenda, Tarjei and Tei'Unwin were also present. Strictly speaking, Tarjei should not have been invited. She had neither the rank nor the experience to warrant her inclusion, but he valued her insights. She was here because he wanted her close, and he was Tei for *Chakra*. If Tei'Unwin didn't like it, he would keep silent if he knew what was good for him. Tei'Varyk had put up with more than enough questioning of his authority. He would allow no more of it.

"Your people would accept this?" Tarjei said.

"They would ### it," James said excitedly.

Tarjei flicked her ears in annoyance at the garbled translation. The Humans did not understand her signal of displeasure of course.

"Say again."

Brenda tried first. "They happy if Shan do this thing."

Tei'Varyk winced at the static coming from his earpiece. Brenda had spoken the name of the race in Shan, and the translator had not understood her mangled attempt.

"How many Humanssss..." Tei'Unwin said trying to think of a simple way to ask his question.

"How many against it?" James offered and Tei'Unwin gratefully accepted that. "We have two hundred and thirty-four worlds, Tei. ### one ### billions of Humans. I ### tell you ### ### figure."

Brenda added her thoughts. "Only fifty-eight worlds ### against coming here."

"Only fifty-eight?" Tei'Varyk said slowly. Did he have that right? "*Only?*" he said exchanging a concerned look with Tarjei. "These fifty-eight would stop us?"

"No," James and Brenda said together, but James went on. "One hundred and seventy-six in favour of us coming here, Tei. It is enough."

"Your elders allow this?" Tarjei said in dismay. "You do not care about the fifty-eight worlds against us?"

"We care, but the Alliance is ### by ### vote. All worlds agree to ### by a ### vote. You see?"

Tei'Varyk believed he understood. Two hundred and thirty four elders led the Alliance, but as with everyone, they did not always agree. The Shan system was better. Kajetan always spoke the final word of decision. The other elders helped her to decide, but she, and only she, decided what was to be done.

"I understand," Tei'Varyk said. "We have two worlds. We have two votes?"

"Ah... no, Tei. The twin worlds of the Shan are..." James looked flustered and Brenda spoke up.

"All Alliance systems have one vote. Your system is the only one with two ### worlds that we ### ever discovered, but the pattern is set. One system, one vote."

Tei'Varyk thought that was probably best. Two votes might mean Child of Harmony voting *against* Harmony at some future time. He could not conceive of a situation that might warrant it, but best to rule it out now.

"What of our fleet?" Tei'Unwin said. "We will not give up

our ships."

Tei'Varyk couldn't prevent his shock from betraying itself at the thought. His ears plastered themselves against his head, and his nostrils flared as if facing into a strong wind. He was embarrassed when his lack of control allowed his tail to wind itself around his leg. A cub of two orbits could control himself better. He took a deep breath and forced himself to relax. His tail uncurled slowly, and he was finally able to listen to James. Thankfully, Tei'Unwin was too intent on the Humans to notice his immature reaction.

"All our worlds ### their own soldiers, but there is only one Alliance navy—" James began.

"We will not give up our ships," Tei'Varyk snapped.

James raised a hand. "You won't have to, Tei. Your fleet is yours to do with as you wish, but I hope ### ### will join it to ours to protect us all. We will help you build bigger and better ships; ships with FTL capability. Do you want this?"

"Very much," Tei'Varyk said and the others agreed. "Very much, but we will not give up what we have without a fight."

"Nor should you," James said but Brenda did not look happy.

"Brenda does not agree?" Tarjei said picking up the Human's scent. She was not in harmony.

"I agree you should not give up your weapons, but why ### we ### talk of war and hurting? Why not talk about nice things?"

"Such as?" Tarjei encouraged.

"### for instance."

"What is *nanotech*?" Tei'Varyk asked sounding the Human word carefully.

"What is the average lifespan of your people, Tei?"

What did that have to do with anything? "Fifty orbits," he said and wondered at the shock on the Humans' faces. "Kajetan is very old. She is sixty one orbits, but that is very rare."

Brenda nodded. "Through the use of ###, James and I

live one hundred and fifty years, and ### even more. ### is ### ### ### improved all the time. A standard year is equal to one point three Harmony orbits, Tei. That means we should live, barring accidents, to the age of one hundred and ninety-five orbits."

"*One hundred and ninety-five orbits!*" Tei'Varyk gasped. How was it possible? "You will give us this *nanotech*?"

"We will. All ### citizens receive ### treatments as children. I hope it can be adapted for your people."

One hundred and ninety-five orbits with Tarjei. He had to make Kajetan agree. Tei'Varyk glanced at Tei'Unwin, and saw the same kinds of thoughts in the slant of his ears and twitching whiskers. Tei'Unwin went still and his ears twitched upright. It was time.

"You must speak to Kajetan," Tei'Varyk said.

"Your elder?" James said.

"She is eldest," he agreed. "You ### speak with her and make her see."

"Don't you think it ### be better if you—" James began.

"No," Tarjei blurted in her agitation. "No. You ### do it, *James*. Tei'Varyk isn't an elder."

"Neither am I."

"But you are alien. Varyk is one Tei among many; you are something other. She will hear you."

James glanced at Brenda uneasily. "All right. When?"

"Now," Tei'Varyk said instantly and was echoed by the others.

* * *

James was nervous as hell. Thank God Brenda was with him. He stood before the blank screen with Brenda on one side and Tei'Varyk on the other. The other Tei, Tei'Unwin, was standing with Tarjei in the background. They had wanted to be present and Tei'Varyk had thought it a good idea. The more the merrier as far as James was concerned.

"I don't know what to say," he whispered. "I wish Bindar was here."

Brenda squeezed his hand reassuringly. "Just introduce us and be polite."

"Oh *thank you*. I had that part figured out."

"You'll be fine," Brenda said. "Just listen to what she says and wing it. She's an elder, she must be a reasonable person."

"Why?" James hissed as the screen flickered on.

Tei'Varyk stepped forward and bowed quickly. James stayed where he was hoping Kajetan and the other elders would not notice him. No such luck. He watched with a sinking feeling as Kajetan's ears lay back in shock. The other elders stared with white-rimmed eyes at the first alien face they had ever seen. James hoped he and Brenda wouldn't be the last.

"Honoured Kajetan, honoured elders, I have disobeyed you. I could not follow your orders." Tei'Varyk bowed twice in apology. "I could not destroy our chance, perhaps our last chance to become what we are meant to be. The Humans offer us a way to make the Great Harmony greater than ever."

There was silence from the elders. They were still in shock at Tei'Varyk's betrayal. James thought now would be a good time to take charge and stepped forward. He tried to imitate Tei'Varyk's bow, but then turned to him in confusion when the screen darkened.

"What has happened?"

"I don't know," Tei'Varyk said and spoke in rapid Shan to Tei'Unwin.

James could not follow what was said, but whatever it was had Tei'Unwin racing out the door in a scrabble of claws.

"I think we're in trouble," Brenda hissed and nodded at the stricken look on Tarjei's face. "She's afraid. Tei'Varyk disobeyed—" she broke off as the screen re-activated. "*James...*" she hissed.

"Tei'Varyk, attend," Kajetan said imperiously. She was alone now and by the tone of her voice, she was not pleased.

Tei'Varyk bowed. "I hear, Eldest."

"By what right do you choose what is best for our people?"

"By clan right and my authority as Tei, Eldest."

Kajetan's eyes blazed. "You *dare*. You dare use clan right for *this!*"

"I dare, Eldest. For this nothing else will suffice."

James had no idea what clan right was, but by Kajetan's reaction, he knew Tei'Varyk was on thin ice. He was about to introduce himself to take Kajetan's attention away from Tei'Varyk, when she turned to him.

"Speak."

James raised an eyebrow at that. Who was she to order him? Brenda shoved him forward, and he swallowed his protest. He stepped forward and performed his bow, but made it less than before. Kajetan would have to earn more from him. So far she had failed to do that.

"Eldest, I am called James Wilder. This is my mate, Brenda Lane," he said and pause to allow Tei'Varyk to interpret. "We were sent here by the Alliance to contact you in hope of making new friends."

Kajetan listened to Tei'Varyk's translation with ears and whiskers twitching. "What is this *Alliance?*"

"The Alliance is comprised of two hundred and thirty-four Human populated worlds living in harmony," James said not wincing at the exaggeration. "We are governed by the Council, which is like yet unlike a Council of elders. Our elders wish to extend the hand of friendship to all Shan."

"Friends do not invade our space. Friends do not skulk about and spy."

James winced at Kajetan's vitriol. "We have learned to be cautious, Eldest. Two hundred years ago, my people met a race that tried to kill us all. You know them as the Murderers of Harmony. They are Murderers in truth. We call them Merkiaari."

Kajetan hissed and spoke with Tei'Varyk. "You believe this—why?"

"I have spoken with James and Brenda for many cycles, Eldest. I have seen what they brought with them. They would offer us a place in their Alliance, but more than this, they offer FTL for our ships and something called nanotech. Eldest I... the Great Harmony can be built anew, built among the stars."

"This is true?" Kajetan said.

James nodded. "I give you my word that what I say is true. I would not lie to you. FTL is one of many things we offer, and nanotech is available providing it can be adapted to work for you. I have been assured by people I trust, that it will simply be a matter of research and reprogramming. Biologically, our two peoples are fundamentally the same. I do not foresee a problem."

Kajetan listened to the translation. "What is *nanotech?*"

Oh yes!

James felt like dancing with excitement. He had her, he was sure he had her. Kajetan was no longer belligerent; she was curious. Brenda seemed to agree, she was fidgeting as if she couldn't keep her feet from dancing.

"Nanotech is a medical process designed to prevent illness and extend life," he said simply when he realised Kajetan was still waiting for an answer.

"Extend life?" Kajetan said with her whiskers twitching. She glanced from James to Tei'Varyk and back. "How, and by how much?"

"I am fifty-two years old, Eldest. That is the same as sixty-eight orbits. I will live, barring accidents of course, for another hundred and twenty orbits... perhaps more if fate is kind."

Kajetan hissed in shock. "You are an elder of your people?"

James smiled. "No, Eldest. I am young yet."

Kajetan blinked at that. James was almost her age yet he was too young to be an elder. "What is your proposal?"

James closed his eyes in abject relief. "First, Eldest, I must ask that my ship be allowed to emerge and be given safe passage. Second, I ask that you and my Tei discuss the future of our two peoples face to face. Third…"

* * *

Aboard ASN Canada, in orbit of Harmony

Never had the launching of a drone had such ceremony surrounding it, Colgan mused. Next to him stood Tei'Varyk of *Chakra*, gazing with pride at the viewscreen where the six heavy cruisers, heavy *fangs* he should say, of *Canada's* escort were displayed. Six heavies as escort should have filled him with pride that his ship was viewed with such respect, but all it did was intimidate him. He wished he had a carrier here, that would even things up right nicely.

Jump technology wasn't everything, he had found. Good weapons and good sensors made up for a lot, and those ships had both in abundance. He had learned a great deal since detecting the probe Wilder launched to survey the agreed upon asteroid. The signal might have been agreed upon before hand, but it was still a tough decision to make. When he finally did come out of hiding, he was greeted by that little lot out there. Colgan remembered thinking he was a goner for sure, but then the lander suddenly appeared out of the shadow of the heavies, and Mark received a tight beam message…

"Hello Captain," Wilder said. "I've brought some friends over, if that's all right?"

"Friends?" Colgan said as his crew ran futilely to battle stations. "Are you sure?"

"I'm sure, sir. Tell the Chief the Box worked great." Wilder grinned and pulled Professor Lane into view of the pickup. "Can we come in?"

That had been two weeks ago. Two weeks of discussions with the elders of the Shan—sometimes heated, sometimes not, but always ending amicably thank goodness. Today was the day to consummate the agreement hammered out by his team. It was far from what they had wanted to accomplish here, but they definitely had a foot in the door. All in all, Colgan felt he was ahead of the game. After all, *Canada* was still in one piece and so was he.

"Contact Kajetan please, Mark," Colgan said.

"Aye, sir," Lieutenant Ricks said and used the jury-rigged equipment donated by Tei'Varyk. "On screen, Skip."

"I greet you, Kajetan... elders," he said standing and bowing to the screen.

The elders were wearing headsets modified by Shan from the Chief's originals. They listened to the translation and bowed to him in return.

"With your permission, we are ready to launch the drone," Colgan said, careful to enunciate the words clearly for the bridge recorders and the translation package.

"I would speak to Tei'Varyk, Tei'Colgan," Kajetan said.

"As you wish, Ma'am," Colgan said and stepped to one side giving Tei'Varyk unrestricted access to his elders.

Tei'Varyk spoke rapidly in his own language. Colgan cupped his earpiece, and concentrated trying to ignore the gaps that Bindar had managed to reduce, but not eradicate.

"...I stand ready to verify the agreement we have with the *Humans*."

"Good," Kajetan said. "But that is not what we wish to discuss with you. I trust Tei'Colgan to do as we agreed; whether that means his people will also... we shall see. You have served well, Tei'Varyk. You have served our people better perhaps than we ourselves have."

The elders standing with Kajetan mumbled their agreement.

"I thank you, but I did not follow your orders."

"That is not known outside of this group," Kajetan said sharply. "It will remain between us. However, *Chakra* is for Tei'Unwin."

Tei'Varyk's stood stiffly with his ears flattened tight to his head and his nostrils flared wide as if facing into a gale. He was hurt by the loss of his ship, as any Tei or captain would be. Colgan stepped forward to protest, but Kajetan surprised them all by waving her ears in amusement.

"Be not so distressed. Have I not said you have served well? We have two new tasks for you and any who will follow you from *Chakra*."

"Tasks?" Tei'Varyk said hopefully.

"Yes tasks. The first is that you be the eyes and ears of the elders…"

That translated as ambassador, Colgan was pleased to hear. He liked Tei'Varyk. Their discussions regarding the cat and mouse game they had played over the past few months were interesting. Duty permitting, he looked forward to a great many more discussions on many subjects.

"The second task is to oversee the completion of *Naktlon*," Kajetan said.

"A heavy fang for me?" Tei'Varyk gasped.

"Why so surprised? You would have moved on from *Chakra* in an orbit's time, two at the most. Did you plan on leaving space and the fleet you love then?"

"*Never!*" Tei'Varyk said horrified at the idea. "My mate and I wish always to serve in space. It's where we belong."

Good answer. It was something Colgan would have said himself if asked that question. Space was his home, exploration his life and goal. He supposed he would be given another ship someday—a heavy cruiser like Tei'Varyk probably, but when that day came, he wanted to be able to say he had made the most of his time aboard *Canada*. This mission would burn brightly in his memory that was for sure.

"Tei'Colgan," Kajetan said. "You may proceed with your launch."

"I thank you, Kajetan, elders," Colgan said and bowed. The screen cleared and returned to showing the heavies hanging in space. "Download the logs please, Mark."

"Aye, sir, downloading… download complete."

"Very good," he said and was about to give the next order,

but he hesitated and turned to Tei'Varyk. "Would you give the order for the elders, Tei?"

"Honoured," Tei'Varyk said and turned to Lieutenant Ricks. "Download the elders' message to your drone *please, Mark*," he said saying the last two words in English. Already his grasp of English was improving.

"Aye, sir, downloading... download complete."

"Set drive to eighty percent," Colgan said. "Coordinates: Alliance HQ."

"Aye, sir, drone programmed. Destination: Alliance HQ."

"Give the launch order please, Tei."

Tei'Varyk flicked his ears in acknowledgement. "I hear. Launch the drone."

"Aye, sir, launching. Drone away... drone has entered fold space, sirs," Lieutenant Ricks said.

"Very good," Colgan said at the same time as Tei'Varyk's, "I hear."

They smiled at each other. A Human smile, reflected against a Shan's ear-twitching jaw-dropping grin.

"Well done everyone," Colgan said to his crew. "Nothing can go wrong now."

The bridge crew cheered.

* * *

17~Answers

James stood upon the taxiway and breathed deeply. The chill air was full of alien scents that delighted his senses. After so long aboard ship walking under the open sky was a relief and a pleasure. The breeze picked up and he faced into it. He could smell the ocean, but could not see it from here even though it was only a few short kilometres from the port; he had crossed the coast on his approach.

"It's beautiful here," Brenda said smiling with eyes closed into the sun's warmth.

"You're beautiful, but I agree it beats living aboard ship."

"Flatterer."

Brenda took his arm and they walked slowly toward the busy buildings. The port was a huge place, and although the Shan were different in many ways, some things were similar. Zuleika spaceport had a control tower with a three hundred and sixty degree view just like a Human port, and the taxiways and runways could have belonged to any number of Alliance worlds. The buildings were not the same, but even here James could see they had the same purpose as those found at a Human port. Hangars and maintenance depots were little different wherever you happened to find yourself. They had to be. The ships they serviced all had similar requirements. Things like repairs and refuelling.

The architecture was unlike modern Human buildings. Back home, they would be made of steel and glass, but here he saw a lot of wood and stone. It looked odd in such a high tech setting as a spaceport, but pleasing to the eye all the same.

"We have a reception up ahead," Bernard said from his place next to Janice. "More speeches I shouldn't wonder."

"You know very well that the Shan do not go in for such things," Bindar said promptly.

"I meant us, my friend!"

James chuckled. Captain Colgan had asked him to give a speech to the crew when Brenda and he had first arrived back aboard *Canada*. He gave a second more detailed report at his debriefing with the senior officers, and after that, another debriefing by his colleagues in the contact team.

When the news broke that contact had been made with an alien race, there had been a great deal of unrest among the Shan. There had been panic in the cities with thousands of Shan simply dropping everything and running for the hills. They were understandably afraid of aliens. They remembered the Merkiaari too well to believe Humans were friendly.

Kajetan and the Council of Elders had made broadcasts one after the other to calm their people, but it wasn't until George Colgan and Janice Bristow were called upon that calm began to return. George had helped the elders by answering their questions during live broadcasts. He explained about the Alliance, and how the Fleet protected it against the Merkiaari. His willingness to meet and talk with the Shan alone and on their own turf helped the situation immensely.

As the weeks past, each of the contact team's members had played their part in the broadcasts. James had drawn on his knowledge of history to paint a picture of the Alliance and how it came to be. David held a class on Human physiology, mainly due to some highly respected Shan healers asking their elders to facilitate it. The session was recorded and broadcast the next day and had been repeated pretty much every day since then. Bindar had found himself trying to teach the Shan the rudiments of the English language, while Sheryl was inundated with requests about her knowledge of science and technology—especially nanotech. The Shan were fascinated by everything Human related.

There were very few Shan who did not know at least one Human name, and many of them knew them all. Cubs would choose their favourite Human to learn about; they took pride in their knowledge and made a game of besting each other with questions on the subject.

He'd had enough speechifying for this lifetime, James decided. "I vote Brenda gives the next one, if one there is."

Brenda punched him on the shoulder. "Hey no fair!"

"It's fair. I haven't heard one speech out of you this entire trip!" he said, rubbing his arm as if in pain, but he was joking.

Brenda had chosen to teach the Shan about the plants and animals found by the Alliance on alien worlds. The Shan were fascinated by her and who could blame them? He was too. A small group of Shan approached to greet them. James stiffened when he recognised the aged Shan female at the centre of the group. There could be no mistaking that patterned pelt and grey speckled muzzle. It was Elder Jutka. This was the first time Jutka had deigned to meet the whole team. Before this, only James and Brenda had spoken with her, and then only via the comm.

James bowed deeply. "You honour us, Elder."

"You honour us, Elder," Brenda said with a bow. "May I introduce my colleagues?"

"You may proceed," Elder Jutka said, her nostrils flared as she gathered alien scents. Her whiskers, grey with age drew down at something she smelled, but rose again a moment later.

Brenda inclined her head politely and introduced the

others. "Janice Bristow, professor of exobiology."

Janice bowed. "You honour me, Elder."

"James has spoken highly of you," Jutka said and touched her paw to Janice's palm in greeting.

"David Harrison, professor of biology," Brenda said and David stepped forward.

"You honour me, Elder," he said and bowed.

"I look forward to hearing your thoughts on what you have discovered," Jutka said inclining her head in return before touching David's hand.

"Sheryl Linden, professor of physics and engineering," Brenda said ushering Sheryl forward.

"You honour me, Elder."

"Ah!" Jutka said, her ears quivering and straining forward. "I look forward to discussing this thing called nanotech with you. It is a fascinating concept. To think such tiny machines can exist..." Jutka twitched her ears in puzzlement. "How can it be possible?"

"I have my reference texts aboard *Canada*, Elder. They are all in English, but perhaps you would like copies? I'm sure you can have them translated, or perhaps I could go through the relevant sections with you?"

"Yes, yes!" Jutka said excitedly and shocked everyone— especially the Shan accompanying her—when she bowed to Sheryl. "You honour me with your offer of teaching, Sheryl."

"The honour is mine," Sheryl said solemnly.

Brenda was at a loss for a moment and it took a nudge from James to put her back on track. "Ah... I... This is Bindar Singh, Elder. He is our professor of linguistics. He's the sole reason we can converse and understand one another."

Jutka bowed even as Bindar did. "I thank you for bringing our two peoples together, Bindar."

"You honour me, Elder," Bindar bowed again. "I could not have accomplished my goal without a great deal of help from the others."

James smiled. "You must excuse Bindar, Elder. He is too

modest, but we love him anyway."

Bindar's face heated in embarrassment. His friends chuckled and murmured their agreement. Jutka dropped her jaw in a grin and her ears flicked and twitched in what was great amusement in a Shan.

"I understand you are here for just a short time."

"That is true Elder," James said. "We cannot leave our work unfinished for too much longer. The Council will require a complete report before they can brief the next team."

"It is important work," Jutka agreed. "I have arranged for you all to stay in Zuleika with me and my mate. I have planned a tour of our city and of the Markan'deya. You will find it interesting James, considering your area of study."

"The Markan'deya?" James said uncertainly. "The... ah... memory of the people?"

"The memory of the *race*, I believe," Bindar corrected. "A museum perhaps."

"Museum?" Jutka said trying the Human word carefully.

"A place where records and items pertaining to our history are displayed," Bindar explained. "People visit a museum to learn about our history."

"Then you have your own Markan'deya."

"We have many museums, Elder. On Earth—our homeworld—there are hundreds. Some are dedicated to Human history, others to natural history. There are even some dedicated to past wars—lest we forget how terrible war is."

Jutka's ears went flat. "You must see our Markan'deya. If you want to learn what it is to be Shan, you must."

"We all wish that," Janice said.

"Come then, let us go now," Jutka said turning away.

James exchanged glances with the others before they all hurried to catch Jutka and her escort. The elder had been very grim. James was careful to stay behind the Shan, but Jutka imperiously motioned him and the others forward so she might speak with them.

"Tell me of the Alliance."

Janice took up the question and launched into their well used explanation. She knew it by heart. They all did by now. "The Alliance is composed of two hundred and thirty-four—"

"No, tell me of your *people*. I have heard enough of your Council and Fleet for now. What are your people like? What do they do, how do they live?"

Janice smiled. "People are people anywhere, Elder. Some live in cities, some in space on our stations and ships. We have teachers and soldiers, factory workers and farmers, actors and musicians, scientists and doctors... the list is endless."

"Actors?"

"People who entertain others, Elder," Brenda said. "We like to write stories and watch people pretend to be the characters. We have plays, and holodramas written to mimic real life, but often the story is fiction."

"Lies used to entertain?" Jutka said doubtfully.

The Shan had a rich aural and written history. Those stories were re-enacted at special times, but James only now realised they were all factual accounts of real historical events. His mind raced over the data he had been compiling for months aboard ship. No fiction at all. None. Why hadn't he realised what that could mean? If looked at from a Shan point of view fiction was another name for lying.

"Not lies, Elder," James hurriedly explained. "All those who watch them know the stories are not real life. The holodramas work because people willingly submerge themselves in the stories. Humans enjoy them. I always like to imagine myself as the hero who gets to save the Alliance."

"Ah! You wish to be other than you are, I can understand the fascination. If the Harmonies had not chosen my course, I would most likely have become an engineer as my father was. I sometimes like to imagine myself inventing some great new thing. Something so special everyone would know my name." Jutka smiled remembering her younger self. "The Harmonies however, have a way of guiding us along unsuspected paths."

Jutka stopped beside a big ground car waiting to take them to Zuleika. It hovered above the ground on a cushion of air. No anti-grav meant no flying and a longer trip.

"Sometimes we all feel that way, Elder," James agreed with a nod. "I like my life and my work, but it does no harm for me to imagine what would have happened had I taken another path."

Jutka climbed aboard the car followed by the ladies; Bernard and David were next, followed by Bindar and James last. There was plenty of room to sit comfortably and they continued their conversation uninterrupted by the quiet power up of the hover car. It glided smoothly along and James thought the Alliance should take note of this mode of travel. Alliance roads were notoriously uncared for and hence travel upon them was often uncomfortable and noisy.

They drove into Zuleika and James split his attention between Jutka and her people going about their business outside. He felt truly privileged to be here. Zuleika was a lovely place full of open parks and delicate seeming buildings. The Shan did not go in for mile high towers or anything near it. Instead of building vertically like a Human city, the Shan had chosen to build Zuleika horizontally with many connecting bridges between buildings spanning wide streets. Those bridges were a marvel in themselves. There did not seem to be anything holding them up! The spans could almost be made of air they were so fragile seeming.

James watched dozens of Shan crossing a bridge and knew it was not air they were walking upon. It must be some kind of metal—a super strong alloy that could be used to construct such wonderful things as those bridges out there, yet not clutter the city with supports and pylons. Sheryl would be fascinated when she noticed them, but she was deep in conversation with Jutka and all her attention was focused upon the elder.

"Look there," Brenda whispered to him and pointed at a group of young Shan chasing each other in a park. "Are they playing?"

"Not playing," Jutka said raising a paw in apology to Sheryl for interrupting her. "They practice the hunt."

"The hunt? They are still cubs!"

"Barely two orbits old I would say," Jutka said glancing at the cubs as they passed. "We begin training early."

"Two years old…" David said in astonishment.

"Shan grow very fast compared to us," Brenda said. Xenobiology was one of her disciplines. "Six years old is adult for Shan."

"*Seven* orbits," Jutka corrected.

"I thank you, Elder," Brenda said inclining her head.

Seven Shan years was adult? James wondered how old Tei'Varyk and Tarjei were. If seven was adult then they might be as young as ten! No, that could not be right. It would surely have taken Tei'Varyk longer than that to learn everything he needed to know. Then of course there was the experience necessary to be promoted to command a ship in the first place. The Shan only had forty-one warships at present. Forty-one captains from among millions of Shan made Tei'Varyk a very special man—Shan.

The Markan'deya was different to the other buildings in Zuleika. It was a large round building separated from the rest of the city by wide boulevards and set in the centre of a forested park. Access was by foot only, and to this end, their car pulled into a space beside another similar car. The Shan seemed to prefer walking or running to riding in cars. James had seen very few on their way to the Markan'deya. He gazed at their destination trying to reconcile the differences he found in this one building. It looked nothing like those in the city.

There were no bridges this time, and no sign of the light and airy feel of the city. It was all heavy stone columns and walls as if belonging to an earlier age. It *was* striking, but ugly in a way James could not put his finger on. It was as if the Shan had deliberately made it this way as a warning. He did not like what that said about its contents.

The Markan'deya had been deliberately set apart from

the rest of the city, yet it was still at its heart. There was a symbolism here that was not lost on Bernard. His area was cultural studies specialising in the Merki. The President had decided his expertise on an alien culture would be valuable to the team.

He was right.

"Harmony again," Bernard rumbled quietly. "You set your past at a remove, Elder. It's as if you wish to separate yourselves from those living back then, yet you do not wish to forget them. Is that not so?"

Everyone was quiet. Bernard was greatly respected and he was always worth listening to. This time they waited with baited breath to see if Jutka would answer the one question that had stumped them all. Where was harmony in Shan culture?

"I believe the Human word for Zuleika would be *lovely* or am I wrong in this?" Jutka said seemingly avoiding the question.

Bindar answered, "Not wrong Elder, but I believe a closer approximation would be the word *fair* or perhaps even *intelligent*. Intelligent city?"

"No," Jutka said. "Zuleika then means fair city, but there is nothing fair about the Markan'deya Bindar. We remember, but it is a hard memory and one without harmony. That is why this place is separate from our city. The Markan'deya is at the heart of things, at the heart of all Shan. By coming here we remember our past, and what was lost. Our past *is* the Markan'deya."

That was as long a speech as James had ever heard from any Shan barring Kajetan. They all silently exited the car and followed Jutka toward the Markan'deya. All of them were apprehensive about what they would find and took no notice of the crowd beginning to form in their wake.

Jutka stopped at the huge door. "*This* is what we are," she said and opened it.

They followed Jutka inside and were confronted by the

snarling visage of a huge Merki female. James and his friends froze in shock.

"Be not alarmed," Jutka said grimly satisfied with their reaction. "It is not real."

"It looks very real to us, Elder." Janice stared with fascination. She moved forward to view it from all sides. The Shan had set the figure in the centre of the room. It gave the impression that it was barring the way further into the building.

James meanwhile was looking around the anteroom. There were relics displayed in glass-like cases all round the room. They were remnants of weapons almost exclusively, but the walls were what fascinated him the most. There were scenes of Shan life lovingly drawn and painted covering the walls. The artistry was excellent, but James found the contrast between the scenes on the walls and the broken beamers and launchers in the cases both striking and puzzling. There seemed nothing to link the two.

"They were painted from memory by the survivors of the war. This one..." Jutka said gesturing at a pastoral scene. "This one shows my people living a simple life. We knew nothing of technology and did not care. We were happy in our villages. We raised our cubs and hunted when we were hungry."

Jutka moved to the next scene showing some kind of meeting between elders.

"Here we see my people have prospered, but the clans were becoming too large for the range they claimed. A meeting of elders was called and a solution was sought."

"What was the solution?" Bernard asked, studying the artwork with interest.

"The clans were made into one with each of the elders working together to govern all the clans equally. It was the birth of the Great Harmony. The clans themselves were joined by blood when mates were chosen from different clans. If not for the creation of the Great Harmony, we may well have starved as we depleted more and more of our resources. There were many times more Shan in those times."

Bernard was nodding enthusiastically. "Your people turned away from the hunter gatherer life and towards permanent settlements and farming."

"Had we not learned to farm and husband the animals we fed upon, we would surely have starved," Jutka said and move to the next scene. "This one shows homeworld many orbits after the founding of the Great Harmony. We extended our settlements more and more until they became towns and then cities. We had learned to feed ourselves and were no longer chained to the land. We had more than enough for everyone and had more time for other pursuits.

"Here we see my people discovering electrical power. Before that time, we had used the wind or muscle power to do what was needed."

"How long after the founding did this occur elder?"

"Many generations," Jutka said. "Almost three hundred orbits."

"Three hundred!" Bernard gasped.

"Yes, a long time."

"That was not what I meant elder," Bernhard said. "You advanced from a hunter-gatherer society and into an industrial one in just three hundred years. That is amazing!"

"Why?" Jutka said with interest. "Three hundred orbits is almost six generations of my people."

"Yes, but you see elder, it took Humans many times longer to reach the same level."

"I see, and you believe this is significant?"

"Well… yes!" Bernard said. "Don't you?"

"No. We are all of us different from one another. How much more different then must two races be?"

"Well said," James said.

There were murmurs of agreement from his colleagues but Jutka simply twitched her ears and moved on to the next to last scene. James judged from the subject matter that this one depicted more recent history, and Jutka confirmed it a moment or so later. James listened to her describe the launching of the first probes to the outer planets of the Shan system while he studied the images. The scene showed the actual launching of the probe against a backdrop of cheering Shan.

"And the last one," Jutka said moving to stand before the picture. "This is an important time in our history. Homeworld was becoming overpopulated and we desperately needed new range. The probes gave us the data we needed to find Child of Harmony, and our scientists gave us the means to reach and land here. This ship was the very first to be launched to Child of Harmony, but it was not the last. As you can see, we began building ships as fast as we could in an attempt at colonising this planet. We succeeded."

The painting showed a large fleet of ships assembled above Homeworld with others already on their way to Child of Harmony. On the surface, a city—Zuleika perhaps, was already under construction. The colonisation was an amazing achievement for any race, but for the Shan it was survival. Shan females gave birth in litters. Six cubs was the average and overpopulation had obviously been a concern.

"How long ago was this?" James said already guessing it would be around a century. The Shan had met the Merki around then.

"One hundred and twelve orbits."

"Just before the war?"

Jutka did not answer. Instead, she moved to the door guarded by the Merki statue. "In here are the answers to your questions," she said and entered.

* * *

KACHINA MOUNTAINS, CHILD OF HARMONY

"It's very beautiful here elder," Brenda said looking around her. "It smells wonderful."

Jutka raised her muzzle to scent the wind. "There are

many such places on Child of Harmony, but we have come here for a reason other than the scenery."

"Of course, forgive me."

"There is nothing to forgive. Beauty is always worth noting, but come, let us go on."

Brenda and the others followed the elder and her entourage along the rock-strewn path, if path it was, and up into the foothills of the Kachina Mountains. It was slow going, Jutka was old for a Shan and so were Janice and Bindar, but there was no hurry. The Markan'deya was a horror but it had one redeeming feature. It had given them an excuse to find out what a Keep was like.

As Brenda climbed higher, she could not help remembering what Jutka had shown them inside the Markan'deya. Jutka said they would find answers through that door, the one guarded by a Merki female. They had found answers all right, but Brenda had found sadness and pain—and nightmares...

They had followed Jutka through that door and found the end of the Great Harmony. Hundreds of cases filled the hall and thousands of horror stories were painted on the walls. It had made her sick to her stomach and Bindar was white-faced. She had wanted to run away from what she saw, but she felt almost obligated to look.

"The Murderers came and destroyed our ships," Jutka said indicating the first images. "We had no weapons, no defence against them. On the surface of Homeworld, there was panic and disbelief. We did not know what was happening, or why it was happening. The Murderers bombed our major cities and then descended to the surface to round up my people. Millions upon millions of Shan were killed before we learned to use the Merkiaari weapons against them."

"What of this one?" James whispered loath to break the horrified hush that had fallen.

Jutka turned to see what James had found. "My people fled to the deep forests where they hid from the Merki and slowly starved. While those lucky enough to acquire weapons fought the Murderers, their mates and cubs starved."

Brenda studied scene after scene of atrocity. Cities burning, Shan fighting unarmed and dying against huge Merki, cubs running as Merki ripped apart their parents... it was horrible.

"And this?" Bindar said.

"The first Keep," Jutka said.

"What is a Keep?"

"A refuge—merely deep caves. My people were dying in their millions, we had no choice but to hide. If we had not, you would have found our worlds empty. We would all be dead."

"I understand, but may I see this cave?"

Jutka was still and so were those with her. Bindar was about to apologise when she twitched her ears in agreement. "I will arrange it."

Brenda stumbled up the rock-strewn path and thanked James as he saved her from an embarrassing fall. She needed to keep her attention on the here and now, and not on the Markan'deya's upsetting images.

"Are you all right?"

"I'm fine, James. I wasn't watching where I was going. I can't help thinking about the Markan'deya."

"I know what you mean. I dreamed about it again last night."

"Me too," Brenda admitted though she had not been aware of James awakening. "Did you get a few hours?"

"Ummm, about four or five... minutes."

"Yeah."

Jutka led the way up into higher elevations until they reached a kind of plateau. A cliff-like wall of rock, the beginning of the mountain proper was a sheer barrier before them, but the so-called path did continue by turning hard right and following the base of the cliff. The plateau was a small flattish outcropping of rock with large boulders seemingly scattered around at random. Appearances can be deceiving however.

"We must wait a few moments to be recognised," Jutka said and sat upon a boulder with the aid of her friends. She was very old for a Shan and was tired.

"I do not see the Keep, Elder," Bernard said looking around. "Are we close?"

"Very," Jutka said dryly and her companions dropped their jaws in amusement. "You will see it soon, do not concern—"

A rumbling split the air and the cliff opened. Brenda watched in amazement as a huge section of rock slowly slid into the ground revealing a lighted passage that ran deep into the mountain's bones. Jutka rose to her feet and led them to the welcoming committee just now approaching from within the Keep. There was a moment of confusion as Jutka's companions moved ahead with the Shan equivalent of *The Box*. The newcomers were outfitted with earpieces and pickups so Brenda and her team might understand them.

"Honoured Elder," a Shan from the new group said. "Welcome to Kachina Twelve."

Twelve? Brenda blinked in amazement. The opening in the mountain was huge with the passage disappearing into the distance hinting at the size of this place. How many Keeps could there possibly be?

Jutka introduced Brenda and the others then introduced the leader of the newcomers. "—and this is Tei'Kerttu. She has the honour of being Tei for Kachina Twelve."

"Honoured," Brenda said with a bow.

"A very great honour," Bindar said.

"Honoured,"

"—noured Tei," James said.

"Honoured to meet you Tei, I have many questions," Bernard said.

"Welcome, welcome all," Tei'Kerttu said in reply. "Your wish, Elder?"

"Our new friends have many questions about our past,

Kerttu. I want you to show them what a Keep is, what it does, and how that is achieved."

"At your command," Tei'Kerttu said with a bow.

Jutka turned away and addressed herself to James. "I will leave you with Kerttu. She will see to your needs and your return to my home."

"Thank you, Elder."

Jutka and her escort left then and Tei'Kerttu took charge of Brenda and her friends. They were ushered inside in order to close up the mountain. Kerttu explained that the Keeps were always sealed to prevent detection. They should only be opened in an emergency, but an elder's word was law and this was a special circumstance.

Brenda followed Kerttu into the mountain listening to her explanations of what they saw. In a spare moment between questions, she asked what she had been wondering about.

"How many Keeps are there?" Brenda said. "I mean, this is Kachina Twelve. Is there a Kachina Thirteen or even a Kachina Twenty?"

Kerttu hesitated but her elder's words had been specific. "There is a Kachina Twenty," she admitted reluctantly. "There are hundreds of Keeps on Child of Harmony, and hundreds more on Homeworld. Some are even larger than Kachina Twelve, not many to be sure, but some. Forgive me for not saying more, but I am not comfortable discussing this."

"We understand Tei," James said and the others murmured agreement. "If we had such places, we too would keep the information secret. You have my word of honour that I will not reveal what I see here," he said and the others were quick to agree.

Brenda was not sure they should agree to that actually. They were here to learn about the Shan and report to the President and the Council. Swearing not to reveal what they learned was a little too much like disloyalty for her peace of mind. Unfortunately, it was obvious she would learn nothing further if she did not agree.

"You have my word, Tei," Brenda said a little late and felt guilty for saying it.

"I thank you," Kerttu said, "but I will not reveal anything that might compromise Keep security or their locations."

James was a little put out by that, but Brenda actually felt happier with the problem out of the way. If Kerttu did not reveal any secrets, she did not have to worry about reporting what she did reveal.

They had to stop briefly when they reached a huge vault door. Kerttu was required to input some kind of code to open it. The door reminded Brenda of an airlock from the outside, but when it opened she realised no air lock was ever built so strong. It was designed like a cork. It was round and stepped down in diameter with the largest size outer most.

"That is the biggest blast door I have ever seen!" Sheryl said in awe. "How heavy is it?"

"I do not know," Kerttu said in surprise. "I am a warrior not an engineer, but I am sure I could find out for you."

"No, that's all right." Sheryl said as the door completed swinging open.

Kerttu led them inside and the door slowly swung closed with a hiss of compression seals. "This is a vacuum chamber. If ever the door is attacked, it is hoped the lack of atmosphere in here will prevent the shock being transmitted to the inner door."

"It has never been put to the test?"

"A prototype was tested in the outer belt where it was bombarded by the fleet. The results seem to indicate the inner door can resist a ten-megatonne detonation but only as long as this chamber remains uncompromised. Should the outer door succumb, there are two more of these chambers to breach before the Keep itself is breached."

Sheryl was an engineer chosen to join the contact team to evaluate the Shan's technical knowledge. If anyone was qualified to judge the effectiveness of the Keep's defences, it was she.

"An impressive system, Tei, but have you hardened the Keep against other forms of attack?"

"Such as?"

"Were this on an Alliance world I would expect to see shields, heavy weapon emplacements, and perhaps even nano assemblers."

Kerttu was interested. Her ears were pricked forward and her nose was twitching as if she scented something on the wind worth her time. "Weapons we have, but I do not know what shields and nano assemblers are. You must explain these things to me."

"I would be honoured to do so, but to understand my discipline you would need to study for many orbits. Let me see if I can simplify what I mean," Sheryl said with a frown. "Nano technology is simply the use of microscopic robot machines to perform pre-programmed tasks. We use them for all kinds of things from performing intricate surgery to building components for an Alliance dreadnought. In your case, you could use them to repair damage to the door the instant it was detected by the nanites. If set up properly, they can be used to reverse the damage even as it is occurring, which would increase the life of the defence this door represents."

Kerttu's nose was twitching and it was obvious how pleased she would be to have nanotech to enhance her defences. "And the shield?"

"That is both easier and harder to explain. Shields are three fold. First is the physical armour to withstand impact forces, but you have that. Alliance armour is designed to resist energy weapons as well. The surface of the armour should be as reflective as possible to deflect the beams, and finally we have shield generators, which produce extremely intense magnetic forces using the jump vanes of a ship to deflect charged particles. Shields are best used on spacecraft, but they can be adapted to work in a planetary environment... after a fashion. They are rarely used in atmosphere, and to be blunt Tei, I would not recommend doing so."

"Why not?"

"Because, should the unthinkable occur, the generators could be destroyed liberating all the energy they have stored. Aboard ship there are ejection mechanisms and blow out panels to reduce damage, but within your mountain here it would be a disaster."

"Dangerous indeed, Sheryl." Kerttu said. "More dangerous than it is worth surely?"

"Not aboard a warship going into harms way, Tei. A ship without shields would be easy meat for the Merkiaari."

"Our fleet does not have these shields, but the Murderers will not find them easy."

"I did not mean to imply—" Sheryl began as she realised that her comments could be taken as a condemnation of Shan defences.

Tei'Kerttu's ears twitched. "Be at ease. I have heard the Alliance will help us in many ways if we join."

"That's true," James said as the inner door opened and they progressed further into the Keep. "You have done wonders here, but with the help of the Alliance I believe you will create many more."

Brenda smiled at James's eloquence. He had come a long way from the shy professor of history she had known back in Oxford. Somehow, James had become the unofficial leader of their group and he was good at the job.

Kerttu escorted them through each of the blast doors and vacuum chambers and into a lift that went down deep below the mountain. Brenda stepped out of the lift and into the Keep proper. It was truly huge just as she had guessed. Sub-level one was the equivalent of twenty stories below the main entrance, a very long way, but there were ten more levels containing living areas, workshops, hydroponics, schools, weapon storage, life support, kitchens… everything needed for the Shan to live separated from the surface for years.

"Each level is hardened against penetration by the Murderers and can survive independently of the others for as many as four turnings."

"Only four days?" Sheryl said in disapproval.

Kerttu's ears flattened to her skull at Sheryl's tone. "That is the maximum time we estimate it would take the Murderers to find and kill everyone on a single level. If we cannot re-take the infested level in four days, my people would be dead and more life support capacity would be pointless."

Brenda moved to the safety railing that edged the walkway and looked over into the abyss. The floor was so far down it was almost out of sight. She thought she could see water shimmering down there, but could not be sure. She counted the levels down and came up with all ten, but the visible sections were as nothing compared with the areas hidden in the depths of the mountain.

In the roof of the cavern were huge lights, but most were unlit, the orange glow coming from those that were powered was just enough to see the details. In the centre was a huge round pillar gleaming metallically; it reached from the roof all the way down into the depths.

"What is that?" Brenda said pointing.

Kerttu joined her at the rail. "The core; power generation, water recycling, and primary life support. My control room is there and of course the security centre including barracks and weapons storage."

James moved to the railing beside her and leaned over the edge. "I assume you have enough weapons for all your people Tei."

"There are weapons caches on each level, but all my people carry their own. Everyone knows they are to bring their beamers with them when the time comes."

"So it is true," Bernard said. "You do train all your people to fight."

"It's true. Only cubs below the age of five orbits and those too old do not fight."

"The central area is too open," Sheryl said. "A bad weakness in the Keep's design. It provides a possible access for

Merki wishing to move from one level to another."

Kerttu dropped her jaw in a grin. "Any Merki showing itself would die instantly. The core is the most heavily guarded section. Do not be fooled by what you see here. The Keep is on power down. When fully activated these walkways can be sealed off—see the shutters?"

Brenda looked up at the overhead. Along the edge of the walkways were heavy looking blast shields that could drop down just past the railing she was leaning against. The effect would be like adding a steel wall along the walkway to create a corridor with no other exit from the level but the lift.

"If the shutters are breached the Merki will find themselves under fire from every quarter by automatic weaponry controlled by security."

Brenda squinted at the walls trying to make out details. They were too far away to be sure, but she could see dozens of hatches that she assumed housed beamers and other weapons designed to protect the Shan. Brenda nudged James when she noticed the others drifting away to follow Kerttu, and he left the rail to join them.

Brenda took one last look at the cavern before trotting to catch up.

* * *

18~Doomsday

It was a small thing at first; a barely detectable blip on a display in the heart of a heavy fang that had alarms wailing. Moments later, the alarm was silenced when the ship was blown to pieces by capital ship missiles.

The destruction of *Vasuk* was noticed, and the Shan fleet turned to investigate. It took the destruction of another heavy fang for the horrible truth to dawn.

The Murderers had returned.

Tei'Kerttu hurried into command central, and stopped to stare up at the huge screen displaying a system wide scan. Glaring red icons winked at her as they advanced in system, while a pitifully small number of cool blue ones, heavy fangs of the Fleet, moved to intercept them. She shivered in dread. There were so few. Even counting the light fangs and the Human ship, the Murderers outnumbered them.

The elders had yet to contact her, but already it was obvious what must be done. The Murderer's ships outnumbered the Fleet. She must proceed with the assumption that landings would take place. Her hackles rose and her tail lashed in agitation. She hoped to be proven wrong, but it was safer to err on the side of caution. She dragged her eyes away from the screen, and looked over the railing at the floor below the command platform she stood upon. There was no overt panic among her staff, but she could feel it all the same. Everyone was tense. She heard it in their whispered announcements and reports, saw it in the cant of their ears, and scented it upon the air.

"Bring us to alert status one," she announced.

For just a moment, all eyes were focussed upon her, and silence greeted the announcement. The order was hardly unexpected under the circumstances, but to actually hear those words was something everyone had hoped never to hear. An almost audible sigh swept command central, punctuated by her staff turning back to their consols.

"I hear," Kon'Tirun said from behind her, and keyed a security sequence into a terminal. Tei'Kerttu moved to join her.

Throughout the keep, alarms sounded and personnel ran through corridors to arm themselves. Thousands of warriors threw on their harnesses and checked their beamers, while technicians closed circuits long dormant. Lights throughout the facility came up full, punctuated by the still strobing emergency beacons that had been designed to lead people deeper into the keep's protected environment. Pumps began pumping, air filters long unused within the deepest levels of the keep, began filtering out non-existent radiation and poisons. Nonexistent, but perhaps not for long—the Murderers of Harmony were coming. Blast doors rumbled open throughout the keep ready to accept the millions of frightened people destined for Kachina Twelve, while above ground, hidden within the surrounding forests and hills, missile silos powered up awaiting the launch command.

Tei'Kerttu watched in silence as her command centre came to life around her. Lighting remained subdued, but the view screens provided more than ample with which to see. One section remained dark—fortress control. Its operators watched their comrades working from a sea of darkened screens. Their section was by far the largest. It commanded awesome firepower, yet they remained inert.

She flexed her claws and made a decision. "Power up orbital defence net."

"I hear," came the quiet response from Kon'Danu at fortress control, and the lonely island of darkness was gone, replaced with busy paws and flashing symbols upon computer screens.

Another huge viewscreen burst into light overhead. This one was a diagrammatic representation of Child of Harmony. In orbit of the planet, huge fortresses were even now powering up—their computers and weapons running complex self tests. Fire control computers reached out to their brothers in the neighbouring fortresses until, with their defences now linked, Child of Harmony was ringed with targeting sensors reaching into the depths of space looking for something to kill.

Tei'Kerttu watched as one after another, the fortresses populated the viewscreen, but suddenly her attention was taken by another screen showing a situation map of the Kachina Mountain range and its hidden keeps. Kachina Eight was fully online according to the information displayed. One through six were at alert status two, well on their way to full activation that was alert status one. Blinking icons, representing still more keeps, informed her of facilities still at power down.

"This is not happening fast enough," she growled. "Any word from the elders?"

"No, Tei," Kon'Tirun said. "Should I try to contact them again?"

Tei'Kerttu tapped a claw in irritation upon her panel. "Why are so many keeps still at alert three?"

"It takes time, Tei. We were already at alert two because of the Humans."

"Too long... it's taking too long! Contact Kajetan. Insist that I speak with her if you must, but hurry."

"Yes Tei," Kon'Tirun said and her paws flashed over her panel.

* * *

Aboard Naktlon in orbit of Harmony

Tei'Varyk crawled through the opening followed by Tei'Colgan. "...and from here back to ammunition storage bays. Should it happen that this area is breached, the transfer system is fully automated."

"Very impressive, Tei. I'm thinking our R&D people could learn a few things here."

That pleased him greatly. Tei'Varyk was proud of his new ship and was glad to hear others found merit in *Naktlon's* innovations. *Naktlon* was the newest and most powerful heavy fang ever to leave the shipyards. He was just about ready for testing. Kajika had howled in pleasure when he saw the size of his ammunition storage. He had three times *Chakra's* torpedo capacity, and twice his energy range. *Naktlon* was the most combat capable heavy fang yet built. Even so, Tei'Varyk secretly missed *Chakra*. Many of the crew had stayed with Tei'Unwin, and he missed them. He was thankful the command crew had come with him in its entirety.

"When do you plan on taking her out?" Colgan said.

"*He* is ready now," Tei'Varyk corrected. "Kajetan has ordered a patrol of the outer asteroids."

"Good choice. You can test his guns out there."

He flicked his ears in agreement. That was the main reason for choosing the asteroids. They were a perfect testing ground for this kind of thing.

Tei'Varyk led the way through the ship towards the command deck. "Let us see what James is doing."

"You know, when my people arrive to talk with the elders, I'll most likely be ordered outsystem."

"Where will you go next?"

Colgan shrugged. "We had just jumped into an unexplored system when we received your transmissions. We'll go back to finish our survey. It's roughly thirty light years from here. *Canada's* mission is exploring new systems, cataloguing what we find and sending the data back to the Alliance."

"It must be an amazing experience. I would give anything to be there with you."

"Perhaps one day you will be."

Tei'Varyk grinned. "I look forward to that day. What is the name of the system?"

"The one I was exploring?" Colgan said and Tei'Varyk flicked his ears in agreement. "It doesn't have a name. We use catalogue numbers. There are billions of suns, and perhaps seventy percent have planets; too many to name my friend. Even our capital system has a number, though it has a name as well of course."

"Ah?"

"Earth is the capital world of the Alliance as well as homeworld to the Human race."

"And the system?"

"We call it Sol, named for its sun."

"Sol?" Tei'Varyk sounded the name experimentally. "A good name."

Colgan smiled. "We like it. I've not heard the name of your sun."

"It is simply The Sun. What need for another name when it's the only one?"

"When your fleet journeys beyond Shan space, your people will find new homes and will name them as we have done."

"And the Great Harmony will be reborn," Tei'Varyk said almost seeing that day. "Not in my lifetime, Tei'Colgan, but perhaps my cubs will see it."

"Perhaps it will be sooner."

"Let us hope." They entered the command deck. Jozka was at his station talking quietly with the maintenance crews.

"Jozka?"

"Tei?"

"Where is James and his people?"

"They have just landed, Tei."

"Landed? Landed where?" Tei'Varyk said looking back at Colgan who shook his head. "Why was I not informed?"

"I did not know you wished to be," Jozka said. "Have I failed you?"

"No. I should have asked you to inform me. Where have they gone?"

"Zuleika... should I contact them?"

Zuleika was a city on Child of Harmony. The main port was located nearby on the coast. The city was a very fine place to visit and he was glad James would see it.

"No. Continue your duties."

"I hear," Jozka said and turned back to what he had been doing.

"It seems we have missed them."

Colgan shrugged, and then grinned. "Not to worry. Ships are my passion, not cities."

"I hear," Tei'Varyk said with a jaw-dropping grin of his own. "Perhaps you would like to go outside?"

"Love to. It just so happens that I have my helmet with me."

Tei'Varyk twitched his ears in amusement. He liked these Humans, more and more. "Let us go now..."

Jozka yelped in surprise. "Tei!"

Tei'Varyk spun away from the hatch, and was back at Jozka's side in three strides. His heart sped when he saw the shock on Jozka's face. "What is it?"

"The Fleet just went to alert one," Jozka gasped quivering in shock at the news.

"What does that mean?" Colgan said to Tei'Varyk's back as he hurried toward his station.

"Sound alert," Tei'Varyk snapped as he sat in his chair and brought his station's screens to life. "Alert one is war,

Tei'Colgan."

A siren growled throughout the ship making hackles rise. The crew stared at each other in disbelief. The ship was at power down and still docked. Moments later their training took over, and they scrambled to get to their stations.

"But who are you fighting? Not... not my people," Colgan said in a shaken voice.

"I don't know yet."

"Tei'Colgan?" Jozka said sounding more composed now. "A message from your ship: We are coming."

Colgan blinked. "Is that all?"

Jozka flicked his ears. "That was all."

"Contact them and ask for clarification, please."

"Tei?"

"Do it," Tei'Varyk said and turned to Tarjei. "Give me a full power scan. Jakinda, go to internal power and disconnect all umbilicals."

"I hear," Tarjei said and quickly bent to the task. "Scanning at full power and resolution."

"I hear, Tei," Jakinda said. "Umbilical disconnect in progress. Main power online. The station grapples are not under my control, Tei."

Tei'Varyk chewed his whiskers in agitation. He pointed a claw at Jozka. "Fix that."

"I hear," Jozka said and tried to contact the stationmaster just as Kajika ran onto the command deck and took his place.

"Bring all weapons online."

"I hear, Tei," Kajika said panting from his run. "Primary and secondary weapons at standby," he said and then snarled a curse under his breath. "Feed jam on magazine two!"

"Unjam it," Tei'Varyk hissed. "Tei'Colgan?"

"What the hell is happening?" Colgan said. "Where's my ship?"

Tei'Varyk pointed a claw at one of his screens. "There is *Canada*, but look here."

Colgan bent to look. *Canada* was manoeuvring, obviously intent on making rendezvous with *Naktlon* to pick him up, but it was the host of glaring red icons on the edge of the system that claimed his attention.

"Jesus…" Colgan hissed. "We're outnumbered."

Tei'Varyk agreed. "Could they be your people?"

"Have they tried to establish contact?"

Tei'Varyk looked the question at Jozka.

"Nothing yet, Tei, but I have more bad news. Two heavy fangs are reported missing. *Atarah* and *Vasuk*."

"Not my people's doing, Tei. Absolutely not my people," Colgan said anxiously.

"Jakinda, status?"

"Thrusters at station keeping, Tei. Ramp and grapples retracted."

"Break dock!"

"I hear. Manoeuvring thrusters engaged. Port ten…" Jakinda said as his claws danced over his controls, and Naktlon smoothly eased away from the station. "Thrusters ahead one third… we have cleared the station."

Colgan leaned down again. "I need to be on my ship, Tei."

Tei'Varyk knew how Colgan felt, but he had other priorities right now. "Set a course to join the Fleet. Jozka, any word from the Human ship?"

"They say they will match our course and speed. They ask permission to send a cub lander for Tei'Colgan."

A Human lander would not be able to dock with *Naktlon*, but it could come alongside and pick Colgan up if he was willing to chance a spacewalk. Knowing Colgan, Tei'Varyk was sure he would be.

"Tell them to hurry."

"I hear."

* * *

ZULEIKA, CHILD OF HARMONY

For Shima, that orbit had already been the most memorable of her short life. She had moved her entire world to Child of Harmony—her research, her home, Chailen. Everything was here. Her father was the only thing missing, but even he was just a short flight away. He had taken up his duties on Hool Station now. It was ironic really. Tahar had told everyone that he worked aboard Hool Station, and for orbits he had lived the lie. In reality, he had been working on an ultra secret project. The FTL project was no longer a secret. It had failed, and the research teams were disbanded. Now he really did work on Hool.

Her move to Child of Harmony was important enough, but it was nothing compared to the momentous news of first contact with another alien race. She had watched the broadcast announcing contact with the Humans. Everyone had of course. Every Shan in the Twin Worlds had watched spellbound as Kajetan explained in detail just who these strange creatures were, and why they had come. Her calm tones were at odds with the historic news. Shima had been fascinated by it all, but others were afraid. There had been disturbances. Frightened people had run in every direction expecting alien landings at any moment. Thousands had fled into the mountains. Every keep was inundated by frightened people seeking sanctuary. It had taken a string of broadcasts by the Council of Elders to calm the situation. Every warrior and every ship was on alert, they said. Be not afraid, they said. Humans are our friends, and they will speak to you soon.

And they had spoken.

Shima had lived through those days hardly able to work for fear she might miss the next broadcast. Kajetan said the Humans had been studying them so that they might speak well enough to make themselves understood, but for now they must use devices they had brought with them. The translators were not perfect, she warned, but with time and patience on both sides, understanding could be achieved.

A Human male with two names had spoken first—*two names!* Jeff Colgan was his name he said, and he was Tei for his ship. *Canada* was his ship's name, and it was built for exploration among the stars. He went on to introduce some of his crew, and it was a female named Janice Bristow (*two names again!*) who had explained about the Alliance.

Broadcast followed broadcast, as each day led to greater understanding between Shan and Human. Alien names and faces were memorised by cubs, just in case the chance to meet one occurred. Everyone knew at least one Human name, and many knew them all. Some even had their favourite Human. Shima liked James Wilder for the way his name sounded, and for his deep voice—so alien it was. Then came the day that everyone had waited for. A message was sent to the Alliance inviting another ship to come. No doubt it was important, but by that time she had been hearing the call of her work again. She could not stay away any longer. Her life, and the lives of her co-workers settled back into normality and harmony. The Humans were relegated to an interesting topic to discuss in their spare time.

Shima was hard at work writing her report on variant three-one-five on that fateful day. It had proven itself the most promising variant of grain she had yet worked with. Genetics was still in its infancy, but already the benefits of hardier grain with higher yields was eagerly anticipated. Weather patterns differed greatly, and mean temperatures were higher on Child of Harmony. Food crops from Harmony did not prosper so well here, but if variant three-one-five was any indication, that would not always be so.

—successful. I therefore recommend assigning Area Six to variant three-one-five. If, as seems likely from available data, variant three-one-five prospers in the unprotected environment of Area Six, I can foresee farm trials beginning with next orbit's

growing season—

"...must get to the keep!" a voice screamed followed by crashes as something smashed. "Quickly, take this and this... where's Shima? Has anyone seen Shima?"

Shima looked up in irritation at the noise. She rose to see what had caused it, but just then her terminal chimed announcing an incoming call. She hesitated a moment, but decided to take the call first. She would see what the fuss was about later.

She pressed the 'accept call' button on her computer. Her work was automatically saved, and then replaced by the image of her father. His ears were flat and his eyes were... she had never seen fear on her father's face, but she knew it all the same. When she heard the booming voice in the background of the transmission, her heart sped as her own fear leapt to match his.

"...levels Six through Eight. Levels Nine through Twelve will evacuate via Red Sector..."

"Thank the Harmonies!" Tahar yelled over the frantic announcement. "You have to get out of Zuleika!"

"What? I don't understand," Shima cried. Behind her father, she saw people running by. "Are you all right? Is the station in danger?"

"Listen to me," Tahar said in a hard voice. "Forget about me. This place is finished. All that matters is you and Chailen. She is with you, yes?"

"No. She's visiting friends. What do you mean forget about you? What has happened—" the door behind her slid aside. She spun in a defensive crouch with her lips rippling back in a warning snarl.

"Shima," Adonia gasped from the open door. "For Harmony's sake what are you doing? We have to get to a keep!"

Shima's ears were plastered tight against her head, making her almost deaf, and her vision was tunnelling. She desperately fought the hunt/kill reflex of her people, and tried to stop the rumbling growl that was forcing its way up from her chest.

"Shima!" Tahar cried as he was buffeted by running people. "The cities near the ports will be hit first. You have to get as far away from Zuleika as you can. The Fleet is fighting to give us time to evacuate the—"

The screen cleared and the calm face of Kajetan appeared.

"My people," she said solemnly. "I have just been informed that the Fleet is under attack, and that our brave warriors are fighting for their lives. From the descriptions received, we believe the Murderers have returned. Our allies, the Humans, have vowed to stand with us and fight. Tei'Colgan informs me that a drone to the Alliance will be dispatched at once, but the Human fleet will take time to reach us. I am therefore ordering a system wide evacuation. Please assemble at your evacuation zones for immediate transport to your assigned keep. I say this to the warriors among you: Protect our young ones, and may the Harmonies be with you all."

The screen cleared, but Tahar did not reappear. The report Shima had been working on suddenly blinked back to life on the screen awaiting her input. She turned away, and forced herself to walk calmly out of the room, when all she wanted to do was run.

"Wait, Shima. Where are you going?"

"Zuleika," she said dully.

The Murderers were coming, and her father was dead. He had no chance aboard an unarmed station and he knew it. That was why he had called her instead of trying to escape with all those running people. Those poor people. Forget about me, he said, but she vowed she would not—not for as long as she lived.

"...heard what she said. The cities are not safe."

"I don't care. Chailen is there. My only sib is there!" she said angrily. She should have demanded that Chailen accompany her to work that morning, but she hadn't. "I'm taking number three," she said jumping into the car.

"You can't do that!" Adonia snapped. "What about the rest of us? We have to evacuate."

"You have the other three. Take the loaders too. You might as well save the grain while you're at it. If any of us survive, we will need it. Three-one-five is stable."

Adonia gaped. "Good idea." She ran off shouting about saving variant three-one-five on the loaders.

Shima lifted off and accelerated hard to gain altitude. She ignored the local traffic pattern to cut straight toward Zuleika. An alarm sounded when her course and speed were noticed, but she didn't care about fines. She shut down the guidance computer and its alarm. She knew the way, and flew the car as if guiding a missile.

She had to find Chailen. Nothing else mattered.

Zuleika was surprisingly orderly. There were heavily armed warriors at every intersection directing people to their evacuation zones. It would take longer than they had to evacuate the city completely, but there was enough time to get the young ones and their mothers out. Shima hoped so anyway.

She had no way of knowing what was happening elsewhere in the world. Had the Murderers already landed? She glanced around through the domed glass of the car. Somewhere up there her father was waiting to die along with thousands of others. The Fleet was fighting and dying to give her time to find Chailen, and she would do that. She would not fail her father or those who were even now dying to protect her.

Shima landed outside her home, and entered to find it empty. It was exactly as she had left it when she awoke this morning, but it felt different—abandoned already. No one had been here. She was certain. Wherever Chailen was now, she had not had time to collect her beamer.

Shima stripped off her harness. Digging tools and seed would not be needed for a long time, if ever. She dropped it on the floor unheeding, and put on her hunting harness.

The knife and other things might be useful. Her beamer lay beside Chailen's weapon in the drawer. The box held spare energy cells and a cleaning kit. The charger was too bulky to carry, but she secreted the spare cells into every available space on her harness, and quickly attached both holsters. She felt uncomfortably weighed down. The harness was not heavy even yet, but it felt cumbersome. It had never felt so before, it had always fit her like a second pelt, but the addition of the holsters made it look like a warrior's harness. She wasn't a warrior.

She felt... wrong. Just wrong.

Wrong or not, she wouldn't give them up. If she was to find and protect Chailen, she would need the beamers to fight the Murderers. She took off her vision enhancer and looked blearily around her home. She never wore it on a hunt, but this was different. Shima wished again that she did not need it, but wishing did no good. She put it back on and left her home for the final time. She doubted that she would be back.

The street was empty when she reached it. Shima couldn't believe that someone had taken her car without asking permission. That just wasn't done. She stared at where she had parked it as if expecting it to reappear, but of course it did no such thing. She studied the street both ways, and then set off for Sharn's house. Sharn was Chailen's closest friend. They did everything together. Tahar had suggested that Chailen and Sharn might mate next orbit. Shima secretly thought so too. They were a good match and she was jealous. Shima hoped that was also a secret. She thought it was, but Chailen had a way of surprising—

CraAAAAacK! CraAAAAacK! CraAAAAacK!

Shima ducked instinctively. She had never heard a noise like it. She looked around, but saw nothing that could be responsible for it. Then she looked up and trembled. There were dozens and dozens of Shan flyers chasing a huge ship.

CraAAAAacK! CraAAAAacK! CraAAAAacK!

The noise came again, and this time Shima knew what

it was. It was the sound of a flyer's lightning weapon. Those huge beamers could smash buildings into molten rock, but the massive alien ship continued on its way unaffected. The Murderers were making their landing right in the city... no, they were going for the port, just as Tahar had predicted. Shima was relieved and felt guilty for it. There must be people at the port. They would die. Yes, but she wouldn't and that meant Chailen would not. Whatever happened, Chailen must not die.

She was all that mattered now.

Shima ran on.

* * *

Hool Station, in orbit, Child of Harmony

Tahar ambled along the echoing corridor alone with his thoughts. He didn't want to watch all the screaming and crying people trapped on the docks. There had been easily three times more people on the station than they had ships for.

He wished he could have just a little longer with Shima. She lacked confidence in herself and still needed him. Chailen was more resilient for all she was the younger. Ordinarily he would have no concerns for her. She would have comforted Shima at his death, but the situation was not ordinary. With the Murderers in system, he could only hope that his children would find some way to survive.

Tahar turned down another corridor toward a place he remembered, they served the best meals on the station, when he heard it—the sound of a cub whimpering in fear. He stopped and listened for the sound again. His ears swivelled and pricked up. The sound was coming from his left. He opened the hatch and a pair of frightened eyes looked up at him.

"Hello," he said trying not to frighten her. "Are you all

alone?"

Her tiny ears flicked and quivered only half erect. "I came back for my present. It's my name day, but now I can't find my sibs."

Tahar swallowed the howl of despair he wanted to voice. All the cubs had left first. Their parents had followed packed to the bulkheads in an old ore transport. It was hoped some would survive that way. Staying behind was certain death.

"Not to worry," he said with false cheer. He bent to pick her up. "You can stay with me until your mother comes." He hugged her tight where she clung around his neck. "Are you hungry?"

"Can I have anything I want?"

"Anything at all little one," he said continuing on his way.

"Even Shkai'ra?"

His ears twitched. "You like that do you?"

"Yes."

"We can have that then," Tahar said cheerfully. "I have cubs you know. They like Shkai'ra too. I used to take them hunting when they were your age."

Tahar and his new friend died holding each other. They did not eat Shkai'ra. The Merkiaari guard ship smashed the station before they reached the dining area.

* * *

Shima streaked along the road on all fours. She had never run like this. She had never needed to. Her people were fast, just how fast she was only now coming to realise. Her ancestors had known of course. An empty belly had often goaded them into such bursts of speed as they attempted to take down Shkai'lon on the run—a particularly foolish thing to try under other circumstances. Shima had motivation for her speed, but it wasn't an empty belly. She had Merki warriors on her tail—

not literally thank the Harmonies, but they were close enough to make speed essential.

Sharn's home was already abandoned when Shima had arrived, but at least she now knew where to look for her sib. When she had searched the house, she found the computer blinking a message.

Kachina 12... Kachina 12... Kachina 12...

The blinking message could only be for her. At least, Shima wanted to believe that Chailen had gone with Sharn's family to the keep. She had to believe it. If Chailen was in the city alone, Shima would need exceptional good luck to find her. No. Chailen was sensible, more sensible than her older sib. She would have seen the need to evacuate with the others.

With a scrabble of claws, Shima made the turn into another street without tumbling into a sprawling heap. She had lost some speed there, but she soon made it up. Thank the Harmonies she had not lost her vision enhancer. Without it, she would not be able to run like this for fear of getting lost.

And she did need to run.

Merkiaari warriors had landed at the spaceport despite all the warriors could do to stop them. A single huge landing ship had settled there, ignoring the Shan flyers pecking at its shielded hull. The underground missile silos had been another matter entirely. It had not ignored those. As soon as the enemy ship was in range, a row of switches had been flipped deep within the mountain's bones at Kachina Twelve. The switches closed, and missile after missile was launched from dozens of underground silos. The parks and open fields suddenly erupted with fire as the Merki computers tracked the missiles and found the launch sites. Barely half the missiles launched in time, and none struck their intended target. Every one of them died uselessly against Merki point defence laser clusters.

Shima had witnessed the launches and the results. Later,

she saw the Murderers in the flesh, and that was the real reason for her speed. She still didn't know why she had done it. She wasn't a warrior. She was a scientist—a gardener for Harmony's sake. Why had she felt the need to kill that particular Merki? Was there a reason to choose that one over another? She decided there wasn't. The thought of her father trapped on the station had enraged her. Tahar was stuck up there waiting to die, while his Murderers were down here looking to kill everyone and everything he loved.

She had been so angry. She had watched the Murderers from hiding, and her vision tunnelled with her rage. She had spat trying to get the taste of Merki out of her mouth. Their reek was everywhere. She had gone deaf—her ears were flattened hard against her head. It was a holdover from the primitive past. A Shan's ears would flatten as a way to protect them from an enemy's shredding claws. She saw nothing but the Merki warrior standing in front of the others. The next moment, she was firing both beamers into his back. She didn't remember drawing them or even aiming. One moment was tunnelled vision with her prey centred, the next he was falling, and she was running with a beamer in each paw. Merki warriors gave chase of course.

Now she was racing through the burning city on all fours trying to lose them, but they had some kind of device that could follow her at a distance. She would have to hide. Running, though absolutely correct according to instinct, was no good in this situation. She needed a place to lay low and attack from concealment. When night came, she would find a way out of the city.

* * *

19-Desperate Measures

"Fire as your guns bear!" Colgan shouted over the noise of damage alarms.

"Multiple contacts," Commander Groves sang out. "Contacts closing fast. Tentative assessment: Merki cap ship missiles."

Colgan froze for an instant. "For God's sake bring us around, helm!"

"I'm trying, sir. She's sluggish as hell."

"Drones have entered fold space," Lieutenant Ricks reported. Out of ten launched, only two had survived long enough to make the jump to fold space.

Point defence missiles sleeted out in their hundreds to meet the incoming missiles. Proximity fuses closed, and detonations pocked the tactical display. Dozens detonated to kill a single missile, wasteful as hell, but cap ship missiles were beyond dangerous. Some of *Canada's* counter missiles killed each other as the force they unleashed washed over nearby missiles on their way to kill their targets. Some lost lock or failed to detonate for one reason or another, but most did their jobs as designed. Most wasn't good enough.

Canada's laser cannons left off their programmed fire mission, and swivelled under computer control to pick off targets that evaded her point defence missiles. It was an awesome sight, and a frightening one. When a ship's computer aborted offensive fire in favour of defensive, that ship was in over its head. Lasers designed to penetrate the armoured hide of a Merki destroyer, flicked out and wiped away one missile after another. The energy in those beams was so huge, that the missiles were vaporised instantly, leaving the beams to stream onward into space for the milli-seconds it took the computer to take note of the kill. Priorities changed, and the mounts swivelled their cannon onto new targets.

"Where's *Chakra*?" Colgan said as *Canada* finally responded to the helm and healed over. She took the single hit on her undamaged starboard shields and rolled drunkenly out of the nuclear fire boiling around her.

"Shields holding," Ivanova cried. "Merkiaari cruiser bearing zero-two-seven by two-seven-five degrees. Target locked. *Firing!*"

Canada spat her own missiles, and changed course heading away from the threat of return fire. Colgan studied his displays looking for something he could kill. He found one.

"Helm, new heading: one-two-eight by zero-one-five."

"Aye, sir. Coming to new heading, one-two-eight by zero one-five."

"*Chakra's* burning, Skip," Groves said from her place across the bridge at scan. "I can see escape pods jettisoning."

"Christ," Colgan hissed under his breath. "Where's *Naktlon*?"

"She's still on our tail, Skipper."

Colgan nodded, thankful for small mercies. Tei'Varyk was covering *Canada's* damaged rear while his people struggled to repair the shield generator for that quadrant.

"Concentrate all fire on the heavy cruiser," he snapped and saw *Naktlon* was already doing that. Tei'Varyk and he thought alike.

Canada went to maximum rate of fire on all energy batteries as she ran by the crippled cruiser. Ivanova used raking fire from her forward mounts, opening the Merki ship like a tin opener opens a can of soybeans, but she kept her starboard batteries concentrated on the ship's drive section.

The eruption when it happened was catastrophic.

"*Evasive,*" Colgan snapped as the Merki ship disintegrated, and chunks of its hull flew outward.

A section of drive shielding slammed into *Canada,* but her shields held and she continued her turn. *Naktlon* miraculously escaped damage as he swept through the wave front of shrapnel. *Canada's* scan fuzzed and the display flickered, as her computer fought to penetrate clouds of metal and ice particles. Data denoting headings and vectors of enemy ships, constantly changed colour, flickering indecisively between the red of certainty and the amber of estimated values.

"What's left?"

Commander Groves studied the battlespace her station was displaying, and then looked up from the plot grimly. "*Naktlon,* bearing one-eight-zero. *Hoth,* bearing two-zero-five. *Hekja,* bearing two-zero-five."

The bridge crew fell silent.

"Three ships?" Colgan said in shock. "Three heavies... what about light units?"

"*Chakra* was the last one, Skipper."

"Word just reached us from the elders, sir," Ricks said. "They've ordered evacuation of the towns and cities."

Colgan paled. "My God. We can't stop them."

Silence greeted his shock statement. Colgan studied his displays and saw three Shan heavy cruisers and *Canada.* They were all that stood in the way of the remnants of a Merkiaari squadron. That the Merki hadn't sent a fleet made no real difference, or that the Shan had destroyed most of their heavy stuff. There was still more than enough firepower to take out the entire system. Four heavy cruisers, or what would be a heavy cruiser in the Alliance—who knew or cared what the

Merki called them? All four had battle damage, but nothing severe. Screening them were the light units—three fast attack frigates, and two badly damaged destroyers.

"Send to all remaining Shan ships," Colgan said.

"Ready, sir," Ricks said switching his position to use the Shan equipment installed next to his station.

"The elders have ordered evacuation of the population to more secure areas. I suggest we concentrate our ships, and attempt to break for the inner belt. If successful, we can strike as opportunity permits."

Ricks listened intently for a reply. "*Naktlon* on screen."

"Tei'Colgan," Tei'Varyk said wearily. "I have spoken with the others. We will join forces and attack as soon as the Murderers are in range. I advise you to return to pick up James and the others. If you're quick, you might escape."

"Don't do this, Tei," Colgan pleaded. "Don't throw your life away. My people will *come!*"

Tei'Varyk's ears struggled erect, but then flattened again in distress. "Not soon enough to save us. Leave us to our fate, Tei'Colgan. Warn your people that the Murderers will come for them next. Good bye my friend. May you live in harmony."

The screen cleared to show a tactical schematic of the system. Merki ships burned red as they advanced cautiously toward the Shan homeworld, and three blue blips manoeuvred to engage. *Naktlon* moved away from where he had been covering *Canada*, and left her to voyage on alone.

Colgan glanced unhappily at Commander Groves. She nodded her agreement with Tei'Varyk. "Charge the jump drive," he ordered and winced at the looks of shock he received.

"We can't leave them," Lieutenant Ricks blurted. "For God's sake, you know what they'll do to these people. We can't *let* it happen!"

"As you were, Lieutenant," Groves snapped.

Ricks surged to his feet, and slammed a fist down on his

consol. "No! I say we stay and fight. We're Fleet. Fleet fights Merki!" He stared at the others, demanding they agree, but no one did. They looked guiltily down or away, not willing to meet his accusing eyes.

"Helm," Colgan said reluctantly. "Set course for the third planet. We have the contact team to retrieve."

"Aye, sir. ETA, two-niner minutes at max speed."

"Very good." Colgan turned to Ricks. "Contact Professor Wilder, and tell him to come back up as soon as we're in range. He can dock on the fly."

Ricks sat slumped at his station in dejected silence, and stared at Colgan with accusing eyes.

"You heard me, Lieutenant," he said angrily.

"Aye, sir," Ricks said, sitting straighter and turning back to his controls.

Colgan looked around at his crew, but none would look him in the eye. Didn't they realise he had to leave, even though he might want to stay? He did want to, but *Canada* would be destroyed to no purpose. If he could be certain that his ship's sacrifice would save the Shan, he wouldn't hesitate, but he knew it wouldn't.

"Continue on course," Colgan said and stared bitterly at nothing.

* * *

Aboard Naktlon, Shan system

Tei'Varyk glared at the tactical situation on the main viewer as the Murderers advanced. His people were silent, having made peace with the fact they were about to die. The fleet was gone, all except *Hekja*, *Hoth*, and his own *Naktlon*. Fifty orbits of work gone in a single cycle, and only three ships remained to save the Shan.

They had been so close to gaining the stars, but the Humans had come too late. One orbit earlier, just *one orbit* might have made the difference. He sighed into the silence, and watched *Hekja* and *Hoth* attempt the impossible. They had all agreed it was the only chance that two damaged heavy fangs had to disable the murderer's ships, but it was a slim chance only. If it worked, *Naktlon* would move in with every weapon firing at maximum. If it did not, *Naktlon* would move in with every weapon firing at maximum.

There were no choices left.

"*Hoth* and *Hekja* engage," Tarjei said into the silence.

"I hear," Tei'Varyk said. "We will go in with all weapons firing at maximum. Torpedoes, missiles, particle cannon, beamers—everything."

"I hear," Kajika whispered.

"Are you sorry you chose to follow me?"

Kajika's ears flattened. "*Never.* You are my Tei."

Tei'Varyk inclined his head, and Kajika bowed in return. He turned back to the screen in time to see *Hoth* and *Hekja* accomplish their part of the plan.

Two heavily damaged heavy fangs entered the Merki formation at preselected points knowing they would not emerge from the other side. They went in with every weapon reaching out to rend the Murderers of their people. Heavy fangs were awesome weapons. Torpedoes spat from every surviving tube as the ships absorbed hit after hit from the Merki ships. The torpedoes were set to lock onto any Merki target, and hundreds did that. Two Merkiaari battleships blew apart as two hundred torpedoes, each having a two megatonne nominal yield, detonated as one. Space went mad as ship after ship was rent and spat out of the nuclear fire smashed beyond recognition. *Hoth* blew apart from the results of her own fire. *Hekja* reeled, bent and broken but still under control. He trimmed course and rammed a Merkiaari heavy fang. Both ships disappeared in the flash of ruptured fusion cores. With them went a light fang.

They had failed.

"Three heavy fangs and two lighter units remain," Tarjei

reported.

"Which are the most severely damaged?"

"Both light fangs appear unable to keep pace with the heavies, but all are still combat capable."

"It doesn't matter then. We kill the ships with the most Murderers aboard."

"I hear, Tei," Kajika said. "Targeting heavy fang... target locked."

"I hear," Tei'Varyk said and waited in silence. "*Open fire!*"

Naktlon erupted in fury. His torpedo launchers went to rapid continuous fire attempting to saturate the defences of his chosen target. As the range closed, his beamers and particle cannons spoke. The Merki heavy cruiser blew apart, but even as she did, missiles infinitely more powerful than any Shan torpedo hammered *Naktlon* closer to destruction. Closer and closer, but finally the fire ended and he was still there. Though battered and bleeding atmosphere, he continued to pour fire into the remaining Merki ships.

"Magazines destroyed or depleted," Kajika reported.

"I hear. Continue with all remaining weapons. Kill them all," Tei'Varyk ordered, as his ship slowly died around him.

Naktlon bucked and reared at the centre of nuclear fury sent by the Merki. He was blinded to starboard, and nearly so on his portside. His great engines propelled him into the heart of the storm to kill his enemies even as he was hammered into uselessness.

"Take out those honourless light fangs," Tei'Varyk said, as they pecked away at *Naktlon's* armoured hide.

Kajika did not respond, but *Naktlon's* particle cannons swivelled and targeted first one, and then a second light unit. Both blew apart as energy beams designed to strip the hide from a Merkiaari dreadnaught ripped through them.

"Target the next—" Tei'Varyk began, but that was as far as he got.

Naktlon, broken and barely making way with a single drive, was hit amidships. The beam sliced through deck after deck, killing his crew and severing control runs. His particle cannons locked and fell silent, as power cables were turned to slag. His remaining torpedo launchers, had they ammunition, would have been useless as power runs to the launch rails were cut, but by far the worst damage was to his fusion room. The beam reached the core of his reactor, and *Naktlon* erupted with super hot plasma eating everything in sight. Blast doors slammed and alarms screamed, but it was all for nothing.

Naktlon broke in two.

* * *

ABOARD ASN CANADA, SHAN SYSTEM

"He did it," Colgan whispered as *Naktlon* broke apart. His aft section blew up in a flare of plasma, and his forward section tumbled wildly away.

"Not quite. Two heavies remain operational, Skipper," Groves said. "One is critically damaged. The second has moderate damage."

What do I do?

Colgan stared at tactical trying to make a decision. "Time to pickup?"

"ETA is one three minutes, sir."

Colgan clenched a fist and pounded his thigh in frustration. Thirteen minutes. If he picked up Wilder, the enemy would be thirteen minutes closer to the Shan homeworld, leaving him even less room to manoeuvre.

"Set an intercept course," Colgan said finally, and a sigh swepped the bridge. "Weps, I want that piece of scrap out of my sky." He highlighted the critically damaged Merki ship with his wand. "Do that first. Then pump everything we have into the other one."

"Aye, sir," Ivanova said eagerly. "Targeting solution locked in. Time to target... two niner minutes... *mark*."

"Run a plot on *Naktlon*. There may be survivors."

"I didn't see any pods jettison, Skipper," Groves warned.

"Just do it."

"Aye, sir. I have him."

"As soon as we hit the range, I want maximum rate of fire. Don't stop until they're dead or we are."

"Aye, aye, Skipper," Ivanova said.

Canada raced into battle, and the moment arrived. Missiles flew from her, adding more acceleration to that imparted by her launch system. Merki point defence missiles and laser clusters attempted to intercept them, and *Canada's* tactical display was suddenly populated with detonations. Only a third of Ivanova's missiles made it through. Merki decoys deployed attempting to suck the missiles off target, but they could not save the first cruiser, which blew apart after only two hits by the megatonne range missiles. The second Merkiaari ship however, was almost untouched.

Canada deployed her own decoys, and ECM hashed targeting sensors trying to blind the Merki sensors, but for all of that she wasn't a true warship. Her counter measures and weapons were designed to hold off an attack for the minutes she needed to jump, not defeat a heavy cruiser with more than three times her firepower. *Canada* bucked as lasers and grazers slashed at her. Her shields held, but still she was shaken and slammed by incoming missiles. Point defence frantically beat them back, killing dozens and then hundreds, but then the inevitable happened. A missile got through and detonated.

Canada lurched and damage alarms screamed; yet her section seals held and she continued to fight. Crewman fought to save friends trapped in the debris, but all too many died from the sudden decompression when razor sharp shrapnel careened through compartments breaching their uniform's integrity. On the bridge, Colgan was white faced at the catalogue of damage being reported. His ship was being destroyed before his eyes, and it was his fault. He could have jumped outsystem, he still could if his displays were correct, but no, he had to be a hero and his people were paying for it with their lives. The lights dimmed, and flickered back to half intensity as something failed. He looked up wondering if this was the end, but as the lights failed completely, emergency lighting took over.

"Report," Colgan barked.

"Merki cruiser badly damaged, but still combat capable," Ivanova said. "We're down to one more salvo of missiles and our lasers."

The lights suddenly flared bright again as damage control repaired the power feeds to the bridge, but Colgan hardly noticed.

"Save the missiles until I give the word. Continue action with energy mounts."

"Aye, sir."

"Helm, take us in to point blank range at max. I want you to scrape the fucking paint off her!"

"Aye, sir," Wesley said and rolled ship.

"Weps, give them every missile we have at point blank."

"Aye, Skipper."

"Are you sure, Captain? We'll not escape the blast wave," Commander Groves said.

"We will." Colgan prayed he wasn't lying. "We're going in at max. With luck we should be clear."

Canada bore in taking hit after hit. Her shields began to fail even as she reached the cruiser. Ivanova smashed a button flat, and *Canada's* missile tubes spoke. The Merki ship shuddered and spewed atmosphere, as the missiles slammed home before any defence knew they were there. Hit after hit went home as the ship tried futilely to track *Canada* as she raced on by.

One of *Canada's* missiles did not launch; the power runs to the accelerator rings in the tube were down. Chief Williams, trying vainly to resurrect the shield generator for the aft quarter, was up to his elbows in circuitry when he knocked a severed cable. He jerked and bit his tongue with a yelp as the current arced through him. He survived with his hair smoking and standing straight up, his team barely survived his cursing, but the Merki cruiser had no chance. The missile spat forth and slammed into the enemy ship. So close was *Canada*, that the missile actually penetrated the Merki's hull before it detonated within the ship.

The enemy ship erupted in nuclear fire.

Canada was racing away, but she did not escape unscathed. Pieces of wreckage impacted her unprotected aft quarter. Blast doors slammed, but many closed upon compartments already open to space. In all too many cases, those compartments were crewed by dead men and women now. *Canada* rolled presenting her port shields to the wave front, and that saved her. The fury of exploding magazines and fusion reactors washed over her, but as it receded, she limped onward with two drives down, and one fluctuating so badly that it was cut from the circuit a moment later.

"Target destroyed," Ivanova reported, her voice heavy with satisfaction.

"Good," Colgan said. "Very well done, Weps. Francis, pass the coordinates of *Naktlon* to the helm."

"Aye, sir."

"Course laid in, sir," Janice Wesley said a moment or two later.

"Execute at best speed." Colgan turned to Lieutenant Ricks. "Get me damage control."

"Aye, aye. On screen, sir."

Chief Williams appeared on the main viewer. Behind him, he could see space suited figures hurry by.

"Chief, I know we have damage all over the place, but I want you to concentrate on the jump drive. We seem to have won the war here, but I don't trust that. I want to be able to jump if I have to."

Chief Williams frowned in puzzlement and looked aside at his boards. "But there's nothing wrong with the bloody…" his face flamed. "There's nothing wrong with it, sir."

"Are you sure?"

"Yes, sir. My boards show it's operational *and* charged. Have you tried it, sir?"

"No of course not," Colgan said, his face heating in embarrassment. He had assumed that after the pounding they had taken, it must be offline. "Carry on, Chief."

"Aye, sir," Williams said in a puzzled voice. He was replaced on the viewscreen by a tactical overlay of the system.

"What happened to his hair?" Groves said with a grin. "It looked like someone tugged him through a mouse hole backwards."

Colgan chuckled.

"*Naktlon* dead ahead… what's left of him," Janice announced.

"On screen."

Everyone groaned when they saw what was left of *Naktlon*. The forward half of the cruiser was tumbling away on a course that would see him exit the system eventually. It was so badly battered that Colgan doubted there could be survivors.

"Try to contact him."

"Aye, sir," Ricks said doubtfully, but a moment later, a fuzzy picture appeared.

"Tei," Colgan gasped in relief when his friend appeared. "Hold on, I'm coming to get you out."

"Tei'Colgan. You should have left when you had the chance," Tei'Varyk said in a dead voice.

"We destroyed the last one for you."

"And what of the ships landing troops on Harmony?"

"*What?*" Colgan yelped and turned to Commander Groves at scan. She was punching in commands at her station like a demon.

"Do not *Canada's* sensors reach so far? *Naktlon's* are destroyed, but we're still receiving intermittent transmissions of the landings."

"Oh my God," Commander Groves said looking up from her position at scan in horror. "We have Merkiaari in the inner system, Skipper. They must have slipped through when we went after those two cruisers."

"Class?"

"Troop transports with escort, but they're too much for us. A kid with a slingshot is too much for us now," she said bitterly.

* * *

20~Hope

"He left us," Brenda said with tears of rage in her eyes. "After all we did for him, the bastard left us."

"He had no choice," Janice said sadly. "None at all."

James nodded. He glanced through the open hatch at his friends sitting in the cabin and then back to Janice. "What do we do?"

"What *can* we do?" Brenda spat. "He abandoned us."

"We hide as the Shan are doing. I want a gun," Janice said staring at the images coming in on the monitors. "A very big gun."

James turned back to watch the Merki landings on one of the lander's monitors. The cities were a chaos of running and fighting people. The Shan military had deployed to slow the Merki troopers down while the cities were evacuated, but the Merki had the advantage of being able to pick and choose their landing sites. The Shan had to remain mobile and not dig in, or else risk annihilation from above. Shan civilians had banded together to fight, and were dying in their millions as untold numbers of Merki gravsleds poured out of the grounded landers. The gravsleds spread out and flew slowly down the streets firing at anything that moved. James was sure they had their reasons for hitting certain buildings while leaving others untouched, but for the life of him he couldn't understand their tactics. The buildings seemed chosen at random. Some collapsed immediately burying those hiding within, while others burned. Clouds of smoke and ash billowed up and filled the sky.

James felt his emotions welling up when the monitor showed him heaps of dead Shan. They lay where they had fallen still clutching their mates and cubs. The picture suddenly whirled crazily and then stabilised. Whoever was manning the camera was taking a hell of a risk. The picture blurred and zoomed in upon a gravsled just turning into the street. On the ground in front of it, a large formation of Merkiaari troopers led the way. Suddenly they came under fire and scattered into cover. Explosions dotted the street zeroing in upon the gravsled. It was hit multiple times and lost power. It slammed into the street carving a trench in the road before rolling and bursting into flames. A Merkiaari trooper jumped out of the shattered wreckage waving his arms and roaring in agony. His armour had not protected him from the flames, his entire body was alight. His fur fed the flames until another trooper shot him in the head.

James changed to another channel, and flinched at what was being shown. Someone was hiding in a building and filming the street outside. The scene could have been culled from any one of a thousand newsreels shown during the Merki War in the Alliance, except this one starred Shan not Humans. He had no idea which city was being shown, or on which planet. It didn't matter. Similar scenes were being played out everywhere the Merkiaari had landed. He reached out to select another channel, but Brenda stayed his hand.

"I need to see it."

He was reluctant, but hiding from the truth wouldn't help matters. He nodded and watched trying not to let Brenda see what he was feeling.

Merki troopers were firing into the packed street cutting Shan down by the hundreds. They fired their plasma rifles and gauss cannons non-stop. Blood coated every surface until it looked as if some mad artist had painted the street red. James covered his mouth with a hand and swallowed sickly, trying not to vomit. He glanced at Brenda only to find her crying silently. The camera shifted. It focused on the other end of the street, where Shan bit and clawed at Merki troopers in a desperate attempt to escape slaughter. He watched a huge Merkiaari female grab a Shan cub and tear it in half above her head. She did the same thing to an adult a moment later when he attacked her. He might have been the cub's father. There was no way to know.

"Oh God, Oh God, Oh God…" Brenda chanted. "Please make them stop…"

James shook his head. Nothing would make them stop. They would come here next… if they hadn't already. He craned his neck to look at the sky through the cockpit windows. It was just blind luck he had chosen to visit here, and not Harmony while the Merki chose the opposite.

"What are we going to do?" Brenda whispered unable to look away from the horror.

"Hide, that's all we can do. Hide and fight when the time comes." James flicked switches bringing the navigational computer and sensor arrays online, and then started the engines.

"Where are we going?"

The lander lifted and hovered over the landing pad.

"The mountain keeps. It's the only place."

"Will they let us in?"

"I hope so," he said and concentrated on flying low. He had no real idea if the Merki had sent ships to Child of Harmony, but if they had, he wanted to stay low and unobtrusive. "Better go back and tell the others what's happening."

"I'll go."

"Thanks, Jan." James glanced at Brenda's tear streaked

face. "It will be all right."

"No it won't," she whispered. "They'll kill everyone on Harmony and then they'll come here and kill us."

There wasn't anything he could say to that. She was right.

Flight time to the keep was less than an hour. He could have reduced the time to almost nothing if he had dared boosting for orbit, but that would have been suicide. He flew fast and low, with the shuttle's sensors on passive. The Merki troop ships were huge things, and they showed up clearly whenever he got within range of one. The gravsleds were insects in comparison, but their drive systems used a lot of power. As long as he concentrated hard on their output, the sensors gave him just enough time to divert wide around them. To James, the hour seemed to crawl past, but eventually his destination loomed ahead of him.

The mountain range would have been impressive if he hadn't been looking for a landing place without being shot down. On his final approach, he had to bank sharply when targeting sensors locked him up, and sirens wailed throughout the cockpit. With his heart pounding fit to give him a heart attack, James checked his monitors and reluctantly turned back. He never wanted to go through that again.

"I'll have to land in the foothills."

Brenda grunted unhappily, but she didn't object as he set down not far from the tree line. "I'll collect some supplies."

"Tell the others to grab the Box. We're going to need it."

"Yeah," she said in a subdued voice.

James waited for everyone to climb out before he eased the lander off the ground, and slowly worked his way under the trees. It was a tight squeeze, but he managed to get under cover before he ran out of places to go. He landed and quickly shut down the engines. He powered down everything he had access to. He had no idea how stealthy the lander was, or how easily the Merki might find it, so he did his best to make it invisible. The only thing left was the maintenance system, but he couldn't shut that down without risking being unable to restart it. Besides, he didn't know how.

He jumped to the ground and keyed the hatch closed before resolutely turning away, and leading the others toward the mountains. At first he set a fast pace, but he soon realised the others were out of condition. Their progress slowed to a crawl. He said nothing, but Brenda could see his concern.

"They can't help it."

"I know," James said. "I didn't say anything."

"No, but I could feel you thinking it."

He laughed and hugged her to him as they ambled through the woods. "How did it happen?"

"What?"

"How did we happen so fast? We've known each other for years, but we've only really known each other for a few months."

"I guess it must be love," Brenda said.

"Must be," James said and kissed her.

"Really," Bernard said, with an exasperated sigh. "Must you two do that at a time like this?"

"What better time?" Janice said eyeing Bernard with speculation that made him flush. "There might not be much left."

Bernard nodded sombrely. "Did you know that I'm unmarried, dear lady?" he said with a grin, and took Janice's hand for a kiss.

"Why, sir. You do take liberties. Do it again."

"Delighted," he said and obeyed.

They made their slow way through the forest. James walked with an arm around Brenda's shoulders. Janice and Bernard held hands chatting and laughing quietly. Bindar walked alone carrying the Box, closely followed by Sheryl and David. They were not a couple, but they walked arm in arm seeking mutual comfort in unknown surroundings. The other members of the team walked in a nervous knot through the shadows of the forest. All had packs on their backs containing a few meagre supplies, but none had anything close to a weapon.

The forest was densely populated with trees and heavy undergrowth. More than once they stopped in fearful silence listening to something rustling in the brush. On closer inspection, they found traces of some kind of animal, and from then on they were more watchful. As the sun lowered in the sky, James called a halt and they made a cold camp. He explained that having no idea whether the Merki were near, he didn't want fires lit and perhaps attracting them.

"What about the animal tracks we found?" David said peering nervously into the trees.

James peered into the darkness uneasily, but then he shrugged. "There's nothing to be done, David. I think we'll be safe enough. The tracks were shallow. Probably made my something small."

"You hope."

"Yes, I hope."

After eating a meagre meal from the emergency rations they had brought from the shuttle, James lay down with Brenda snuggled up close to him. It was a pleasant night, thankfully not cold, but he found himself unable to sleep. What had happened to *Canada*? Had she been destroyed, or had she jumped outsystem as Brenda believed? He hoped it was the latter, but he doubted Colgan would do that without a very good reason. Maybe he went for help. If he did, they wouldn't see any for a couple of months, plus however long it took to assemble sufficient forces to contest the system's ownership. He had no doubt Admiral Rawlins would want to fight, but would the Council let him?

He hoped so.

The next morning they set out again. As before, James led the way and they were soon out of the forest and into the foothills. This was the most dangerous part. There was no cover here, and if anyone looked down at the right time they would be spotted. Their pace fell to a crawl as they struggled into higher elevations and gasped for air. He relieved Bindar of the Box, and continued his stumbling way ever upward. Brenda took a turn for an hour, but although the Box wasn't heavy, it was an awkward size, and struggling up a steep trail with it took its toll. Around midday, James began actively looking for one of the entrances to the keep. Sheer rock walls and rubble strewn goat paths were all he found. Did this planet have a goat analogue?

"I know it's here," James said worriedly. "She showed me right to it, but it looks different."

"Are we lost?" Brenda whispered as the others sat down to rest.

"No-no," James said quickly.

"We are, aren't we? If we are, you would tell me right?"

"We're not lost. I think they might have sealed the keep already."

"Oh."

After a short rest they moved on until they entered a canyon that looked very familiar. The sheer cliff-like walls towered high into the air making James feel very small. He found a distinctive outcropping of rock below which the entrance to the keep should have been, but when he reached the rock face, there was no evidence that it wasn't a natural rock formation. He ran his hands over it, trying to feel any difference in texture or temperature... anything that might reveal the entrance, but there was nothing. Bernhard waved him over, and pointed out a peculiar pattern in the rock. James nodded. It *was* the right place, he remembered the pattern. He pressed an ear to the rock trying to listen, but he couldn't hear a damn thing. The Shan had designed it that way, and they did fine work.

"Anything?" Bernhard said. "This looks right to me."

"Yeah, I'm pretty sure they've sealed up the place."

"Well then," Bernhard said cheerfully. "All we have to do is sit tight and wait. I'm sure they must be monitoring the area."

James nodded. It made sense. "What if they don't open

up?"

"They will," Bernhard said, his smile slipping. "They won't leave us for the Merki."

"I hope you're right."

As it happened, Bernhard was right but for the wrong reasons. The night came, and a grumbling earth shaking noise split the silence. A dozen Shan warriors slipped out of their mountain fastness levelling beamers at them. James stood, and they nearly shot him when a rock shifted under his foot causing him to lurch toward them.

"Don't shoot," he cried in badly accented Shan. "We need sanctuary from the Murderers. Please, for harmony's sake take us in."

One of the warriors edged forward. "I am Tei'Nelrik. You are the beings called Humanssss?"

"That's right."

"Your ship, he fought well for us. You may enter."

James sighed in relief, and gestured everyone into the keep. Brenda stayed by his side. "Brenda, this is Tei'Nelrik. Tei, I'm called James."

Tei'Nelrik bowed. "Honoured. Quickly, we must seal the mountain lest we be sniffed out."

"Yes, you're right." James ducked into the opening.

It was pitch dark inside. The blast door rumbled into place and the lights came slowly up. Hundreds of beamers were levelled at James and his friends. They stood absolutely still while Tei'Nelrik explained the situation. Ears twitched in recognition, and slowly the weapons were put up.

"I thank you for opening the door for us," Brenda said carefully. None of the Shan they had yet seen were equipped with the new translators.

Tei'Nelrik's ears went back then struggled erect. His tail lashed from side to side betraying his agitation. "We did not open for you, but for us. If the Murderers had seen you, they might have found the keep."

"I see," Brenda said sounding a little put out by that.

"We understand, Tei," James said. "Can you tell me more of our ship?"

"The Murderers have the only ships in system."

"The Fleet?"

"Gone, and so is your ship. He fought well."

Tei'Nelrik led the way into the mountain. The others moved to follow leaving James staring at Brenda in stricken silence. They were here to stay.

* * *

21~Extermination

Shima lost her pursuers after a long chase. In the end it was through no action of hers that the Merkiaari lost interest in a single reckless vermin. No, they had something more interesting to do apparently.

Shima kept running, but she no longer felt panic forcing her on. She had the wit to think and plan again, and perhaps the time to do it as well. She slowed her mad dash and focused her thoughts upon the Harmonies, sensing the insanely dark minds of the Murderers behind her, knowing they were tracking something more to their liking now. Probably more of her people, Shima realised, and felt guilty for her part in bringing the Murderers here. The hateful alien mind glows felt like poison, it hurt deep in her head to watch them this way. Any member of the healer caste would recognise the jagged edges and dark colours as something requiring the attention of mind healers... *if* the afflicted had been Shan, but the Murderers were alien and insanity was their natural state. The horror of such a thing was so vast, Shima could hardly conceive of it. Youngling lessons did not do the reality of the Merkiaari justice.

Shima snarled and her jaws snapped, biting the air in mindless fury when her inattention dropped her into a fight for her life. Stupid, stupid, *stupid!* Her father would be ashamed of her for letting what was behind her distract from what lay ahead. And what lay ahead was bad, very *very* bad indeed.

Shima tried something she would never normally do, but her situation was dire. She had been running on all fours, not at her best speed but close; now she needed her hands. Badly. She forced herself up onto her hind legs without slowing, snatching desperately for the beamers holstered securely on her harness, and staggered forward trying not to sprawl tail over nose into the chaos.

Snarling and screaming people fought for their lives against Merkiaari warriors in the street while Shan warriors sniped at the grav sleds from the buildings. Merkiaari gunners in the sleds returned fire and buildings burned. Beamers flashed back and forth, people died hideously burned or missing limbs, their blood painting the ground red. Others fought with tooth and claw carrying the Murderers of their cubs and people down into death with them. There must have been hundreds of people already dead and more were piling up as the Merkiaari's superior weapons raved, sweeping the crowd with unstoppable destruction.

Trying to slow down, change her stride from a four legged run into a two legged one while arming herself proved too much for Shima. Her right hand grasped a beamer but to her dismay it squirted from her grasp. She had never dropped a weapon. Never! But it had happened now and at the worst possible time. She staggered forward trying to regain balance, but she was unable to keep her feet under her. Already falling, she did manage to turn onto her right side so that her left hand could finish reaching for her other beamer. The impact jarred her to the bone, her speed was such that she slid along the road losing fur and skin, but the burning pain of abrasion was nothing to the disaster that befell her next.

Her vision enhancer flew from her face and skittered away.

Tahar had made it for her with love in his heart, but how she hated that thing. The visor-like device marked her as defective, a cripple among her people, and she loathed it, but now was not the time to be rid of it. Without it, she was as near blind as it was possible to be. Instead of buildings and people, she saw dim shadowy shapes where they should be. She kept low and scrambled along the ground in the direction she thought the visor lay. Lucky she did, because the Merkiaari turned their weapons in her direction. She hissed as a hot wind blasted past her to hit a target behind her. Any closer and the beam would have crisped her ears or taken her head off outright. She couldn't see a Harmonies cursed thing now, the smoke from burning buildings choked her and dimmed the street so badly that everything blurred into a single hazy shadow.

Patting the ground and sweeping the road with her spare hand, she vowed that if she survived the cycle, she would nail the cursed visor to her head to prevent a situation like this ever happening again. She loved her father and would love him for as long as she drew breath, but she would never reconcile her need for his creation. Her current distress was a mere taste of what the future had in store for her, and she had always known and dreaded it. She would have given anything for a healthy pair of eyes right now.

Someone grabbed her and jerked her roughly back just as a building exploded in front of her. Shima gasped as the pressure wave sucked at the air and flinched as the heat of the sudden blaze slapped her face. She closed her useless eyes and turned away from the blaze. Even to her eyes, it was bright.

"Th... th... thank you," Shima gasped.

"Welcome," Shima's helper said. He sounded calm, but Shima could scent his fear and hear the panting of someone forcing himself to be calm. He took her free hand and wrapped her fingers around her visor. "This thing yours? What does it do?"

Shima's relief made her muscles go weak. She gripped the hated thing hard and tears of relief burst from her suddenly hot eyes. Her hand shook violently, but she managed to put the visor on. It was still working. Thank the Harmonies it wasn't damaged. She looked around and found a pale furred male watching her quizzically. He had pulled her into cover behind a smashed ground car and was about her own age she judged, but unlike her, his pelt was a startling light tan colour without any other markings. He would be very visible in the forest wilderness where Shima hunted, but almost invisible in the desert where she was sure his ancestors had roamed free. He was pureblood and very beautiful.

"It lets me see. My eyes are bad without it," Shima said, trying not to see the pity she was sure she would find upon his face. "My name is Shima. Thank you for helping me."

"Honoured to be of service, Shima. I am—" a huge explosion drowned out his words and they both cowered as debris rained down upon them, pattering upon the ground like hail. "I am Kazim, this is my ground car, but I fear I cannot offer you a ride in it."

Shima blinked at his dropped jawed amusement. "Perhaps some other time," she said. "You were driving when this happened?" The car was on its side and obviously damaged by weapons fire. It would never work again. "The Harmonies must watch over you if you were."

"Happily I was not inside when this happened. I caught the entire thing on camera. My supervisor was very impressed. She said it went out live."

That was when Shima's addled brain realised Kazim was not holding a weapon. It was a camera he was pointing at the fighting not a beamer. He was braver than her to calmly film the massacre of their people and not have a weapon out. Thoughts of weapons reminded her of the lost beamer.

Shima scanned the ground and found her missing weapon in the middle of the street. She glanced around, tensed her muscles, and sprang out into the open at full stretch. Kazim cursed in surprise at her move, but before he could do more, she had snatched up her beamer and had leapt back to join him.

"Next time warn me, I missed the shot," Kazim said doing something to his camera before panning it around at the burning buildings and fighting people. "That would have made for a very dramatic sequence."

"Do all journalists talk out of their tails the way you do?" Shima grumbled as she checked her weapons.

Kazim flicked his ears in agreement. "Most I would say. It's a very competitive environment."

Shima snorted. She wondered what Kazim's parents and sibs thought of him choosing the arts for his caste. She would wager a handsome sum that his clan did not have many people like Kazim within its ranks. Shima's clan had always specialised in science and engineering, and had done very well by that. She couldn't imagine what an itinerant life like Kazim's would feel like. Waking each cycle not knowing where he would go or what he would see, or even where he would sleep the next night. It was hard to imagine. Shima's life was orderly, and she liked it that way. Her research had logical steps and goals. She liked goals, and she liked knowing what to do to reach them. Her only goal right now was finding and protecting Chailen.

Chailen was all that mattered now her father was gone.

"We should get out of here," Shima said aiming at a particularly large Merki. Nice big target like that. Would be a shame not to take advantage. She fired both beamers into the alien, but felt only mild satisfaction as it died. She had Chailen to find. Killing Merkiaari didn't bring her sib closer. "This won't end well."

Kazim flicked his ears in agreement. "You go. I'll stay and film for a while longer."

"You want to die?" Shima killed another alien, this one a smaller example. A male she guessed if her lessons were right about females being bigger. "Haven't you seen enough here, don't you want to see what happens tomorrow?"

Kazim's jaw dropped in a laugh, and he abandoned his filming. He slid down behind the car and into cover. "You think there will be a tomorrow? Don't you know the Murderers landed warriors on Harmony too? These are the end times, Shima."

Shima's whiskers drew down as if scenting something foul. "You can't believe in that drivel. Prophecies are a product of delusional minds, Kazim."

"Look at them!" Kazim said gesturing toward the fighting. "How can you doubt this is the end?"

"Easily. My father taught me common sense! Our people survived this once, we will again. The Murderers won't take our worlds easily, certainly not today, Kazim. Don't you want to be there?" Shima took aim and fired both beamers, and added slyly. "Don't you want to film it all as it happens?"

Kazim waved his ears jauntily. "I should probably consider it my duty to record the end times, no?"

"Certainly! It would be a crime not to. Future generations of younglings are relying upon you, Kazim."

Kazim smirked, but his tail lifted to shoulder height and gestured acceptance. "No need to lay it on any thicker. I will come with you... where might that be and how do we get there?"

"Kachina Twelve... and ummm," Shima faltered and looked around for inspiration. "Through there," she gestured at the collapsed building closest to them."

"You're joking," Kazim said. "You do see the flames?"

"We can make it into the next district and find somewhere to hide until night. We can't stay here, Kazim. These people are brave, but they are not thinking."

"They have lost home and clan—"

"I know, I do not lay blame, but we must think long term not short. This is the first cycle of a new war. We will not win it in this street."

Kazim agreed reluctantly. "It feels wrong to leave them to

die."

Shima silently agreed but kept her thoughts to herself. They had made their decision to fight and die here. She had Chailen to protect, and did not have that luxury. There would be other times and other fights, she vowed, after she made Chailen safe.

"Follow," Shima said and ran in a crouch toward the burning building.

Behind her she head Kazim scramble to follow.

The rubble was easy enough to climb; it was the fire that made things interesting. She avoided the obvious dangers, leading Kazim wide around them, but she couldn't escape them all. Rubble shifted beneath her weight opening voids beneath that seethed with flame. The fresh air caused the fires to flare anew and Shima cowered away from them. The piles of masonry were hot beneath her paws and she flinched, her hands burned when she pulled herself up and then over the last barrier. Kazim hissed as he burned himself similarly, but said nothing as he rolled over the top and part way down the far side.

Shima scrambled after him. "You alright?" Shima asked him, his pelt was blackened and filthy now. As was hers. "We can't stop here."

"Fine... I'm fine. Just a little scorched," Kazim said raising his blistered paw. "You?"

Shima winced, that must hurt. Her burns certainly did. She ignored his question. "Come, we need to find somewhere quiet to hide until dark."

Shima led the way down and into the street. The sound of the fighting was muted here, and the district seemed all quiet. They stayed on two legs and ran directly away from the fighting, their ears flattening when larger explosions elsewhere in the city sounded. Shima used the Harmonies to steer them both from danger. Although they saw no one, they were aware the Murderers could appear overhead in their grav sleds, or march around any corner at any time.

Shima kept them moving, staying close to buildings and using them for cover as much as possible.

"You have a plan?"

Shima didn't, but no need to say that. "Of course. As I said, we will hide and travel at night. My sib is waiting for me at Kachina Twelve."

"Kachina Twelve," Kazim mused. "I was allocated Kachina Eight, but twelve is better. It's sector command for the entire continent; I should be able to get better access to information there."

"How do you know that?" Shima asked in surprise. "Not saying you're wrong, but that sort of thing is supposed to be secret in case the Murderers catch us."

"My mother's third cousin's best friend mated outside the clan. Big scandal at the time. He was always a little too adventurous. Any way, he mated a warrior caste female. Fierce little thing, you would like her... if you didn't kill each other first. You remind me of her."

"You calling me fierce?"

"Brave," Kazim corrected. "And you fight well. You killed those two Merkiaari as if you do it every day, but you're not warrior caste are you?"

"Are you interviewing me, recording are you?"

"Always," Kazim said without any sign of embarrassment. "You never know what will be important later. Not warrior caste, but something related I bet. Are you Fleet?"

Shima made a rude noise. "Hardly. I'm scientist caste. Agricultural geneticist."

"Ah..." Kazim sounded gratified. "I knew you were out of the ordinary. Such a new field, comparatively speaking of course."

Shima kept them moving at a good pace and pointed toward the outskirts of the city and the mountains that lay at least five cycles beyond it. The Harmonies let her know that others like her had the same idea of heading for the mountains. The district seemed deserted, it wasn't, but by the evidence of her eyes and ears it was. Many people were hiding in the buildings, lots of them underground where she would like to be.

"This one will do," Shima said and trotted through a nice relaxation grove to the door of a dwelling. "No one else is near."

"And that is important why?" Kazim said following her inside and panning his camera around.

"It's important because the Murderers have devices that can track us better than our best hunters could do. We need to stay away from large groups of people. No sense making it easier for them to kill us."

Kazim aimed his camera at Shima. "You did well in the fight earlier; can you explain how you came to be there?"

Shima's ears went back and her muzzle rumpled showing him her killing teeth. It was not a friendly gesture. "You think because we are no longer running for our lives that we are safe here? I don't have time to play to your audience."

Shima turned away, not caring that Kazim followed her still filming. At least he was quiet about it. She went through every room checking doors and windows, familiarising herself with the layout and every conceivable exit. She took her time and was methodical about it, as if this was one of her projects and would need to pass oversight inspections. The front windows overlooked the grove that she liked. In the growing season, it would be very pleasant to meditate upon the Harmonies out there. The rear windows looked upon a park, and she was very pleased. It was no wilderness, but there was still plenty of cover if she needed to flee, and more to the point it was in the right direction. Shima was too far from the fighting to sense the Merkiaari now, but they were out there.

She had always been very strong in the harmony given talents of her people, and that had given her an advantage today. Her father had taught her how to track and hunt; how to live and even prosper in the wilderness with nothing but a knife and piece of spark rock. Escaping pursuit even here in a city should have been easy, but it hadn't been. The alien's devices turned them into superlative trackers without needing the true skill of a hunter.

Shima stared into those trees and wondered who was hiding in there, perhaps staring back at this very window. From the evidence of her eyes, Shima and Kazim were the only two people left alive in the district, but using the Harmonies she was able to find many others hiding nearby. The gentle pastel coloured mind glows of other Shan were soothing to her frazzled thoughts after watching the dark insane-seeming alien mind glows of the Merkiaari for so long. She could tell some of them were sleeping, probably because they planned to travel all night. Others were alert, perhaps guarding the sleepers. She would have planned similarly in their place.

"Get some rest, Kazim. I will watch."

"I am not tired," Kazim protested.

"We will be travelling all night. If you don't sleep now, you won't get another opportunity for a few cycles. A seg or two now will help. You will be surprised by how much."

Kazim hesitated, but he switched off his camera and flicked his ears in agreement. "Wake me if something interesting happens, Shima. I don't want to miss anything."

"I will," Shima lied smoothly. If she woke him it would be because she was ready to leave or they were about to be discovered.

Kazim fell asleep quickly after making a nest in the corner of the room with pillows and blankets. Shima watched over him allowing her thoughts to slow and be soothed by his sleeping mind glow.

Tahar... oh Harmonies Tahar!

Shima clenched her jaws shut preventing the wail of grief escaping. He must be dead by now. Her father dead, it didn't seem real. He had always been there. He was timeless and unending... a foolish youngling's fancy. Shima snarled, disgusted with her self-pity.

He would tell her to focus on her own survival. He would

expect her to be strong for Chailen. Yes, Chailen was what mattered. Shima had to survive to find and protect her sib. She should search for things that might aid her she decided. Shima realised she should have done that first thing. Her failure to do that earlier when she looked around was testament to how rattled she really was. Her extended run and inability to lose the Murderers had scared her more than she had thought. Such a simple thing as searching for supplies should have been one of the first things she thought of.

She made up for her lack quickly and efficiently. Weapons, water, food in that order followed by luxuries. She had no plans to carry any luxuries, but perhaps medical supplies could be justified if small enough to fit on her or Kazim's harness. She dared not encumber herself too much; her speed had been the only thing to save her earlier, but Kazim needed at least a knife and preferably a beamer or two as well.

Shima did not find any weapons worthy of the name. Knives for cooking and other utensils could be used at a push, but she had two proper hunting knives on her harness along with her beamers already. She would give one of her knives to Kazim when he woke. She left everything as she found it and explored the other rooms. In one of the sleeping rooms, she discovered something useful in a cupboard. No weapons, the owners had obviously taken their beamers with them as they should, but like her, they had left the charger behind. She quickly swapped the energy cells in her beamers for new ones off her harness and inserted the old ones into the charger. She watched the indicators and nodded. It wouldn't take too long to top up the cells to full charge. Turning slowly on the spot, Shima wondered if there might be more cells here, but decided after a moment they would have been kept either with the beamers or the charger as Tahar had taught her to do. No doubt the owners had taken them and were safe now in their assigned keep watching the news and waiting to learn what the elders planned to do.

Shima's whiskers drew down as if tasting something

noxious. What could the elders realistically do? The Merkiaari were here on the surface in force, which meant the Fleet had been defeated already. That left only those in the warrior caste chosen to protect their people on the ground, or the permanent forces assigned to each of the keeps, to fight on. Shima had no doubt that everyone, adult or child, would fight when the time came, but that didn't make them warrior caste. They had their beamers and the training to use them, but no experience. Real warriors trained constantly and fought each other in huge complex mock battles. Warrior caste lived for the time they would be called upon to fight for real.

"Well, this cycle might seem like a dream come true for them, but I doubt they will think so tomorrow," Shima said to herself. She took a last look at the charger's progress, and left the room.

Shima found little that she wanted to take with her. She could hunt for food once out of the city, so she made no effort to gather some to take with her. Instead she gorged herself upon the bounty of Shkai'ra she found in the cold room, putting some aside for Kazim to eat later. The tender meat was one of her favourites, and together with fresh fruits and vegetables made a feast. She forced herself to eat more than she normally would, gorging until uncomfortably overfull. She had burned a lot of her reserve fat since coming back to the city and needed to replenish it. If she didn't eat more than her usual amount over the next few cycles, she would lose muscle mass. It was inconvenient but part of what it was to be Shan.

Her people had evolved to survive lean times in a number of ways. One was by consuming vast amounts of food in good times and building a reserve in the form of fat, the other way was a type of hibernation. Shan did not sleep like Shkai'lon did in winter, but they could slow their metabolism so much that the difference was hard to determine. But there *was* a difference and an important one. Shkai'lon were completely vulnerable while they slept the winter away, Shan were not. With their bodily functions slowed, it left their minds free to ponder the Harmonies and allowed their senses to wander far afeild. Hence they were forewarned of approaching danger. The ability was how so many Shan had survived the last Merkiaari invasion.

Shima spent the remainder of the cycle resting, readying herself for night and her escape from Zuleika. She forced herself to drink a lot of water and even managed a few more morsels of food when Kazim awoke to join her. She made him stuff himself and drink lots of water, and would not hear his complaints that he would not be able to run with such a full stomach. He would learn as she had just what a terrified Shan could accomplish when necessary.

In the end the only things Shima decided to take were her weapons, her harness, and a small water bottle she had found in one of the rooms. She didn't need anything else to survive the journey to the mountains, and if Kazim stayed with her, he wouldn't need anything either. She could hunt for two as easily as for one.

Shima was sitting quietly in the main living space in the trance-like state her father had taught her to use before a long hunt, when darkness fell. It was the best way to attune oneself with the Harmonies, and made her gifts easier to use. Stronger too. Her senses were always at their strongest when used this way. She noted the sleepers in the park and other nearby buildings were stirring, readying themselves to leave. Kazim had some ability with the Harmonies, enough to notice the exodus, but Shima said no when he suggested they go.

"Not yet, they are too many and might attract attention. We will give them a seg to clear our path."

"We don't know where they are going."

"True, but they will head for a keep and the nearest is in the Kachina chain. It's safer for them and us if we spread out. The gunners on just one of those grav sleds could kill us all in two bursts if we don't."

"Are you sure you're not warrior caste, Shima? You sound just like those I have met."

Shima noted Kazim's camera was active again, though he had tried to be discreet by holding it low in his lap. She said nothing. If his work comforted him, who was she to say no? She could wish for some comfort herself, but a gardener like her wouldn't be needed for a long time to come... or ever? Shima shook off the sudden chill that came over her. She was a scientist not a superstitious fool who feared gloomy thoughts would encourage them to come true.

"Not a warrior, sorry to disappoint. I'm a gardener."

"That's not all you are. There's more."

Shima's tail gestured a shrug and her ears flicked agreement. "There's always more. Scientist, agricultural geneticist, hunter, daughter of Tahar, sib to Chailen... the list is extensive for any of us."

"Interesting that you list hunter before daughter," Kazim said. "Why is that?"

"Tahar, my father works—*worked* on Hool Station. We spoke just before..." she waved a hand around. "All this. He was trapped up there with the others."

Kazim's ears struggled half erect. "I am sorry."

"So am I, he was a wonderful person and father. Many fathers died when the Murderers came. I'm not the only one to lose family."

"No, but sadness is not lessened by having company."

Shima agreed.

Kazim shifted and raised the camera. "Do you mind so very much?"

Shima felt like asking what he would do if she said that she did mind, but perhaps he was in the right with this. If her people survived the Murderers a second time, wouldn't it be a good thing to have a record of events? She couldn't see how her actions could contribute to Kazim's historical record of the second alien war, but who was she to say? Her youngling lessons had included trips to places like the Markan'deya where she was shown lowlier things than Kazim's recordings. Perhaps in the future his films would be played in the Markan'deya dedicated to this new war, and younglings would watch and learn about the true horror of war.

"I do not mind," Shima said, "But we must find you a beamer. I would give you one of mine, but I suspect you would be too busy recording the aliens killing you to use it."

Kazim laughed. "You are right. When I heard what was happening I fetched my camera first thing. I did not even remember my beamer until after my car blew up."

Shima was secretly appalled by Kazim's admission. How any Shan could be so lax when the Merkiaari breathed the same air with him was frankly incomprehensible to her. Everyone was taught Shan history. No one could be unaware of what a fresh incursion would mean to them, their families, and their clans.

"I see I have shocked you." Kazim said ruefully and Shima agreed with a flick of the ears. "Tell me the story of our meeting, Shima. Tell me of your father and how you heard about the murderer's return, and I promise to kill the next alien I see before trying to film it."

Shima did.

* * *

22~The Wilderness

"... and we stopped here to await the night," Shima finished her recitation of events noting how dark the room was. "And now we go, Kazim. It's full dark, time to leave the city."

Kazim did something to his camera and rose to his feet. "Do you think the others are far enough away?"

"I hope so. I will look ahead when the time comes and steer us away from anyone I find."

"You are strong in the Harmonies, Shima. I noticed before but didn't want to ask."

Shima knew what he wanted. "No, they did not invite me. My uncle is Tei, but my eyes..." Shima gestured 'what can you do' with her tail. "The clan-that-is-not has certain expectations and standards I do not meet."

"I'm sorry."

"It's an old hurt, but seriously, I'm not sure what I would say now if they did invite me." Kazim regarded her sceptically. "I mean it. I love my work; I would not want to give it up."

"You wouldn't have to. As Tei your choice of profession is yours to make and no other can gainsay you, not even the elders have that right."

"Oh I don't mean that, of course I would follow my heart and stay in my caste. No, it's the expectation that as Tei I must lead the others. I would have no time for my own research projects."

"Hmmm," Kazim said sounding unconvinced.

Shima wasn't surprised. Tei were honoured and held up before all as the epitome of ambition. But she had secretly held the view for quite some time now that it must be a very tiring way to live. People's expectations could be draining. It would take a very strong person to live that way, which was yet another reason to admire them and venerate them. The word Tei meant 'one who leads' but the true meaning was farther reaching than that. Being Tei meant leading others by example, motivating others by one's own actions to strive, to be better than they think they can be. The clan-that-is-not held a special place in Shan society, one that even the council of elders did not equal.

"It's time we were gone," Shima said leading the way out the back and into the night.

Shima didn't hurry into the park. Stealth was preferable to speed now. She used all her skill to move silently amongst the trees, and tried not to sigh audibly when Kazim made a noise. He wasn't loud but compared to her silence he seemed it. Her skill was her father's, taught to her from almost the moment she could balance on two legs. Kazim could not be blamed for being lesser in this. He was competent, no worse than average, and all Shan were hunters by instinct. It was just that her instincts and skills had been honed to a fine edge.

She said nothing.

"Sorry," Kazim hissed under his breath, sensing her tension. "It's been a while for me."

"Nothing to be sorry over," Shima whispered back. "I hunted often with my father."

"You are very good at this, all of it I mean, not just the silent stalk."

Shima did not answer. She supposed she was good at it in

a way. She did not doubt her ability as a hunter, for her father would be remembered by his clan as one of their greats despite his demurrals, and she took for granted her harmony given gifts would not let her down. They never had before so why would they now? No, Kazim was right, but being good at it did not mean she liked the necessity right now.

They travelled through the park and beyond into the last district of the city. Fires illuminated the streets, and revealed only the dead. The Merkiaari warriors had swept into the city via this district using the road from the port to speed their way. They had destroyed many of the buildings, though not all, and their targeting puzzled Shima. The buildings had no strategic value that she could see, they were just simple homes.

Kazim was grim as he used his camera to record everything they saw. He almost seemed to will Shima to comment on the massacre of their people. She walked amongst their dead and said nothing. What was there to say? Should she say it was horrible? It was, but saying it did not change anything. Should she point to this or that person, this or that dead youngling... and say what? Vow vengeance maybe. Perhaps Kazim was silently vowing it now, calling upon his ancestors to witness the oath. Swearing by his clan name even. Shima said nothing and vowed nothing, but she knew deep in her heart there would come a reckoning. Once Chailen was safe, surely it would not offend her father's kah to come back and claim a little justice for his death. He would not approve of anything that put her in danger of course, but surely he would understand her need to fight. Any Shan would.

"We need to move, Kazim."

Kazim nodded. "There is nothing we can do for them and there are too many to send to their ancestors properly."

"They will find their way to them, the Harmonies know their own."

Kazim followed as Shima chose a path. "You truly believe that?"

"Yes. The ceremony is for those left behind, not the one journeying on. My father is with my mother and our ancestors now. I know it."

And she believed it to the core of her being. Tahar's body would never be ritually cleansed or placed in the clan's grove for three cycles to free his kah. He would not receive the honours due him, nor would his ashes be mixed with the ashes of their ancestors. None of that mattered. Shima had seen death; she knew Tahar's kah would not really have been released by the rituals. Her gift had shown her they moved on very quickly after the mind glow dimmed, not lingering for even a single cycle let alone the three cycles bodies were customarily laid in the grove. Tahar was with her ancestors now, watching over Chailen and her. She knew it beyond question.

Shima and Kazim studied the empty road from concealment of the trees, but there really was no option but to venture out and cross over into the country on the far side. It was a bit of a stretch to call the land there wilderness—the word seemed to conjure an image of a barren land, which this was not, but it was wild in the sense it had never been settled or cultivated. There were no cities or even large towns between Zuleika and the mountains, so it was in its natural native state; heavily forested with open plains far to the south. A good thing, because the native wildlife was extremely tasty to hungry Shan, and there should be plenty on the hoof for a hunter to track. The road led to the spaceport where she was sure the Murderers would be doing alien things that made sense to them, but no sense to anyone sane. She wanted nothing more than to be far from there and under a trillion cubic tonnes of rock in Kachina Twelve, but that would take a few cycles more and some careful work on her part. Kazim was a good sort, but obviously needed care. Shima would provide, who else was there?

The Harmonies revealed Kazim's anxiety. He had been like that since discovering the massacred people. She thought until then Kazim had been treating the new war as some kind of adventure, exciting and possibly a way to advance in his clan, but now the reality had him by the tail. He had realised that labelling events as the end times didn't make them a neat and tidy thing. There was blood, and there was pain, and there was death. A great deal of death.

There was no choice, Shima decided. The Harmonies assured her no one was close, but that didn't mean they were safe. Her gift could reveal living things, but it could not show her devices or tell her if the area was being observed from a distance. With the Merkiaari in control of the orbitals, if any of them had been spared, they could have surveillance of anywhere on the surface they wished. Even if they had destroyed everything in orbit, a situation Shima deemed likely, the Murderers still had their ships watching. Still, how likely was it for two people to be detected from orbit way out here?

Shima would have been very surprised to learn it was in fact highly likely, because the Merkiaari were already tracking various groups leaving the cities and had set a continuous over watch of both inhabited planets. It was standard doctrine to track vermin migrations to aid in extermination missions.

Shima did not know anything about Merkiaari standard doctrine or procedures. She simply had the Harmonies and her instincts. She felt uneasy, but had felt that for most of the cycle and so dismissed the unsettling feeling as her imagination. Besides, even if the Murderers appeared before her on the road in plain sight, it didn't change her need to head toward the mountains. She was sure to feel better once deep into the trees and hidden under their concealing canopy.

"I'll go first," Shima said. "Don't follow me right away. Wait and watch half a seg before leaving cover. I will wait for you."

"Half a seg! Really? Don't you think that's over the top?"

Shima hesitated and then reluctantly agreed. Her paranoia was getting the better of her. They really did need to vacate the area. "Let's say... a tenth seg then?"

"A tenth it is," Kazim said.

"If something happens, run Kazim. I will find you."

Kazim's ears went back briefly at the thought of running away, but then he agreed with the necessity. He was armed with a knife and nothing he could do would help Shima if she was seen.

Shima crept into the open on four feet, keeping her tail tucked and her belly low to the ground. It reminded her of past hunts with her father, and she could almost see him in her mind's eye, his translucent kah just ahead leading the way. Right fore-foot left hind-foot and pause. Left fore-foot right hind-foot, and pause to listen. She kept her head held low between shoulders, ears swivelling listening for any sound, muscles taught with tension ready to launch her into a sprint in any direction. She lowered her face to the road and breathed in, rolling scent markers over her tongue and the glands at the back of her throat. A growl rumbled deep in her chest, but the stink of Merkiaari was old. She raised her head as tension eased a little, and with more confidence, she trotted across the road and into the trees. She allowed herself a sigh of relief, and lowered herself to the ground in some brush to watch Kazim's crossing.

As planned, he waited a tenth and then crept out into the open. She watched with her eyes and the Harmonies, but as far as she could tell, Kazim was safe. He did all the right things, and it wasn't long before they were moving together under the safety of the trees. Shima only looked back once to see the red glow in the sky as Zuleika burned.

They stayed on four feet that night, ready to flee at top speed on the instant; besides that, it was easier to negotiate the wilds that way. Shan had evolved to walk upright yes, but they were still at their physical best on all fours. It allowed them faster responses, allowed them to use sensitive noses and glands in the throat to snuff the ground seeking scent trails. Even their tails became what they were meant to be rather than just another appendage for gesturing. A Shan's tail was quite muscular but hadn't evolved to hold things, though it could do that in a clumsy way. It was for balance. When a Shan ran at high speed and needed to change course abruptly, something hungry Shan in the past often needed to do while chasing canny prey, the tail became a way to help balance and steer.

They didn't stop that night, neither did they hunt. They had both eaten heartily back in the city and could go without food for cycles at a push. Shima would prefer not to fast for that long, she had used her reserve escaping the Merkiaari, but she could if she needed to. Without discussion, they kept moving until dawn approached. When Shima sensed it was nearly sun up, she began actively seeking water and a place to stop. It took no effort to find a stream, barely a trickle of water above the surface but good enough for their needs and after drinking their fill they burrowed into dense underbrush to rest.

Kazim took first watch, and Shima gratefully allowed her thoughts to slow enough that she could attempt sleep.

"Shima?" Kazim whispered. "Please Shima, wake up. Something is coming."

Shima didn't grown, though she wanted badly to do just that. The way she felt—weary to the bone and aching in muscle groups she had over used—she couldn't have slept for very long. When she opened her eyes though, she could tell by the level of light and shadow that it was mid afternoon. Kazim was supposed to have woken her to trade watches much sooner than this. She felt anger stir but then fade, defeated by tiredness. What was the point in anger now the damage was done? No point at all, and besides, Kazim probably thought turn about was fair considering she had let him sleep in Zuleika yesterday

Stifling her groans she stretched each leg and opened her eyes. "Mmmmmffffph, whatsit?" she mumbled around a tongue that felt thick in her mouth. By the Harmonies she wanted a drink.

"Hush!" Kazim hissed under his breath. "Something's out

there... I *feel* it."

Shima stiffened and her eyes opened wide in alarm as she remembered the situation. Tahar, Merkiaari, Chailen...

She rolled over to find what had Kazim so worried. He wasn't strong in the Harmonies; if he had been he would have noticed the newcomer long before this. Shima sampled the mind glow and relaxed a little. It wasn't good, but it wasn't a danger to them.

"It's one of us, not Merkiaari," Shima said. The mind glow felt light as a breath of wind and the colours pure pastels of orange and yellows, unsullied with the jewel colours of adult experiences. "Young I think... male? Yes male, and barely old enough to be out alone."

Kazim nodded, taking her word as absolute fact. He was recording with his thrice cursed camera again, Shima noted and sighed. He was useless. The beamer she gave him to use while on watch lay beside him on the damp ground absorbing moisture. She retrieved and holstered the weapon sparing a brief glare for Kazim as she did so. She might as well not have bothered. Her disdain just bounced off. He would never understand why seeing the weapon not in his hand and aimed made her angry. He had no fear, none, but it was the bravery of absolute faith in another's abilities, not in the belief of actual safety. He was too trusting, and that endangered her as much as him. It was patently obvious she could not trust him on watch alone from now on.

She held back a sigh. Why was she even bothering to think about it? She had known from the moment she met Kazim that he needed someone to lead him to safety. He was not wilderness wise or trained in the ancient skills as she was. It was her failure letting him stand watch at all, not his; she could have meditated instead of sleeping and kept a better watch than he could wide awake. Not boasting or false pride. Simple fact.

Why did she always find herself in the position of den mother like this? She wasn't a clan matriarch—mother to generations—and never would be, so why did she feel the responsibility she imagined they must feel toward others? Why did she want to reach out and make it better when she saw someone in need? She wasn't a healer with their compulsion to take away pain and coddle everyone. Frankly, she found that trait in healers annoying if anything. She certainly didn't feel that way did she?

She was scientist caste as were many in her family. She fit the life perfectly. Surely she had chosen the right path. She loved her work. Research was her life, genetics her chosen field. Besides, she had never shown any talent the healers would own. Perhaps it was losing her mother at such an early age that awoke this in her. Perhaps looking after Tahar and Chailen did it, but whatever caused it had made her want to save Kazim despite himself. She couldn't save everyone, and had lost Tahar already, but she wouldn't let Kazim sleep walk into death. He was hers as much as Chailen was... for now anyway.

"Don't move from this spot, Kazim. I will fetch him. And when I give you a weapon, if I ever do again, you by the Harmonies will at least pretend to know what to do with it!"

Kazim's nostrils flared wide and his ears went back as if facing into a stiff wind. "What did I do?"

Shima growled low. What was the point? He was clueless. Kazim was looking around in bewilderment trying to discern what was amiss. He hadn't even noticed her taking and holstering the beamer right in front of him! Utterly clueless, it was simply staggering how any Shan could be this oblivious to danger.

"Just..." words failed her. "Just... don't move. Don't do anything, nothing at all. Don't help me... by the Harmonies please don't try to help me!"

Kazim blinked, seemingly at a loss to explain her sudden change of mood. "I'll stay here if you want me to, but whoever he is will find us on his own. That's why I woke you. He is coming this way."

"I know he is, but is he leaving a trail a wild Skaggikt could follow?"

"Skaggikt are not indigenous to this—"

"It's an expression, Kazim!" Shima hissed. "There are others we don't want following him to us."

Realisation dawned and his eyes widened, "You mean Merkiaari."

"Yes. Aliens here would be bad... besides, Skaggikt aren't the only creatures I don't want on my tail and some *are* native to this region."

"Really? What—"

"Later." Shima said cutting him off. Really, his curiosity would be the death of him, of both of them. "I'll fetch him."

Shima left her beamers holstered, and on four feet trotted away to fetch their visitor. Kazim was right, the newcomer would have stumbled upon them anyway, but she wanted to be sure his back trail was clear. If she had to take in another stray, she wanted to be sure his baggage was all in order so to speak. She didn't much like surprises anymore. They could kill you.

She circled wide around him, keeping his mind glow centred within her search perimeter. No one was on his trail, which was good, but said trail was glaringly obvious, which was bad. Shima didn't sigh. Another city bred mouth to feed. Seriously? Why wasn't she surprised? The trail he was leaving meant he was like Kazim, not wilderness trained. Maybe Tahar was right when he said hunting was the past, but surely moving stealthily was Shan nature?

There was no time to debate nurture over nature right now, but if there ever came a time for such things, she would tell the elders what was what. Training in the ancient arts needed to be put into the youngling's curriculum if parents couldn't be trusted to teach their cubs properly. She was being unfair, Shima knew. All Shan were instinctive hunters, but that meant there was no formal schooling for it, which in turn meant a huge variation in competence. Survival could depend on such things now.

Shima took a little time to blur the youngling's trail. Easily done, it took no time at all before she was ready to approach him. That she did, from behind and to his left. Never surprise a Shan from the front if you don't want your ears shredded. Tahar taught her that when she had tried to use a tree and long leap to surprise him. He had known she was there of course— he really had been one of their clan's greats—but he had acted as if surprised only pulling his blow at the last instant. With claws in, it had only made her eyes cross not drawn blood or shredded her ears.

"I am Shima. You need help?" Shima said standing in deep shadow, using her colouring to blend.

The youngling spun about and rose up onto two legs in one motion, the claws of his hands ripping the air looking for his enemy's eyes. Shima approved of his technique. He was quick and agile. He had instinctively gone for a crippling strike rather than risk a disembowelling move that could so easily have gone wrong and left him open to a counter.

"Where... who?" he stammered searching the shadows.

First lesson then, Shima decided. "Take a deep breath; roll the air over your tongue and you should scent me."

He peered into the shadows, not quite directly at Shima, ears swivelling constantly. Shima held her breath to make the lesson stick. He was forced to try for her scent, which he finally did. Shima knew the instant he had it. His mind glow would have told her, but it wasn't that. He simply lowered himself to all fours again and looked into her eyes... or rather where her eyes should be if the shadows had revealed them. Shima decided he'd had enough for now and stepped forward.

"I am Shima. You need help?"

He obviously did. His harness had nothing useful on it. The holster she expected to see was there, but it did not contain a beamer. It was empty.

"I... Merrick, my name is Merrick. I am," he swallowed thickly. "I *was* going to be warrior caste next nameday, but

Fleet is gone now. It must be don't you think?"

He had asked the question hoping she would refute him, but Fleet was obviously destroyed before the landings. Shima couldn't imagine the Merkiaari trying to land their warriors before that was done. She knew he knew that as well as she did, but there was no need to destroy what little hope he had left.

"We will rebuild Fleet bigger than ever after we win this new war. We did it before, we will again."

Merrick's ears flicked agreement, but his face was grim. "The Murderers are hard to kill. I tried but... they captured us." He looked down as if ashamed. "My parents and sibs. The aliens took our weapons."

Shima's ears went back at that. Captured? Since when did Merki do anything but kill Shan? Why take prisoners, and do what with them once taken?

"Are they dead?"

"No!" Merrick snarled, his muzzle rumpling to reveal killing teeth. "Captured like I said. I snuck away... like a coward."

This was not her concern, Shima hurried to tell herself. This youngling could join Kazim under her protection, that would be no hardship really, but... she sighed. No, no, no she had to think of Chailen. She couldn't get involved! She mustn't only...

"How long ago were they taken? How many Murderers? Which direction were they heading? How armed? Did they have a grav sled?" She heard herself saying, and railed at her foolishness.

Shima prayed to the Harmonies that Merrick's answers would make it easy to walk away, but it was cowardice to think like that. But Chailen... she had to get to the keep for Chailen and—but Chailen would be ashamed of her sib if she heard her thoughts. Shima couldn't bear that. Her sib was all she had now. She mustn't make Chailen ashamed of her, and so she had to help this youngling, right? Not for her own honour's sake but for her sib? She told herself that Tahar would have understood that logic.

"No sled and there were ten, all males carrying those mass drivers they use. It happened about a seg ago, and they made us walk back toward Zuleika."

"Just the mass drivers, no flamers or beamers?"

"No, just the mass drivers but they were more than enough. Including mine we had six beamers. They took us by surprise while we slept. Father was on watch. They... hit him, hurt him badly but he wasn't dead!" Merrick hastened to add. "They carried him, so he must be alive. They wouldn't carry him if he was dead would they?"

Shima didn't know but it seemed unlikely. Then again, taking prisoners seemed an unlikely thing for them to do as well. "They wouldn't bother," Shima assured him. "Come with me. I have a friend waiting not far from here."

Shima led the way back to Kazim and introduced Merrick. Kazim was pleased to have another person to film and question. Shima listened only absently to Merrick's story a second time, but she noticed Kazim's eyes gleaming as they watched her not Merrick.

"What?" Shima said.

"You have a plan to deal with this, I can tell."

She didn't have a damn thing, but saying that wouldn't help matters. "Don't know what you mean."

"You plan to get Merrick's family," Kazim said and swung the camera back to Merrick in time to catch the youngling's excited face. "Tell me I'm wrong."

"If you had bothered to bring a weapon, and if Merrick still had his, I might have risked it. With only me armed? It would be foolish."

"Yes," Kazim agreed. "Foolish, but you are still going to do it. I can tell."

How? How did he read her stupidity so easily? Was it written upon her face that she was suicidal enough to try this? She scowled.

"If I were to give my beamers to you, one each, can I count on your accuracy? How good a shot are you, Kazim?"

"I scored in the nineties once," Kazim said proudly. "Merkiaari are big targets. I won't miss I promise you."

Shima sighed. "I don't want your best score. I want your average, as in what can you do consistently?"

Kazim shifted restlessly. "Low eighties, but Shima, those targets are harder to hit than the aliens are. They are much smaller."

"Yes smaller, but they don't move or fire back at you." Shima looked at Merrick. "And you?"

"High nineties most of the time," Merrick said without pride. "I really was going to be warrior caste, Shima. I'm better than all my sibs."

Shima flicked her ears in assent. She believed him, but again it wasn't target shooting they were speaking of. "If I do this, I'll need you both to do exactly what I tell you. No wild heroic charges. We are not trying to kill Merkiaari, we are rescuing our people. If we can do that quietly without blood, we do it and thank the Harmonies for it."

"But you don't think that will happen," Kazim said, his camera zeroed into Shima's face in a tight close up.

"No I don't, but the principal stands. I need your word you will do as I say and nothing more. If we find the situation different to what we expect, or we can't rescue the prisoners, I need to know you will accept it and escape to the keep. We can fight and avenge them another time. Do I have your word?"

Kazim was quick to agree, but Merick was slower.

"Merrick, your word?"

"My family…"

She felt bad for him, but she could not budge on this. "I know, and we will do our best but dying ourselves against impossible odds won't help them. Now, your word or we part company and Kazim and I head for the keep."

"You have my word that I will follow you and do as you command, Tei."

"Don't call me that!" Shima snapped, and Kazim laid a hand on Merrick's shoulder as he jumped in surprise.

"I'll tell you later," Kazim murmured to Merrick.

Shima stroked a hand over her harness and counted the loops holding her only chance at success. She ignored the significant glances the two males were passing back and forth.

"Fine. We try," Shima said, and prayed her father and her ancestors weren't scolding her for acting foolishly. "We need to move fast. I will lead you closer. I will tell you what to do when we get there."

Shima raced into the trees back the way she had come with Merrick, using her own scent to find where they had first met. When she reached the spot, she switched to Merrik's scent and followed that to the place he had been captured. The stink of Merkiaari saturated the place along with Shan pheromones of fear and desperation. Shima's vision threatened to tunnel, but she forced away the fight/kill reflex and found a trail to follow.

Shima pushed the pace beyond safe limits. She knew she did and tried to compensate using the Harmonies. It was harder to do than she thought it should be. It was the combination of distractions she decided. Trying to sense danger with the Harmonies, trying to use scent and her tracking skills to follow the trail left by the Merkiaari, while at the same time running through wilderness with not one but two untrained males... well, it was a wonder she could do it at all.

Finally she found them.

"Stop here," Shima panted. "They are not far ahead now. Take these." She gave each of them a beamer. "Have you ever seen what happens when a beamer cell is overcharged, or burned?"

Merrick gulped and Kazim's jaw dropped. Shima started plucking free all the spare cells she had loaded her harness down with. She kept only two back for later, if there was a later. She gave each of the males half of the cells.

"This is what you will do..."

The fauna and flora of Child of Harmony was different to the homeworld, and well did Shima know that. Those differences played a large part in her research. Modifying food crops to thrive here in this environment was the goal of her research. But a tree was still a tree, no matter how different its form and those oddities played no part in the current use Shima had for them.

Shima followed the Merkiaari patrol high in the trees, using the canopy to hide her movements and the thick chunky branches as her highway. Shan as a rule were more comfortable on the ground, but hunting and pouncing on prey from above was a valid skill. Her ancestors certainly thought so, Shima mused. She doubted Kazim's would, but then the deserts of Harmony had no trees, just scrub and brush, and lots of sand. Hunting there was more about finding prey to kill than combat. Desert clans hunted fire lizards and the like. Hard to find in the first place, but not hard to kill once found. Fire lizards were fast like most species back home, but they had few defences once cornered.

Shima paused, gauged the distance to the next tree, and leapt, landing with claws out to gouge into bark and secure her grip. She was above the prisoners now, and Merrick was exactly right in his description of what to expect. Five Shan, four females and one male. The male was awake but not well. The Harmonies told Shima he was in pain, and her nose told her he was bleeding though not how badly. The Merkiaari warrior closest to him was no longer carrying Merrick's father. He simply prodded the injured and stumbling male forward, snarling words that only another Merkiaari would understand. The intent though was obvious. Move faster or die, seemed the likely translation.

Shima could have killed this warrior easily from where she was, but that wasn't the plan. She had to save them all, not just one injured male, and to do that she needed Kazim and Merrick to do as she had bid them. It shouldn't be long now.

Shima used the trees to move ahead of the column and circle around, scouting the problem from all sides. This wouldn't end bloodlessly she decided, not entirely unhappy with the decision. If she could see a way to save the prisoners without fighting, she would use it. She meant what she said to Merrick. Anything could happen in a fight. The only way to ensure everyone's safety was not to fight, but that wasn't an option now. With two warriors so close together and near Merrick's father, she couldn't possibly spirit him away without being seen.

It was nearly time. She readied herself by removing her visor and securing it on her harness. She hadn't forgotten the desperation she had felt when she thought she had lost it, and hadn't yet found a solution to let her wear it in the kind of fight she was anticipating here. She had never used it while hunting with Tahar, and although this was a different kind of hunt, she wouldn't need her eyes to find the aliens. If all went well she would have the advantage regardless. She had planned for it at least.

The first explosion took even her by surprise, but she was falling upon her prey just moments later. The flash as the energy cell exploded blinded all within sight of it, but not Shima. Her eyes were so bad in the dark without her visor that she could have stared right into the explosion without discomfort. Not that she was going to do that. She was busy killing her prey.

The Merkiaari she landed upon had no time to scream. Shima landed on his back already reaching around his neck and ripped his throat out with the claws of both hands. He was already choking on blood and dying as she sprang away directly at another alien shaped blur. More flashes lit the trees and plunged them back into deep shadow as Kazim and Merrick threw beamer cells and shot them, causing them to explode. Beamer cells contained enough energy for hundreds of shots. Liberating all that at once made for an energetic display. Flashes of light lit the night, making shadows leap up and cavort amongst the trees. Mere moments later, the trees were plunged back into darkness all the deeper for the brief display.

Merkiaari roared in anger and surprise, firing indiscriminately into the trees at targets they couldn't see. Trees soaked up the damage, some cut in half beginning a majestic fall, but the forest was dense and they couldn't complete their descent, branches tangling with their brothers.

Shima disembowelled her second alien, not slowing to watch him die. The scent of Merkiaari and blood made her rage, and Shima let it take her. It was a liberating and fearsome thing, allowing her primal self to come to the fore. This must be what her earliest ancestors felt when the clans fought each other before the Great Harmony.

The fight/kill reflex of her people tunnelled her vision and clamped her ears tight to her head. Her muzzle gaped wide, her lips rippling back exposing killing teeth. She screamed her rage into the night sky. It was her battle cry, her first ever, and was the scream of a hunting Shan giving challenge to all enemies within hearing.

Shima was essentially blind now, but as her father had maintained she didn't need eyes to hunt her prey. She had the Harmonies. She sought out the insane mind glows using her gifts, and raced madly into the trees aiming for the knot of alien mind glows. Behind her, she left two dying aliens and a bewildered Shan male in her wake.

Shima slashed into the aliens, darting between them and splashing blood in all directions. Not stopping, she raced into the trees and circled back to attack from another direction over and over, whittling the enemy down with quick hit and run strikes; none of them instantly fatal, but all debilitating and confusing. Merkiaari weapons raved chaotically, blasting the trees to kindling as they sought targets that were simply not there. They did not know a lone Shan female was responsible for the carnage.

More explosions and flashes of light courtesy of Kazim

and Merrick lit the dark, and suddenly Merkiaari were falling to beamer fire as well as claws. Shima was lost to the madness. She danced in the dark amongst the trees. Strike, strike, jump, spin and slash. Alien blood sprayed, she spit it from her mouth and screamed her challenge again, but this time it was not answered by weapons fire.

Silence.

Spinning on the spot, claws still extended, Shima barely had time to close her fists. Her attack thudded home into Kazim's belly and he folded with a grunt of air expelled. He fell to his knees groaning. Shima stood tall above him and screamed one last time, arms held wide with claws extended. It was not a challenge, but a cry of victory.

"Shima, it's done. You killed them all," Kazim said gently. He didn't try to stand, perhaps realising that in her maddened state she might take it as a challenge. "It's over."

Shima glared down at him, panting hard and still raging in her thoughts, but his words almost inaudible with her ears still tight to her head began to make sense. Over? It was over already? She blinked trying to see into the trees, but it was so dark. Dark? Her visor!

She reached for the visor still secure on her harness, but paused staring myopically at her hands. Her claws were thick with blood and bits of meat and alien fur. Her hands were dripping red onto the ground. She peered down at herself, forcing a semblance of calm into her thoughts and her tunnel vision began to recede. Her pelt was matted with blood, and she swallowed remembering the fight at last.

Shima's ears struggled up, and swivelled at a sound behind her. She spun falling automatically into a defensive crouch, but this time she found more of her people staring at her. Merrick's mother looked upon Shima with a kind of fascinated horror, her cubs though were frightened. It made Shima want to hide her bloody face. Merrick's father bowed to her when she met his eyes, and Shima bobbed one back quickly in reply. He shouldn't bow to her that way. He was older than she and surely wiser. He was due her respect, but he didn't seem to see it that way.

Shima looked beyond her audience and into the trees, not finding whom she sought. "Merrick? Where's Merrick?"

"I don't—" Kazim began to say.

In a sudden panic, Shima reached out with the Harmonies and found a lone Shan mind glow. It was dim and fading. "He's hurt!" Shima shouted and dashed into the trees.

Shima found Merrick amid broken trees on his back blinking into the night sky. He still had his beamer, and he made her proud by aiming it steadily in her direction as she rushed toward him. He lowered the weapon when he saw who she was.

Shima crouched over the youngling, looking for wounds and found one. A huge splinter of wood had speared him clean through close to the hip joint. Shima chewed her whiskers. She dare not remove it for fear of blood loss, yet he was literally nailed to the ground by it. She was no healer, but the Harmonies had already prepared her.

He was dying.

No! There must be something I can do, some trick Tahar taught me, or something Sharn said about blood loss. Please... Ancestors help me!

"My father?" Merrick whispered.

"Lives," Shima assured him. "All of them. You saved them, Merrick. You did. You will make a great warrior one day."

"No," Merrick said, his voice already fading as his heart pumped what little blood he had left onto the thirsty ground. "I was a coward. I ran away."

Shima's eyes burned and she clutched his hand in hers. "No young warrior, no. Your ancestors sent you for help... you came to get me, you see?"

"You think so, Tei? I don't want to die... a... coward..." Merrick's hand released Shima's and his eyes stared at the sky unseeing. His mind glow faded to nothing.

Shima stared into his face, burning the image of the

youngling she had failed to save into her memory. He was dead. It was her fault. She had taken him under her protection as she had Kazim, and failed him. What had she been thinking, bringing two untrained males into this? Worse, what had possessed her to bring a youngling? Kazim at least was adult, able to make his own decisions, but Merrick...

"Merick, please forgive me..."

"There's nothing to forgive, Shima." Kazim said. He was half carrying Merrick's father and that slowed his approach. "He was a warrior, and you were his Tei."

"Don't..." *call me that.* Shima didn't say it. Merrick had been young, too young, but he had chosen her to follow. The knowledge cut her all the deeper for she had proven unworthy of him. "Just don't."

Shima took the beamer from Merrick's other hand and holstered it upon her harness, before rising to her feet. She braced herself to meet Merrick's father's eyes, and the accusations she was sure would be there. She put her visor on to see them all the better, but the truth was she wanted to hide her own eyes for shame.

"I... Harmonies forgive me," tears began to fall and she let them. "I killed your cub. I have no words to express how sorry I am. I owe you a life now and submit myself to your justice. I swear by my clan, my life is yours."

Kazim gasped as Shima spoke the old formula, but Merrick's father had attention only for his dead cub. Behind him, his mate and other cubs arrived and the night was filled with wails of grief.

Shima let the sound wash over her, and cried silently for Merrick, for Tahar, for her people.

* * *

23~Going Underground

They couldn't take Merrick with them, there was just no way it would have been safe carrying him for cycles to the keep. Shima had hated the thought of leaving him for scavengers, of which there were many on Child of Harmony, but he would have understood the need. Thankfully, his father, Nevin, and his mother, Marsali, took charge of Merrick and they were the practical sort. They knew what had to be done.

Shima was silent, her ears constantly swivelling listening for approaching danger while Merrick's parents dug a pit using their claws. They would leave a marker of some kind so they could come back and take Merrick home when it was safe.

Shima kept her head turning, watching for movement. She had both beamers in her possession again, in hand and ready to fire. She was wired, very tense, and feeling jittery. The Harmonies were screaming at her to move. Leave this place. Go. Go now was the message she was getting. There was no sign of more Merkiaari in the area, and she was watching with every sense she had. She knew they were safe for now, and yet the Harmonies were screaming of imminent danger. She wanted to run far and fast just as the Harmonies urged her to do, but they had to do right by Merrick first.

Kazim was on the far side of the pit talking quietly to Merrick's sibs. Kazim had asked Nevin if it was all right to record, and he said it was. It surprised Shima that he had agreed so easily, until she realised he wanted his cub to be remembered. Shima thought the three younglings looked a lot like their mother, but then so had Merrick. Inaki had her mother's patterning on her flanks, and so did Rahuri. Merrick had that distinctive pattern too. Miamovi lacked the pattern entirely, but she had her mother's ears. In fact, her head matched her mother's in shape and feature, not just colouring. The younglings had their mother's looks, no question, but their manner was all their father. They walked softly like him, spoke with gravity as he did, and Shima felt certain they would take after him in their opinions. At any other time, they would seem reserved, Shima felt sure, but with Merrick's death, emotions ran high and close to the surface.

Shima froze for a moment when she saw it, but then continued her watch without a word to the others. It wouldn't help anything to tell them that Merrick's kah was standing there watching them. This wasn't the first time she had seen one, and with the new war just starting, she doubted it would be her last. It would go to the Harmonies soon.

Shima had seen kah before, but she had never seen one do what this one did next. One moment it was standing near Kazim, the next it was a pace away and in Shima's face trying to talk. It gestured urgently and tried to say... something. There was no sound of course, and the kah seemed frustrated by that. It walked past Shima looking back at her with a pleading look when she stared. It held out a hand to her, still with that pleading expression upon its immaterial face.

Shima was shocked motionless, her thoughts in chaos. Kah didn't do this! They just didn't! They weren't people. This kah wasn't the youngling she had met so briefly and failed to protect. It was... it was a memory of him, like one of Kazim's films. That is what she had been taught when her father realised she was strong enough in the Harmonies to see them, and had invited his mate's favourite sib to visit their home to teach her. Only Tei were ever taught about kah because only Tei were strong enough in the Harmonies to see them, but she was a special case. Strong enough to be Tei, but flawed in herself and unwanted by the clan-that-is-not. Tei'Thrand had been kind to teach the scared youngling she had been, and had broken many an unwritten rule to do it. Such deep knowledge of kah and their link to the Harmonies was held exclusively by the clan-that-is-not.

This kah was all wrong. It was not playing by the rules, she thought plaintively. That thought was so absurd that at any other time she would have laughed, but not now. There was nothing funny about burying Merrick, or running for their lives from the Murderers, and there was nothing funny about this kah. It... she couldn't think of it as a he. It wasn't Merrick, it wasn't! Despite its strange ways and looking like the youngling, she had to cling to her lessons. It wasn't him, but it seemed not to know that or care. It acted like Merrick, wanted her attention like he had, and Harmonies help her she felt herself wanting it to be really him. That was so wrong.

She couldn't talk to him... it! It was an it, wasn't it? She couldn't talk to him with the others nearby, but when she checked they were busy lowering Merrick's body into the pit. Shima holstered one beamer and gestured surreptitiously behind her back, wanting the kah to move behind a tree. Shima almost gasped when it did what she wanted. They don't do that, she wailed silently in her head.

Shima followed it behind the tree and stopped to watch its antics. "I don't understand."

The kah... oh Harmonies, call it Merrick. She was already losing her mind, what difference did it make? Merrick raised his hands and let them fall in defeat. He looked very upset.

"You can't tell me, can you show me?"

Merrick's face glowed brighter as if suddenly excited. Shima swallowed. He moved away and looked back. His expression asked if she was coming. Shima used her gift to look for danger, and gave herself over to the madness. She followed him through the trees, already guessing where he planned to lead her. Maybe she was asleep and dreaming? She stumbled over a hidden root barking a shin painfully.

"Not dreaming," she muttered and rubbed the pain away. "I couldn't be that lucky."

Merrick stopped by the dead aliens and looked at her.

Shima and Kazim had dragged all the bodies together before deciding to just leave them for the scavengers. They'd had some vague notion of hiding them, but it would have taken too long. Better to bury Merrick and vacate the area quickly than spend time hiding dead aliens she had decided.

"What?"

Merrick pointed urgently to one of the aliens.

Shima raised her beamer, suddenly wary. Had it somehow survived? No, not possible. The Harmonies showed Merrick glowing very brightly and nothing else. They were definitely dead.

"They're dead."

Merick raised his fists at the sky and shook them. Then he pointed at the alien again.

"All right, all right... no need to get testy about it. I'll look at your stinky alien if you will leave me alone and join your ancestors like you're supposed to."

Merrick grinned at her. Grinned!

Grumbling about getting even more blood on herself, she holstered her beamer and rolled the stinky and definitely dead alien onto its back. Kazim had stripped its weapons and shared them out, just as she had done with the other aliens, so she didn't expect to find anything.

"Now what? There's nothing here."

Merrick crouched near her and mimed undoing its clothes.

"I am not stripping this foul thing naked!"

Merrick's ears went back at that, and he looked disgusted.

He gestured slowly and Shima finally understood.

"Oh, sorry," Shima said and reached for the flap of material attached to the Merkiaari covering.

Merkiaari didn't wear anything like a Shan harness with its loops and pouches, but they still needed to carry things. Like the new aliens, the Humans, they wore coverings they called clothes and those had built in pouches. She undid the flap securing the pocket and reached inside. Her hand felt something and she stilled. Had they missed a weapon?

"What is it?"

She looked for Merrick but he was gone. Had he gone back to the others? Somehow she knew he hadn't. He was truly gone to his ancestors now. Shima looked back at the alien and withdrew the item. It wasn't a weapon, she was sure of that. She suspected it was some kind of minicomputer. She turned it this way and that, wondering why this thing was important enough for Merrick's kah to break all the rules to get it into her hands.

She turned it over and stared at her face reflected in the shiny surface. There were no controls, but if this really was a computer... she touched the shiny part and things started happening. She watched coloured icons and blinking graphics move over the screen. She cocked her head trying to understand the display, and her ears flicked at the nasty alien speech sounds coming from the device. Suddenly things rearranged themselves in her mind. She turned the device ninety degrees and her breath rushed out as the electronic map made sense and she associated the graphics with the real world.

"No..." she said in horror.

She dashed into the trees carrying her booty.

Shima threw herself onto her knees at the edge of the pit and unceremoniously began pushing the mound of earth into it with her hands.

"Shima!" Kazim said.

"Help me!" Shima snarled at Kazim. "Merkiaari heading this way. She passed the device to Nevin. "We can't let them find Merrick or us. They will chase us forever using one of these things. It happened to me before in Zuleika."

Nevin stuffed the device into a pouch and started shoving at the loose dirt. His family followed his lead and the pit was soon full. Shima kicked away the excess dirt, spreading it out to hide it.

"Kazim, lead them away from here. The stream. Take them to where we stopped yesterday. I'll catch up."

"But—"

"Go!" Shima screamed.

Kazim stumbled back in surprise. "This way." He ran and everyone rushed to catch up.

Nevin stopped to look back. "Don't do anything foolish. You owe me a life, remember?"

"I remember," Shima said grimly. "I remember everything. I must hide our presence here, and blur your trail. Now go."

Nevin dropped to all fours and raced after his family.

Shima used deadwood and underbrush to cover Merrick's pit. That was the easy part. The ground all around the area was scuffed and trampled. She didn't know how good at tracking the Merkiaari were. She hoped they relied upon technology and not natural instinct. Using primitive methods might fool technology, probably would, but she had to do the best job she could in case the aliens did know how to track prey without their devices.

She drew her knife and leapt into the air, aiming and swinging the knife at a low branch of the nearest tree. The blade was very keen, made of the best steel. It was one of a matching pair Tahar had bought her one nameday. She landed neatly and caught the severed branch in her free hand. Using it like a broom, she swept the entire area so that fallen leaves and other forest detritus spread evenly over everything. To the casual eye, no one had been here. To Shima, it was still obvious that people had been here but that was training and the scent left behind by the others. She could only hope the aliens weren't her equal.

Shima backed away, still brushing furiously, following Nevin's scent. She did that for a long time. Probably too long, but she was determined that any curious Merkiaari would not get any help from her inaction to find Merrick's family. Finally she climbed into the trees, taking along her branch with its tell-tale freshly severed end. She wedged it in the crook of more branches to hide it, and then sprang into another tree heading toward the stream and the others waiting for her.

It didn't take long to find them. Shima dropped out of the last tree to land lightly a few hundred paces from Kazim and the others. Wonder of wonders he had the Merkiaari mass driver aimed rather than his camera. The others were inexpertly holding the Merkiaari weapons they had liberated from their captors; the aliens had broken the beamers they had brought with them from the city. None of them knew how to use the huge weapons; they were used to hand beamers, which had no recoil at all. But mass drivers very much did, especially Merkiaari mass drivers. Merkiaari were big creatures and their weapons matched them in size and power. They couldn't be held and fired like a Shan beamer, but Shima could tell no one had thought about that yet.

Shima didn't have time to tell them now.

"May I see the alien computer?" Shima asked Nevin. He removed it from his pouch and handed it to her. "We might need to put greater distance between us. Let us see."

Nevin watched as Shima touched the shiny surface and the display brightened. She pointed to the icons and looked the question at Nevin. He flicked his ears and his tail rose. Its dark tip curled and made a short slashing motion. He was right, the aliens were about to discover their dead. She flicked her own ears and her tail mimicked his. They turned back to the display and watched the alien lights stop at the place where the fight occurred.

"Watch, they will spread out and search the area. Probably in twos."

Nevin flicked his ears in agreement. "Will they find

Merrick?"

"I'm hoping not. If they do, it tells me something. A lot actually."

Kazim joined their huddle around the computer. "How so?"

"If they find Merrick after all I did to prevent them, then it means they are skilled trackers. We already know from history they are hunters... mindless predators, but can they track us without one of these?" Shima said raising the alien device slightly. "If they can't, we will lose them in the forest. If they can, we will still lose them I promise you, but it will be harder and I will have to be very careful."

"And if they keep following?"

Shima wished Nevin had not said that. It was one of her greatest fears about this. She dare not lead the aliens to any keep. She remained silent and looked hard at Nevin. His ears went back just a little as he realised what he'd said, but they came up quickly. His tail gestured understanding but worry too; for his mate and cubs no doubt.

"Let us worry about that if it happens."

Kazim finally realised the problem. His nostrils flared and his eyes flicked from Nevin to Shima and back. "We..." he swallowed hard. "Shima and I could lead them away if it comes to that. Nevin can take the younglings to the keep while we distract the Murderers."

Shima felt a sudden burst of affection for Kazim. He could be clueless at times, but none could say he wasn't brave.

"Yes," Shima said. "That's the plan."

The aliens split into search parties; they searched in pairs as Shima guessed they would, and were methodical about it. They were using a grid pattern, logical enough, but Shima was very interested to note how exacting their spacing was. That kind of accuracy was machine-like and it made her grin. She looked at Nevin, but he hadn't caught the clue. He noticed her expression and cocked his head in query.

"They're using their machines to search. I'm certain

now."

"How can you be sure?" Kazim asked.

"The spacing. It's too regular. I think they're using a computer like this, rather than their eyes or noses. They won't find us that way."

Kazim looked unsure. "I don't know, Shima. Maybe I'm missing something, but if we can see them with this thing, can't they see us?"

Shima began to say of course they couldn't, but why couldn't they? She had assumed the Merkiaari could not because they had stopped to search instead of chasing them. Was that good enough? She looked at Nevin. He was watching the Merkiaari icons thoughtfully.

"I assumed they stopped to search because they couldn't see us, but..." Shima gestured frustration with her tail. "Everything is a guess where aliens are concerned! I don't like not knowing."

"Scientist," Kazim said and laughed. "Don't scowl at me. You know that's part of it."

It was, Shima admitted privately. It was the curse all scientist caste suffered from—ever questioning, wanting to know the answers and reasons behind everything. It was often said that a cub's caste could be predicted by the first word out of her mouth. Future scientists were born with the word 'why' on their tongues.

"The Murderers know their devices better than we," Nevin said thoughtfully, slowly feeling his way to a conclusion. "Could it be as simple as that? Could they be using it differently?"

"Yes!" Shima said excitedly. She scrutinised the computer. "This one could indicate a wide area scan," Shima pointed a claw at one of the icons running down the short side of the map. There were two circles one inside the other. The outer ring was filled with colour, the inner empty. "Perhaps the Murderers are watching for danger close by."

Kazim flicked his ears in agreement. "That makes a lot of

sense. They're looking for what or who killed their friends."

"Yes," Nevin mused, "but that means they only have to touch this icon on their computer to see us."

"Right," Shima said. "We must run until we can't see them on ours anymore, then we rest and wait for night again. "One of us remains awake to watch the computer."

"Agreed," Nevin said.

Shima studied the display a moment longer and chose her direction; away from the mountains and the safety of the keep. They dare not be seen heading to a keep. Even if the Murderers did not guess they were looking for safety of some kind, it wouldn't take much for them to project forward and notice the mountains. Shima decide right then to turn toward the mountains only if the map remained clear for a cycle.

"This way," Shima said, putting the computer in her pouch and dropping to all fours. "We move fast and hard, and then review our direction. Let's say two segs before our first stop, which gives us roughly two more before dawn to find somewhere to rest."

"Good," Kazim said. "I play rear guard this stretch."

Shima flicked her ears and tail. She was pleased he was taking some responsibility for the group. She left Nevin to organise his family how he would, and set off into the trees. A moment later, she heard the others move to follow. She set a rapid pace, but not so fast that she risked exhausting everyone. The wilds could be dangerous. They might need to fight or run from predators, or Merkiaari, or both.

Dawn found Shima safely hunkered down with the others. Rahuri and her sibs were tangled together in a pile, sleeping the sleep of the exhausted. The sight made her smile, but it faltered as she remembered Merrick. He should be with his sibs, no doubt in the centre with the others on top and spilling around him. Female sibs tended to be that way, very protective of a brother especially if he was their only brother. They would have doted on him, looked out for him, boasted of and about him. It made Shima want to weep.

Chailen was wonderful; a beauty in her personality to match her sleek form, but a brother would have been very special to both of them. They would have raised him together, though of course Tahar would have final say... well mostly. Sibs were always close, their bond as strong if not the same as parent to child. Yes, a brother would have been good. Tahar had told her of her dead sibs only recently. She didn't know any details except they died as a result of the failed FTL project, the same that crippled her. She didn't know if one or more of those dead sibs had been male. She didn't have names for her dead. Suddenly that lack mattered. It hadn't before, but with Tahar gone and now Merrick, it mattered a lot. She should at least have names to think about, to imagine what might have been, but she didn't. She wished she had asked Tahar. It was possible her parents had not named them. She didn't know, but they had surely chosen names in anticipation of the birth. If Shima knew the names, she could pretend she had a brother once.

Shima sighed quietly, trying not to disturb the others, and studied the alien map. All clear, as it should be. She wondered what the other control icons did, but she dared not change any settings. For one thing, she might not get the ever so useful map back. For another, she had heard alien speech come from it so she knew it was a communicator as well as a map. What if she accidently transmitted her location? No, the two icons they had decided were long and short range scan would have to do. She would give it to someone at the keep. Let an engineer figure it out. Tahar would have loved investigating its guts, like that time with the droid.

Shima smiled remembering his delight in the strange device. They didn't know then of course, but they had played a tiny part in the arrival of the Humans. Her smile faded. Where were the Humans now? Had they escaped the Murderers? Kajetan said in her broadcast the Humans would fight, but had they? Surely their ship could not do so well as the Fleet. Everyone said the Human ship was designed for surveying new worlds not fighting. Shima gazed upon the fading stars as the sun came up and wished the Humans well.

At least she was clean now. They had a good source of water and cover. The spring was icy cold; supplied no doubt by snow melt from the mountains, but all she had cared about was getting the stinky alien blood out of her pelt. She loved that spring for being here. The cave was a boon too of course. Shima had stationed herself just inside the entrance to watch the game trail she had used to find it. It was perfect. They couldn't be observed from above, they had water, and the cave was close to game trails fresh from regular use. Native animals must use the spring, and that meant she would have an easy time feeding everyone.

She checked the map again. All clear.

She closed her eyes and settled into her meditation sleep. Not truly sleep, her lessons were clear on that, but it was restful for the body if not the mind. She was determined not to make any more mistakes as she had with Merrick. She would let the others help, but she would not relax her guard until they were safely in a keep. Her muscles relaxed, the map device settled a little in her hands and lap. Her breathing deepened and slowed as her mind wandered. Images of Tahar, of Merrick, of Chailen flowed through her thoughts, but none lingered. The fight with the Merkiaari briefly flashed by, broken static images shocking. Her claws buried in the eyes of an alien, another of her claws already running red ripping open a throat. Another, another, another... her hand in the guts of a Merkiaari. That one almost made her lose her trance. She hadn't noticed at the time, but she must have been aware enough to strike beneath the alien's breastplate to disembowel him. Gradually the violent images gave way, and the Harmonies showed her the world around the cave.

She was right, Shima sluggishly mused, her thoughts slowed to match her breathing. The local wildlife was abundant. The animals would not come near the cave now it was occupied, but they still needed water. She watched as they followed their usual trails, and noted the point at which they scented the Shan hiding in the cave. Shima wondered what the little mind glows were thinking. Probably they were scared or annoyed about the interlopers sleeping here. The creatures waited a short time before turning aside. Shima followed and watched as they found a second source of water. It was a shallow pond, just a low place in the forest that ground water had filled.

Shima opened her eyes, not losing her calm and slowly looked down. Yes, the little creatures were clear on the map. The icons were a different colour, and the alien text attached to them was different than she saw previously attached to the Merkiaari icons. She couldn't read the text, but she would bet it said the animals were not Shan or something of the kind. Non sentient maybe, though Merkiaari didn't seem to care they were killing sentient beings. Or perhaps they did, and preferred to kill them. Who knew?

Shima studied the map, took note of the pond's location by the simple expedient of comparing where she knew the animals were and where they appeared on the map, and then closed her eyes to continue her watch.

In this way, alternating eyes open observation of the map and cave entrance, with eyes closed observation using the Harmonies, Shima kept the group safe through that morning. Kazim came and took over charge of the map. Shima didn't move or bother to say anything when he quietly took it out of her lap. He knew she was aware of him, but didn't speak. He sat inside the cave entrance on the opposite side to her, probably using her position as guide. They sat like two statues, guardians of the clan, though their small group was no such thing and the real clan guardians were wooden, cut from trees in the various clan groves.

The day passed slowly for Shima. She did not allow herself sleep. She kept her vigil, noting Kazim handing off his responsibility of watching the map to Nevin. She ignored their whispered converse. They were simply speculating about what was happening elsewhere. To Shima that was a little pointless when all that mattered for now was surviving to reach the keep. Besides, homeworld was far away. It was likely the Merkiaari were doing the same there as here. Considering what happened when the Merkiaari last made war on them, Shima didn't doubt her people were fighting for their lives everywhere.

Kazim left to get more sleep. Nevin watched for a couple of segs in silence, and then gave his place to his mate. They had decided not to include the younglings in the watch, though next nameday they would be seven cycles old and adult. They were not adult quite yet, though probably more than capable. It was their parent's decision in any case, and they had decided to prolong their cub's innocence for as long as they could. Shima sympathised. If this war progressed as she thought it might, Merrick's sibs would be fighting very soon. Let them remain innocent for as long as they could.

"You killed my cub," Marsali said.

Shima said nothing.

"Making him fight was wrong. He was too young. I hate you for that."

"I know," Shima said, her eyes still closed keeping her watch. There was no sign of Merkiaari, but some of the larger predators were starting to concern her. "I know."

"You saved us."

Shima did not reply, but wondered where this was going.

"My mate, my cubs... we would all be dead if not for you and Kazim."

"Don't credit me with saving you. It was Merrick; he died for his family. He loved you all very much. If not for him you would be dead. If not for him I would not have turned back to find you." Shima opened her eyes and turned to Marsali. "I killed Merrick and will never forgive myself for that. Nothing you say can make me feel worse than I already do."

Tears welled from Marsali's eyes and fell. Shima watched her weep silently, but then stood. She moved to take the alien map away, but Marsali held it tight.

"I need to do something," Marsali said clearing her throat and scrubbing away tears. "I need to be useful, to help save my cubs. To be worthy of Merrick."

Shima blinked feeling flustered. "I... you have nothing to prove to any of us."

"To myself," Marsali insisted. "I need to not be a burden. I need to help save them."

Shima released the computer into Marsali's care, but she did take a very quick look at the display; as before it showed no sign of Merkiaari. It did show something was out there. The predators she had found using the Harmonies.

"Keep it and watch then. I am going hunting. We need to eat before we leave."

Marsali clutched the computer and indicated agreement, her ears flicking in the common gesture, but her tail also curled around one leg. She was nervous indeed; it was a youngling thing to do. Shima wanted to find Nevin and ask him to watch with his mate. Marsali didn't seem completely confident of what she wanted, but Shima decided to see how she performed. No point in undermining her before she even tried.

Shima slinked silently through the trees, keeping low and moving slow as she stalked her prey. It was a decent sized male Shkai'lon, and could be dangerous. They were fast too. She was upwind of him and determined to hamstring him on her first pass. Shkai'lon weren't indigenous to Child of Harmony, but they had thrived here. The first colony ships had brought all manner of animals from Harmony for the colonists to eat. Back then no one knew if they could even eat the native plants and animals. As it turned out, certain species were poisonous, but in the main they could. When the Merkiaari came, everything was shattered. Farms and towns were abandoned. Animals such as this one's ancestors had escaped the pens and bred in the wild. No doubt some of the native life had lost their place in the ecosystem, some even becoming extinct as Shan nearly did, but a surprising number did not and fought back until the current balance was reached. All of which was good news from Shima's point of view. She was hungry and Shkai'lon were tasty.

Shima stopped, buried in shadow and underbrush, only her gleaming unblinking eyes visible in the gloom. She had taken off her visor as she always did on the hunt, but this time it was for a different reason. Since her accident in Zuleika she had entered a whole new realm of paranoia where her sight was concerned. She had always feared blindness ever since she learned the long term prognosis of her condition, but now she'd had a small taste of it. She never wanted to be so helpless again. The hated visor was now a lifeline she dare not let out of her possession, but at the same time she feared damaging it. Tahar would not rescue her with another visor or repair it if broken. So once again it was safe on her harness.

Like Shkai'ra, Shkai'lon were herbivores, but unlike their smaller cousins Shkai'lon had formidable weapons and bad dispositions to match. They were dangerous as all get out, and would fight even when the odds were bad. A bit like her people in that way, Shima mused watching the delicious creature use his spurs to grub in the dirt for roots. Those spurs were deadly in a close in fight, the only kind to be had between Shan and Shkai'lon. The rack upon his head and the sharp hooves were also something to be wary of. If a Shkai'lon was cornered or chased toward exhaustion, they would turn at bay and put up a murderous blur of flashing hooves and swinging antlers. Many a hunter had died to pull such a beast down.

The great head dipped to eat the now exposed roots. Shima gathered herself and sprang with fore-claws out already slicing toward the back of one hind leg, but the creature had the luck of the Harmonies on his side. At the very last moment he must have picked up her scent. He shied sideways, his rear legs kicking out. Shima tucked her head taking a glancing but painful blow to one shoulder. She tumbled, rolled on her back then to all fours. Her rumbling growl climbed into a scream of pain, as feeling slowly returned to her arm. Her own coppery blood perfumed the air.

Shima dodged left, right, left. The Shkai'lon backed away swinging his head to keep her covered. Canny beast, Shima thought in admiration. She pivoted aside and ran straight up a tree. Just as gravity decided that no, she could not run up a vertical surface for so long, she pushed off turning in the air with all four legs spread wide and claws out. The marvellous beast ran, but too late. Shima landed just behind him, catching his haunches with the claws of her hands and digging in.

The Shkai'lon bounded through the trees, crying its distress call, alerting any of his herd to scatter. Shima didn't care about that. It was all she could do to hang on. Even dragging her he was fast! She knew that Kazim would not have been able to keep up. Kazim was not here, only she was and dinner was bleeding under her claws. It was up to her.

Her back legs scrabbled trying to run, but there was just no way. They were moving too fast. She was barely hanging on. Her weight, borne by the claws embedded in the Shkai'lon's tough hide threatened to tear loose as she was dragged through the forest. She winced as her legs hit all manner of roots and brush, but even as she considered letting go, she managed to pull herself up higher onto the beast's back. She bit down, trying for a better hold with fangs so that she might at least reset her claws, but the tough muscle around the animal's spine resisted her. She couldn't get a decent mouthful. She spat blood and bit harder.

Blood slicked its hide, and Shima knew if she could hang on long enough it would weaken, but she didn't have that luxury. Knowing her luck, the beast would run right through a Merkiaari patrol. Finally she managed a decent hold with her teeth and withdrew the claws of one hand. She reached higher on the beast and clawed his back, ripping his hide and making him cry out in terror. She was about to pull herself fully onto his back when he slammed into a tree.

Shima flew over his shoulder and hit the ground rolling. The impact winded her, but she had enough awareness to move behind the tree before the Shkai'lon stomped her. It hooves barely missed her, but they did miss and Shima was able to get to safety. The Shkai'lon was enraged now. Its panic had turned to fury, and Shima's heart sank. This was why her ancestors hunted in packs and not alone. It would kill her now if it could.

It slammed its antlers into the tree, tearing bark free, and then reared onto its hind legs to rake its spurs at Shima. She dodged, and circled the tree keeping its bulk between them. The Shkai'lon rammed the tree again, this time with a shoulder, and Shima swung around the tree to land a blow. This time she didn't miss. The hamstring let go and the leg collapsed under the furious beast. It squealed and snapped at Shima as it fell. She jumped clear and stopped to consider her next move.

Shima rubbed her shoulder and warily stepped away as the crippled beast tried to reach her. He was one very angry dinner, Shima thought ruefully. She inspected her injury and decided that, although bloody, it wasn't serious. The Shkai'lon bellowed at her, then hissed and snapped his teeth at her. Shima growled, the noise might attract unwanted attention. She darted forward and back, her claws dripping scarlet, and the beast quieted. A spray of blood pulsed from the artery in its neck. It moaned plaintively and slumped. Shima edged forward to provide the killing blow, and howled as the beast had his revenge. The spur caught her in the thigh, and ripped a ragged line through her hide. Shima yelled and leapt clear, ready to fight anew, but it was all over. The Shkai'lon was done. He fell on his side panting and pumping the last of his spite and blood onto the ground.

Moments later his fierce mind glow dimmed and was extinguished.

"Harmonies be praised," Shima said wincing as she put weight on her leg.

It would be her back leg, she thought unhappily. She needed to walk upright if she was going to carry meat back to the others. She looked thoughtfully at dinner. Or did she? She had her knives. She could clean her kill here, butcher it, and take the best cuts. Why not make an old fashioned drag sled? Tahar had shown her how, though it was really for dragging someone who was injured to safety. It was one of many things she had learned as part of her hunting and survival lessons.

She quickly set about her task.

Shima dragged dinner back to the cave and found Kazim waiting for her. He had his thrice cursed camera out and filming her. What was it with that male? He seemed unable to lay it down for longer than a seg or two.

"You're hurt!" Kazim said, still recording.

Shima sighed. "That's all right, I can drag this myself. No no! You don't need to help, thanks for the offer."

She glared at him as she struggled past. The sled with its burden was cursed heavy. Her fault for loading too much of her kill aboard it, she admitted privately. She had wanted to impress Kazim, she realised now. He didn't seem impressed however.

"How bad is it?"

Shima sighed again, and stopped struggling with the sled. It was just inside the cave. Good enough, she decided.

"I'm not hurt," she said and stood up, letting go of her burden. Pulling the sled on four feet had definitely been the right way to do it, but now she winced as the ragged tear in her leg made itself felt. "Much," she added at Kazim's sharp look.

Kazim examined her kill and his jaw dropped into a laugh. "Oh this is good. You forgot, didn't you?"

"What?" Shima said looking at her kill. "There's enough here for all of us. Plenty to reach the keep."

"No, you forgot we're in the wilds not a sanctuary."

Shima rolled her eyes, as if she didn't know they were in the wilds. They were hiding from Merkiaari in a cave for harmony's sake. She let Kazim see her derision and he laughed again.

"If you knew, oh wondrous hunter of fine meat, why didn't you just shoot it?"

Shoot it? Shima suddenly realised what he meant and her ears sagged in embarrassment. She could have used her beamer to kill it the first moment she saw it. They were in the wilds and hunting laws didn't apply. Besides, even if they had been in a sanctuary, no one would have expected her to follow the law under these circumstances. Her spirits sank as she realised what a fool she had been.

"Don't feel bad," Kazim said kindly. "I'm sure it was an epic fight."

That made her feel worse. The Shkai'lon could easily have killed her during his run, and later she had stepped into his range to deliver the killing blow when a single blaster shot would have done just as well. She hadn't even thought of the beamers holstered on her harness. She had hunted without her visor on as if it had been just another hunt like those she had been on with Tahar. If she had kept her visor on maybe she would not so easily have fallen into old patterns, but maybe not too. She sighed morosely.

"It nearly killed me more than once, Kazim. I was stupid. You are right."

"I didn't say that!" Kazim protested.

"No, but you should have. I hunted the way I was taught. I should be thinking clearer than that. It won't happen again." Shima promised herself not to forget herself again. If she had died, who would look after Chailen? Sharn would, she supposed. "Help me take this to the others?"

Kazim picked up the two largest and heaviest portions, the back legs, and took them deeper into the cave. Shima followed with other portions, leaving the rest for later.

Marsali was watching the map intently as Shima and Kazim came in view. She didn't look up, but her shoulders relaxed a little. She had obviously seen Shima approaching on the screen, but hadn't been sure it was her. Probably that was why Kazim had come out to greet her. Nevin came to investigate the meat.

"There's more back there," Shima said indicating the entrance with her tail. "If we need it."

"I'll get it," Rahuri volunteered and headed that way.

"Don't go outside!" Nevin called after her.

"I won't! Don't worry, father."

Shima watched the youngling go then handed her burdens to the others. "I should go back to my watch."

"But you're injured," Nevin said.

"It's nothing," Shima said.

"At least bathe them. They might get infected."

Shima hesitated, but it was time she started thinking and acting smart. Nevin had a valid point, so she would take his advice and do the smart thing for once. She flicked her ears in agreement, and headed toward the spring.

"Are we to eat this raw, father?" Miamovi said doubtfully.

"Yes, 'movi. It won't hurt you to eat as our ancestors did. Try a little, you'll like it."

Shima paused to watch, smiling inwardly. The youngling was in for a treat. Fresh meat seasoned only by still warm blood was delicious. The youngling tentatively bit into the dripping haunch of meat, her ears halfway back, but as soon as she had the taste, she ripped a chunk free and chewed with eyes narrowed in pleasure.

"It's wonderful!" Miamovi enthused. "We should eat this way all the time!"

"No," Shima said. "It's only this good when the kill is fresh. You should try meat that you bought in the market and see."

"Bad?" the youngling said taking another bite.

"Let's just say it loses a lot in processing."

Nevin growled and laughed at the understatement.

Shima shared the joke. Processed meat never tasted good unless cooked well and was heavily seasoned, but that was the price of civilisation and animal husbandry.

"Actually, we could cook some of this," Shima said thoughtfully. It would help preserve the meat. "This fresh it will taste great either way."

"But a fire here, what about the smoke?" Kazim said.

"No fire!" Shima said in alarm. "Absolutely no fires until we are safe. Gather a bed of rocks and heat them with this," she said and gave a beamer to Kazim. "Cut the meat about a finger width thick, and cook it on the rocks. The juices will sizzle a bit, but there won't be much smoke."

"If you're sure?"

"Positive. I saw Tahar do it once."

"I wish I could have met your father," Kazim said softly.

"So do I, Kazim. You two would have become fast friends." Shima looked back as Rahuri reappeared with more of the meat. "I'm going to wash."

* * *

24~The Keep

Shima stood guard at one of the many tunnel entrances to the keep, not caring about, and not really understanding, the strange looks she was getting from the warriors sent to greet her. She had vowed not to relax until Kazim and the others were safe. The warriors would just have to understand. Besides, Nevin would be joining his family inside in a moment, and Shima was sure Kazim would get tired of fiddling with his camera shortly. He would want to contact his own family to tell them he was safe, and after that, he would be busy talking to anyone who would answer his questions. They would probably never meet again. Keeps were big places after all. Shima told herself she would welcome the peace his departure would lend her.

"You have harboured and protected my mate and cubs, risked your own life to bring us to safety," Nevin was saying. "I call you friend, Shima, and would be honoured if you will consider me yours also. There is no debt between us."

"But Merrick—" Shima began.

"Died a hero's death to free his sibs," Nevin said firmly.

Shima did agree with him about Merrick, but... "If you are

sure you want it that way."

"I'm sure."

"Then I agree there is no debt, but call on me at need. Friends help one another, and you are one of mine."

Nevin bowed and took his leave of her.

Shima watched him go thoughtfully. He was a very proud person, yet had bowed to her as if she were the superior. It made her vaguely uncomfortable, as if she were pretending to be other than she was.

"Well," Kazim said. "You did it."

Shima looked at him sideways. Wonder of wonders, no camera. "It?"

"Dragged me to safety."

Shima rolled her eyes. Kazim couldn't see that of course, her visor hid her eyes. "Truly, it was a feat worthy of the sagas. You were determined to kill us so often."

"Sarcasm is for the weak minded," Kazim said loftily. "I wasn't that bad." The watchers all laughed and laughed harder at Kazim's outrage at their mockery. "Well I wasn't!"

Shima wondered exactly why they laughed. It wasn't as if they knew what she had to do to drag Kazim to Kachina Twelve. Well, one of its many access points actually. The mountains and surrounding area was riddled with tunnels. Not all led into the keeps of the Kachina chain. A lot did of course, but many were traps for the Merkiaari; others led to supply bases and defensive installations. Access to those was restricted to warrior caste exclusively. No others had the codes necessary to enter them. Shima and the others had been led to this entrance by a patrol whose mission it was to gather strays like Shima's group. In the chaos, many people had been caught out of position and unable to reach their assigned keep, but the likelihood of such a thing had been planned for. Shima had meant to search for a patrol just like this one when she was close enough, and for once everything had gone to plan.

As they followed the warriors along the tunnel and deeper into the ground, she felt tension ease and her step become lighter. The Harmonies were telling her all was well now, even thoughts of Chailen failed to make her anxious. The Harmonies were with her sib, not the other way around. She was certain now. She hoped for Chailen's sake that Sharn was well, and that his family were also. Chailen was sure to have heard about the destruction of Hool Station and Tahar's death by now, but at least Sharn was there to comfort her.

"Why are they looking at me like that?" Shima said feeling faintly annoyed as they passed through another security checkpoint with its massive door and heavy beamers tracking them all. The warriors stationed here were whispering and pointing at her. "What's their problem; is my face dirty or something?"

Kazim's tail lifted and signed over his shoulder in the universal gesture that meant, "don't bother me, I haven't got a clue."

"Yeah well, I don't like it," Shima said, quietly. At least she thought so, but evidently not quietly enough because Patrol Leader Kotanic dropped back beside her.

"It's the broadcasts," Kotanic said.

"Huh?" Shima said confused. "What is?"

"The reason for their interest in you. It's the broadcasts."

Kazim's ears gave him away. Shima stopped and grabbed his arm. "What did you do?"

Kazim brushed off her grip in evident annoyance. "You knew I was recording, Shima. I interviewed you more than once and how many times did you tell me to turn it off? You knew."

"Recording yes, not broadcasting!" Shima said angrily. "Don't you know how dangerous that was? The Merkiaari might have tracked your signals!"

Kazim sighed. "Give me some credit, Shima. I did realise what could happen. I transmitted every morning just before we broke camp. And before you ask, yes I did scramble the signal and send it by burst transmission!"

Shima snapped her mouth closed. Well, Harmonies smile

on him. He was starting to anticipate her objections. "All right then, but why are your recordings the cause of all this?" Shima pointed to the staring and whispering warriors. "Tell me that."

Kazim flicked his ears. "No idea," he laughed at her outraged expression. "Come on Shima. I was with you the entire time. What, you think I had the time to edit everything ready to broadcast? No chance! You hardly let me stop running long enough to sleep."

Shima didn't dispute him, though he was exaggerating outrageously. She turned to Kotanic for her explanation. He obliged after a moment for consideration.

"You have to understand how it was that first day," Kotanic began. "Chaos doesn't begin to describe what happened when the first landings occurred."

"I know, I lived it," Shima said impatiently.

"Maybe so, but you were reacting to things you could see and affect, all we could do was watch. If not for the reports and broadcasts being sent to us, we would have gone mad. They flooded in from all over the planet. The fighting was fierce almost everywhere, and our people died everywhere they met Merkiaari. Fighting or running, even hiding, made no difference. But then something happened, we received Kazim's first report.

"At first it was like the others. Full of horror and destruction, but a little further on it changed in tone. It showed you, Shima—that first meeting with Kazim in Zuleika when you convinced him to follow you. We cheered when you killed those aliens. Reports of other small victories like yours came in later, some not so little, but yours was the first we saw and from then on we wanted to know what you and Kazim were doing." Kotanic turned and inclined his head to Kazim. "You are famous, Kazim. You and Shima both."

Shima's ears went hard back and her whiskers drew down as she imagined what she would like to do with Kazim's camera.

"Don't be angry with him, Shima. He was doing what he knew to do in a bad situation. He did what most of us did when the world we knew ended—his job. We need people to go on doing that. If they need heroes to make them feel that their lives are still worth living, that there is still hope, who are we to say no?"

"That's easy for you to say, you're not the one being made a spectacle. I'm no Jasha at the gate, Kotanic! I'm just me, Shima the gardener. By the Harmonies, I won't let you make a fool of me."

"By what I have seen of you, you are far from a fool, but you do have something other than your clan in common with the great Jasha, Shima. He was a hero none can deny and a great hunter, as you are. He denied it often, as I suspect will you."

Shima growled deep in her chest and spat dryly to one side. "That for your stupidity!" She glared at the amusement she saw on the faces of the other warriors. "Harmonies take it, I'm not a hero!"

"Yes you are," Kazim said firmly, and the warriors mumbled agreement. "Do you know what they call you?" he asked flicking a look toward the warriors.

Shima just stared mutely at him. Appalled at the turn things were taking. She wanted not to hear this. She wanted to find Chailen and hug the breath out of her, and then watch as her sib laughed and Sharn told her all the news of their friends that she had missed. She wanted to disappear into anonymity, and just be Shima.

"They call you The Blind Hunter, just as Jasha was The Great Leveller."

"I'm not blind yet," Shima said feeling a pout coming on. Couldn't they have at least thought of a name that didn't label her with her disability? Would she never out run her shame? Kazim just looked at her knowingly. He knew she was as good as blind already without her visor. "Well I'm not!" she added, this time hearing the defensiveness in her voice. "You did this to me. You... you... *don't talk to me!*" Shima stormed past Kotanic and left them all standing there.

"She'll come around," Kazim said confidently, and projecting his voice so that Shima heard even as she stalked away. "She will."

Kotanic started them following her. "If you say so, but heroes are notoriously hard headed I've heard. Jasha could hold a grudge like you wouldn't believe, or so they say now."

Shima growled a curse under her breath, but her ears swivelled to catch Kazim's reply.

"She likes me. I'll be forgiven by morning, you'll see."

"Huh, fat chance," Shima snarled under her breath. She glared at a warrior who stared at her too long as she approached him. "What you looking at?" she snapped.

"Identity," he said faintly, obviously recognising her.

Shima waved a hand at her escort arriving at her back. "Ask them," she snarled. "Apparently the name my father gave me isn't enough anymore."

"Don't be like that, Shima," Kazim said. "It's not his fault."

Shima rounded on him, her muzzle rumpling, and her ears flat to her skull. "No, it's yours!" She spun away, glared at the warrior daring him to intervene, and stormed past.

"Stand easy, she's with us," Kotanic said to the guard. "Just found out about the broadcasts. She's a little... upset."

"Upset?" the guard said faintly. "I thought she was going to rip my heart out."

Shima spat dryly at the amused chuckles. It wasn't funny curse them all. As she made her way through the tunnel not letting the others join her, she had time to reflect on everything that had happened and a new concern raised its ugly head. Chailen must have seen Kazim's recordings. What must she think? Would it seem to her sib that Shima had abandoned her to care for strangers? Would Chailen understand that all Shima had been trying to do was reach her, and all the other stuff had just happened? Blind Hunter indeed, Shima snorted.

Blind Fool more like it.

* * *

James craned his neck to see what had caused the agitation, but saw nothing unusual. He snorted in amusement. Nothing unusual? He was deep inside a secret alien facility surrounded literally by aliens wanting to chat, while millions more went about their lives above, below, and all around him for kilometres in every direction. Unusual didn't begin to cover it.

James turned back to Zylaric. "Forgive my rudeness."

Zylaric shrugged in the Shan manner, ears and tail gesturing.

James was beginning to learn what all the twitches and gestures meant, and briefly wondered if Humans seemed unemotional to the Shan. Having no tail to express themselves, Humans must seem bizarre indeed to them. If not that, then... stoic? Yes stoic, and perhaps guarded. James was sure the Shan would learn Human body language, but until they did, Humans would be very frustrating to them, lacking as they did the important appendages that Shan used so much to express themselves.

"Curiosity is no bad thing," Zylaric opined. "Questions lead to greater understanding. What was your interest?"

"People seem excited. Is there going to be another broadcast?" James said, his translator faithfully converting his English into passable Shan. They were a godsend, and James once again prayed that Chief Williams, the engineer most responsible for the translator's creation, had survived. "I don't remember seeing anything scheduled."

"Ah no, not a broadcast but something better in my opinion."

The Shan standing nearby agreed with varying amounts of enthusiasm. James smiled at all the differing expressions, barely remembering in time to keep his teeth hidden. Baring teeth to a Shan was not an indication you were amused.

"What do you mean?"

Zylaric gestured at the excited people. "The Blind Hunter has arrived in the flesh. We are lucky that one of our patrols ran across her trail and not one from Kachina Eight. Our patrol radius intersects with theirs you know."

James nodded though he in fact had not known that. Humans were considered honoured guests within the keep, but there were limits to hospitality James had found. Anything related to keep security was off limits to any but warrior caste. Patrol schedules and routes were classified even within the caste and restricted to the Tei directly responsible for overseeing them. Shan were exceptionally paranoid regarding such data. They feared the Merkiaari would somehow gain access to it. It was a genuine concern, James supposed, though Merkiaari rarely if ever questioned the vermin they hunted. They simply slaughtered them. Still, better safe than sorry James supposed.

"She's here now?" James said, his interest quickening. "Might I meet her?"

"I think that's an excellent idea," Zylaric said. "It will be interesting to see her reaction."

Everyone laughed, and James frowned. What didn't he understand here? The translator often missed nuances that could prove important. Still, it was laughter not concern on their faces. What could possibly go wrong?

"We can see her now then?" James asked hopefully.

"Yes, now would be good I think," Zylaric said leading the way. "She should be passing through here soon. No doubt she will be going to visit her family."

"I wouldn't want to get in the way of that," James said. "Perhaps we should wait and send a message?"

"Too late," Zylaric said and flourished his tail to point ahead.

James stopped when he saw Shima striding toward

him followed by a crowd of other Shan all talking amongst themselves. Shima was easy to recognise. Her visor shone dull gold in the keep's lighting. James recognised Kazim not far behind her. Anyone who had seen the broadcasts would recognise him. His monotone pelt, so light in colour, was distinctive. Shima seemed in a hurry, and James was reconsidering the meeting. She had only just arrived. He could introduce himself later, but just as he made that decision, Shima froze. She was still at a far distance; too far to talk without shouting. Her companions fell silent and stopped behind her, all eyes on James.

Oh well, time for my dog and pony show.

James moved forward, alone this time, but very aware of all the watching eyes. He almost laughed when he saw Kazim reaching for the famous camera that had been such a bone of contention between Shima and him, but the urge passed when he finally registered Shima's posture. She was statue still, her head cocked to one side. James assumed she was staring at him. Her covered eyes made it impossible to say for sure, but who else would she stare at when he was the only Human here and the first she had ever met.

"I greet you, Shima," he said to break the ice as he had done so many times before. "May you live in harmony."

Shima shivered, the individual hairs of her pelt rising in a wave from the top of her head down her body and finishing at her tail. James was fascinated. He had never seen that reaction before from any Shan. It made her seem suddenly larger. Was it a threat display, or something else? He didn't feel threatened. He knew what anger in Shan looked like, and this wasn't it.

"You burn," Shima whispered. "In my head, you burn..." her words trailed off, but then another shiver more like a full body shake and her pelt settled into a more normal dimension. "So bright, the colours... why did no one mention the colours?"

James blinked. He didn't think she was talking to him. "Are you alright?"

Shima straightened and seemed to come back to herself a little. She approached James and held out her paw. James touched her palm with his. "You are the Human called James," Shima said. "I recognise you from the news casts."

"That's right," James agreed. "And I also recognise you from the broadcasts. You are Shima, The Blind Hunter."

Shima growled deep in her chest and the hair on James' neck stood up. "Don't call me that!" She looked back and found Kazim with his camera. "No one call me that!" She faced James again. "I am Shima. Just Shima, that's all."

James laughed when every Shan but Shima disagreed either by voice or gesture. Shima snarled, and James took her hand for a companionable squeeze. "Ignore them, Shima. I have found it's the best way to deal with this sort of thing."

Shima squeezed back, and then took James' hand in both of hers. She pulled it closer for inspection. James had had similar experiences before, and didn't react when she raised his hand close to her mouth. The first time had been startling, but now as she drew air into her mouth so that she could taste his scent with the glands at the back of her throat he just waited.

"Huh," Shima chuffed lowering his hand but not letting go. She manipulated his fingers noting, he was sure, the range of motion. "No claws," she said looking at his blunt fingernails. She sounded disapproving and James smiled.

"No tail either I'm afraid," he said apologetically as he had done so many times before.

"Yes, I knew that. I have tried to keep up with things. Are there more of you here? Can I meet Bren-daaaar and Jah-neeeece?"

"Brenda and Janice," he corrected and she flicked her ears in acknowledgement. "I'm certain you can. They're both here at Kachina Twelve. My entire team is here. We were left behind when *Canada* jumped outsystem."

"Your ship, he survived?" Shima said sharply. "He has gone for help?"

"We lost contact, but believe *she* has, yes."

"Huh, she is it?"

James nodded.

"Very sensible," Shima opined and everyone laughed. She ignored them. "You were waiting for me?"

James shrugged. "I was walking. I do that a lot to meet people and find out things. I heard you had arrived and wanted to see you, but I don't want to delay your meeting with Chailen. We can talk later."

Shima released his hand. "You know my sib?"

"Know *of* her, yes. She is well known here because of you."

Shima groaned and turned toward Kazim who raised a hand in apology. The other still held his camera as it recorded her first meeting with a Human.

She turned back to James after a moment. "Would you have time to meet Chailen?" James nodded but then wondered if Shima knew what his gesture meant, but then she said, "Good. She would enjoy meeting you."

"And she won't chastise you for your tardiness," Kazim interjected, still filming. "Good plan."

Shima pointed one finger at Kazim, right between his eyes. She held the gesture in silence with her teeth bared. Kazim laughed but didn't say anything more. James grinned at the familiar by-play. The broadcasts had prepared him, but in person, Shima and Kazim were even funnier.

* * *

25~Rescue

"Is this everyone? You're sure?" Colgan said in a sick voice. Forty-three weary looking Shan stood before him. Forty-three from a crew of hundreds.

"This is everyone," Tei'Varyk said with slumped shoulders.

Colgan waved his people forward to see to the wounded. He took his friend's arm to ease him out of the way. He watched Tarjei being rushed to surgery. Others were given similar treatment leaving the walking wounded standing silently slumped and dejected in their defeat. Tei'Varyk watched his people leave until he was left with fifteen uninjured including himself.

"Your people will be shown to a place to rest," Colgan said.

Tei'Varyk gestured to his people. "Go with the Humans. You will be cared for."

The Shan bowed once and followed Baz Riley to quarters, but it was obvious they were far from happy about it.

"Come to my quarters, Tei. We need to decide what to do." Colgan set off with his friend by his side. "You know

Canada is the only ship left?"

"Yes."

"You know that I can't stop the Merkiaari?"

"Yes."

They entered his quarters. "Take a seat. Or on the floor if you prefer."

Tei'Varyk threw a cushion from the chair onto the deck, and sat staring at nothing. Or perhaps he was seeing again the last transmission from his homeworld, as the Merkiaari landed looking to kill his people. Harmony's orbital defence net had lasted no longer than the time it took to target the fortresses. The fighting at the landing zones had been ferocious, and was still being waged.

The Shan had been unable to predict where they would land, so any kind of defence had to be mobile. Entrenching Shan warriors had simply been impossible. They had met the Merki without the benefit of fixed defences, and their losses had been simply staggering. Hundreds of thousands of Shan warriors and civilians had died within minutes, and the war had only just begun. Neither side would stop until one or the other was utterly destroyed. Missile installations had targeted the landers and knocked down some of them, but such victories were few.

Far too few.

Colgan sat cross-legged in front of his friend, and saw the despair there. The flattened ears, the claws working in and out of their sheaths, the restless tail tip. It was the posture of a defeated man—*Shan*.

"I can't take you home, Tei," he said quietly.

"Tarjei is dying."

Colgan drew a sharp breath. "Perhaps not my friend. Our medics have been studying with your healers. Doctor Ambrai is very good…"

"No. I know when one of my people will die. Send me home to die with them, with her."

"I can't, I *won't!* You and your crew might be all that's left of the Harmony of Shan soon. Think about that."

"I am thinking of it," Tei'Varyk said with his eyes blazing. "Don't you think I know the Murderers will do their evil work right this time? I *do* know it."

"Well then. It's your duty to save what you can. This ship is a wreck, but it's still jump capable. I can't take you home Tei, the Merki would destroy me before I came close, but I can take you to my home."

Tei'Varyk's ears were quivering, and almost flat to his skull. His eyes were white-rimmed. His fur was standing up making him seem larger. He was on the killing edge. Colgan went still, trying to appear harmless. After a few seconds, that to Colgan felt like hours, Tei'Varyk spat dryly and his ears struggled erect. Slowly his eyes returned to normal.

"Take the others, but give me a lander. I'll get there."

"I haven't got one, Tei. James and the others are marooned on Child of Harmony with the only one not destroyed. Even if I did have one, I wouldn't give it to you. I don't hold with suicide."

"No? Then what was that attack if not suicide?"

Colgan shifted uncomfortably. "I calculated the risks and they were favourable. Putting you in a lander is not. You have no choice. This ship is jumping outsystem as soon as I give the word, but I wanted you to agree."

"Then, as I have no real choice, you have my agreement for what it's worth."

"It's worth something to me, Tei." Colgan rose to his feet. "Come to the bridge with me."

Colgan led the way to the bridge, and asked Tei'Varyk to sit in the observer seat. He racked his helmet beside his command station and slumped into it. He was tired, but he couldn't rest yet.

"Prepare for jump."

"Jump drive hot, Skipper, all jump stations report manned and ready," Lieutenant Wesley reported.

"Referent?"

"Referent locked in, destination Sol."

Colgan glanced at Tei'Varyk where he sat staring at his homeworld on the viewscreen. "Execute!"

ASN *Canada* twisted and was gone. Where she had been, empty space remained.

* * *

26~Blown

Eric crossed the open compound appearing casual and uninterested in anything going on. It was the middle of the night, but you wouldn't know it by the activity under the harsh white floodlights on the towers. Night was when the work was done; daytime was for sleep and relaxation

The buildings, shacks at best, were constructed of materials scavenged from the jungle locally. A matter of both convenience and security. There was always the chance that supplies could be traced to the base, though Eric found it unlikely. It was impressive foresight regardless. All the important equipment was kept underground in the old mine itself. The command centre, barracks, motor pool, commissary... all were in the various tunnels and caverns protected from dinos and discovery both. Above ground, the shacks contained various stores mostly awaiting use in raids or shipment elsewhere. The only way in or out of the compound was by road, the only one was little more than a single lane dirt track. From the air it was invisible until it joined a properly paved road leading from active mining facilities to the east. From there it led to a small airfield able to handle transports and shuttles. Eric had travelled that route to reach the base.

Eric kept his steps casual. He was a well known face and people nodded or raised a hand in greeting as he passed. He smiled and nodded in return, or gave a brief wink and grin if it was a pretty girl. He was liked, and he made sure never to destroy that image. He blended. He was one of them. They trusted him, and were even a little in awe of his skills because when they went on raids he planned, no one got dead. He was indispensable now. As planned.

Eric paused as his sensors detected a weapon system coming online. He turned slowly, making it seem he was looking for someone. In reality, he was turning to watch as the sentry guns powered up. There wasn't a test scheduled as far as he knew, and he made it his business to know such things. He squinted in the bright light of the floods, and watched. The guns were tracking something, but the jerking hesitating way they moved told Eric this was a malfunction not a test. He readied himself to run for cover, but then he realised the guns really were tracking but not firing. Not a malfunction then. He ordered his processor to run a sensor sweep. Multiple unknowns dotted his display and they were close! His right hand twitched, but he managed not to pull his gun. The unknowns had to be native wildlife, some kind of nocturnal flying dinosaur or bat. Did Thurston even have bats? He had no idea.

He watched the sentry guns tracking the sources of his unease and knew what the problem was. The gun's sensitivity had been dialled way down because they had kept fragging the wildlife and getting on everyone's nerves. Sentry guns were noisy and burned through ammo at a horrendous rate. Now though, an unknown threat had been detected within a hundred meters and the gun's programming said threats must be eliminated, but the sources were smaller than the new limits that had been imposed to prevent false alarms. The guns were stuck in a logic loop. They tracked, tried to fire, were prevented from firing, tried to power down, and looped back to detecting a threat and tracking again. That was why they were moving spasmodically when normally they would be smooth.

"God damned junk!" someone cried heading toward one of the sentry gun towers.

Eric nodded as if he agreed, but in fact he didn't agree. Those guns were good tech and dangerous in professional hands. It wasn't their fault they had been deployed in the wrong environment. Even here in the jungle they would do the job, they just needed a little care and tinkering. He could have had them running as smooth as can be in a few hours, or he could tell the techs here how to do it. He wouldn't though. He wasn't here to help them, he was here to bring them crashing down. He was here to end them, and had spent months here putting a plan together to do just that.

Killing everyone here would be a short term solution. He had considered it a few times, but he wanted long term. He was tired of people making the same mistakes over and over, undoing his work and making him come back for a do over. He needed to change the political system, or aid President Thurston in his efforts to do so. A simple massacre here wouldn't do it, wouldn't even make the evening news. He needed a big splash, something big enough to tip the government over the edge and force them to take the leap into full Alliance membership instead of just talking the matter to death in Parliament.

Eric turned back to his walk, letting his sensors map the minefield as he walked the perimeter. It was stifling hot under the camo netting and the nano net beneath it. Simple is efficient, Eric mused, taking a moment to look up. Funny how such a low tech solution as netting strung overhead could fool high tech observation from satellites or navy air patrols. The camo netting fooled the eye, and the nano nets fooled any sensors that relied upon heat, magnetic, or electrical emissions.

When he had climbed aboard that transport at Zhang's

factory months ago and headed for the port, he had wondered then how the Freedom Movement had managed to hide a base on a planet with modern satellite communications and its attendant surveillance capabilities. What impressed him about the Freedom Movement's solution was that the old mining facility had been hidden years ago, long before the Freedom Movement even existed. King had been planning and scheming for decades. He must have hidden the place in case he ever needed it, and somehow destroyed any record it had ever existed. To do all that just in case? Amazing.

Had King always intended to overthrow the government, even as a young man? Why? Back then, democracy on Thurston had been a distant dream; not even that. President Thurston's father had been a dictator, one of a handful of men who owned the company which in turn owned most of the below ground resources of the planet. He'd had no intention of ever joining the Alliance and must be spinning in his grave at his son's antics. Writing a constitution based upon the Alliance constitution and then upholding it! Ye gods. He had even given away his own lifetime Presidency in favour of a five year term and proper elections! So King didn't want Thurston to join the Alliance; what did he want?

Eric had no idea, but he had used his time trying to find out, and had learned a great many things. He now knew names in the government secretly dealing with King and helping the Freedom Movement, he knew everything there was to know about the base here and its resources. He knew where all the terrorist cells were located and what their missions were, but he still had not fathomed King's motivation. It didn't matter. All that did was Stein's marines taking King and the other government conspirators out. And they would. As soon as he reported in, Stein would move. Just a matter of time now.

Timing was the thing. He hadn't reported in yet, because he didn't have a long term solution to the government's dithering. If Stein moved now and decapitated the Movement, the underlings would fade away only to re-emerge years later, probably stronger, certainly wiser from experience, but worse than that would be the government's reaction. He could see it clearly. They would relax; believing the emergency over, they would go back to business as usual. Might even withdraw their application to join the Alliance, probably would because what need now eh? Now the emergency was over and the terrorists taken care of? Foolish to think that way, but Eric had seen it many times. Easy to forget when immediate danger passes. So he held back his data, stalled the marines leaving them in a guard position and reacting to events instead of preempting them. Not something they liked, to be sure. Marines preferred well defined goals... go here, destroy that. Take that hill. They were damned good at it.

"Hey Eric, give a hand here could you?" Reiner said from across the compound.

Eric lifted a hand and went to join him. "What's up?"

"Got to get this stuff squared away," Reiner said struggling to drag a crate off the battered loader's forks. "Goddamned pile of junk ran dry before I finished."

"Power cell dead again? Should have charged the mother before you started, my man. You know what this heat does to a cell's efficiency," Eric said getting a grip on the other side of the wooden crate and lifting. He groaned and cursed for effect, when in reality he could have carried it alone with ease. "Damn me, what's in it?"

"Ammo," Reiner grunted, his voice strained. "Over there with the others."

Eric shuffled in time with the man. Ammo stores was a simple shack with canvas roof, and was stacked high with all kinds of crates; some wooden like this one, others metal, but most were the olive green fireproof plastic cases that told an experienced eye they were out of an off world Alliance weapon's factory. The codes were in Eric's database, and the sight of so many RPGs (Rocket propelled Grenades) and SAMs (Surface to Air Missiles) stockpiled here and in the mine had angered him when he first realised how well supplied the Movement was. They were for killing marines and navy pilots, especially the SAMs. Off world backing again. He saw the like more and more

They manoeuvred down a lane left open between stacks for the purpose of moving stuff around, and had just navigated the corner safely when Reiner tripped. Staggering backwards he let go of the crate, trying to keep his feet out from under it. Eric should have held the weight easily, but the suddenly unbalanced load bit into his hands and tipped. Before he knew it, the crate had smashed upon the ground spilling cases of loose rounds onto the dirt floor. Hot blood scolded his palms and he scowled at his hands.

Bloody wooden crates in this day and age. Bloody Border Worlds in the bloody Border Zone, bloody primitives...

He muttered curses as he pulled out the long slivers of wood. He didn't notice Reiner staring at him, at first. He looked up from his ripped flesh and saw Reiner staring at his hands. Eric looked down again and... oh shit. The synthskin glove on his right hand was ripped and the gold contacts of his weapon's bus were clearly visible. Dammit, not now! He wasn't ready. Ready or not, his cover just went bye bye.

"You're a—" Reiner began, shocked and horrified, but he said no more, and wouldn't ever again as Eric leapt forward and broke his neck.

Eric held the body sagging in his arms; maybe he could salvage this. He could hide the body; dump it in the jungle as a free meal for passing dinosaurs. The others would miss Reiner eventually, but maybe they would think the wildlife got him. It would be the truth...

A shout, and the sound of running feet had Eric spinning in place, but it was too late. Another man was running for his life and screaming the alarm. Eric cursed, dropped Reiner, and hurried deeper into the ammo store heading for the far wall. He kicked his way through the wall and ran for the wire fence. It was a simple chain link affair, not meant to keep men in or out, just the smaller jungle creatures attracted by the chance of easy food. He chose a blind spot in the fence, a section the sentry guns didn't cover very well, and ripped it down with his bare hands. He called up his map of the minefield, and started picking his meandering way through, while behind him, men grouped up and began their pursuit.

In a matter of moments he was into the minefield following his safe route. Safe was a relative term, but his sensor sweeps had been thorough. He had everything well mapped and knew his own abilities. He could pass through, but his pursuers would need to turn the field off before they could follow. They must have realised, because they stopped at the boundary and ordered him to stop. He didn't of course and they fired a warning shot. He kept going.

Eric leapt over the last mines and ducked into the trees just as the enemy finally organised itself and opened up on him. He put the trees at his back and ran. Hard. No one could catch a Viper in flight, but they didn't know what he was and would try. He watched them on his sensors as they entered the minefield. They didn't know what he was or why he had killed Reiner, but they didn't need to. All they needed to know was that he was running away with knowledge they couldn't let him spread.

Shots rang out unaimed. Surely they must be unaimed with the trees between him and them. They couldn't see him, but they might get lucky. He couldn't run full speed. The jungle was too dense. He changed course, heading away at a tangent hoping they would keep going straight. His sensors updated and Eric cursed. Someone was thinking back there. They were following using motion detectors or other sensors.

Nothing for it, he needed extraction and fast. He made the call to Stein using internal comms linked via satellite.

"I'm blown," Eric panted. "Need extraction fast."

Stein snarled a curse. "Do you have what we need?"

Eric wondered if Stein would leave him hanging if he said no. He grinned. Good thing he had the data then wasn't it? "I have it, I have it all."

"Understood. I'll have a team cover your withdrawal. Coordinates follow..."

Eric adjusted his route and added the rendezvous to his map. It would take him less than an hour to reach, but the marines would take longer to get there even if Stein had a team on standby. He needed to delay his pursuers.

"I'll be there."

"Stein out."

Eric increased his lead and started to think seriously about using the road. He could really pile on the pace if he did, but the road went the wrong way. He could still use it to lose pursuit, and then double back. No, he didn't need to give them even more opportunities to find him. According to sensors, they were already breaking up into teams and spreading out. Damn them, now wasn't the time for them to show some competency.

Eric was so busy watching what was behind and trying to plan an escape, he failed to note what was waiting for him up ahead until it was too late. He skidded to a halt and looked up and up...

"Fuck me," he whispered, his face draining of colour. "Desmond!" His hand was a blur reaching for his gun, but it was too little too late. The huge dinosaur's jaws snapped forward. The crocodile like teeth ripping and tearing.

The screaming began.

* * *

27~A Cry for Help

> *Falling...*
>   *...Twisting, and falling...*
>   *...Down, and round...*
>   *Twisting, and here!*

ASN *Invincible* staggered and bled away the awesome speed a ship could attain in fold space with a blaze of light, her impossibly fast motion—impossible now she had re-entered real space—was instantly converted to raw energy and blasted away from her into the void. She seemed to twist along her centreline one last time as if shaking off the last traces of fold space from non-existent coattails. The blue energy discharge that always accompanied translation gradually dispersed. That discharge would be alerting beacons and system defence nets of an intruder throughout the system, but not quite yet. The light-speed wavefront, though fast, would still take a minute or three to hit the nearest beacon.

Captain Monroe retched into her helmet and groaned at the smell and burning in her throat. With shaking hands on seemingly boneless arms, she threw the disgusting helmet away and coughed racking her chest with every breath. The steady beeping from the communications consol told her of a beacon query, but no one silenced it. Martin was out of it, and so was the rest of the bridge crew. Groans and coughing came from her left front as Keith Hadden tried to wake from the stupor that fold space had put him in.

Monroe had never, *never*, experienced a worse translation. The speed she had forced out of *Invincible* was the cause, but the emergency translation back to normal space was necessary to save time, and time was in short supply.

The beacon… she thought mushily as her people groaned and began to rouse. She stood on legs gone wobbly and tottered to the communications panel. Keying in *Invincible's* security sequence, she dumped the prepared message into the queue and transmitted it to the beacon—fleet priority one.

That done she staggered to her seat and collapsed into it. She had done what needed to be done. It was up to the authorities at Northcliff now.

* * *

Aboard ASN Sutherland, Northcliff System

Northcliff was a beautiful planet, Lieutenant Commander Oakley thought, and he was stuck up here in this tin can! He sighed. His work was important, it was necessary and most times very interesting and rewarding, but at zero-three-hundred on the bridge of an Alliance carrier, the only thing rewarding enough would be a long sleep in his rack.

"Sir?" Communications specialist Guauri Kistna said, frowning at her panel.

"What is it Guauri?" he said turning toward her station.

"I have an emergence at the edge of the zone, sir, but no response to the beacon hail. Northcliff Port Control has requested I.D but received no response."

That's odd.

"Hmmm, put it up on the threat board and give me what you have on my number two monitor."

"Yes sir," Guauri said and did that.

Lieutenant Commander Oakley, third officer of the battle group carrier *ASN Sutherland* turned to the information plotted on his monitor and studied what it showed him. He stiffened when he noted the ship was wandering from the lane. It didn't appear in control, and *Sutherland's* sensors reported battle damage.

"Wake the Captain!" He snapped and slammed his fist down on a red button. The battle stations alarm began wailing throughout the ship.

END

Also available from Impulse

If these books are not available from your local bookshop, send this coupon together with your check made payable to:

Impulse Books UK

At the following address:

Impulse Books UK
18, Lampits Hill Avenue,
Corringham
Essex SS177NY
United Kingdom

Please send me the following great titles from Impulse Books UK

Tick as approrriate:

The God Decrees (Pb)
ISBN: 0-9545122-1-9 £10.99 _____ ☐

The Power That Binds (Pb)
ISBN: 0-9545122-2-7 £10.99 _____ ☐

The Warrior Within (Pb)
ISBN: 0-9545122-0-0 £10.99 _____ ☐

Hard Duty (Pb)
ISBN: 0-9545122-3-5 £11.99 _____ ☐

Wolf's Revenge (Pb)
ISBN: 978-1-905380-43-5 £11.99 _____ ☐

NAME _____

ADDRESS _____

_____

_____

I have enclosed a check for the sum of £ _____

Please be sure to add £2.25 to your order to cover shipping and handling charges.

Made in the USA
Lexington, KY
08 March 2013